Collide

J.R. LENK

Harmony Ink

Suna Tabag 3709. Castle Hill Blvd.

Published by
Harmony Ink Press
382 NE 191st Street #88329
Miami, FL 33179-3899, USA
publisher@harmonyinkpress.com

Collide

Cover Art by Anne Cain   annecain.art@gmail.com
Cover Design by Mara McKennen

ISBN: 978-1-61372-473-6

Printed in the United States of America
First Edition
April 2012

eBook edition available
eBook ISBN: 978-1-61372-474-3

Dedications

As the first, of course part of this page is reserved for my mother and father, and my aunt, who never laughed at my silly dreams.

Next it's for Galadriel Brown, who a while back put on the editor pants and told me everything that was wrong with the initial draft of this story. Thanks for that slap in the face.

And lastly it's for Brittany Jung. God knows this project would never be anywhere without you, just like everything else I do in life.

Okay, my part's over. You can read now!

Chapter 1
December

"OH, *DAMMIT*—"

One moment, he was dreaming about being at a Nirvana concert (which would never happen because it was 2004, after all), and the next, he was curled up in bed with his eyes wide open, looking at the digital clock by his bed and realizing that he'd hit the snooze button exactly four times already. He didn't usually do that. He had a good habit of getting up on time. But that explained the dream about Nirvana, seeing as his alarm was set to FM and they were playing "About a Girl."

Hazard didn't scramble out of bed, but he hurried. He hated being late.

"I was wondering when you were going to get up," his mom said when he scampered into the kitchen for cereal, which he ate out of a coffee mug instead of a bowl. He'd picked up that habit from Emery.

His dad was gone, off to work already. His mom leaned against the counter, polishing the earrings she was going to wear for the day. She was already dressed, sterile blue polo and white capris. She pursed her mouth to the side in thought as she studied Hazard through her lashes, adding, "You have to be at school in, what, forty minutes?"

"Thirty-five," Hazard corrected with a sigh, adding sugar to his Cheerios. "But Emery and Russell should be here any minute to pick me up."

Letting his radio play, he made his bed before his mom could mention it and dug around for some clothes. He changed his shirt three times before finally deciding on one to wear, washed his face to wake himself up a little more, brushed his teeth, then tried to fix his unruly cowlicks. His hair never wanted to lie down the way he wanted it to. It was always a dark tousled mess that just crowded in on his face.

He watched the morning news with his mom as he put on his shoes, both leaning against the counter on opposite sides of the kitchen.

Everything he needed for the day was neatly organized in his backpack; he checked twice. Finished homework, textbooks, binder, notebooks. He ignored the notes of scorn in his mother's morning conversation, and he glanced out the front window repeatedly to make sure his ride to school wasn't there yet. God, he hated feeling *rushed*.

"Be good" was what his mom said when Emery and Russell showed up, instead of "I love you, have a good day." Hazard didn't take it to heart. It wasn't like he was a bad kid or anything.

"Hey, did you get your history homework done?" Emery asked as Hazard struggled to put his coat on and get into the car at the same time while Russell idled at the curb. Russell was old enough to drive. Emery was old enough to forever claim shotgun.

"Thankfully," Hazard grumbled, hurrying to buckle up as Russell pulled away from the edge of the driveway. "Do you need it?"

Emery wilted with a guilty smile around his simple breakfast of a cereal straw. He ran a hand through his mess of hair and nodded. "Yes."

Hazard handed his backpack up to the front seat so Emery could copy his history homework on their way to Bethany High. They had the same history teacher, anyway, just different periods.

"Thank you, I owe you—" Emery cried, and above the rustle of papers and zippers, Russell made a sound of distaste at the whole thing. Hazard didn't care.

Hazard leaned back, looking out the car window as Russell drove and Emery copied his homework answers, at the same time regaling them with the witty remark he'd made to his stepdad, Andrew, the night before, something about going and watching *The Godfather* for the millionth time instead of wasting his breath trying to get Emery on the wrestling team. That was funny, because Andrew was totally New York loud, and his nagging was annoying. Hazard had never liked Andrew, anyway.

The morning was cool and pale and a little foggy, as it usually was in a winter by Puget Sound, the neighborhood and city quiet. The world was still waking up. "Longview" buzzed from the car stereo and Hazard sighed, realizing he'd forgotten to stop his alarm while he got dressed. He slumped down and rubbed the last of sleep from his eyes. His mom would probably say something about it later, like she'd had a headache all day from the racket or something.

It felt like it was going to be a long day.

IT DIDN'T really *start* that winter, but it was safe to say that December was the crux. It was the turning point of it all.

THERE was nothing really special about Hazard Oscar James.

In December of his freshman year, he was fourteen years old. He was an only child born at Swedish Medical Center in Seattle after two miscarriages, and he'd lived in the same house on the same street in Bethany, Washington, for his whole life. That winter, Hazard didn't drink yet, he'd never gotten high (except for maybe a contact buzz), he'd never been to a party, and his best friend was Emery Benjamin Moore. Sometimes he felt like Emery was all he had.

Hazard's family was the perfect family, except nobody was ever home. His dad was the head of an advertising company in Seattle, so he spent a lot of time working and commuting. His mom didn't have to work, but if she did, she wouldn't have liked it. She liked cleaning the house and getting her nails done, and watching *Entertainment Tonight* and talking politics with her friends, who'd all married businessmen and preferred the pampered life too. The house was always spotless and Hazard had grown accustomed to the scents of air freshener and cleaning products. Everything had to be in order, everything had to be neat, and everything had to be in the best working condition.

Hazard was smaller than he thought was very good for his reputation, five foot two and just under 125 pounds. He had thick, messy dark-brown hair that was always in his eyes, which were blue and big in a pale, kind of petite face. He thought it made him look a little too girly, which wasn't cool because his name already made him different enough.

He wasn't very good at science. He had to pay a lot of attention in history, although he liked it, but his favorite classes were art and English. Admittedly, he was kind of quiet and kind of moody, and maybe a little

anxious sometimes. He liked alternative rock (his favorite songs then were
"All That I've Got" by The Used and "Heart-Shaped Box" by Nirvana),
Vanilla Coke, and Chuck Taylors, and his jeans were always too loose on
him. He wasn't super cool, but he wasn't a loser either. Nobody even
recognized him as a skater, even though he'd hung out with them the past
year and a half. Sometimes people in class stared at him, but otherwise he
was just kind of there and nobody noticed—except for Emery, of course,
and Emery was the sort of best friend you could call your brother.

Emery wore shirts from the kids' section of Target. His mom raised
him on Jewel and Tom Petty. He wore surfer necklaces and hemp and
sported bumps and scrapes from friendly scraps with pals. He had a
collection of Converse in every color and design he could find. He was
honest, funny, and had a hot temper, and nobody could resist his roguish
smile, so older kids at school treated him like a well-loved little brother,
which made him just a stone's throw from being relatively popular. He
drew on his hands in ballpoint pen when he was bored in class, and he'd
just turned fifteen, but from some angles he still looked like he was
twelve.

Emery and Hazard liked to go to the bookstore to sit around and
read. They liked to stop in the stores in the mall where the massage chairs
were set up to try, so they could drink slushies and get back massages and
snicker together while they people watched. They liked to shoot basketball
in Emery's driveway and play video games until late at night, and when
they were younger they'd thought Jesse Camp was ridiculous in a good
way.

Hazard had met Emery in second grade. He knew Emery like the
back of his hand—how he liked horror movies and Swedish Fish, how he
knew just how to sneak out of his bedroom window, how he'd broken his
wrist in fourth grade, how he hated his stepdad, Andrew, and especially
how Emery idolized Russell Leroy, whom he'd known since kindergarten.
If Emery wasn't hanging out with Hazard, he and Russell were practically
a boxed set, and everyone knew that if you wanted to get on Russell's
good side, you had to go through Emery because Russell only ever
listened to him.

"Russell is so cool," Emery said a lot. He'd always thought that,
even when they'd been in grade school and they'd all made blanket forts
in his living room to watch scary movies. Russell never jumped at scary

movies. Hazard always jumped.

Russell was a year older than them. Hazard didn't really like him, mostly because Russell was kind of aloof and he'd known Emery longer than Hazard had. He'd been Emery's friend forever, and Emery thought Russell was even greater now that they were in high school. Russell was suave and cool. He was good at sports, he was good at guitar, he was good at French (only because his grandparents were from Canada) and probably just about everything else that mattered. He had blond hair somewhere between surfer and rocker, electrifying blue eyes, quiet commanding stares, and an apathy that for some reason drew everyone in. He wore thermals under all his T-shirts and yellow shoelaces with smiley faces on them, and all the girls liked him, but he didn't care.

Hazard hated Russell.

But that was when Jesse Wesley showed up, after all, with his red leather and cigarettes—that December.

THE noise in the cafeteria of Bethany High was a roar, too many restless students ignoring the way eating teachers glared at them. Outside the wide windows and glass doors, the sky was cold and gray, pale sunlight filtering through during a lull in the Washington rain. At the lunch table, Emery's face was pinched in frustration, and he grumbled, "I can't learn anything in math class because my teacher has this dumb lisp."

"What do you mean?" Hazard asked.

"Instead of saying 'slope', she says 'schlope', and I can't concentrate because I'm constantly trying to figure out what she just said."

"So ask someone if you can copy their homework questions."

"Ha, ha, you're hilarious," Emery huffed, referring to all the homework he'd copied from Hazard. "Do you have Mr. Rippe for math?"

"No. Sorry. But I heard he's open to tutoring through lunch."

"Did you know Mrs. Whitehead *charges* you for tutoring?"

"That's stupid. No, Mr. Rippe is cool."

Emery looked up hopefully as Russell sank down beside him with a tray of food, having finally escaped the slow-moving lunch line and the group of girls in it who insisted on talking to him. Russell glanced over skeptically, like he was suspicious of Emery's imploring stare.

"Would you help me with geometry?" Emery pleaded.

Russell sighed, pushing white-blond hair out of his eyes. He opened his chocolate milk and took a long drink. "Yeah, sure," he finally said after subjecting them to his usual nonchalance. "Get out your homework."

"Thank you—"

"Maybe you should worry about this *before* lunch, seeing as you have math *next*."

"Leave me alone, Russell."

"I can't. I have to help you with geometry."

Hazard ate, watching as Russell tried to explain to Emery how slopes and their formulas worked. Grunting something about how math sucked, Russell's friend Clay plopped down beside them, followed by Becca and Cody. Hazard didn't know why, but watching them kind of made him mad. He thought slopes were incredibly easy. He wasn't going to tell Emery that, though.

The table filled up with more students, some kids Hazard knew from Biology and English. He greeted them, then ate in silence, offering Emery his last tater tots, although Emery was concentrating very hard and had barely touched his own.

Hazard passed the skaters' corner of the cafeteria on his way to toss his trash and return his lunch tray. Some kids sat near the vending machines and on the steps down toward the hall, eating their lunch there with trays resting on their backpacks or skateboards, which would probably be confiscated soon judging by the way Ms. Cavanaugh was eyeing them unsympathetically from the teachers' tables.

Hazard paused by the table nearest to the stairs to say hi to his friends Tom and Peyton and Olivia. In eighth grade, he'd fit in perfectly with them at the lunch table with the rest of the skaters and underachievers, but not so much anymore. That was okay.

"Tommy," Hazard said, leaning down next to him, "I can smell your gum all the way over there."

"Shut up," Tom snorted with a grin, elbowing Hazard away. "I can chew gum all I want. It's lunch."

"Ms. Cavanaugh's coming," Olivia reported, playfully acting inconspicuous. But Ms. Cavanaugh didn't come toward them; she went to the kids at the stairs and asked them to put their skateboards in their lockers or in the office until classes were over, and Tom patted Hazard on the shoulder as Hazard hurried off to the trash cans with his tray.

Closer to the big windows of the cafeteria, where the rain was starting again, he could see Russell and Emery and Clay still hunched over Emery's math notebook. Clay seemed a little amused. Russell looked tetchy, hand buried in his hair, while the expression on Emery's face read frustrated impatience, and Hazard didn't really pay attention to the guy who'd come up to the trash cans beside him until he said with perfect disgust:

"Oh God, you really ate that mac and cheese?"

Hazard bristled, looking over with wide eyes. He vaguely recognized the guy who stood across the trash can from him, but he was more offended by the way the guy's face held perfect revulsion and the way that cocky disparaging expression could make Hazard feel like such a loser. What was the guy's name again? He was a junior. Hazard had heard about him plenty of times. Red leather jacket, patent attitude. He was tall and thin; the top of Hazard's head only reached his shoulder.

Jesse. That was it: Jesse Wesley. Even though he wasn't the *most* popular, like Blake Monroe, everyone knew Jesse, and everything he did or said was worshiped in one way or another. He was notorious, and for what, exactly, Hazard couldn't even think of at the moment. Getting in trouble? Beating people up? Partying and screwing girls? All of that sounded right enough.

Hazard looked down at his lunch tray, a few tater tots left on one side and the remains of mac and cheese on the other. Admittedly, the noodles had been so dried out, except for a residual puddle of cheese, that it hadn't tasted as mac and cheesy as it should have, but it hadn't been that bad, and it was more identifiable than the cafeteria's frequent beef stroganoff, so—

Wait, that wasn't the point here.

Hazard frowned, meeting Jesse's eyes. Jesse was chugging the last of his chocolate milk, staring with irritating self-importance.

Hazard glared across the trash can at Jesse. "Yeah, but I overheard Mr. Nash talking earlier about how they're worried the school's milk cartons have a false expiration date on them, which means everyone's drinking bad milk, so I'd be more worried if I were *you*."

Jesse lowered his carton of chocolate milk and stared at Hazard across the trash can. He looked as if he hadn't swallowed his mouthful of milk yet and seemed a little surprised by Hazard's reply. Truthfully, Hazard was a little startled by his own comeback, too, but he tried not to seem that way.

Jesse dropped the empty milk carton in the trash and swallowed deliberately, holding Hazard's stare the whole time. "That's a good one," Jesse said, not at all humbly, shoving his hands in the pockets of his jacket. He narrowed his eyes and peered at Hazard some more with something like appraisal, mouth set in a hard line. "*Except*," he added, "that if they really thought that, they wouldn't have allowed us to take milk today. And also, you have chocolate milk on your tray. Nice try, though. Seriously. I applaud your efforts."

Hazard stiffened against a tiny pang of embarrassment, dumping his tray and the milk carton on it into the trash can. But Jesse didn't seem to be finished. He lingered there on the other side of the trash can, staring. His eyes were a piercing green. They made Hazard nervous. He had a straight nose and thin lips and softly angled cheeks, like what some people called a *pretty boy* except with a viciously cocky frown. His lashes were dark. So was the skin around his eyes, like he worried too much or didn't get much sleep. He looked like he'd fit in with pretty much anyone he wanted to, not because of clichés but because he'd take over. His hair was dark and choppy and tucked behind ears pierced just like his left eyebrow. Hazard had heard he was really rich, but he looked pretty normal with the baseball tee and neat jeans below his renowned red leather jacket.

"What?" Jesse grunted, raising his brows.

Hazard's stomach sank. God, he was staring like an idiot. He wracked his brain for something to say, frowning darkly. "Nothing, just that—I've heard you're such an asshole, and it's true."

"Oh, like nobody's said that before. Honestly, I like to think I'm just conversationally blessed."

"More like conversationally cursed."

"One person's trash is another person's treasure."

"That doesn't even apply here."

Jesse raised his brows as if to say *You don't think so?* and pointed at the wide trash can between them. Hazard rolled his eyes. He laughed a little, scornfully, and Jesse smirked while he scratched idly at the bridge of his nose. Hazard caught a tiny flash of black, the symbol for Scorpio, on Jesse's middle finger. Maybe he drew on himself like Emery did. Or maybe it was a real tattoo.

"Oh, I'm funny now?" Jesse muttered, somewhat to himself.

Hazard frowned just to spite him. Across the cafeteria, he could see Russell and Clay laughing at a very flustered Emery over his homework. Hazard's stomach soured a little. "Look," he said with a sigh, shifting from foot to foot. He was still holding his lunch tray, stupidly. "I'm sort of in a bad mood already, so just—if you're done bugging me...."

Jesse raised his brows, smirk still lingering at the corners of his mouth. He held his hands out, stepping to the side. "Carry on," he said.

Hazard wandered off to return his tray, but he wasn't dumb. He could feel Jesse's eyes following him. Apparently, their rocky conversation was not over yet, because as he passed the trash cans again, Jesse made him stop by gesturing demandingly.

Hazard sighed again and stepped out of cafeteria traffic, crossing his arms where he stood next to a poster for the Secret Santa party the Spanish club was having.

"What—?" he started, but he shut his mouth halfway through his question because he realized with a sudden pinch in his gut that Jesse was looking at him with no scorn and no arrogance anymore, just a spark of curiosity. That was sort of alarming and flattering all at once, and Hazard wasn't sure what to think of it or the way a few people at a table just a couple rows away kept glancing at them.

Other kids passed them arbitrarily, dumping the trash from their lunch trays. Jesse grunted, "So... you know Clay Bentley?"

He knew Clay a little because Russell knew him, but Hazard shook his head. "Not really. Why?"

"Because I know Clay's friends are sort of stuck-up, and I've seen you around him before, so I was just wondering."

Hazard laughed, because Russell was Clay's friend and Jesse had just called Clay's friends *stuck-up*. But then he paused, glancing at Jesse skeptically. *I've seen you around him* meant that Jesse had noticed him a few times before. Hazard shrugged, dismissing that because it was weird-feeling, like the way people stared at him in class sometimes. Jesse Wesley, noticing him?

"Do *you* know Clay?" Hazard asked.

Jesse shrugged, rocking back and forth with his hands in his pockets. He looked totally indifferent to their conversation again, like now he was just waiting to go back to his table. "I had gym with him last year. Why?"

Hazard raised his brows. "He's a sophomore. I thought you were a junior."

Jesse's complacency faltered a little. Something shifted in his expression, and with a cruel light in his eyes, he briefly looked Hazard up and down. Hazard leaned back a bit, wondering if he'd just stepped on a landmine. But if Jesse didn't like his prying question, he didn't show it any further than that.

"I failed gym freshman year. I had to repeat it." The tone of Jesse's voice declared that that was the end of *that* discussion, but then suddenly his face changed, softened a little, although his eyes still felt like they burned right through any pretense to the core, and he asked, "You're not afraid of me, are you?"

Hazard shrugged. "No," he lied, because he couldn't deny that Jesse was sort of intimidating, but he wasn't going to *say* that.

"Why?"

"What's there to be scared of?"

"Oh, damn! Silver tongue you got there."

"Look, I told you, I'm not in the best of moods right now—"

"I made you laugh earlier."

Hazard blanked. He looked at Jesse, brow knotted, and he could feel the incredulous impatience on his face as he said, "You're an idiot. That's why."

"Whoa! Oh, yeah?" Jesse scoffed a little, hands deep in his leather jacket's pockets as he shifted from foot to foot. But the way he was looking at Hazard wasn't at all vindictive. It was interestingly sly and innocent at the same time, that spark of curiosity, and cowing as it was, it seemed authentic enough. Jesse's cocky scowl transformed suddenly, becoming another smirk as he said, "Hey, you're ruining this *mean* thing for me, you know. You're too funny to be annoying."

"Oh, I'm so sorry," Hazard mumbled sarcastically, glancing over his shoulder at the lunch table where Emery and everyone else were. And there, those people who kept glancing at them looked away quickly like he wouldn't notice their stares. He met Jesse's eyes again, realizing with a little blush of embarrassment that the subtle shift he felt in his chest was that of making a friend.

Hadn't his attitude pissed Jesse off? It occurred to him then that it was a joke, that some other juniors had sent Jesse over and they were going to use Hazard for entertainment during lunch. What else could possibly compel someone like Jesse to talk to him? Most juniors— especially cool ones—hated freshmen.

Jesse stared at him hard for a moment, thinking. Then he declared, plainly enough, "You should hang out with me and my friends sometime."

"What?" Hazard gawked. He raised his brows dumbly. *Hang out* with Jesse Wesley? He didn't believe it, but he understood all of a sudden that there was no joke. Jesse was completely serious.

Jesse shrugged limply. "Yeah," he said. "I mean, Brianna would probably like it. Do you know Brianna? Brianna Macintosh?"

"No."

"Well." Jesse shrugged again, glancing around almost impatiently before catching Hazard's stare. "You'll meet her. Hang out with us or something."

Hazard didn't mean to sound reproachful when he grunted doubtfully, "Why?"

"Usually people don't argue with me. But you do, and it's hilarious."

Jesse said it like it was something cute or endearing, probably to make sure Hazard understood that they weren't on the same level yet. Hazard already understood that. He also understood, by the look on his face, that he'd piqued Jesse's curiosity. He eyed Jesse from below his lashes: messy hair, red leather, irritating nonchalance. A teacher walked by, lanyard swinging.

Hazard could tell by his peripheral vision that everyone at that table a few rows down was glancing at them again. He thought about Emery and Russell and the way all the sophomores talked to Emery because he was Russell's friend. The same thing would probably happen to Hazard— if he was Jesse's friend, all the juniors and other cool people would notice him. Something kind of warm and curious swelled in his chest. He glanced at the clock on the far wall of the cafeteria; lunch would end in ten minutes. He said, more bravely than he'd expected, "Give me your number, then, if it's not a joke. Because I don't believe you."

Jesse scoffed. He dug in his red leather jacket pocket and pulled out his cell phone, handing it to Hazard discreetly, so teachers didn't see. "Give me *your* number. If you think you're worth it."

Hazard hesitated, heart pounding. *Hang out with Jesse Wesley.* He took Jesse's phone and started to program in his number with clammy fingers, glancing over at the lunch table where Russell and Clay were still trying to help Emery understand geometry. Something wicked inside him begged Emery to look up and see them and get jealous because Jesse was cool, and he was talking to Hazard.

"Oh, yeah? You think you're worth it, hunh?" Jesse curled into an infectious grin, somewhere between honesty and a smirk, as Hazard handed his phone back. He ran his hand through his hair and regarded Hazard through his lashes in an altogether intimidating and evocative stare. It struck a chord somewhere in Hazard's chest, maybe something like the *click* when it just felt natural to talk to someone.

Jesse shrugged idly, looking at the entries in his phone. "I'll text you, loser. I think you already know, but I'm Jesse. Hey, where's your name in here?"

Hazard shrugged too, pointing. "I'm Hazard," he said, and just as abruptly as it had begun, it seemed their conversation had drawn to a close.

Jesse laughed as he walked away, heading for the vending machines as he muttered, "Seriously, who names their kid Hazard?"

Hazard felt bruised in the chest, strangely insulted and embarrassed and yet totally thrilled at the same time. Was that normal? He lingered there stupidly for a moment, then wandered back through the tables to where Russell had finally gotten Emery to see why some lines had undefined slopes and others had a slope of zero.

"Did you get lost?" Emery grumbled absently, not looking up from the problems he was trying to finish before lunch ended.

Hazard laughed, slumping down beside him. "No, but I talked to Jesse Wesley."

Emery glanced up skeptically. Russell looked up too, arms crossed and head resting on his backpack like a pillow.

"*Jesse Wesley?*" Emery said, raising his brows, not without a hint of distrust.

"Yeah, why?" Hazard asked, frowning.

"I don't know." Emery shrugged. He seemed to notice that he'd offended Hazard a little. He looked apologetic. "Just—Lily said Sophie said she saw him once at a party and he's pretty out of control—"

"He is," Russell confirmed, nodding on his arms but still looking kind of bored with everything. "Clay had gym with him and—"

"I know," Hazard interrupted, throwing a sharp glance at Russell. He didn't want any advice from him. Russell glared back, but Hazard ignored it. "He's an asshole, I know. But he said he wants me to hang out with him and his friends sometime. What am I supposed to say? *No?*"

Emery stared, but he seemed lost in thought, like he mistrusted Jesse or didn't understand why he wanted to hang out with Hazard. Maybe a tiny bit of it was jealousy, but most of it appeared to be concern. Russell slouched on his backpack and frowned, fiddling with the key chains he'd put on his zipper.

Hazard shrugged in response to both of them. "I'll be careful," he promised. "If he's even telling the truth, I'll just hang out with him once or twice. Just to be nice. Because he asked."

The bell rang, and the commotion in the cafeteria rose to mayhem as throngs of students filled the space between tables with startling speed. Emery hissed, *"Shit!"* and hurried to put his things back into his bag. Russell helped him. Hazard waited patiently so he could walk with Emery to fifth period.

JESSE LOGAN WESLEY was not at all the kind of boy anybody wanted their kid to be friends with. He was a partier, and Hazard had overheard once at an assembly that he'd gotten suspended last year for punching a teacher. There was also speculation he'd been busted for drugs. In the bathroom near the auditorium, where the lights flickered over the back stall and everyone wrote gossip on the far wall, Hazard read that a girl claimed a while ago to be carrying Jesse's baby, but lots of scribbles underneath argued the falsity of that because "the girl is a skank anyway." That was a direct quote.

Hazard had to admit he was a little leery still, but Russell was tutoring Emery on slope all week, and Tom and the others weren't skating because it was too rainy, and part of him wanted Emery to be jealous, so Hazard gladly took Jesse up on his offer.

Jesse texted him. Hazard texted back. It was intimidating but kind of exciting to have somebody so popular and wild talking to him casually. He was a little cowed by Jesse's friends, who looked unruly or at the very least too talkative for Hazard's comfort, so he didn't sit with Jesse at lunch, but they texted.

Hazard added Jesse to his phonebook under the name ASSHOLE. He was confident there was no joke being played on him, nothing clandestine or malicious at all. He didn't know how he knew; he could just tell. Jesse's attitude was a little daunting, but he was sarcastic and funny and Hazard was hooked. They bantered together through texts for two hours one night.

On the Friday the week before winter break started, Jesse stopped to talk with Hazard at lunch. Hazard was startled. Emery stared and Russell scowled, then went on talking to Becca and Clay.

Jesse leaned down by Hazard and ignored Emery's wide, curious eyes. He said, "There's a party tonight. You wanna come?"

"Sure," Hazard mumbled, a little flattered and sheepish, and very nervous because it hit him then that Jesse was his ticket to a different side of high school.

Jesse said, "Cool, I'll text you," and left, clearly satisfied.

Hazard looked over at Emery.

"I'm not jealous, because I don't like partying," Emery snapped immediately. He looked tense. "But that's just my opinion. You have to tell me what it's like to hang out with Jesse."

Hazard mulled it over for a minute. "Could I stay at your house afterwards, Em?"

"Sure." Emery took a long drink of his chocolate milk, glancing away. "There you go, you rebel. You have an alibi and everything."

JESSE tried many nicknames before finally finding one that he liked. One of his friends suggested Rookie or Dukes because of *The Dukes of Hazzard*. Hazard frowned. Jesse tried Biohazard, but Hazard did not approve. Jesse tried H, which he pronounced Hah. Then he tried Z. After that was Haz, which quickly became Has-Been, but none of them seemed to work right except for the last:

"Have you ever been to a party, Danger?"

Hazard sighed curtly. "I told you my name is *Hazard*, not *Danger*."

Jesse scoffed. "Seriously, who names their kid Hazard?"

Blue eyes clashed with green as Hazard met Jesse's disdainful stare. "My mother," he said miserably, and he could see in Jesse's eyes that he was amused by this game. Hazard frowned tightly, wondering whether or not he should answer the question. *Have you ever been to a party?*

"Yes," he whispered, following close after Jesse. They'd parked a block and a half away from the house they were headed to, which was in the more redneck part of Bethany. Jesse's other friends walked a few paces ahead. "I've been to a party before," Hazard said, a little louder. He was lying.

Jesse grinned, as excited as a five-year-old with a surprise. It reminded Hazard of Emery.

Jesse's friends stopped at the curb outside their destination to light a cigarette or two. Lights spilled forth from the windows. Cars were parked up and down the sidewalk, and there was the muffled sound of organized chaos that rattled Hazard down to his bones. He began to panic for the second time that night. He'd breathed through it in his bedroom an hour earlier, getting ready to go and frantically trying to decide which shirt made him look coolest while he insisted to his mother that he'd be fine eating something at Emery's house even if it meant a late dinner, and yes, Emery's mother was okay with him staying over. Seeing Jesse in his red leather and Calvin Klein jeans had made Hazard nervous all over again, but not compared to this uncertainty he felt as he followed Jesse to the door of a stranger's house. He was afraid of making a complete idiot of himself.

Jesse rang the doorbell three times and then just opened the door of the house. The sleepiness of the street was butchered by the sudden rush of loud music and voices.

Two people brushed past Hazard rather rudely, bumping into his shoulder. Hazard scowled after them. They were the boy and girl who had been in the car when Jesse picked him up—*Hey, Mom, this is my friend Jesse. We're going to see his aunt at the hospital. Emotional support and all, and Emery's meeting us there and I'm going back to his house with him to stay the night, and yes, his mom is okay with it, I swear.*

Hazard stood in the light falling out on the stoop, a little cowed and a bit anxious as he gawked in at the party. He could already smell the alcohol and cigarette smoke. He could see the milling bodies; he could hear the laughter and friendly shouts. The scene inside tempted him. It looked fun and inviting and totally worth it.

Hazard squeezed through the doorway with Jesse, eyes wide as he took it all in. It felt surreal. Somebody almost ran into him, and Jesse tugged him out of the way at the last second. It was a small house, living room and kitchen already packed. Hazard recognized mostly juniors and seniors, but he saw a few sophomores and even a couple freshmen passing in and out of the crowd. There were people from all over the spectrum of clichés. How many were there? Thirty or forty, all smashed into this house, and whose house was it, anyway?

He was very curious, but his stomach flipped. The music was blasting a song with a good beat. There were cans and bottles of beer sitting around, half-gone or empty. The cigarette smoke was horrible because everybody was smoking inside but nobody had opened a window at all. Everyone was loud and laughing and having a good time. Some people were dancing.

"Hey," Jesse grunted, capturing Hazard's attention again. "Look, don't let me down, okay?"

Hazard frowned defensively. "What are you talking about?"

The front door slammed as a few more people squeezed in. The music's volume increased with the intensity of the song, and Jesse leaned down so Hazard could hear him clearly. His breath tickled the cartilage of Hazard's ear, striking him motionless as he said, "I just get this vibe from you, like you'll fit in with us, like you won't freak out." Jesse paused. "You can handle this, right?"

Hazard was surprised but flattered and still very nervous. That was a lot of pressure on him: the pressure of impressing everyone and making sure he didn't embarrass himself. He frowned, looking at Jesse over his shoulder. "Of course."

"Listen," Jesse husked. His eyes were smug. "You're here with me, so all I'm saying is don't make a total loser out of yourself, because it'll reflect badly on me and my friends, and I don't want that. You get it?"

"What, you think I'm gonna get totally smashed and start dancing on the table? I'm fine. You're an asshole, Jesse."

Jesse seemed a little caught off guard by the blunt, moody insult. Hazard fought a smile. Jesse straightened up, looking amused. "Good movie reference," he grunted, then sighed dramatically and ruffled Hazard's messy dark hair. "Ah, shit, I feel like a mentor."

"An—"

"Asshole, right." Jesse smirked ever so gently. He wandered off and left Hazard trying desperately to fix the mess he'd created by touching his unruly hair.

Hazard watched as a group of guys welcomed Jesse with pats on the back, calling out his name. Hazard frowned darkly. He didn't know what to do. He kind of wished people would welcome him like that—that everyone would light up when he walked through the crowd or forget what they were doing just to say hi. Hazard wondered what even made people do that when Jesse moved through the room, anyway.

Hazard went into the kitchen. He tried to avoid the regulars and the weirdos, debating nervously whether or not to grab a drink while there was no pressure on him about it yet. He'd never really had alcohol before, so he didn't know when the *drunk* point came. He and his friends had always wondered about it, but nobody had ever braved Peyton's dad's cooler of Bud or Emery's mom's vodka cabinet.

He tried to be inconspicuous. He looked around, peeking silently at the other people in the kitchen, who really didn't seem to notice him at all. Each hand had a fresh bottle or cup of *something*, and nobody was paying attention to him.

Demurely, Hazard looked at all the bottles of liquor and cans of beer and tall mixer bottles with gleaming silver tops. Who had even bought it all, anyway? Quickly, Hazard grabbed a bottle off the counter. It was slick with condensation. He examined the label curiously: Smirnoff Ice, watermelon flavor. It tasted good, even with the bite behind the watermelon.

Two guys came to his side of the kitchen to raid the fridge. They were very loud and obnoxious and probably jocks. Hazard slipped back out into the living room. He looked around for Jesse, trying to avoid people and nursing his drink absently. He was still freaking out, but he hoped he didn't look it. He hoped he looked comfortable with the lack of space and crazy people everywhere.

Hazard looked down the hall. There was an open doorway at the end of it from which a haze with the pungency of pot was beginning to creep toward the living room. Some of the bedroom doors hung open. There was toothpaste all over the bathroom mirror and a few girls sitting in the tub laughing hysterically. Hazard got out of the way of people worming down the hall into the living room.

The cigarette smoke made his nose stuffy. Hazard found Jesse again, sitting with a few others in the corner of the living room, leather jacket draped over the arm of a chair. He was wearing a faded T-shirt that looked like he'd gotten it off the racks at Goodwill. It had two cherries on it and said *hole*. There were more tattoos on Jesse's arms. Hazard wanted to see them, but he kept himself from looking. He didn't want to stare.

He sat down beside Jesse quietly. Jesse looked happy to see him, like he hadn't even left him in the first place. He held his drink out. "Want a sip?"

"No, thanks." Hazard held up his own bottle, showing Jesse he'd really just started it.

Jesse properly introduced Hazard to his friends: Felix Wilton, Lexie Morgan, and Brianna Macintosh. Brianna was a freshman too. Hazard remembered Jesse mentioning her in the cafeteria, and he didn't feel so mistrusting anymore. He actually felt kind of proud to be the other freshman Jesse had invited to hang out with them.

They sat together in the corner of the living room where the music was loudest and Hazard had to lean forward to hear them clearly. Somebody put on a CD with a good beat, and a couple of people started dancing around again.

Jesse and his friends talked about everything. Hazard talked with them. They talked about music. Hazard told them his favorite bands. They commended him on his great taste. They talked about movies and which were the best and which sucked. They talked about idiots at school. They laughed at party fouls like the girl who kept spilling her drink everywhere.

Hazard got drunk quickly. He didn't mean to. He was just having fun, and when Lexie made trips back to the kitchen to grab everyone more to drink, she made sure to bring Hazard a fresh bottle too. Jesse and his friends were loud and fun. Hazard liked them. By the time he was starting his third drink, Hazard wasn't nervous anymore. His face felt hot. He felt super comfortable, like everything was okay and he could fall asleep or think forever.

"He's a lightweight," Jesse's friend Felix said, which he looked like he thought was adorable.

Jesse slung an arm around Hazard's shoulders. Hazard could smell his cologne, his laundry detergent, cigarette smoke on leather, and alcohol and warm skin.

"We like you, Danger." Jesse leaned down to say it so Hazard could hear.

Hazard stiffened. He swallowed hard, glancing up at Jesse. "What do you mean?"

The girl named Brianna started laughing really hard with Felix about something. Lexie got up and left for the toke room. Hazard felt kind of edgy, kind of thrilled, kind of confused, and kind of impatient all at once. He wanted Jesse to stop breathing down his neck, because it sent chills along his spine and it was weird.

Jesse smirked. With it, Hazard relaxed completely. "I just meant that you're kind of cool," Jesse murmured, like it wasn't something he usually said. Maybe it wasn't. That meant something, right?

"What?" Hazard mumbled, muscles tingling from the alcohol, or maybe because Jesse's words made him feel shy. He wondered what Emery would say when he heard that Jesse Wesley thought he was *kind of cool*.

Jesse looked at him curiously, then smirked like he was trying to win a game. "So, Danger," he said next, casually, "are you gonna be our rookie?"

Hazard sighed heavily. "My name isn't *Danger*. It's *Hazard*. My mom read it in a book when she was younger and...."

Jesse wasn't really listening. Hazard frowned. His brow furrowed. *Rookie*. What did that mean? Was Jesse officially asking Hazard to be one of his friends? Jesse said they liked him, after all. He was *kind of cool*. Hazard found that a little hard to believe, but he wasn't going to argue.

"I'll hang out with you guys," Hazard agreed, hoping that was a good enough answer.

Jesse seemed satisfied with it. He got up and started dancing around with Felix to the rock song someone put on.

Jesse dropped Hazard off at the corner of Emery's cul-de-sac around one in the morning. Emery helped him climb through the window. He was his alibi, after all, and Hazard thanked him over and over for being such a good friend.

Chapter 2
January and February

ALL through winter break, Jesse texted him. A simple

What up?

quickly became long conversations rife with witty remarks and quips and one-liners that made Hazard forget about being nervous. Jesse talked to him like they hadn't just met three weeks before, joking and complaining and teasing. Things like

Oh man, my dad just scored
me a wicked pair of Doc Martens,

or

I like rib sandwiches and pizza for
school lunch but otherwise count me out

and

So booored, I feel like I'm in Mr. Crenshaw's class and it's fucking Sunday,
nothing to do, I demand you amuse me.

They were little glimpses of a tangible Jesse that made Hazard excited to talk to him, to learn more, and if that was Jesse's strategy to keep Hazard on his toes, it was working, and Hazard let it.

"You sure are texting a lot," his mom said the day after Christmas, watching him from the dining table, where she was flipping through a magazine. "I hope you're not running up the bill."

"Sorry," Hazard mumbled, sprawled on the couch. "I'm not."

"I said *I hope* you're not," his mom reminded him with a curt sigh, "not that you *are*."

"He's fine," Hazard's dad grunted from the easy chair on the other side of the living room, turning up the TV. Hazard's mom gave another sigh.

Emery and Russell argued a lot most of winter break. Hazard had no idea what they fought about. He didn't want to get involved—and, guiltily, inevitably he wanted to know if they were going to hate each other or make up and stay friends. When Hazard hung out with Emery, he didn't answer Jesse's texts. He thought it would be rude. His phone would vibrate over and over for each new message until Emery asked, "Who the hell is texting you?"

"Jesse," Hazard answered invariably, waiting for Emery to scoff. Emery never did.

There were four good parties over winter break, and Hazard went to each with Jesse and his friends. Partying wasn't their only favorite pastime, though. They liked to cause trouble during pep rallies, collect detention slips, disgust preps and jocks, vandalize small corners of the world like street signs, light poles, and bathroom walls, and steal snacks from gas stations too.

In the bitter soggy cold of a night near the end of winter break, Hazard waited in the back seat of Lexie's car with his feet propped on the middle console and his heart pounding. His fists curled and uncurled nervously. The dark of evening was flushed out by the glare of the Chevron's lights, and he'd been so mortified of looking like a loser but *more* mortified of getting arrested for shoplifting that he'd insisted the other four go inside and do their thing because he had to make a phone call.

Nobody gave him a problem, but he didn't really have a call to make, so Hazard sat in the back seat of Lexie's little Eclipse, tapping his feet on the middle console and sweating and swallowing and staring through the windshield and into the gas station beyond it.

Jesse and Felix made faces at him through the window over the magazine racks, sticking their tongues out and crossing their eyes and giggling to themselves when Hazard rolled his own eyes at them and made dismissive gestures. They were like little kids, he was coming to find. They gave off these airs of being badass and angry, but they were like little kids.

Felix, Lexie, Brianna—they were Jesse's closest friends. Lexie idolized Pink and wore baggy, tattered jeans and push-up bras (when she wore a bra). She had a lip ring she constantly toyed with if she didn't have anything else to put in her mouth, like gum or a pen, and Hazard had only gone to four parties so far, including the one in December, but it seemed that Lexie was always the hostess of the toke room no matter where they were. Brianna was like Lexie's sidekick, except that Lexie didn't boss Brianna around. Brianna was just quiet. She was tiny and frail looking, with very long blonde hair, but she could hold her liquor like nobody would guess. If her nails were unpainted, which was rare, she liked to color them with Sharpies. She played flute in the school orchestra and came across as gravely serious, but she actually danced on tables after her third drink—on purpose, because she liked to.

Felix was tall and sculpted, with perfectly styled hair and a klutzy kind of charm. He liked tie-dyed shirts with safety pins in them and *American Pie*, and Jesse claimed that he and Felix had been inseparable since fourth grade, partners in crime or something like that. Hazard sometimes found that hard to believe, because it was obvious that Felix wore his huge heart on his sleeve, and how somebody like that could be friends with a stubborn jerk like Jesse, Hazard wasn't sure. But Felix was, and Felix had frowned upon everyone teasing Hazard twice now, so Hazard kind of liked him, and he couldn't blame Felix for being friends with Jesse because there was just something about Jesse that nobody could resist.

Messy hair and intense green eyes above a crooked smile—Jesse Logan Wesley with his red leather jacket, slim-fit Levi's, smug attitude, teenage rebellion, and the fake ID reserved for smokes. Hazard discovered quickly enough that Jesse wasn't *exactly* what the rumors made him out to be, but Jesse was just Jesse, and that was all that could be said.

Hazard watched everyone as the tops of their heads bobbed through the little aisles in the gas station, pausing here and there, disappearing now and again. He watched as the four of them congregated around the cash register and Jesse bought two packs of cigarettes. Once they were all back in the car, they unloaded their pockets, dumping a bounty of candy and crackers and even a pack of condoms onto the car's middle console.

"It's just too easy," Lexie cooed, taking the cigarette Jesse handed her and tucking it behind her ear. She rode shotgun, grinning broadly. Hazard shrank into the back seat between Felix and Brianna. Jesse smirked, sifting through their stolen goods and picking out a little golden Ferrero Rocher. Rich tastes for a rich boy.

"Are you gonna join us next time?" Felix asked. Hazard's brow knotted because Felix sounded so hopeful.

Join us next time. Join them in what? Petty shoplifting at a gas station? Lexie and Jesse looked at Hazard pointedly, and Felix and Brianna watched him silently from either side of the back seat. They were all waiting for his answer because his place in their group sort of depended on it. Either he joined in their fun and was truly one of them, or he was the awkward goody two-shoes who condescended to hang out with them. He thought of Jesse saying *You're kind of cool* and *We like you.*

"Sure," Hazard mumbled, shrugging idly. He felt like he couldn't let down the open look on Felix's face, anyway.

Hazard didn't lie. The next time they hit up a gas station, he joined them. After three times dawdling around with his hands in his pockets and stealing nothing, he finally dared to use the five-finger discount and was praised by the rest of them when he returned to the car with a pack of Swedish Fish and a bottle of Mountain Dew. He gave the Swedish Fish to Emery later. Emery loved Swedish Fish.

SOME teachers started a fundraiser for Sri Lanka after the Indian Ocean earthquake. Jesse dyed his hair punk red, like a fire engine or an alarm. It made him look more badass. It made him look *good.*

What else was there to do for fun in a cold, wet Northwestern winter than party? Hazard felt totally insecure and out of place the first couple times, hoping he seemed cool and hoping he impressed Jesse and his friends and hoping Emery wouldn't be mad about being his alibi again. But after a few weeks, Hazard didn't need to have finished off a drink or two before he started dancing around to the music too.

Somewhere between the first party Hazard went to and the last one in January, Hazard changed. All of a sudden, his last walls just crumbled and he felt good, conditioned to the scene. He liked to dance with people to the music blasting through someone's tiny living room. He liked to drink until his knees shook. He liked to laugh with people he didn't really know and follow Jesse and his friends from room to room, and he liked to flirt with people because he was cool and it made him feel great. Sometimes people tried to kiss him, and they weren't always girls. Hazard let them now and then. They weren't his first kisses, after all. If he was drunk enough, he kissed back. It was a party. Nobody cared. Hazard liked that.

Waking up and remembering what he'd done while drunk was sometimes miserable, and Hazard was always terrified that he'd made an idiot of himself. But despite Jesse's relentless teasing about *this one time* or *the other night*, the pictures Felix collected from each party, and the stories that circulated through a party's crowd the morning after, Hazard still felt pretty cool just to be hanging out with Jesse and his friends at all. He felt cool coming into the party with them, blowing dark hair out of his eyes and throwing back a drink, bopping along to the words of whatever song was playing, and recognizing more and more familiar faces to wave at and laugh with. After three drinks, Hazard was usually drunk. Not yet to the threshold of being utterly trashed, but far enough past buzzed. He caught Jesse smiling at him sometimes, when he wasn't dancing close to or making out with some girl. He wondered if Jesse was proud of asking him to be their rookie or if Jesse even remembered telling Hazard not to let him down.

Hazard ran into Russell once, near the end of January at a house on Maple Ridge Street.

Hazard had been in the rec room sitting cross-legged with Brianna, where behind all the laughter and conversation was casual music, not dancing music. They had Dixie cups of Mountain Dew and vodka that had a little too much vodka in them. They played card games while Jesse explained to Emily Thompson, Mark Graham, and Lexie's gangster cousin Jeff Morgan that Hazard was a *natural,* and once he got two drinks in him, he'd do *anything.*

"We're training him to hold his liquor," Lexie announced.

"I'm not a dog," Hazard grumbled, but he laughed with them all. It felt good that they thought he was a *natural.*

He found Russell in the living room, where the lights were off and everybody was either really drunk or making out with each other. Finding Russell there made Hazard furious. He knew how Emery looked up to

Russell. For Russell to go to a party without Emery seemed like the biggest slap in the face, especially because the two of them had been fighting for a few weeks about Russell dating Beth Nye, and now Russell had gone to a party with her. Hazard wanted Emery to hate Russell, so he kissed Russell in the dark of the living room while Beth was in the bathroom, because they were both drunk and it seemed the best way to take advantage of the situation. Russell didn't even seem to know what was going on, just that he was pissed off and so was Hazard. Either way, Hazard made sure Russell had a safe ride home before he left.

The last party of January was at Ashton's house. Ashton was Felix's friend. Hazard sat with Jesse for a while, crowded around the table in the atrium-crowned dining room. They laid out hands of solitaire with Ryan and Luke. There were girls making out in the kitchen and a lot of jelly sex bracelet snapping going on. Over solitaire, they spoke in low voices of rumors that someone had heard police sirens nearby, but they didn't really worry about it because the party was good and the drinks were expensive.

Hazard got bored of that quickly and wandered off. He was nursing his fourth bottle of Mike's Hard Lemonade. He ran into Liam, a junior closer to the prom king's side of popularity than the underbelly's. They compared their best dance moves, trying not to run into the sophomores playing Twister. Liam's cell phone rang. His ringtone was Eminem. For some reason, it made Hazard laugh really hard. Something changed in Liam's eyes with his laughter, and the next thing Hazard knew, Liam's tongue was in his mouth, and Hazard fought to keep his Mike's from spilling as Liam crushed him down against the arm of the couch.

Liam's phone kept ringing. His hands slid around Hazard's sides, and Hazard didn't stop him. Liam was a lot stronger. It made his heart race like every new kiss did. The music faded away as the track switched, the noise in the house going from a gentle hum behind the beat to a roar in the silence.

That was the night Hazard's last walls of uncertainty fell. It was something inside him, internal and significant but too complicated for him to name. It just shifted—and that was it. The change was made.

Hazard wanted that. He wanted to be wanted like that, and he wanted to be part of this world where everybody did what they wanted and nobody cared because there was good booze, good music, and stuff like that was the latest trend. He wanted to be surrounded by people. He wanted to kiss and have fun and sleep it all off like the alcohol.

"My turn," Jesse grumbled when he intervened, grabbing Hazard's arm and yanking him off the couch. Liam looked irritated by that. Hazard grunted, stumbled, scowled, and began to resist, but then they danced, and Hazard forgot all about Liam. He danced with a girl named Christina and a girl named Amy, and Amy said, "That was really hot, you and Liam," and, "I mean, you're not gay, right? It was just a party kiss—you guys are just shitfaced, right?"

"Yeah," Hazard agreed, nodding. Just a party kiss. Amy kissed him too, just another party kiss. She wanted his number. Hazard gave it to her. He understood that as long as he got close to a girl at some point during a party, nobody but the bored obligatory gossipers would really call him *gay*. They'd blame it on the alcohol because nobody cared who was gay and who was straight at a party, as long as you were straight again when you left. Then everything was just a skeleton in the closet or a funny story to tell. It was cool to be *open* like that.

It was a Friday night. Emery let Hazard take a shower and borrow some clothes later when Jesse dropped him off after the party. Hazard called him a sweetie. With the lights off, they played Mario Kart on Emery's old Nintendo. Emery's parents had already gone to bed, but they still tried to be as quiet as possible, snickering together in the shadows of Emery's room because Hazard couldn't play very well when he was so drunk.

Amy called him the next afternoon. Hazard pretended he didn't remember her.

"WHY won't you let me kick her ass?"

Gravel crunched beneath Felix's feet as he tightened his grip on Hazard's shoulders and pressed him back against the passenger door of his car.

"Because," Felix snapped. "Because you don't get it, Hazard."

"What don't I get?" Crisp winter wind swept across the parking lot and tossed dark hair off his forehead. It bit at his skin where it was not covered by his jacket. Eyes narrowed, shaking with fury, Hazard glared between Felix and Jesse and back again. Trying to pry Felix's hands off his shoulders, Hazard settled his wrath on Jesse now.

Jesse stood just behind Felix, not looking at either of them but peering out at the busy street beyond the school parking lot. This was his smoke break, and he wasn't going to let Hazard ruin that. His cigarette burned between his fingers, free hand in his hip pocket. The breeze pulled his red jacket away from his body, twisting his T-shirt against his frame. He ignored Hazard's stare.

"What don't I get?" Hazard demanded again, this time using a knee to try and create distance between himself and Felix. Felix grunted, swerving his body away, and Hazard yanked free from his hands. More gravel crunched, rocks spitting away from his Converse as he stumbled forward.

Jesse turned slightly, cutting a sharp, scornful glance in Hazard's direction. Hazard stopped short, glare faltering just a bit.

"Jesus Christ, Haz, just listen to Felix. He knows what he's talking about."

Felix reached for Hazard again and Hazard jerked away, casting Felix a warning look below his lashes. Nevertheless, he backed up and leaned against the car, crossing his arms. Felix scowled, but his eyes were hurt. He looked worried. That was just how Felix was, Hazard was learning. He cared a lot.

"The same rules don't apply," Felix said.

Hazard's brow knotted. "What?"

"The same rules don't apply, Haz." Felix adjusted his coat, frowning. "Gossip will start and people will call you names, but in the end you're practically immune to it. The more gossip rages, the cooler he gets."

Hazard tensed, feeling his skin ice over. His stomach dropped in confusion. *The cooler he gets.* His gaze flickered over Felix's shoulder, and he watched as Jesse blew a stream of cigarette smoke toward the car next to them. Someone had written *Reno luvs ya bay-bay!* on the back window. Jesse. The *he* Felix referred to was Jesse. *The more gossip rages, the cooler he gets.*

"That's what I mean when I say the same rules don't apply," Felix explained, watching the connections form in Hazard's eyes. "Because of gossip, everyone knows what he does—what we all do—and people make comments and spread rumors, but look at how it ends up. Everyone still loves him. He's still one of the coolest kids ever."

"Could be because he's rich," Hazard grumbled, but both Felix and Jesse ignored him. "Could be because he's a train wreck," Hazard added, but they ignored him again because they knew that, either way, money or social label, what Felix was saying was absolutely true.

"The more you're with Jesse, the more gossip doesn't really matter. Pretty soon, the same rules don't apply to you either. You're *cool by association*, or something. The more people gossip, the cooler we all get. Fucked up, hunh?" Felix laughed, but he sounded tired. "It didn't always used to be like this, you know. It started around seventh grade—"

"Who said what, Hazard?"

Both Felix and Hazard looked to Jesse, silenced. Felix frowned at the interruption. He'd been talking about something important. Hazard just frowned at the whole thing.

Jesse put out his cigarette on the window of the car next to them, looking at them from the corner of his eye. "Who said what?" he repeated.

"Um.... This girl," Hazard mumbled, feeling very cowed by this newfound value of Jesse and his camaraderie and Jesse's interest in what had hurt Hazard so much. Hazard glanced at Felix but found no support there.

"What'd she say?"

Hazard shuffled his feet in the gravel of the parking lot, watching the toes of his shoes as he did so. "That I'm just a closet case and a big attention whore."

"Well, that's okay. They called Felix worse things a couple years ago, because of Ryan—"

"Jesse, shut up!"

"Did you hear this girl say it, Hazard?"

"Yeah, as she walked by, and I—"

"He was about to clock her," Felix filled in, running fingers through his hair where the wind was beginning to mess it up. "So I grabbed him and brought him out here to you. I mean, Jesse, he was gonna do it. He was gonna hit a *girl*."

Jesse brushed past Felix and fixed Hazard with a stare, arms crossed. Hazard tipped his head back against Felix's car. Jesse held his eyes for a long moment. His stare pierced right into him, a mesmerizing green. "Are you in the closet, Hazard?"

Hazard jumped, offended. *"No."*

"Are you an attention whore?"

"No!"

"Well, there you go. You just disproved the gossip, so you shouldn't let it bother you." Jesse propped his hands on his hips, smiling as if those simple words soothed the sting completely.

Hazard stared back, incredulous. Simple words *didn't* soothe the sting; he wanted *action*. Albeit, Jesse was trying to make him feel better, and that was something.

"The same rules don't apply," Hazard said slowly, trying to believe it.

"Pretty much."

"So I should just brush it off?"

"Yeah. Hey, what did the girl look like, Felix?" Jesse motioned for Felix to come closer. Felix had been fixing his hair in the side mirror of a car. Jesse broke into a grin, swinging an arm around Felix's neck and putting on an air that was clearly supposed to be mocking that of a gang member. It worked because Jesse was an intimidating person. "We'll make sure she never says anything about you ever again, Danger. Just brush it off when something like that happens, then come and tell me. And I'll *take care of it*."

Hazard watched as they wrestled together, Jesse hanging around Felix's neck, Felix overpowering him because he was just slightly bigger. They staggered around and play-punched each other. Crunching gravel and their laughter echoed. Hazard swallowed, shrinking back against

Felix's car. But he had to admit he did feel a little relieved.

The same rules didn't apply, and Jesse would take care of anyone who wasn't aware of that. That felt good.

A THIN blanket of snow had fallen, but rain turned it to icy slush. There was a long weekend for teacher's meetings, and nobody was going to let an extra night of freedom escape without a party. Emery kindly agreed to be Hazard's alibi again, as long as Hazard helped him with his English project on *Romeo and Juliet*.

Hazard found that most of the parties were the same, no matter who was throwing them. Dark, music pounding, booze and smoke and everyone laughing like they knew what they were doing, and sometimes people started dancing around, and sometimes they all just sat in someone's house and got drunk to the beat of the song. One thing was for certain, though, and that was that Jesse and his crew always left just before everyone started puking.

There was a haze in the living room from countless cigarettes, and beneath it all, the smell of pot snuck in from the kitchen. The joints had been rolled on the counter between a bowl of soggy potato chips and a bottle of Absolut. The chips had been abandoned after someone spilled their entire drink in them.

It was stuffy. The lights were down, music cranked. The house wasn't very big, but somehow, those in attendance made it work—and if they ran into someone while they were dancing, or upon an innocent navigation from one end of the room to the other, so be it, because the energy bounced off bodies and circulated, spreading around the party like a contagious disease.

The ceiling fan was on, stirring the smoke that settled. It stung Hazard's eyes and made his skin feel hot. The beat rattled through him. Sisqó, the Gorillaz, Outkast—Hazard was new to this, the swiveling of hips as he worked through his second rum and Vanilla Coke, the game of flirting everyone seemed to play while he blushed and talked, laughed, smiled politely. He wasn't new to partying anymore, but he was still getting used to it. It still made him a little nervous when Jesse found him again an hour or so later, but Hazard was beginning to feel like he'd known Jesse for a lot longer than just five weeks.

"Lexie's opened up shop in the back bedroom if you wanna light up," Jesse grunted as he came near. He took a sip of Hazard's drink. Hazard let him. Jesse tossed his pack of Camels down and kicked a foot up on the arm of the couch to retie his shoe.

"No, thanks." Hazard sat on the arm of the couch next to Jesse's foot. "Not tonight."

"That's cool. Hey, are you having fun?"

"Yeah."

Jesse looked up at him. His glances always commanded attention, even unintentionally. "I saw you with, um—oh God, what's her name? Brandi."

"Yeah. I recognized her from school."

"She's cute, hunh?"

"She's pretty."

"Oh, yeah? You're such a gentleman. Hey, will you grab my cigarettes?"

"Sure."

"Get one out for me, will you?" Jesse asked distractedly, having caught sight of someone familiar. It was a rather hard-looking girl with a pinched face and sharp eyes, and dark-brown hair she tossed over her shoulder as Jesse greeted her. She grinned and wrapped her arms around him, laughing as he returned the rough and friendly embrace. He said, "Janelle, what's up?" and she drawled, "Nothing much. I didn't know you were going to be here."

Pretending he wasn't watching from the corner of his eye, Hazard leaned across the couch and grabbed Jesse's pack of cigarettes. He held them for a moment, passing them from hand to hand and watching Jesse and Janelle catch up until some of Janelle's friends arrived, looking like copies of her but with different shades of hair. They pulled her off somewhere else. Remembering Jesse had asked for a cigarette, Hazard tapped the pack of Camels into his palm, pulling his feet up to sit cross-legged on the arm of the couch so people would stop running into his ankles.

He didn't really think about it, tapping the pack of cigarettes. It was just something he'd seen people do before taking one out, but for some reason Jesse was totally affected by it.

He looked at Hazard curiously, a dark, covetous kind of curiosity, although Hazard wasn't sure of it at the moment. Jesse looked at him like he'd never seen him before, and Hazard frowned, pulling out a cigarette for him and hoping nobody stole his drink where he'd set it down over there on the bookshelf.

Jesse took the cigarette and leaned down swiftly. Hazard bristled as their noses bumped, and then Jesse's mouth was a firm pressure on his, soft and hot. A dangerous chill zipped down Hazard's spine at the same instant that his heart jumped and his stomach flopped, which was all at once quite a sickening sensation.

Jesse stepped closer. Hazard leaned back on the couch. His eyes shut. He didn't fight it. He didn't think about people seeing or saying something mean or thinking he was *that way*, because Jesse's hand was tender as he touched Hazard's cheek, and Jesse's lips were wet as he moved them to soften the kiss. Hazard tried not to crumple the pack of cigarettes as his hands twitched nervously and he craned up into Jesse's kneading mouth.

They kissed for just a moment, warm pliant lips and the graze of teeth. Hazard's face was hot when Jesse pulled away, looking at him with that same strange curiosity and his head tipped to one side. He reached down and took the pack of cigarettes from Hazard's hand. His fingertips made Hazard shiver, and he pulled his hand away instinctively. No, bad touch. No, don't be seduced. Think about how many girls Jesse has been with, maybe even that Janelle girl. What would Jesse's friends say? Look away from those deep eyes and ignore the flutter of the heart, the urge to kiss again, because—

"I'm just drunk," Hazard mumbled, brow knotting. He pushed the cigarettes into Jesse's palm.

Jesse smiled like he didn't believe him. "I believe you," he lied. "Hey, what happens at a party stays at a party. It's like Vegas, right?" He gave Hazard one last tender look, and then suddenly he was nothing but a cool guy again. He pushed away from the couch and wandered off to find an ashtray so he could have his cigarette.

Hazard couldn't breathe for a moment. He sat on the arm of the couch and stared at his tennis shoes and wished he knew why he felt so stirred up—stirred up by the feel and the taste still on his mouth, the way he felt sick with shyness, the way Jesse gave him goose bumps with that cat-eyed smirk and profound stare. Hazard watched from across the house as Jesse lit up in the corner, laughing with a few other people, running a hand through his punk-red hair, looking so damn cool in his hemp and dog tags and button-down shirt with the sleeves rolled up. It was just a party, it was just a kiss, it was just Jesse, and Jesse was revenge for Emery having Russell.

One of Jesse's favorite songs was stuck in Hazard's head. *Go on, take everything, take everything, I want you to.* Hazard grabbed his drink after a moment, took a long sip, and then he tried to find somebody he knew from school to distract him from his thoughts. Brandi would do again.

"HAPPY Valentine's Day!"

Jesse's friend Brianna stood post at the front door, wearing a cute little dress and strap-on wings. She had a heart-shaped barrette in her blonde hair. She was bored, Hazard remembered that much, but when he and Jesse had walked in behind Felix, Brianna had lit up and thrust the bowl of party favors at them. The bowl was full of condoms.

"Courtesy of Lexie," she scoffed above the echo of Nine Inch Nails from the stereo. Jesse had laughed and grabbed two fistfuls of condoms, so Hazard snatched up quite a few in turn and shoved them in his back pocket, following Jesse as he got Brianna a beer and then walked around, talking to people and throwing condoms back and forth. It was Valentine's Day, after all.

Hazard could still see Brianna now, from where he lay on the sofa. He wasn't sure how long poor Brianna had been wandering around welcoming people in, but it must have been a while if he was measuring by sobriety, or the lack thereof. He was starting to feel a little out of focus after his third Dixie cup of—what was it? "Cupid's love potion," Lexie had said when she gave it to him, and thinking about it now, it was really funny.

Hazard saw Jesse pass by the couch and cast a smoky glance in his direction. Hazard waved. Jesse didn't wave back. He disappeared beyond Hazard's peripheral vision, and Hazard frowned. The couch sagged behind his head as somebody sat down beside him. Hazard rolled over, looking up at the girl joining him there. She had dark eyes and razored hair and a little too much eye makeup on.

"Hi," Hazard said.

"Hi," the girl replied.

The party swirled around them. The girl got up and left after a while. Hazard watched Brianna dance around by herself with the bowl of condoms, nursing a beer. Lexie went over and talked to her.

Hazard stood up and wandered through Lexie's house. In her bedroom, people were getting high. He watched them for a minute or two, remembering how he'd almost tried it once with Tom in eighth grade, back when he'd hung out with the skaters a lot more. He recognized Benny Petrovich from Biology, and Benny saw him too.

"Hey, come here." Benny waved at him. Hazard drifted in and sat down beside him. There weren't a lot of others in Lexie's bedroom, just another boy and a girl who was falling asleep against the bed, and Benny held up a half-smoked joint for Hazard to take.

Hazard tried it, nervously. It was the first time he'd touched a joint. He didn't even smoke cigarettes like Jesse did. Benny and the other boy couldn't stop laughing at him because it took him three times to finally learn to hold the toke in long enough.

"Like this?" Hazard mumbled, squinting in the dark room at the smoldering end of the joint.

"Yeah," Benny said. The other boy scooted around to help, snickering endlessly below his breath. He had a beanie on and untamed curls. He said his name was Chase.

Hazard took a pull off the joint and held in the smoke for a moment, tasting the paper and the pot. It burned in his throat. His eyes watered as he let it all out, pushing the joint at Benny again. Chase laughed. They traded the joint back and forth a few times until Benny took the last hit and then smashed it out on the sole of his shoe.

"Benny just raped you, man," Chase snickered.

Hazard's brow knotted. "What?"

"Ignore him. Do you feel it yet?" Benny asked.

Hazard shrugged. "I don't know. I mean, I'm really drunk. Maybe I won't feel anything because I'm drunk."

Benny snorted, shrugging in turn. They waited together. Benny played with his lighter. Hazard thought about Benny in science class, sitting in the back of the room snickering with his friends while they wrote notes in the textbooks—*turn to page 289* and *u r a loser*. It was funny. Hazard laughed at it. Benny looked at him, startled, then started to laugh too, even though he didn't know why. The room began to tip and sway, something Hazard felt most certainly right at the base of his spine, and the taste of pot was dry in his mouth, and he said, "Oh my God, Benny, I don't even talk to you in science class."

Benny thought this was just as hilarious, and they laughed until Hazard couldn't breathe. He had to lie down to get rid of the stitch in his side, but the room still spun like crazy, and he laughed because it wasn't like he was unaware of what was going on around him. He was perfectly aware. He just couldn't stop laughing. The more he laughed, the more embarrassed he got, because he didn't want to be cliché, except the more embarrassed he got, the more he laughed. He knew exactly what was going on, even when Benny left to get a glass of water and Chase, the boy with the beanie, immediately seized the opportunity to pin Hazard down on the floor and start going through his pockets.

"No, dude, give it back," Hazard groaned when Chase took out his wallet and started fumbling through it. There was nothing in it. Nothing important, really. Some of the condoms from Brianna were in it. There was no cash. Hazard had spent the last of his allowance with Emery at the bookstore.

Chase didn't answer. The girl asleep against the bed snored a little. Chase tossed the wallet aside and reached up Hazard's shirt, and Hazard remembered something he'd heard once while watching *Dateline* with his mom: something like sometimes it wasn't about boys or girls but about power and shame. Like prison. That was what Chase wanted. He wanted to scare him. That disturbed Hazard.

He heard the bedroom door open again. He saw the slant of hallway light on the carpet. He tried to wrestle away from Chase, but the room spun so much he didn't know if he was wrestling up or down or left or right. Chase's hands were clammy on his skin. He unbuttoned Hazard's pants, mumbling, "Shut up, it's okay, we're alone."

And to think, just last year, Valentine's Day was all about handing out cards and candy to your classmates.

Hazard watched as somebody grabbed Chase and pushed him violently to the side. His beanie fell off. It was Lexie, scowling viciously. Chase bumped into the girl asleep against the bed and she swore at him. Lexie cornered Chase against the far wall of the bedroom.

Hazard scrambled upward, eyes widening. He almost lost his balance. A little bit more clarity pierced through him with it. His heart skipped a beat, and he watched in growing horror as a crowd gathered in the hall outside the bedroom because Lexie was screaming at Chase, jabbing a finger in his face. She looked ready to rip him to pieces.

"—*and I let you come into my fucking house and smoke your fucking pot in my fucking room and you think you can take advantage of someone here? Do you even realize that's my fucking friend over there? You faggot, you little piece of spineless shit, you—*"

"Get the fuck out of here." It was Jesse now, pulling Lexie away and shoving Chase to the bedroom door.

"*Hey, lay off!*" Chase roared. There was a brief struggle, and Hazard groaned because he could see everything that was about to happen in his head already. He could see Chase and Jesse getting into it, fighting, really hurting each other, and somebody would call the cops, and it would be all over school, and then Jesse would be mad at him, and—

The girl that was trying to sleep got up and stomped out of the room. Chase followed her. Lexie and Jesse tailed him, and Hazard grabbed his wallet and did the same, fastening his pants again. The crowd in the house parted like the Red Sea for them, and Hazard was terrified. The music was blasting, but nobody was really doing much but staring.

Chase voluntarily went to the door. Lexie, dissatisfied, hurried past Jesse and pushed him out into the cold. She waited as two or three of his friends followed him, a few others who wanted to leave. Lexie waved good-bye and slammed the front door.

"Show's over!" someone yelled. Tentatively, people resumed what they'd been doing before.

Jesse grabbed Hazard by the arm and dragged him roughly to the bathroom.

"I'm sorry," Hazard groaned, stumbling after him. "I'm sorry, I'm sorry, Jesse—"

The bathroom door slammed and Jesse locked it. Hazard rubbed his stinging eyes with the balls of his palms, choking up in his panic. Jesse switched on the light and turned on the faucet in the sink. His fingers wiggled in the air as he searched around the bathroom for a moment, then grabbed the cup sitting next to the sink and plucked out the toothbrushes, filling it with cold water. He pulled Hazard forward and dumped the cup of water over his head.

Hazard sputtered, waving his hands around in shock. He wiped at his face and gave Jesse a rough shove. Jesse didn't resist. He staggered backward into the door and stared at Hazard curiously.

"What the hell was that for?" Hazard cried, flinging water droplets everywhere as he fixed Jesse with a scowl and sat down on the edge of the bathtub. He was far too shaky, far too dizzy.

Jesse shrugged, setting the cup down. "Trying to sober you up."

"I'm *fine,* but now I'm all *wet.*" Hazard grabbed the nearest towel and wiped at his face, then just draped it over his head. His throat clenched up. His cheeks burned as he felt himself begin to tear up again, his breath shallow. It felt like the bathroom was swaying to and fro. "I feel like I'm gonna puke!"

"Good. Do it." Jesse lifted the lid of the toilet loudly. Hazard could tell Jesse was far past buzzed already, because he was too laid-back and a little out of it. "Puke, Haz."

"I don't *want* to!" Hazard stomped his foot, and his voice wavered pathetically. He sounded like a little kid throwing a fit. He threw the towel down, glaring at the toilet. His eyes stung. "I don't wanna puke. I hate it. Jesse, if I ever see that kid, I'm gonna kick his ass—"

Jesse jerked the door open, disappearing out into the hallway. Hazard stumbled after him frantically. "Don't leave me alone!" he hissed, grabbing Jesse by the back of the shirt. Jesse shook him off.

"I'm *not*," he grumbled begrudgingly. "I'm going to get you some fucking apple juice. That's supposed to help too. I'm sure all this bullshit's already killed your high, though."

Hazard miserably followed Jesse to the kitchen. He couldn't fight the feeling that Jesse was mad at him for some reason. He drank the apple juice when Jesse gave it to him, even though each pull on the straw made him nauseous. He let Jesse have a sip, then drank the rest and held his head, slouched against the countertop. Jesse stood beside him, silent. He coughed once or twice. He had that look on his face, that detached look, that halfway connected to the real world but definitely drunk look, and his stern frown made it even more frightening than usual. Hazard asked him to come with him to the bathroom again, but Jesse refused.

Hazard went alone. He'd just flushed after peeing when his stomach gave a rebellious lurch, and before he could zip his fly, he threw up. It was thin and burned his throat. But he felt better. He flushed again and looked in the mirror. He felt lighter. He felt shaky and dizzy, and he had a bad taste in his mouth, but he felt a little better. He didn't look it. His eyes were puffy and looked scared, his cheeks were pale, and his hair was a dark-brown mess all around his face.

Jesse tugged him out onto the porch when he emerged from the bathroom, passing Brianna and closing the door. He shoved his cigarettes and lighter against Hazard's chest and grumbled, "Something about a stimulant."

"I threw up," Hazard insisted. "I drank juice. You dumped water over my head, and it's cold out here. I think I'm about as coherent as I'm going to be before I just sleep all of this off, Jesse."

"Just do it." Jesse waved a hand. "Think about that dick Chase and then you'll need a cigarette. Oh, hey, give me one too. I'm so fucking pissed at you right now. I don't think you even realize it."

Hazard carefully pulled a cigarette out, handing it and the lighter over to Jesse. Jesse sagged down to sit beside him on the steps, hunched forward in the cold as he lit up. Hazard watched, shivering. His stomach turned, but not like he was going to get sick again. He was just scared. He felt violated too. *Think about that dick Chase and then you'll need a cigarette*, Jesse had said.

Hazard pressed his forehead to his hands, listening to Jesse smoke as his teeth chattered. He wanted to crawl into bed and sleep this off. What would people say tomorrow, at school?

"Why are you mad at me?" Hazard croaked.

Jesse shrugged. He avoided the question. "Lexie makes strong drinks," he said.

"Don't let me get this way again." Hazard frowned tightly. "Promise me."

"Okay, okay, whatever. I promise." Jesse held up a pinky finger. Hazard stared at it for a moment before joining it with his.

"Thanks," he whispered. His breath made little clouds on the night air. He was still pretty dizzy, but he felt a little more focused than usual.

"Yeah, well, just remember *your* promise."

Hazard looked at Jesse, lost.

"You promised me that first night—" Jesse paused to take a pull on his cigarette. "—that you could handle this. Don't let me down. I don't need to hear about you losing control and something bad happening to you. I need to know that you'll always be in control of the situation, because you promised me you would be."

The world blurred as Hazard's vision doubled, then trebled. Something about what Jesse said touched him. He thought of the night they'd kissed not too long ago, and his mouth grew dry and his throat clenched, and his fingers shook, not from the cold but from emotion as he pressed his mouth against his knuckles.

Jesse nodded, sighing a stream of cigarette smoke. He set his Camels down between them. "Happy fucking Valentine's Day," he whispered.

HIGH school had its unspoken rules and its universal truths, which were generally understood even with a lack of justification and communication. There were just some things that were unacceptable in some places but totally proper in others. There were social processes and routines and traditions passed down through the generations of cliques, some of which weren't even comprehended by successors, just executed with a livid passion that rivaled that of a wild and irrational animal.

One of these rules was that the bigger bullied the smaller.

"Hey, move it, faggot—"

Hazard tumbled into the locker with a hiss and a growl, recoiling off the thin metal door just in time to watch the perpetrator and his buddies saunter further down the hall. They were already too many steps away to really confront.

Hazard stood next to the locker he'd been shoved against, rubbing at his arm. His backpack slipped off his shoulders a little. Hallway traffic kept moving, unaffected. He scowled after the guys in their letterman jackets as they neared the end of the hall, disappearing around the corner with their blockhead laughter slicing through the rest of the hallway noise. Hazard clenched his teeth, fingers fisting in his sleeve.

God, how he'd love to just sprint after them right now and tell them exactly what he thought about their wannabe jock asses and how they'd never pass their second time through the school year with the few brain cells left in their skulls after all the tackles and touchdowns and head-banging to pointless music while they tailgated with their prom queen girlfriends. Except that they probably weren't repeating their grade, they were just dumb and rude. And also, if Hazard got riled up enough by his own words, he'd probably swing, and there were three of them, taller and bulkier, and just one of scrawny little him, so that wouldn't end very well.

Hazard stood against the locker in the busy hallway with his hand on his sore arm and his throat burning in embarrassment, glowering at the corner like the intensity of his fury could really summon the three guys back around to face him. Somebody had probably mentioned Hazard when talking about Jesse, or maybe some kind of word had finally gotten around about Hazard at parties, and jocks like that didn't like people like Hazard because people like Hazard didn't care about them or what game they'd won lately. Jocks like that had to hide their sensitivity by finding anything to punch—something like a hunter bringing home a buck and hoping for beer and praise—because guys weren't supposed to be sensitive. Maybe it had nothing to do with parties and what Hazard had been doing lately, because Hazard was tinier than they were and tiny guys were automatically categorized as *faggots*, and maybe one of the jocks had just needed to blow off some steam.

Hazard decided that that was what had happened, mostly because rumors scared him. He didn't want to think about them.

Somebody tapped him on the shoulder lightly, and a girl said, "Um, excuse me."

Hazard cut his eyes over to her. He must have looked pretty angry, because the girl standing beside him actually shifted backward an inch or two in surprise. Hazard shuffled his feet.

"What?" he said, brow furrowing further.

The girl stared at him. "This is my locker," she said, her eyes hardening over. "You're in my way."

Hazard blushed. He mumbled a miserable apology and gripped the straps of his backpack with murderous intent as he hurried away to his next class.

Chapter 3
March

JESSE was a good kisser.

At every party they went to, by the end of the night, Hazard kissed him at least once, and dancing with him was just as fun. Other people were just distractions until Jesse was ready to have fun with him again, and Felix and Lexie and Brianna didn't ask questions (at least, they didn't ask Hazard). The only problem was that people talked. It wasn't like nobody knew what happened at the latest party or what Hazard did.

It was okay for Jesse, because he was a top, so he was still cool. The guys that weren't grossed out thought he was a god because of it, quick-witted and flirting with girls and boys left and right. He had power.

Hazard, on the other hand, did not get that much respect, because he was small and he was Jesse's sidekick, so that automatically made him a bottom. Which wasn't true at all, but that was the way the mind of gossip worked.

In Biology, Canaan Lutz, a boy who looked and sounded like he'd walked right out of an episode of *Beavis and Butthead*, called Hazard every bad name under the sun. Hazard called him impudent. Canaan didn't know what that meant. Another time, a guy Hazard didn't know sauntered up to him during lunch and told him he was going to kick his ass because he'd made out with his girlfriend at some party. Emery looked over at Hazard with huge eyes, and Hazard had been startled and horrified and grappling for a way out when Jesse walked up, patted the guy on the back, and muttered a threat below his breath, short and sweet. The guy stormed off after that, making sure to turn all his friends against Jesse Wesley and his crew, but Jesse didn't care, and neither did anyone else. When Hazard asked about it, Jesse said plainly enough, "I told him if he didn't back off, he'd better watch himself walking to his car at night because the Seattle gang knows where he lives."

Hazard found out later that *the Seattle gang* consisted of Jesse's college friends, and they had a serious pack mentality. Emery didn't say a word about any of it, which worried Hazard until Emery looked at him pointedly one afternoon and said, "You really take a lot of shit at school, don't you? You know I've got your back, though, right?"

Hazard was relieved. "I've got yours too," he promised, because he knew Emery had heard his share of derogative jokes too. You couldn't be lovable without being teased.

When Jesse wasn't around, sometimes people heckled Hazard with stuff like *Where's Wesley, pal?* and *I heard you kiss like a girl, lady boy*, or empty threats to have a knuckle sandwich for lunch. Once, Hazard was afraid to be alone in the bathroom because Byron and Ricardo had told him to watch out. Another time, a junior named Allen, surrounded by laughing friends, asked Hazard, "Hey, wild thang, could I catch you house-hopping later tonight?" And in the gym one day, as the Lifetime Sports class was coming out of the locker room and the PE class was swarming in, Timmy—one of the arrogant popular kids, tall and tan with blond surfer hair—paused by Hazard and purred, "Hey, little boy," like he was trying to cut a deal or something.

"Don't call me that," Hazard hissed, trying to walk around him.

"What *can* I call you?" Timmy asked.

"Not that," Hazard said.

"Can I call you *cutie*?"

"No."

"Can I call you *sweetheart*?"

"No."

"Can I call you *sugar*?"

"You know what? You can call me your worst fucking nightmare if you don't leave me alone."

Hazard told Jesse about Timmy, and Jesse must have done or said something to Timmy later, because Timmy stopped bothering Hazard. Hazard didn't want to think about Jesse's powers of dissuasion, but it prided him to know that Jesse used them for him.

If Emery heard any horribly incriminating rumors, he never said anything about it to Hazard besides *I've got your back*. Hazard was content with that.

HIS mother had mastered the art of maternal manipulation, a trifecta of tone, glance, and word choice, but only with the most loving of intentions. Hazard had learned to steel himself against it when he didn't feel like clever remarks and battles of the wit.

"Oh, my good boy stayed home tonight," his mom cooed, sitting down beside him on the couch and pulling him to her chest to run her fingers through his hair. She smelled like her perfume and skin cream. Her hair was loose, and she had cotton pants on. She wanted him to feel guilty. Hazard shifted so he could watch TV through the bend of her arm.

"When was the last time you washed this shirt?" she asked. Hazard didn't answer. She was not satisfied with this. "It smells a little funny. You wore it around *that junior*, didn't you?" She wasn't really curious. She was telling him she could smell cigarette smoke or something like it, and she knew it wasn't because he smoked, because he was her good boy, after all.

"What are you watching?" She paused, letting Hazard's chagrin sink in before she spoke again. "Oh, I hate this show," she grumbled. "I hate MTV in general. Remember that crazy kid—"

She didn't have to elaborate. Hazard sighed thinly. "Jesse Camp."

"*Him*," his mother confirmed. "Ugh, he drove me up a wall. I swear he was homeless. And you thought he was *so cool*."

Hazard remembered. He'd been seven or eight, and he watched MTV just for Jesse Camp because Jesse Camp made him laugh really hard. He and Emery used to imitate him, rolling around on Emery's living room floor.

Hazard wasn't sure how she did it, nitpicking and insulting so effortlessly in one breath. A commercial came on for *War of the Worlds,* and she said something about Tom Cruise being short and girls not liking short boys. Hazard felt a little bruised by that, especially because she followed up by telling him he was going to be shorter because his father was shorter. His mom liked guys like Vin Diesel and Ricky Martin, which Hazard didn't understand at all.

Somebody sped by the house outside, and in the quiet of the evening, the sound of the car revving and peeling out was quite audible. It made Hazard think of Jesse and his cool car. His mother made sure to inform him that she hated loud cars, because any loud car was a piece of junk, and the driver was compensating for something. Hazard felt another blow somewhere sore in his chest, and he bit his tongue, wishing that if he turned the TV up, she wouldn't raise her voice further to talk over it.

Jesse texted him about a party. His mom didn't say anything when Hazard got up and left the living room, but when he came back through with his backpack on for his jacket and shoes, she muted the television immediately (having already changed the channel to *Sex and the City*, as if she'd been trying to bug him out of the living room in the first place).

"Where are you headed, Hazard?" she asked. She looked a little tired but very unyielding.

Hazard glanced at her. "Jesse's aunt is back in the hospital. I'm going with him to visit her. I'm staying at Emery's again."

"I just don't know if I *want* you going," his mother sniffed rather sharply. "What does *that junior's* aunt have, anyway? It's nothing contagious, right? And Emery—good God, I'm surprised his mother hasn't called me about you staying over so often."

"You know she doesn't mind. Jesse's really upset about his aunt—" Hazard saw something shift in his mom's eyes, like she knew she'd worn him down and was about to pounce for the kill.

"Are hospital visiting hours even open this late at night, Hazard James?"

And there it was. Hazard was at a loss for a moment, tying his Converse. He frowned, thinking about this. He didn't want to deal with this tonight. He wanted to skate down to Walnut and Wesleyan where Jesse was waiting, shove his skateboard in Jesse's trunk and squeeze into the back seat with Brianna and Lexie, go to a party and dance, get a little tipsy and have fun with everyone. He wanted to go and forget *this*, this annoying way his mother had of making him feel stifled and undeserving.

"Yeah, they are," he said, hoping to God it was true. "When was the last time you visited anyone at the hospital, anyway, Mom? How would you know?"

"I don't like this *attitude*," his mom countered immediately.

"*I'm sorry*," Hazard returned in much the same tone.

"If this *attitude* is a product of the time you spend with *that junior* and his friends"—his mother didn't even seem fazed that Hazard opened the door, ready to go—"then I think we have a problem. You'll be grounded, Hazard, and I mean it. You'll have chores to do, including the bathrooms, and you'll be grounded from *everyone*, even if *that junior's* aunt is on her *death bed.*"

His dad was uninvolved, in their bedroom down the hall. His mother regarded him coolly from the couch, trying to get everything she felt necessary out into the air before the front door closed. This was how it went. Hazard decided that if she really wanted him to stay home, she'd physically keep him from going out the door. She didn't.

"—and we'll have to have a talk about that hair of yours, because it's getting long and you're looking a little scruffy. And we'll have to get you some pants that don't look like they've gone through a shredder. And we'll have to *look into some plan of discipline because obviously you just don't care, and I think we are definitely going to church next week!*"

Hazard opened the front door, feeling very downtrodden. But Jesse and the others were up on Walnut and Wesleyan, waiting for him. His mom hurried to follow him out, clutching the door after he hopped down the stoop.

"*Hazard!*" she called.

"*What?*" he hissed back.

"Call me when you get to Emery's, or you're in *big trouble*," she spat, and Hazard was positive that the entire neighborhood heard her slam the door.

THE sky was a pasty gray and the air was cold, the whole world crisp and damp and lusciously green like it always was in the Northwest. A bitter wind came in off Puget Sound. Hazard was exhausted. He hadn't really had an appetite for days. He blamed it on getting up early after staying up late, but deep down he knew it was the drinking. He was worn out from balancing homework and partying, but after the note his science teacher had sent home with him when his percentage plummeted briefly, his mom was watching his grades like a hawk. "Look this over with your parents and get it signed," Mr. Cowles had said that Wednesday, and Hazard had felt like an idiot staring at his latest progress report and the attached letter, "because we all know you can do better, and I want to see you at least back to a B." But Hazard didn't think anybody, tired or not, found cells and their activity easy to learn about.

His ride home that day was Emery, but Emery had soccer practice. Hazard stayed after to watch, sitting alone on the bleachers with his hood up and hands shoved deep in his pockets. They were going to the bookstore and then getting McDonald's for dinner. And man, did Emery *kill* at soccer. He was a blur all over the field, a scrawny flash of messy brown hair and the white and blue of his team shirt over a thermal. All the white was in danger of permanent mud and grass stains.

Russell played soccer too. He was there, dribbling around orange cones. Hazard bit his tongue against a nasty comment about that all the time—something about the locker room, something about team players.

Below the sound of cars leaving the parking lot behind him, Hazard heard a little cough. There was nobody around him (although he looked around quite stupidly), but under the bleachers in a pocket of cliché, he saw a smudge of white blonde and denim and had to stifle a cry of surprise when he realized it was Brianna.

She sat below the bleachers, cross-legged with fingers curled on the metal beams and watching soccer practice. She looked perfectly content, sitting on her backpack so her pants didn't get dirty, gloves on and scarf wound tight around her neck.

Hazard knew Brianna well enough to call her his friend. She was part of Jesse's crew, and it would be rude to ignore her until they met up on the curb of someone's house, so Hazard gave her waves and smiles when he saw her and offhanded conversations when they sat at the same table at lunch, because that was polite. But today, as soccer practice went on and the sky threatened with more rain, Hazard went down below the bleachers to sit by her.

"Hi," he said, smiling.

She glanced at him like he'd shattered the most important silence in the world. But then she relaxed a little, resting her chin on her arms. She always looked kind of spacey in a dark, intuitive way. "Hi, Hazard," she said.

They were quiet together for a while, watching soccer practice. Hazard thought about Brianna at house parties, dancing with tall guys and throwing back beers and kissing people in the corner. He thought about the way she laughed when Jesse said something only she thought was funny. He thought about her in the back of the car when they made gas station runs to steal candy and pop, emptying her pockets of Baby Ruths and Paydays. He thought about her looking pretty and quiet in the hallway, and about the way she'd looked standing at the door on Valentine's Day with a bowl of condoms.

"What music do you listen to?" Hazard asked, and felt dumb for asking.

"Garbage," Brianna said. Hazard looked at her blankly, not sure what to say. Brianna shook her head, smiling. "No, not like *trash*. The band is called Garbage. I like The Cranberries too."

It was like that one question totally opened her up. Hazard couldn't do much more than nod and listen, commenting now and again when he felt it was necessary. Brianna told him about how she met Lexie, in middle school. She told him she had four older brothers. They talked about foods class and US History, and parties they went to, and she told him more about the scene and their crew before he'd joined them. That intrigued Hazard a lot, especially the part about Jesse being nicer now than he used to be.

"So you're the only girl?" Hazard asked, raising his brows. "You have all brothers?"

"Yeah." Brianna smiled faintly, watching the soccer team out on the soggy field. "So guy code and all the secrets boys have—I know them all."

Hazard smiled dubiously, brow knotting. "What do you mean, secrets?"

She glanced at him through her thick lashes, not at all contemptuously.

There was a little bit of significance there, a depth in her gaze that was sort of cowing. "You know, attitudes that boys have when they wear their hearts on their sleeves." There was a brief, tender pause between them. She was implying she could see right through any act he ever put on, and the same for everyone else—Jesse, Felix, her brothers. Hazard blushed.

"Do you like *Legend of Zelda*?" Brianna asked then, wrapping her arms around her knees. She looked very pretty in the pale light with the cool wind tossing blonde hair in and out of her eyes. "It's my favorite game. I could play it for hours and hours."

"No way!" Hazard relaxed, feeling relieved for some reason. "Me too."

"I'm really happy you're hanging out with us now," Brianna said.

Hazard blushed again. He didn't know what to say. "Who are you watching?" He motioned to the soccer field.

After a long silence, she whispered, "Russell."

Hazard crossed his arms. "He's gay," he said decidedly. He didn't care if it was the truth or not; he just didn't want Brianna to like Russell.

Brianna turned and looked at him, lashes fluttering on dark eyes. She frowned. "So are you, sometimes," she retorted coolly.

Hazard recoiled, a little offended. He looked at her, frowning and feeling very inept all of a sudden. A hush fell between them, not awkward, but notable enough.

"*Sometimes*," Hazard repeated defensively after a long moment, mumbling it like a grumpy child. Brianna started to giggle, and Hazard sat slumped beside her. Her laugh was contagious. Hazard couldn't help it. He laughed with her, relaxing again, and they watched the rest of soccer practice together.

RUSSELL and Emery might have fought most of winter break, but they were still as close as ever. Hazard couldn't begrudge them that.

Somewhere along the way, Russell told Emery about what had happened that night in January, when Hazard had found him at a party and they'd kissed. Hazard wasn't shocked—after all, he never expected

Russell to keep that from Emery—he was just embarrassed because he'd forgotten about it until then. For a week, Emery looked as if he were constantly holding his breath, until finally he broke down and insisted to both Hazard and Russell that if they were *that way*, that was fine with him, he was just pissed off at both of them for not telling him sooner.

"It was just a party," Hazard tried guiltily.

"You only go to parties because your *new friends* go to parties," Emery retorted, which injured Hazard more than he'd expected.

"Bullshit," he hissed. "Your *math tutor* goes to parties."

Emery was offended by that too. "Don't make fun of me because I'm bad at math!"

Russell did everything he could to make Emery believe he wasn't *that way*, like going on dates with a bunch of girls, which only made Emery grumpier. Hazard hated Russell more for it, because Emery was a pain in the ass to be around with his damning glances and obvious grudges, and it put a damper on the coming end of the school year, which was supposed to be a really fun time.

Emery started dating Lily and told both Russell and Hazard that he was straight and didn't give a shit about their sexual activity. Russell nodded quickly, as if to say of course Emery wasn't required to worry about their sex lives. Hazard wasn't sure what bothered him more—that Russell was still sucking up to Emery, or that Emery had heard things about Hazard at parties, and hadn't said anything. He tried hanging out with Tom and Peyton and Olivia again, but it wasn't the same, and he found himself spending his evenings alone watching TV, waiting for someone to text him. Maybe Emery, calling to apologize. Maybe Jesse, texting him to be ready to be picked up by nine o'clock.

The worst was the night near the end of March when Hazard accused Emery of being jealous of him, and if he'd been asked earlier Hazard never would have guessed what the night would escalate into. Emery called him full of shit. Hazard suggested that Emery was dating Lily to prove something, and with a perfect mask of malice, Emery said, "Russell told me that when you guys made out, he was so drunk that he thought you were me at one point. Chew on that, Haz."

Hazard was left in cold, icy rage with the bitter aftertaste of shame.

He stared, completely speechless, not sure what that was even supposed to mean and too stunned and too furious to really come up with anything to say in response.

"Oh," Emery added, and his eyes were bright like he wanted to cry, like he wanted to stop being mean but couldn't help it, "I forgot to mention that he cried too. He cried a tiny bit because he felt so bad for not telling me and for doing such a stupid thing in the first place. Now he's gonna have to tell every girlfriend he ever has that he made out with a guy once when he was drunk."

"*Leave me alone*," Hazard growled, and he slammed Emery's bedroom door behind him when he left. He almost wished Emery would follow him out or something, but Emery was too caught up in the emotion to apologize yet. That was okay. Hazard would forgive him whenever he decided to apologize. He hoped it would be soon.

Emery's mother offered to drive him home. Hazard thanked her but didn't accept the ride. It wasn't a long walk back home.

Already moody, Hazard definitely didn't expect the contention that awaited him when he got home. It started out almost as usual. His dad was still at work, and his mom was eating dinner alone while she watched *Sex and the City* and nitpicked everything. She always tried to tweak him into what she considered perfection, and he hated it. Tonight it was complaints about "irresponsibility" that led along the lines of *ungrateful teenagers, bad attitudes and rebellious stages,* and *no respect at all.*

Feeling patronized, Hazard argued back. His mom plucked at every untied nerve and every unique characteristic, everything different and everything unusual. She flung out every possible criticism, from his clothes to his atrocious taste in music to an alleged lack of generosity, to his one D last year, to the reflection upon her by his skateboarding and his taste in food, to his *friends.*

With a disdainful sniff, she said, "Ever since you started high school and met those friends of yours—"

Hazard flinched. "Mom," he cut in quickly, "I didn't meet Emery and everyone else in high school. I've known them for years."

His mom rolled her eyes, which was childish and rude and not very her. "I'm not talking about your skater buddies, and I'm not talking about

Emery. Emery is a very good friend, and the others are okay. I'm talking about *that junior*"—she eased the word out like it was poison—"with the tattoos and his junior posse. The one with the aunt in the hospital."

Hazard blinked, momentarily confused. Then he remembered. Right, while Jesse's pretend aunt was *in the hospital* dying from the inside out, they went to parties and had a few drinks and danced a little dirty with friends and sometimes with others he didn't know very well. The junior friend with his junior posse and the aunt in the hospital, that's right.

"Ever since you started hanging out with *that junior*"—his mom acted like the words actually pained her—"you've been acting different. I can't explain it, I can only notice it. It's a mother's job."

Hazard could usually brush her words off or shrug them away. Tonight he couldn't. They hurt him. They were sour, but he didn't know why, and that made him tremble. He just wanted her to shut up already, because the more she spoke, the more he felt caged. His head hurt. He was exhausted with the whole thing. So he countered, "You're just picking on me because you don't have a life anymore, and now I do."

His mother froze. She looked at him strangely, as though she wanted to say *Go to hell*. But she didn't. Instead, she iced out, "Go to your room." With the empty chill in her voice, she could very well have said the former and had the same effect.

Hazard stormed down the hall to his bedroom, emptied his backpack out, and shoved some extra clothes in it. He ignored his mom's wavering demands to stop and listen to her. He grabbed his toothbrush and a few other little things. He grabbed his skateboard and told her he was going to Emery's and slammed the front door behind him. She opened it again just to make him promise he'd call her when he got there.

He was too overwhelmed by everything. He just wanted out. Part of him wanted to go back to Emery's even if they were fighting too. He could swallow his pride and let Emery be right for one night. In fact, he kind of longed for it. But he was still too heated. He was shaking from all the arguing, and he had plenty of friends who would be willing to let him stay the night, so Hazard didn't stress too horribly.

He meandered from Easton Street to Walnut. Walnut took him to Redding, which he could follow to Wesleyan and then Rosewood, where Emery lived, and a few blocks up, where Tom was. Redding went to

Berkeley Street, which officially left residential neighborhoods and ended at the intersection everyone called the Four Corners, where Taco Bell, McDonald's, Starbucks, and Carl's Jr. all met.

Hazard went into the 7-Eleven on Berkeley Street. It had a really good cappuccino machine. He bought a coffee. He mixed a bunch of creamers into it, tasting until he was satisfied.

He stood in the bright artificial light of the gas station as the last of early summer twilight disappeared on the horizon and the smell of Puget Sound drifted in on the wind. Slowly, he cooled down, and, of course, then he started to feel guilty for yelling at Emery. He sipped his coffee through double straws and tapped the edge of his skateboard on the sidewalk, bored. He could feel the gas station clerk glancing at him now and again as people passed him, coming and going, and finally Hazard decided to leave before he was accused of shoplifting or something. That would just be his luck.

Hazard rounded the corner of the gas station, where the doors to the bathroom were. There was a generator at the back corner, an ice box set up next to it. People had written all over the wall of the gas station, colloquial graffiti. Scribbled random messages and names, stickers, flyers, threats, and solicitations like *Call me for a good time*. And there, a little higher than Hazard was tall, kind of isolated and written quite neatly, was the phrase:

we all collide

His brows furrowed. Hazard shifted his weight to the other foot. The simple phrase loomed over him, sinking into his heart in an unexplainably profound way. It was soothing and yet somehow damning. Who would put something like that with all the other scribbles and vandalism? *We all collide*. What was that even supposed to mean? It seemed kind of ominous compared to things like *Emily wuz here!*

In his pocket, Hazard's phone vibrated three times, alerting him to a text message. Something pathetic inside him pleaded it to be Emery, even if they were just going to argue again. He opened the new message.

ASSHOLE: *whats up?*

It was Jesse. Hazard frowned, slightly disappointed. He almost closed his phone. What did Jesse want? But even though it wasn't from

Emery, Jesse's text made something eager flutter in Hazard's chest. It wasn't Emery, but it was someone, an opportunity to go relax, and Jesse never texted him for no reason. Instead of closing his phone and ignoring the message, Hazard hit the reply button.

We all collide. It made him think of Newton's third law of motion: for every action there is an equal and opposite reaction. It was like, when you collided with someone, they would not be in the same position as they used to be. Everyone equally affected one another.

REPLY TO ASSHOLE: *why?*

Hazard sat down on his skateboard, tapping his toes absently. He waited patiently for a returned text, watching cars move in and out of the 7-Eleven lot. He tried willing the message to come quickly. He was thinking about what his mom had said and what Emery had said, and he was feeling terrible. He was fourteen; what did his mom want from him? And Emery, what else did he expect? He'd apologized over and over.

His phone vibrated. He had a message.

ASSHOLE: *just wondering whats up.*
its saturday night. anything going on?

Hazard rolled his eyes. Jesse knew that Hazard would never be invited to a party without Jesse being invited too. He was cool only by association.

We all collide. Maybe it meant something like everything happened for a reason.

Hazard stopped wondering about it. He tucked it away in a corner of his mind and texted Jesse back.

REPLY TO ASSHOLE: *gimme your address*

Jesse lived on Elite Street. Hazard found this out ten minutes later, skating down a quiet street to a large house among other large houses. Everyone knew Redwood Court was the Elite Street, because only the very wealthy lived in the neighborhoods of Redwood Court. The development was tiny and surrounded by thick shrubbery. All the houses on the Elite Street were a notch below boasting but too pretty and big to be modest. Their lawns were treeless, and they had homeowners' associations just like Hazard's neighborhood, but he guessed that theirs were a lot stricter.

Jesse had given him specific instructions. Hazard was nervous (he really didn't want to get caught sneaking through Redwood Court, especially because it was so quiet and any commotion he made would be painfully obvious), but he trusted Jesse because Jesse claimed to have experience sneaking out of his bedroom. Hazard didn't doubt that in the least. Little rich kid whose emotional vacancies were stuffed to overflowing with materialistic things, rebelling to fill the voids—that was how Jesse's cliché went, right?

Backpack hooked on both shoulders and skateboard beneath one arm, Hazard jogged through the yard of the address Jesse had sent him. The house was massive. Jesse had a pool. There were lights on in the first floor. Hazard skirted lawn décor and trundled his way around the edge of the polished stone pathway to avoid the range of motion-sensor lights Jesse had warned him about, and finally, shaking with adrenaline, Hazard made it to his goal: the sunroom.

He left his skateboard on the grass and hoisted himself up onto the fragile wooden ladder attached to the sunroom's eastern wall. The ladder brought him to the roof of the sunroom, six feet under a window, the lights off but the curtains open.

"*Jesse*," Hazard hissed, waving his arms around. He gave it a few seconds, but it didn't work. The window was shut and it was dark, and to top it off, he was only five foot three. He lacked nine inches even with the tiptoes and vigorous arm flailing, and he was definitely not going to risk any loud jumping on the sunroom's roof. Trembling, he texted Jesse to open the window.

Jesse's head popped out above the windowsill. He gave Hazard a wholehearted grin. "Yo, Danger. What's up?"

"*Hazard*," Hazard corrected. "I need some help."

"You have to be really quiet."

"I will."

Hazard handed his bag up first before taking hold of Jesse's arms and squirming, shifting, twisting his body up to scale the wall and ease himself through the window with as little noise as possible. Jesse carefully pulled him in over the windowsill, and when Hazard's shoes touched down on the bedroom floor, all the excitement of being a sneaky teenager thrilled him like an adrenaline rush.

"Fun," he gasped, unaware he'd even been holding his breath. Jesse laughed a little. He brushed past him to close the window.

Hazard looked around. Jesse's room gave a lot of insight into him: posters of bands and half-dressed cute girls like Keira Knightley and, of course, one of early-nineties Courtney Love; striped pillow; game consoles and stacks of games. His room had built-in shelves on the far wall. He was watching *Boy Meets World* on the TV there on the second shelf. There were clothes in a pile near his computer chair and shot glasses lined up on his desk with funny messages and cool designs on them.

They talked for a while. They watched TV. Jesse asked why he'd come over, and Hazard explained the fight with his mom. Secretly, he studied Jesse, looking away whenever Jesse met his eyes. Jesse's hair was a mess tonight, loose around his neck. He had a sweater on, so Hazard couldn't see his tattoos, but he looked really good in it anyway. It was faded blue and looked vintage, but Hazard knew it was probably from some expensive store.

Hazard suddenly felt very nervous. It felt like his heart was in his throat. He was completely alone with Jesse. He thought about all the times at parties that he'd let Jesse grab him for a good song and they'd danced tight against each other like nobody was watching. He thought about stealing stealthy kisses here and there or finding a corner to make out in and the way Jesse's fingertips felt when they dusted along the small of his back. Hazard could feel that same familiar volatility on the air then. He felt a little uncertain, and confused, and kind of scared because he was alone in Jesse's room with him, and if he didn't say something soon, the way Jesse was staring at him told Hazard he might be treading in dangerous waters. There was one thing rumored about Jesse that was absolutely true, and that was that he was damn irresistible.

Hazard fidgeted. He got up and went over to his backpack, rummaging through it like he needed something but only needing to recompose himself. He looked over at Jesse, trying to seem confident and cool. He understood the way Jesse was staring at him, and even though his heart pounded so hard his breath wavered on his lips, he said evenly enough, "I just want to be friends."

Jesse blinked, brows furrowing. He looked honestly blindsided. Then he frowned bitterly and tilted his head to the side. His stare was intense. He didn't say anything, but he didn't have to. Hazard fidgeted again.

I just want to be friends was a portentous statement. But as it sagged in the air between them, it only soured into something untrue.

It was a lie. It was a complete lie, and it was totally worthless.

The pressure of the fallacy built on Hazard's shoulders until he broke. In the back of his mind, he thought about Emery, and Emery telling him to be careful around Jesse Wesley. He thought about fighting with Emery, and he thought about party kisses and swiveling hips, and then he just tried to stop thinking altogether.

"We can just be friends, right?" Hazard mumbled pathetically. His stomach flipped in a crazy way as Jesse stood up and moved over to him, sharp stare gone and a soft smile curling at his lips. Hazard was frozen in place, suddenly strung out between convictions and desperately trying to avoid the concerns of any. Jesse craned down and tipped Hazard's chin up. Hazard could smell his skin, and his breath, and the warm sweetness of his hair, and faint cigarette smoke.

Suddenly it was easy not to think.

Jesse wanted him, and he wanted Jesse too. The sensation swelling in his chest was almost overwhelming, thick and ardent and impatient. It scared him, but it made him excited too. Hazard thought that maybe this was what sex appeal felt like, but that sounded horrible, and he was Jesse's friend, after all.

Their first kiss had been just another party kiss initiated out of adrenaline and impulses, but after it had happened they'd both been shy and flustered and giggly, a little buzzed, and had run away to other people to distract themselves. This kiss wasn't like that, though, all butterflies in the stomach and coy breath. This was a manly kiss. Hazard reached up and clutched at the collar of Jesse's sweater, standing on his toes and pulling Jesse down until their mouths met. Jesse moved forward more. His teeth grazed Hazard's lower lip hungrily. He smoothed his palm along Hazard's cheek and led him back a few feet toward his bed. Hazard tumbled back onto the blankets and tightened his grip on Jesse's sweater, tugging him down with.

"Oh, yeah? Get your terms right, Hazard," Jesse breathed out into his ear, straddling his hips and nosing against his jaw line. Hazard's fingers fisted in Jesse's sweater as shivers rattled his frame, lashes fluttering.

"What do you mean?" he whispered, heart racing. In the shadows, he could see Jesse's roots coming back, dark-brown hair that became bright red, slicked back out of his face. He wanted to touch it. He did, tangling his fingers into thick punk-red locks.

"It's called being *friends with benefits*," Jesse husked.

Hazard chuckled, at first thinking it was a joke. But he realized quickly how serious Jesse was—and then he was cut off and tasting those sweet kisses again, body bucking, hands quivering, thighs twitching apart, finally, and he wasn't *that way*. Jesse was his friend, and he just really wanted it—

But Jesse knew how to play the game. An hour and a half after Jesse pulled him through the window, Hazard called home to tell his mother he was staying at a friend's house while Jesse made him a bed out of extra sheets and pillows on the floor. Hazard buried his face in the spare pillow with his breath still coming in ecstatic puffs, turned on and unbearably sensitive. But the blankets smelled like Jesse, and he was lying on Jesse's floor, and he didn't know why, but that delighted him to no end.

"You're an asshole," Hazard hissed at him, and Jesse sounded amused as he countered, "Glad you finally caught on, Danger."

THE days went by.

Hazard met up with the rest of the skaters in the park a few times, exchanging tricks with Tom while Peyton and Olivia looked on. He lied to his mom about staying at Emery's house when in reality he went to Jesse's or they went to a party. It was an escape from everything, laughing and flirting and drinking, breathlessly dancing and joking along, and the mornings after, when he had to own up to everything he'd done while drunk, were paltry in comparison to the way it felt to just have fun and be liked.

Sometimes Hazard picked fights with his mom, intentionally getting on her nerves just to have a reason to grab his skateboard and leave the house. He liked to stop by the 7-Eleven on Berkeley Street, get a drink, and stare at the vandalism between bathroom doors—*we all collide*— before making his way to the Elite Street and wriggling through the window six feet above the sunroom roof, tumbling half into the arms and half onto the bedroom floor of his beneficial friend with the punk-red hair. Now and then Jesse welcomed him into his room with hungry kisses, but sometimes they just read books or listened to music or played video games and laughed together—just stupid, friendly stuff. A few times, Jesse passed Hazard in the hall at school and told him things like *You look good today*, which made Hazard clam up and stare as he rounded the corner, and once, Hazard took a shower at Jesse's house, in the insanely ornate upstairs bathroom with the red curtains, marble counters, and jet bath. He used Jesse's soap and felt deliciously bad.

Hazard hung out with Emery, trying to make up for their recent arguments. They went to the bookstore and the mall, played basketball and street hockey in Emery's cul-de-sac, and went with Russell to the beach, where the water of the sound was still freezing and the wind felt good as it clawed at their clothes and they kicked at smooth, dark, gritty stones. There was a tension there, but Emery gradually apologized, which meant Hazard was officially forgiven. He still said sorry twice more, and even Russell apologized to Hazard, which made Hazard feel like shit for hating him. But things were okay again.

JESSE'S parents had four vehicles: an SUV, his mother's Forenza, his father's sports car, and the car Mr. Wesley had bought for Jesse. This happened to be a sleek red Toyota Celica from 2000. It matched his jacket, and it matched his hair, and it matched his attitude: bright, eye-catching, loud, and memorable.

The interior was off-black, beads and bottle caps and pop-tab necklaces hanging from the rearview mirror. In Jesse's middle console was the library of CDs Hazard liked to dig through on the way to and from parties. The front drink holder was reserved for Jesse's lighter and cigarettes. He was too cool for steering wheel covers, bumper stickers, or decals, but the floor mats had nautical stars on them. The tiny backseat was often littered with notebooks and pencils, empty cigarette cartons, and stacks of schoolbooks that had fallen from his backpack. It smelled like leather and cigarettes, a little bit like the air conditioning, and a lot like the bottle of TAG Jesse kept in the dash. Somewhere over the last year or so, the scents had just become one with the car—like the chip in the upper right corner of the windshield and the faded sticker near the unused cassette player.

Sometimes when the parties were too hard on Hazard and he was so drunk he couldn't even get in and out of Jesse's car without stumbling, Jesse drove him to Emery's and watched from the curb until Hazard had successfully slithered up into Emery's room. Emery was always his alibi, anyway. He was a great friend like that. Other nights, Jesse felt compassionate enough to let Hazard stay at his house. One of these nights happened to be a Sunday night, which Hazard would never hear the end of from his mother because she didn't like him imposing on friends on school nights—and which meant Hazard had to ride with Jesse to school.

Jesse stopped by McDonald's on the way to Bethany High. Hazard loved that. They sat in the parking lot on the hood of his car, eating breakfast sandwiches and drinking orange juice. Hazard's mom didn't like fast food. She said the smell of grease made her sick, which usually made Hazard feel bad eating it.

There was something significant and kind of intimidating about the way everyone reacted that Monday morning when Jesse turned into the school parking lot, spitting gravel. All the not-juniors and wannabes scattered from his parking block as he slid up to it, and a lot of people stared as Hazard got out of the car.

He didn't do anything special. In fact, he tried to be as inconspicuous as possible, but it just didn't work. Hazard opened the passenger door and scooped up his backpack from under the dash. He stood up to more stares aimed in their direction than he could count, and he blushed miserably at the way Jesse didn't turn his music down. Through the commotion of a Monday morning in the school parking lot, Jesse let Brand New's "Sic Transit Gloria" blast. It was like he wanted everyone to notice them as his car idled and he stretched into the back seat for his bag, cigarette clenched between his teeth.

Hazard waited patiently, but he felt totally cowed. He rocked back and forth on his heels and tried to ignore the obvious tension in the air. It was discomfiting, volatile, and curious. Everyone wanted to know who Jesse had driven to school, because everyone knew what that implied, especially with all the talk Hazard knew went around. His heart fluttered below his throat nervously. He wished Jesse would hurry up.

Jesse hissed something colorful about how his things had fallen out of his bag because he'd forgotten to zip it up. Hazard could see students glancing over at him from the sidewalk. He knew some of them would know him from classes, and some of them would know him by name. Students loitering in their cars and parking blocks observed from safe distances. Others walked by slowly because they didn't notice they were staring. Hazard wondered if what he felt was the sensation of a reputation coming into existence.

"*Got it!*" Jesse cried. He was sprawled across the middle console. He had his bag, properly zipped. He turned off the car and elbowed open his door. His keys jingled as he tucked them into his jacket pocket. The music disappeared, and in its place was the buzz of a school morning: people milling, buses rumbling, cars peeling into the lot. Hazard locked and closed his door too, fumbling with the straps of his backpack.

Coming to school with Jesse officially meant he was cool, and everybody noticed.

Hazard inched around the nose of Jesse's car. He swore he heard someone whisper Jesse's name somewhere amongst the other parking blocks. Jesse took one last drag of his cigarette before stomping it out and flashing Hazard one of his patented crooked grins.

Jesse knew. Jesse knew the scene he'd caused, and he'd done it on purpose because he knew the repercussions. Hazard elbowed him gently as they made their way to the building. He felt a curious little sense of pride. He'd been driven to school by Jesse Logan Wesley, *that junior*, that punk-haired god of the school, and now Hazard was cooler than he'd been before. Jesse was king, and Hazard was prince, or something like that, and people knew not to question these things, or else.

Jesse ruffled Hazard's hair, which was already messy enough. Hazard scowled and pushed Jesse's hand away. Felix found them. Jesse disappeared with him to the right of the office, heading to his locker.

Hazard walked with his head high.

On Wednesday, at lunch, Tom bumped up beside Hazard in line, tossing his milk to and fro. They hadn't talked in a while, so Hazard was happy to see him.

"Hey," Tom said.

Hazard smiled. "What's up, Tommy?"

Tom shrugged, glancing over his shoulder at the lunch tables. "Not much. Hey, we were all just wondering, because I mean, rumors are stupid, but—" He met Hazard's eyes. "Are you really friends with Jesse Wesley?"

Hazard didn't know what to say for a minute. He fidgeted. The lunch line moved forward, and they moved with it. He felt a strange pressure on him, heavy and bittersweet. He looked at Tom hard, wondering how much Tom had heard about him and Jesse. There were lots of things to hear. Sometimes Hazard woke up in the morning feeling sick to his stomach not because of a hangover but because of something somewhere between shame and embarrassment curdling in his gut as he tried to trace back everything he'd done the night before. But Tom was only being curious, and rightfully so.

"Yeah," Hazard said. He didn't know why it had been so hard to say until Tom was gone and sitting with Olivia and Peyton again. Then the weight on his chest was overwhelming. Hazard realized that that was the moment he and his old friends parted ways. Somewhere, somehow, maybe after the first few weeks of Jesse and parties and the butterflies, the anxieties and tensions and hangovers, maybe after all that—there was just a gap between them, and the distance was too great.

They hardly even talked. Olivia wore T-shirts of the Japanese shows she watched and Japanese bands she listened to, and Peyton mostly stayed at Tom's house because he hated his family, and Hazard didn't really know what else was going on with them because they barely talked anymore. Sometimes they commented on each other's MySpaces. Sometimes they stopped to chat in the hall between classes. But Tom, Peyton, and Olivia were still outcasts, and Hazard was cool with Jesse Wesley.

It was kind of poignant and cold, like realizing you're no longer young enough to be afraid of the dark or get away with things by crying. Tom, Olivia, Peyton. They still smiled and joked and exchanged milks every now and again, but the middle school days of skating until Emery was available, of watching TV with Olivia and keeping Tom company, were gone.

Hazard didn't care that Jesse pretended he didn't see him, even when he passed by his table with the lunch he didn't even feel like eating. Hazard sat by Emery, and he didn't mind the way Emery goofed off with Lily most of lunch, or the fact that Russell was not even a yard away. He was just thankful that the same embittered distance was not present between him and Emery, and Hazard hoped that, whatever happened, it would stay that way.

Chapter 4
April and May

"*HULLOOO*, nurse!"

"Shh, Hazard, just come inside before my mom hears us down here."

The clock hanging beside the television read 2:10 in the morning. Emery closed the front door as quietly as he could, locking it again. Emery's cat, Dust Bunny, sat on the back of the couch, and Hazard petted him. He started walking to the stairs, humming to himself, but Emery grabbed him by the back of the jacket. He almost tripped.

Emery walked close beside him, leading him up the stairs. The house was dark. "Hazard, you smell like booze."

"I'm *drunk*, Em," Hazard reminded.

"*Shh*," Emery hissed, more demanding this time. Down the hall was the closed door of his parents' bedroom—closed, yes, but not soundproof. "Hazard, please just be quiet for a second."

"Do I smell *bad*?" Hazard whispered, feeling very frantic.

Emery shook his head, pushing him into his room and closing the door behind them. He'd switched on the lava lamp in the corner of the room. It was purple, a low glow, shadows shifting around the floor and walls as the insides of it moved.

"No," Emery sighed. "Just your breath."

Hazard watched the lava lamp, distracted for a moment. He felt deliciously numb and woozy. His fingertips and toes buzzed. He could still feel the beat of a song pulsing deep into his bones and the way it felt to grind along with it. Emery's room felt as familiar to him as his own, all the scribbles, notes, pictures and posters on the walls, the street signs they'd stolen back in eighth grade. There was Russell's old amp, duct-taped and abandoned, in the other corner, working now as a stand for Emery's tiny TV.

He glanced over at Emery. Emery stood with his hands on his hips, looking a little crestfallen and tired. He was in a big T-shirt and boxers. Maybe he'd been sleeping when Hazard called him and told him he was at the door.

"Why didn't you come in through the window?" Emery asked.

"I don't know," Hazard mumbled apologetically. He looked over at the open notebook lying near the lava lamp, on top of a math textbook. There were notes scribbled back and forth in the notebook, and lettered quite largely above them was a scrawled declaration of *Russell knows all, faggot*. Hazard knew that Russell was the only one Emery would tolerate the F-word from. It was something of a term of endearment that Russell had used for years now.

Hazard licked his lips. "You studied with Russell tonight?" he asked. Suddenly he could imagine Emery and Russell making out instead of studying. Maybe it was the alcohol.

"Yeah." Emery moved across the room, pushing Hazard to his bed. "Haz, you need to sleep this off."

Hazard flopped down onto Emery's bed, noticing that the end of his belt was coming out of one belt loop. He hated that. Emery kicked his homework beneath the bed.

"You know…." Hazard frowned, looking up at Emery's ceiling, where there were glow-in-the-dark stars still, after all these years. They didn't glow as much anymore. The shadows danced from the lava lamp, and Hazard felt kind of nostalgic, nostalgic and drunk. "I could have helped you with math," he said, looking at Emery. "You just never asked me."

Emery didn't say anything. He moved over to the foot of the bed and started untying Hazard's shoes. Hazard reached up to help, but Emery swatted him away. Finally, Emery said meekly, "I'm sorry."

Emery dropped his Converse. He motioned for Hazard to sit up, and Hazard let him strip away Jesse's red leather jacket. For a moment, Hazard didn't want to give it to him. It was warm and it smelled like Jesse and it was awesome that Jesse had let him wear it home. Hazard watched Emery neatly fold the jacket and gently put it by his shoes, as if he knew how special it was.

"Time to sleep," Emery insisted, voice thin and unyielding. He sounded bitter or weary. Hazard felt guilty. He didn't want Emery to be mad at him for being drunk or staying over again. He groaned like a little kid resisting bedtime, but Emery pressed him to the pillow, and by 2:35 he was long gone and deep in a dream.

HAZARD did it with Jesse.

It started out the same. Hazard came over and Jesse helped him up through the window, and they talked for a while in the light of Jesse's desk lamp. Jesse told him about how depressing detention was when Mrs. Delaney hosted it, when instead of sleeping in the back of the room everyone had to sort papers and clean the lunchroom. He'd had to stay after school for carving obscene song lyrics into a desk during history class, which was ironic because he'd expected detention for threatening Grant Pollard in front of Mr. Luce, not something as stupid as vandalism. Hazard told him about how sometimes he felt like Emery was still mad at him for what happened with Russell in January.

"Oh, yeah? You should just sit them both down and talk it out seriously, go to lunch or something," Jesse suggested in a mumble, flipping through the channels on the little TV in his room.

Hazard blanked. Why hadn't he thought of that? "That's a good idea," he said. "Thanks."

It was funny how Jesse put on such airs around other people, but when Hazard came over, he just sprawled around his room as comfortably as ever. It made Hazard nervous. It made him wonder if Jesse expected something, or if it was solace of sorts, or if it really meant nothing and he was overthinking it. It made him smile, though, to see Jesse with punk-red hair pulled back in a sloppy ponytail, lying on his stomach in pajama pants and a T-shirt, watching TV and absently wagging a foot. His red leather jacket lay carelessly over his backpack. Sometimes his fingertips twitched together, like he wanted to tap the ash off a cigarette he wasn't smoking. His other tattoos were visible, words on his wrist and stars on his arms, but Hazard still wasn't brave enough to ask about them yet. He was hardly brave enough to let Jesse know he looked around his room, at the posters and video games, the movies, the books and other little details lying around. The desk and the swivel chair, the game consoles, the collection of CDs at the base of the bed by a little house made of playing cards taped together. It smelled like body spray and the very faint stuffiness of recent cigarettes and a familiar scent Hazard was coming to know as the smell of Jesse's skin.

"Do your parents know I come over?" Hazard asked after hearing someone walk by the closed bedroom door.

"Yeah." Jesse didn't look away from the television. "But it's cool. They don't really bother a lot when my door is shut."

"That's good."

It was definitely good when Jesse decided it was time to fool around, turning out the desk lamp and joining Hazard on the floor in front of the TV. And it was all fine, because they both understood their place. Getting tangled on Jesse's floor and loving it would not change the fact that it was a *benefits* thing, and it didn't affect their sexual preference. That was the cool thing about it. It was all impulse, free and clear. And it felt *good*. The heated connection of lips and tongues and teeth as fingertips toyed with the hem of a shirt and knees knocked together was interrupted only by little whispers of "Shh, shh, not too loud" and "Jesse, I *am* being quiet."

In the dancing light of the TV, Jesse looked at Hazard pointedly and whispered, "Danger, have you ever done anything with anyone before?"

Hazard cast him a dark glance, licking his lips. "*Hazard*. Get it right, Jesse."

Jesse smiled faintly. Hazard watched TV for a moment. Jesse waited patiently for an answer.

Hazard swallowed, thinking about the question. He was a little tentative of his own answer and what it might mean. If Jesse were going to start making fun of him, it would ruin the moment and the way the delight buzzed in all his nerves. "Does it matter?"

"Have you? I bet you've been with a bunch of people. You're the quiet type nobody suspects."

"Actually," Hazard snapped, blue eyes clashing with green as he met Jesse's stare sharply, "yes, I've been with someone before. Are you satisfied?"

"You're lying." Jesse grinned. He was like a mischievous child. He tucked red hair behind his ears and leaned down, talking against Hazard's ear: "Come on. Admit it. You haven't done anything with anyone. That's okay, I'll be gentle. But if you keep giving me that attitude, I might change my mind."

For a minute Hazard was just put off by Jesse's idea that he was lying, that he could charm him into anything. He acted like Hazard should be honored to be in his presence, but Hazard begged to differ. And then Jesse's words sank in and he looked up, eyes wide. "What?" he whispered. "What are you talking about?"

The mischievous child was gone. Jesse looked dangerous again. His glance was sultry, shadows moving on his smoothly angled face in the light of the TV. In the hush, the sound of him shifting was deafening, the rustle of clothes, the waver of breath, and Hazard did nothing but lie stiff and stare up at him. His eyes widened, and chills prickled his skin, the pressure settling as Jesse ducked down and kissed him. And it was different. It wasn't *Hey, let's have some fun*. It was significant. It was powerful. It made Hazard's back arch, and he didn't quite know what else to do but succumb to the shiver rattling through him as his heart thundered and he blushed hot, hot, hot.

His fingers tangled in the punk-red hair that was tickling his face. There was the taste of Jesse's mouth—the heat, the wet, resilient feel of it—the rigidity of his teeth and the passion in the kiss. Sinful, oh God. This was twisted. This was too serious. But they were guys. They couldn't just *stop* when it felt this good—

"Your parents," Hazard demurred, locking his arms around Jesse's shoulders.

"They're downstairs," Jesse promised. He seemed a little uncertain for just a moment, but he was not to be deterred.

The friction of grinding together was too much. It was like dancing when he was really drunk, but it was so much better. Hazard's back ached from lying on the floor, but he didn't care, because sparks of delight burst in his muscles and his breath came in hot bursts. He could feel Jesse, stiff against his leg, and it was daunting—it was so daunting and sudden—but what could he do? He wasn't thinking anymore. He couldn't.

There was a commercial for GameCube on the TV when Jesse

reached down into Hazard's pants. Muscles fluttered excitedly. Hazard unfastened his jeans to make it easier. On the bedroom floor, Jesse jacked him off. Hazard consciously came for the third time in his life, and it left him shaking. His back arched up off the floor. His toes curled, and he clapped his hands over his mouth just in case he moaned as he closed his eyes tight and just *felt* it, the waves of pleasure rattling through him, the sense of dizzy, wet release and the way a blanket of shivering numbness settled so quickly with the comedown.

He let Jesse grind into his thigh. He felt bad. He tried to touch him too, but he was nervous. He straddled Jesse's hips and let him grind some more, a devilish dance. It scared Hazard, and it excited him. It felt like wonderfully long minutes, but it was really only a few moments. Hazard worried that he'd never be satisfied, that he'd get hard again and they'd be stuck fucking each other one after the other all night.

It occurred to Hazard suddenly, painfully, that he didn't even know how many people Jesse had ever been with. And now here he was, maybe another notch on the list. Jesse was very popular. He knew a lot of people. He was bold and brazen and bad. How many people had Jesse ever been this close to? How many girls, how many boys? How many *beneficial friends* had he had? How many steady partners?

Hazard rocked down into Jesse's lap. Jesse grabbed his waist and held him there. Hazard let him thrust and grind until he came to a rocking end, which wasn't that much later, and Hazard kissed him and felt the heat between his legs and knew, plainly enough, that he could trust Jesse. He wasn't that complicated; Hazard was sure of it, and it just *felt right*.

"*Shit*," Jesse breathed, lying back on the floor and draping an arm over his eyes. An exhausted silence filled the room. Hazard rolled away and lay spread-eagle on the carpet beside him, catching his breath. His pants were still undone. He didn't even hear the TV anymore. He could see under Jesse's bed, old pairs of shoes and what looked like an abandoned dartboard.

"That...." Jesse looked up at the ceiling, pausing. Hazard glanced over at him, feeling suddenly weak and kind of shy. Jesse looked utterly perfect, staring up at the popcorn ceiling and mulling over his next words. His green eyes gleamed in the erratic light of the TV. He looked somehow both young and very wise at the same time, a curious mix. A real smile pulled coyly at the corners of his mouth, and Hazard swallowed. His chest ached at the sight of it.

"What?" he whispered.

"That was awesome." Jesse spoke as if to the ceiling. Slowly, he looked over at Hazard, and the honesty written all over his face was breathtaking for many reasons: because he'd never seemed so soft before, because he'd never seemed so *real*, because he looked truly satisfied, and because he'd said, *That was awesome.*

Hazard was in disbelief for a moment. He laughed. He raised his brows, skeptical. But Jesse was serious. Hazard felt rude for laughing.

"Yeah." Jesse sat up, grunting as if it were hard to do so. "If my parents weren't home, I'd say that was worthy of an after-sex cigarette."

"I'm flattered, Jesse."

"Oh, shit, don't let that go to your head."

"Shut up." Hazard pushed him. Jesse laughed. Hazard felt sore, the delicious kind of sore he felt after having a good workout in PE. He watched TV while Jesse changed pants, humming "About a Girl" to himself. Hazard took off his jeans and kicked them over by his backpack, which sat below the window. Jesse flopped down by him on the floor. Part of Hazard wanted to tell Emery all about it, but he could never. Emery already hated it when he talked about Jesse. Hazard frowned. Wasn't that what he'd been aiming for? He didn't know anymore. He didn't care.

"I CAN'T stand you sometimes, Jesse."

"Well, I guess that works out, because I can't stand *you* at all."

"Why are you always such an asshole!"

"I don't know. Why are you always so annoying, Hazard?"

"If I'm so annoying, then why don't you stop talking to me?"

"Ugh, I *try*, but you keep texting me."

"Oh my God, that's such *bullshit!*"

"Look, Danger—"

"*Hazard. My name is Hazard!*"

"Whatever. Look, we have a lot of differences. We kick it and have a lot of fun when we hang out and stuff, but otherwise... I just don't think we should be *that* friendly to each other."

"We're not. You're never friendly to me."

"I didn't know I was required to be."

"*Oh my God, you piss me off!*"

"Oh—yeah?—calm down."

"What happened to the Jesse from last night?"

"He's still sleeping. He partied really hard. But I think, if you come to another party with me, he might come back out."

"See, and I *hate* that about you—you're so two-faced—"

"I'm just fucking with you, Hazard. Really, I am. You're too fun to piss off. I can't resist."

JESSE always got what he wanted, in many ways. He had charm and wit. He had connections. He had parents who let him do whatever he wanted and gave him whatever he asked for, and even if he didn't have money, he was good at stealing.

"Here," Jesse said, pushing a stack of books across his bedroom floor at Hazard.

Hazard stared at them for a moment, uncomprehending. He looked up at Jesse and back at the books, and then he licked his lips and asked, "These are for me?"

"Yeah." Jesse shrugged. He grabbed a towel from the back of his desk chair, rolled it up, and shoved it against the crack between his door and the carpet. He went over to the open window Hazard had just climbed through and lit a cigarette.

Jesse watched him from the corner of his eye. Hazard knew. He sat cross-legged on his floor and pulled the books over to look through. The first book of *A Series of Unfortunate Events*, *The Talisman*, a book on the history of alternative rock, and *Z for Zachariah*. At first, Hazard really couldn't believe that Jesse had bought them for him. He didn't read that much, but if a book was really good he'd slam through it. Did Jesse know that? Jesse didn't seem like the kind that cared about books either, having a simple battered pile of them near his CDs—things like *Queen of the Damned* and *To Kill a Mockingbird*—and for a moment, Hazard didn't quite know what to think.

"You got these?" he asked, looking up at Jesse. Jesse flicked ash out his window and onto the sunroom roof. He nodded mutely, glancing back at Hazard.

"For you," he explained. "They're yours. I bought them."

That was it. That was all Jesse said about it. Hazard had no idea what to say. He felt a little cowed, a little sheepish and awkward, but warm deep in the chest. He was probably blushing like a loser. He started flipping through the history of alternative rock first, looking at glossy photographs and skimming chapters. He couldn't wait to show Emery. They looked like good books. It wasn't very often that Jesse went out of his way to be nice to him, so it touched him that Jesse had bought them for him. But why? Did he think Hazard couldn't afford anything? That wasn't true at all.

It wasn't the last time that Jesse suddenly gave him things that he'd bought or stolen—books, T-shirts, CDs, magazines—and part of Hazard thought that maybe Jesse was trying to buy his affection. Another part of him thought that was horrible to think. Hazard wondered what, exactly, it made *him* to accept everything Jesse got for him.

Hazard decided that he wasn't anything different. He wasn't being *bought* or *bribed*. He was Jesse's *friend*.

"YOU'RE not homeless, you know."

Hazard glanced at Jesse as he slammed the passenger door shut behind him, tucking his skateboard between his knees and fastening his seat belt. Jesse's finger drummed on the gearshift. He looked at Hazard, eyes critical with contempt.

"I know," Hazard grumbled.

Jesse shifted into drive and jerked away from the curb, peeling back onto the road with headlights bouncing in the dark between streetlamps. "Then you need to start acting like it," Jesse hissed.

Hazard shrugged roughly, peering out at the night as it rushed by. The 7-Eleven faded in the rearview mirror. The radio was on, music a soft background fuzz. Jesse's car always smelled a little bit like the air conditioning even when he didn't have it on. The beads and strings on Jesse's wrist jingled together as his wrist shifted, hand draped idly over the gearshift, other elbow propped on the window.

Hazard knew he wasn't homeless. He wasn't a melodramatic brat. Sometimes he just really needed to get out of the house. It was stressful being under the same roof as his mother, and he couldn't stand being home alone. Nobody ever wanted to go home just to be alone. Didn't Jesse get that? Hazard picked at the edge of his old skateboard, frowning grumpily. The 7-Eleven on Berkeley was really not that far of a walk from his house. The neighborhood was safe. Or maybe Jesse wasn't worried about Hazard's well-being so much as he was pissed off that he had to take the time to come pick him up and keep him company for a while.

"Listen," Jesse said. "You're going to give your mom a fucking heart attack if you just walk out all the time—"

"Oh, sure, take her side."

"Haz, that's not my point. Throwing *fits* isn't going to help anything. How old are you again?"

Suddenly Hazard regretted ever telling Jesse about his fights with his mom, even if it felt good to vent. He scowled. "Fuck you, Jesse. Just because you can do whatever you want and your parents could care less—"

The car screeched to a stop and Jesse pointed at the door. "Get out of the car."

Hazard stared, incredulous. Jesse glowered at him, all crude teenager again. "*No!*" Hazard insisted after a moment, brow knotting.

"Get out of my car," Jesse repeated in a hiss. He leaned back in his seat and got comfortable, showing he wasn't averse to waiting patiently.

"Fine!" Hazard jerked the door open and grabbed his skateboard. He made sure to shut the door very hard. He started walking, scowling darkly and checking the street sign they'd just passed so he'd know how long the walk to Emery's might be from there. He wasn't ready to go home for the night.

He heard Jesse's car idling for a moment, then accelerating suddenly and jerking to another stop a few yards ahead of him. Jesse threw open his door, leaning out to send Hazard a vicious glance.

"Get back in the car," he grumbled.

Hazard obeyed. He'd hardly closed the door before Jesse started driving again.

"I thought we came to an agreement," Jesse uttered below his breath. "If you want to go somewhere, call me and I'll pick you up. I thought we decided you wouldn't be skating around in the dark alone anymore, like an idiot."

Hazard shrugged. "I didn't think you were so worried about me. I'm annoying. At least, that's what you told me earlier at lunch. That I'm annoying the hell out of you lately."

Their eyes met over the middle console of the car. Jesse looked powerless and irritated. He sighed bitterly, looking back at the road. Hazard got comfortable, feeling victorious. He reached over to the radio, intentionally letting his wrist brush against Jesse's knuckles on the gearshift. Jesse's fingers twitched. Hazard turned the volume up. "Get Low" was playing.

"I like this song," he said.

Jesse rolled his eyes.

JESSE gave him some sex bracelets.

Every color of the jelly bracelets meant something different, something the wearer was willing to do. Jesse gave him yellow, orange, purple, and red, then white, clear, and glittery clear, and Hazard stared at them in confusion for a moment because he knew what they meant, but he wasn't sure he should wear a glittery bracelet. But everybody else wore them, even Jesse, even Russell, and the game of snapping them was cool, and they *were* a gift, after all. Yellow, orange, purple, red, white, clear, and glittery clear—they meant hugs, kisses, lap dances, flashing, feel-copping, and the regular clear meant he had to obey the order of whoever snapped it on his wrist.

"Thanks," Hazard said, putting them on one wrist. He didn't hate them. It meant something that Jesse gave them to him. It felt like an initiation of sorts, and he felt badass wearing them after a while.

"No problem," Jesse replied, reaching over and snapping the red one. Red meant lap dance. Hazard rolled his eyes.

"Do you want sparkly green?" Felix asked, grinning. "I have a million of those."

Glittery green meant sixty-nine. Hazard stared at Felix, then met Jesse's glance and burst into laughter with him. Felix flipped them off.

SCHOOL let out for the summer, and that meant freedom. Freedom from homework, freedom from rumors, freedom from schedule. When they went back to school, they wouldn't be freshmen anymore. They'd be sophomores, and they'd be worth something.

Hazard followed Jesse's advice and went with Russell and Emery to eat lunch at Panda Express, telling them both that he wished everyone would get over the party in January because they'd both been drunk and not thinking straight. Russell agreed with a curt frown, and Emery actually laughed about it. That was something. That meant he was moving on.

"By the way," Emery added, "do you guys know where I should take Lily on Friday? We're going out, and I have no idea what to do. I'm a terrible boyfriend, aren't I?"

The summer went on without many glitches. In fact, it was great.

Chapter 5
Summer

HAZARD met the Seattle gang, and they got high.

Jesse said, "You guys know I don't prefer it, but it's summer, so what the fuck."

It was somewhere in the University District, at someone's apartment. They drove there, and Hazard was nervous the whole time. Jesse said he didn't usually go across to see them. Normally, the Seattle gang drove back to Bethany to hang out. Jesse knew them from school. They'd been juniors and seniors when he'd been a freshman. Lexie and Felix knew them too, and of course, Lexie brought her stash.

The Seattle gang consisted of Sam, Bentley, Chris, Maddie, and Max, except Max still lived in Bethany because he didn't go to the University of Washington. Hazard would get to know Max better later, at a party on his birthday and bashes in his sophomore year. They called Chris *Shirtless* because he had a penchant for walking around without a shirt to show off his tattoos. But for the time being, they were all new faces to Hazard, and Felix kept trying to comfort him by ruffling his hair and throwing his arm around his shoulders because he noticed the way Hazard bit his nails anxiously. Hazard loved him for it. Felix made him think of Soda Pop from that book they'd had to read in eighth grade.

Sam and Bentley looked like they could have been brothers, square jaws and even squarer shoulders, dark hair and goofy grins. Shirtless was a little more narrow faced, with red hair and a rather mousy disposition and tattoos of card suits on his arms. Maddie was a loud girl just like Lexie, with auburn hair moussed into little wavy curls. She looked a little bit like Rachel McAdams, and her belly button piercing was quite obvious below her short shirt. Out of all of them, Max seemed the most mature. He had sandy hair and was laid-back and quiet, his eyes bright with intelligence and his smile knowing even though he never joined in on the conversations.

Hazard sat by himself for a while pressed against the arm of the faded couch in Bentley and Sam's little living room, looking at a fuzzy TV but not really watching because he was too busy listening to everyone laugh and catch up in the messy kitchen. He felt like he'd traveled through time, back into a scene of, say, *Singles*. There were a few holes in the couch, the coffee table was trash, there were water stains in the ceiling, the wallpaper was old, and one corner of the room was covered in creative Sharpie drawings, and there were bottles of Febreeze standing around, but the apartment still smelled a little stale. It was a college apartment. He wished it were cleaner.

Hazard was the youngest, so he felt sort of out of place, staying in the living room and biting his nails, watching the rest of them from where he curled up against the arm of the couch with his knees to his chest.

"Have a drink, have a drink," Sam said, pushing beer around. Lexie took one. Max opened it for her while she dug in her pockets for her bag of weed and all the supplies to roll it out for everyone.

"So how've you been?"

"Lexie, don't worry about it—I got a bowl—"

"Good, actually. Exams *killed* me, though. I mean, *holy shit*. Enjoy your last year of high school, man."

"How's your girlfriend? Skylar, right?"

"Good—"

"Esther's good too. Here, Lexie, give it to me."

"So what's been up in Bethany lately?"

"Dude, it's boring as fuck. Why are you even asking?"

"It's not *boring*. If it was *boring*, there wouldn't be any good parties, would there?"

"Jesse, you dating anybody?"

"Nope. I'm a free man."

"Oh, Lexie, *ugh*—"

The kitchen erupted in laughter as Felix ducked away before Lexie could breathe any more smoke into his face, and with that, most of the important conversation was over, and Jesse waved Hazard into the kitchen. Hazard tried not to think about Valentine's Day and went in, standing very close to Jesse's side and watching everyone else take hits out of the little clay bowl. Jesse took a hit, his cheeks dimpling as he held it. He put the bowl out for Hazard to take, motioning for him to hurry, and Hazard looked at him with wide eyes.

"I don't know how," he whispered, and thankfully nobody was paying attention to him except for Jesse. Maddie was talking about her drama class or something.

"Here," Jesse mumbled, and Hazard's eyes watered at the smell of it. Jesse helped him, holding the carb and lighting the bowl once Hazard's mouth closed on it. "Now," Jesse signaled, and he laughed because Hazard didn't really get anything. They tried again, and Hazard really tasted it that time. It left him reeling for a second, staring at the faded linoleum of the kitchen floor. The bowl moved along to Felix.

It didn't take much longer until Hazard had to sit down on the floor because he was so dizzy. Shirtless said, "He's baked," and Lexie grumbled, "Dammit. Cashed," and started to pack the bowl again.

"He's so little!" Maddie cooed, petting Hazard's cheek like he was a baby or a doll.

"Don't tell me we're babysitting him," Shirtless groaned.

"What?" Hazard asked, laughing. He was too old to be babysat.

Felix and Lexie shook their heads vigorously. Jesse said, "No, we're not."

They laughed. Hazard knew they laughed at him, but he didn't care. At least he was entertaining them. He laughed too, and it was the same as before—he was dizzy and embarrassed and his face was hot, and he didn't want to be typical, but he couldn't stop laughing because he was nervous. The more he tried to stop, the more he giggled, and pretty soon everyone joined him on the floor, and Sam went to put some music on. College rock. Fall Out Boy.

"*Gay*," Jesse said, but he didn't care that it was still playing.

"Hey, look—" Hazard pulled on Jesse's arm when everybody's attention was elsewhere. "Look, I know this is going to sound really high of me, but look at my eyes. Are they really big? Because I feel like I'm looking around with wide eyes, but I'm really just relaxing."

Bentley overheard and started cackling wildly, which got everyone laughing again. "Oh my God, I hate this," Jesse grumbled, rubbing at his eyes. But when he looked at Hazard again, he wasn't mad. He smiled weakly and his eyes were bright. Hazard bit his tongue in apology.

They talked more. Hazard wasn't part of the conversation. He didn't know the times or people or places they mentioned. He lay down on the linoleum, and it was cool on his face. He traced some of the grain in the wall molding, listening to them and feeling the world spin. He wanted to brush his teeth to get rid of the taste and smell of pot.

They talked forever, it seemed. They got out Oreos to eat. They laughed, and the laughter seemed to go on forever, and sometimes Hazard couldn't help but laugh too, because listening to them as high as they were was hilarious to him. Felix started washing the dishes that were piled in the sink because he was paranoid.

Sam let Hazard go through his CDs. Hazard put on Three Days Grace. Maddie and Lexie sang along to every song until finally Max told Hazard to please change it. Hazard put on Green Day instead, grinning. Green Day meant something to stoners, right? He went through the CDs and found Bon Jovi, and then the Foo Fighters, and then a band called From First to Last. Eventually, Bentley told him to put in Incubus.

By then, the high was mostly fading. The Seattle gang was starting to get drunk, though. Everyone else was not. They had to drive home, after all. And Hazard didn't like the taste of beer, probably just like Jesse didn't like getting high.

They stayed a lot longer than Hazard expected. He was still woozy from the pot. Nobody believed that Sam found the porn channels on his TV, so they all crowded into his bedroom to see. Hazard got embarrassed by it, although he was amused by how casually they'd all sat down to watch. He went back out and sat on the couch in the living room. *Roseanne* was on. He thought about Emery and what Emery might be doing then—maybe watching TV too. He wondered what Emery would think of him if he knew what he was up to in Seattle.

"Are you okay?" Felix asked after a while, when he went to the kitchen for juice.

"I'm fine," Hazard promised.

Jesse came out next. He sat down next to Hazard on the couch, sprawling out. Hazard wondered if his eyes were still as red as Jesse's.

"Felix told me you were uncomfortable," Jesse said, meeting Hazard's stare.

"I'm not," Hazard swore. He frowned. Jesse didn't look exactly satisfied either. He thought about Jesse saying *I don't prefer it, but what the fuck.* Hazard said, "You're uncomfortable, aren't you?"

"Nah." Jesse ran a hand through his hair. "I just.... Sometimes I think I outgrew these friends. I mean, I love them to death, and I'm still really close with Max, but—sometimes I just get bored around them."

"That's okay," Hazard assured him. Quietly, as Jesse watched TV, Hazard looked him up and down again: punk-red hair tossed out of his face, band tee, straight-cut Levi's on long, skinny legs. Hazard looked at the smooth angles of his face, his sarcastic brow and big eyes, and the glinting silver of his earrings.

Laughter echoed from Sam's bedroom.

"Show me your tattoos," Hazard asked softly.

Jesse thought about it for a moment, then complied.

Sam had put Fall Out Boy back on, and the lyrics circled around and around in Hazard's dizzy head: *I only want sympathy in the form of you crawling into bed with me.* He leaned back on the couch in Sam and Bentley's living room, hearing but not listening to the music and the laughing audience on *Roseanne* and the voices from down the little hall, and still feeling pretty high and breathless, although maybe that was because Jesse was practically stripping in front of him.

He did it on purpose. Hazard knew that. Jesse moved slow and sexy with full intention, and Hazard hated him for it. Jesse showed him all the tattoos he had: the Roman numerals for one, three, and eight (which he said were his numbers in numerology or something) just below the back of his neck; a nautical star in black and red on the back of both triceps; Leviticus 6:13, *setting my world on fire* on his left inner wrist; a killer little tribal designed like a flame on his left side; the zodiac sign for Scorpio on his right middle finger. Hazard realized that Felix had tattoos that matched a few of Jesse's. They'd probably gotten them together.

"We need a song," Hazard decided suddenly, as Jesse put his shirt back on and Hazard watched the way his muscles flickered beneath his skin. Everybody had a song, even friends. Russell and Emery had a song. He and Jesse didn't yet.

"No, we don't." Jesse fumbled in his pocket for his cigarettes. He started smoking without even asking Bentley or Sam if it was okay. The strident smell of it was hot in Hazard's nose, but it was familiar and comforting. He liked the smell of Jesse's Camels more than the smell of Lexie's pot.

"We do." Hazard thought about it for a moment. There were a lot of songs he could say, ones that made him think of them that he listened to all the time. "How about the one that just played? 'Dance, Dance'."

Jesse jumped suddenly and frantically searched for an ashtray, or something that would count as one for a minute or two. He sighed out some smoke, licked his lips, then leaned down to whisper in Hazard's ear, and oh, familiar clever sarcasm and sadistic glance:

"Oh, yeah? How about 'I Hate Everything About You'?"

It was nearing one in the morning when they left the University District. Hazard fell asleep in Jesse's car on the way back to Bethany.

WHEN Hazard turned fifteen in early July, his parents took him out to dinner in Seattle, Emery made him a cake, and Jesse took him to a really great bash at Max's house.

The roar of the song pounding away amidst a buzz of activity, the howl of the party outside the locked bedroom door, was not so much heard as it was remembered. It started with a no-talking game, in which Hazard tried everything to get Jesse to make a sound, and it turned into Jesse blowing him on Max's bedroom floor.

Hazard knew his shirt was somewhere in the room, but he didn't know where, exactly. Maybe it was with Jesse's. He couldn't breathe. He worried his drink would get knocked over. The air was too hot. His skin was itchy with sweat, and his hips were starting to cramp. But Jesse made him crazy in such great ways, and nobody had to know because it was their secret and they were friends with benefits.

His drink was fine. It didn't get knocked over. Jesse finished him off, and Hazard took care of him after, reaching between his thighs. When they were done, pants back on, Jesse sat up Indian-style and grabbed Hazard's drink, taking a sip. He curdled into a bitter grimace.

"Tell me you didn't make this drink, Stranger Danger."

"I did." Hazard snickered. *Stranger Danger* was a new one.

"Good Jesus, is there any pop in here at all?"

"Yes!"

"Put some more in and it'll taste better."

"Okay." Hazard held out his shirt. "Hey, can you make this right-side-out for me?"

"Hazard, that's already right-side-out."

"It is not! Are you kidding me? I can't see in here!"

"Oh, yeah? I just think you're a little drunk."

"I might be." Hazard glanced over at Jesse. He still had his drink. Hazard smacked him on the shoulder, and Jesse snorted while he took a sip. "Well, shit, Jesse, if you don't like it, stop drinking it and give it to me. It was mine, anyway. Let's get back out there so Max won't get mad at us for taking so long—"

"I think you're forgetting something really, really important, Danger."

"Oh, right. Get your shirt on."

"No, no, no." Jesse smiled, setting the cup down and climbing to his feet. He stretched his arms and legs as he did so. Hazard heard his joints pop. He pulled on his shirt the right way, adjusting the collar and trying to fix his hair. He pretended not to know what Jesse was talking about.

Jesse knew otherwise. He said, "Happy birthday, Haz," and started humming faintly to himself.

Hazard stopped moving, fingers still buried in his hair. He cut coy blue eyes up to scrutinize Jesse, searching for clandestine intentions but finding no such ulterior motives. He relaxed a little, hands falling to his sides. "Thanks," he mumbled, and grabbed his drink as he made his way to unlock the door.

"Wait—" Jesse snatched up his own shirt and looked at Hazard, who leaned on the door and peered back expectantly. "Don't you want, like, a birthday kiss or something?"

Hazard's brow furrowed. He unlocked the door, blushing. He shrugged.

Jesse took it upon himself to solve his indecision for him. He strutted over, smirking softly as he brushed dark hair out of Hazard's eyes. Hazard turned his face up, feeling kind of groggy. Jesse delicately kissed the corner of his mouth, and after a moment, Hazard relaxed into a soft grin, shaking his head and pulling away halfway through the offered kiss. He almost lost his balance, but he managed to keep hold of it until the moment was over. He locked eyes with Jesse, passing thoughts back and forth in the darkness, and then he opened the door and slipped defiantly out into the crowd and loud music to find the bathroom. He always had to pee after coming.

The next morning, Hazard found himself cocooned in a blanket and slumped at Emery's dining table, a cup of coffee steaming in front of him and a bottle of Excedrin on the counter. The original story had been that he was staying the night there anyway. He threw up once at three in the morning before he fell asleep again, pressed up between Emery and the cool plaster of his bedroom wall.

At ten in the morning, Emery's stepdad and mom were at the store, so they went down to the kitchen and Emery fixed Hazard some coffee. He gave him some painkillers—not for the headache but for the agony about to ensue via his furious lecture.

But before he could begin, Hazard looked up miserably and husked, "Please don't yell at me, Emery. It's not like it's my first bad hangover."

Emery crossed his arms and leaned against the counter, frowning. For a moment he looked like he wanted to say a lot of things. Hazard remembered the way Emery had reacted when Hazard first started talking to Jesse, the mistrust and the protectiveness. Hazard didn't feel accomplished, though. He felt kind of guilty. He couldn't help but notice that Emery had a few sex bracelets now too. He wondered if Emery knew what black and red meant.

Emery said simply enough, "It's your life and it's your decisions and you're still my best friend, no matter what. Just be careful with yourself,

Hazard. Seriously."

Hazard nodded and lifted the hot coffee to his lips.

HAZARD didn't want to think of Emery as being capable of social indecencies. But it was undeniable that right then and there, in the dark of the back row of the movie theater, Emery was delighting in some good old-fashioned not-naïve-in-the-least PDA.

Hazard had been excited when Emery invited him to go to the movies Tuesday night, especially because Hazard had been spending a lot of his summer nights with Jesse, and he was missing Emery and all his impish grins. Hazard didn't even care that Russell and Lily were there, because Emery was still dating Lily, and Russell chose to ignore Hazard unless he really didn't have a choice, like when they ordered drinks to share.

They saw *War of the Worlds* first, and it was great. Hazard was on the edge of his seat just like Emery, but Lily was the one who screamed a few times and got them all in a stitch as they tried not to laugh too loud at her.

"I need to see something happy after that," Lily insisted outside the bathrooms, eyes wide and clutching Emery's hand with white knuckles.

Before they were seen, they hurried across the corridor to *Charlie and the Chocolate Factory*. It wasn't that bad, but Lily obviously got bored. Halfway through the film, to Hazard's right, Lily and Emery started whispering. It took Hazard a few minutes to realize it, but the next time he looked over, they'd moved down to the seats in the corner reserved for disabled audience and become two tangled shadows, kissing together in the darkness. Emery's hands were laced at the small of Lily's back. Lily's auburn ponytail bobbed, and they kissed—slow, tender teenage kisses that were lost in the noise of the movie.

Hazard's stomach sank. He wanted to yank them apart. He wanted to yell at Emery. He wondered if that was how people felt when they saw him and Jesse. But he was frozen, candy melting in his hand as he stared at them, a soreness clenching up inside his chest. He didn't know what it was; he just wasn't happy. For a moment, he hated Lily—but that wasn't right. For a moment, he hated Emery—but that wasn't right either. He was left with a childish, lonely anger that he couldn't direct at anyone, and Hazard despised it. Emery wasn't one for PDA. He wasn't like that. This was all Lily's doing. Emery probably wanted to watch the movie—he loved Johnny Depp, after all, and he had Swedish Fish to eat—but Lily wouldn't let him because she wanted to be typical and make out instead.

No, Lily was sweet, with big hazel eyes and a whiskey-and-cigarette voice that just made you smile with her, and she wasn't mean at all, just a little high-strung sometimes. Hazard couldn't be mad at either of them, so he glared at the movie.

Hazard felt Russell move in the seat next to him. He glanced over in time to catch the way Russell's face was pinched up. He looked mad too. Hazard wondered why. Was he mad at Lily, or was he mad at Emery?

Russell looked over, meeting Hazard's stare. Something contrite passed between them, and Hazard shrugged in response, helpless. Russell frowned with all the bitter indignation of a little boy, and to take out his anger, he started to throw M&Ms down at the rows further below them. Nobody seemed to notice. Only one person swatted at their hair absently, tickled by a piece of candy. Hazard had to bite back laughter at it. He joined in, throwing pieces of Buncha Crunch with Russell's M&Ms.

It was something like a truce, Hazard decided.

THE party had been crazy. Hazard managed to sneak back up through his bedroom window, which he'd left cracked, undetected by either parent. That was an incredible feat for as trashed as he was, but the moment his head hit the pillow, everything went wrong, and he stomped over the pile of clothes he'd doffed at the side of his bed as he made a mad dash for the bathroom before he threw up in the hall. What he remembered after was still something of a blur.

He tried to recall what could sober a person up, but he really only managed to make a lot of noise in the kitchen, which woke up his parents, who then became very worried after he announced he'd thrown up. His mom scrubbed his face with a cold cloth. She made him change into fresh pajamas and brush his teeth before she helped him back into bed, and his dad brought him antacids, a towel, and a bowl just in case he threw up again—which Hazard did, a few hours later when he had to pee, because he had a splitting headache and sat up too quickly. But he threw up in the bathroom, flushed, peed, waved good morning to his father, who was leaving for work as the sun rose, then went back to his room and fell asleep again.

His mom promised to be back in the afternoon. It was Monday, and on Mondays she had brunch with Danielle Gallagher. She called around lunch to see if Hazard was even awake, reminded him to brush his teeth, take a shower, use the Vitamin C packet she'd left on the counter, and eat some soup, preferably not the garden vegetable one because that was her favorite, but egg drop or chicken-and-dumpling was there and totally available. Hazard told her he would, but he didn't. It was just a hangover. It wasn't like it was the first one.

He texted Jesse five times before Jesse texted him back to say,

I'm ignoring you, shut the hell up already.

Hazard threw his phone across the couch.

He did take a shower, though. He took advantage of an empty house and blasted the Breaking Benjamin CD he'd borrowed from Emery while he did so.

My polyamorous friend, you've got me in a mess of trouble again.

Hazard stopped in front of the mirror, looking at himself. Shaggy dark hair framing his face in messy locks—eyes the color of a winter sky, the skin around which looked kind of bruised and tired—skinny neck, skinny shoulders, skinny wrists, bony knees. He didn't look that bad, he decided. In fact, he might even be kind of attractive—to girls who liked boys too cute to be sexy or guys like Jesse who could score anyone they wanted.

Hair wet from his shower, Hazard rummaged around for his phone where he'd thrown it earlier so he could call Emery. Emery could always make him forget how irritated he was.

HAZARD and Russell both watched Emery's rushed relationship with Lily shatter. Emery tried really hard, but Lily was too high-maintenance for him. She couldn't help it.

The night they decided to call it quits, Emery shrank away to Hazard's house. Alone with Hazard in his bedroom, Emery choked up. He said, "I'm trying too hard, right?"

Hazard frowned tightly, not sure what to say. He hugged Emery with one arm and fixed his messy hair with the other hand. He dug around in his desk drawer and got out the CD Emery had made him years ago. He put it on and played *NSYNC's "Pop," which made Emery laugh a lot. He was feeling much better by the end of the night. Hazard prided himself for that.

Chapter 6
September

WHEN school started again, the first day hadn't even been over yet before Canaan Lutz flipped Hazard off in the cafeteria to remind him he was still an insufferable dick, and John Henderson informed his row in art class that gay people created AIDS.

In September in psychology class, after talking about tragedies like the Beslan school massacre and Hurricane Katrina, they learned about the amygdala, a little almond-shaped part of the brain that was in charge of impulsive and emotional reactions. Mr. Prewitt said that most teenagers were more likely to use the amygdala than the rational part of the brain, and that was why teenagers didn't make good decisions.

This tidbit started in Hazard a chain reaction of thoughts that bothered him all day. But it was nighttime now, and Hazard sat with Jesse on a gray couch in the basement rec room of someone's house, holding both their drinks while Jesse lit a cigarette. There was a round of pool going on in the middle of the room. A number of guys crowded around the pool table, and a few girls sat prettily on the corners, laughing and batting their eyes and already swaying to and fro with their drinks cradled delicately in their hands.

The rec room was hazy. The sound of the music upstairs bled through the floors and rumbled around the basement, a muffled roar until someone opened the door at the top of the stairs.

Lexie had opened her personal apothecary on the big blue beanbag in the opposite corner of the basement, smiling her way-too-sweet smile. People just like her lounged at her side—girls with short hair, tattered boy jeans, oversized flannels and hoodies with only the bottom few inches fastened, boys with caps backward or long hair in their faces. They added to the haze in the room with an elegance and a pride. Felix was probably dancing upstairs, Ashton was probably pissing someone off, and Brianna was probably shooting someone down while she daintily nursed a beer.

In psychology, Mr. Prewitt also explained that while teens used the overreactive and emotionally charged amygdala, adults tended to use the frontal cortex more, which had to do with empathy, guilt, and reasoning. He explained in the lecture that this was only in most cases, though, statistics and averages gathered from ranging data. It still bothered Hazard.

"Hey," Hazard mumbled, poking Jesse.

Jesse took his drink back from him. "Hnm?" Jesse blew a stream of smoke to the side, away from Hazard's face. He tapped his foot absently. His green eyes were dull and relaxed, his arm slung over the back of the couch. He looked laid-back and tired. He was drunk.

"Do you think I have a dysfunctional amygdala?" Hazard asked quietly.

Jesse cut his eyes over to meet Hazard's, looking a bit confused. Then he seemed concerned, glancing down between Hazard's legs. He looked skeptical and perplexed. "Your *what?*"

"Never mind," Hazard grumbled. After a moment of silence, he got up. He felt Jesse's eyes on him as he wandered off into the crowd. He could still feel them on him as he climbed the steps and went back upstairs, opening the door on an explosion of sound.

Hazard hadn't been upstairs again for ten minutes before he was lost in the dark living room, sitting squished with someone unfamiliar in the little space where two couches met at the corner. The someone unfamiliar said her name was Alex, and her foot brushed against Hazard now and then as she tapped it to the beat of the music, the same music pulsing through the floor and reverberating up through Hazard's tailbone.

They shared a drink and laughed, something about the student council president and how much of a bimbo she was. They both agreed that she only got the title because of who she knew and who she blew. Alex had golden blonde hair pulled up into a sloppy half back that was coming a little undone around her face, and Hazard didn't care if she looked kind of like Britney Spears, because she was funny and smart and he liked sitting there laughing with her, hidden from everyone else.

"Everyone's a product of their childhood," Alex theorized about the student council president. She took the drink from Hazard and sipped from it lazily.

"What do you mean?" Hazard asked.

Alex shrugged, pulling her pants up a little. Hazard blushed. She must have seen him looking at the waistband of her panties, which had been quite visible beneath a sliver of tan skin.

"We're all products of our childhood," she said. "We're influenced by our parents, duh, because of genetics and the way they act, but, um— we're influenced by society too, and culture. We're all molded by, like, what we were exposed to when we were little. When it really comes down to it, at least."

Hazard was quiet, brow knotting. Alex sounded like she was very smart. He tapped his fingers on the rim of his cup as he struggled to fully chew over this with as much as he'd had to drink already. "Do you think that's true?" he asked.

"Sure." Alex nodded sagely. "Like, my mom and dad love me a ton and I get everything I've ever wanted, but they never let me *do* what I want. They want me to be a good girl. Obviously, I don't wanna be. Because of them. I mean, what was *your* childhood like?"

Hazard was fascinated by how easily and casually Alex could evaluate herself. After a moment, though, Alex's question really sank in, and Hazard's brow furrowed further. He stared at his feet as he thought about it. What *was* his childhood like?

Hazard remembered his mom being young and pretty, his dad taking him to the park to play, and that pancake place on the corner after Sunday school, where they made chocolate-chip pancakes in the shape of Mickey Mouse's head—but those things were vague and brief, and only significant because they hadn't happened that often. He remembered daycare the most, and the young woman there with long brown hair who helped him learn his ABCs and to count to ten, and how they had a video game room in the back for the older kids that he'd liked to hang around, hoping the older kids would think he was cool enough to talk to or maybe let him play a game or two.

He remembered once that when his mom came to pick him up, he saw that she'd gotten her nails and her hair done, and Hazard remembered wondering how she'd had time to do all of that between her errands and picking him up. He remembered realizing that she *hadn't* been running errands while he'd been stuck at daycare. He remembered that being the first time he'd been truly mad at her.

By third grade, he hadn't gone to daycare anymore. He woke up himself, ate cereal himself, was patted on the head and reminded to brush his teeth, rode the bus to school, rode the bus home, watched PBS while he did his homework, ate dinner on the opposite end of the table from his parents, played by himself, played at Emery's, watched TV all alone in the big living room, and went to sleep with a cautious kiss and a stroke of the hair. Working long hours and commuting to Seattle meant his dad wasn't home until later, and his mom sometimes preferred leisurely afternoons with her girlfriends to staying home with Hazard.

Hazard stared into his drink and thought with sudden clarity that he was very alone when he was little.

There was a warm pressure on his shin. It was Alex's hand, inching up his leg, her big hazel eyes fixed on him. Hazard gripped his drink. He almost pushed Alex's hand away, but then the track booming from the surround sound hidden around the living room switched to a song he liked.

"Let's dance," Hazard urged. He took a long sip and put his drink down on the end table, staggering to his feet before Alex's hand could move any further up his leg. He reached down, helping Alex up and out of the little nook between the couches. Her hands were soft.

"You're a gentleman," she giggled, suddenly less cynical and full of philosophy. Jesse had said the same thing to him once or twice, sarcastically.

Hazard thought about teens being governed by the amygdala, which wasn't really rational. He thought about how everyone was a product of their childhood. He thought again that he'd grown up very, very alone.

Alex distracted him from this. She snapped a few of his sex bracelets. Hazard ignored it, but she didn't seem to mind. She was a good dancer. She didn't lose the beat even if she was drunk, and she made it fun, her arms in the air. They laughed, moving around the dark living room together, bumping into people but staying close enough to each other. Alex was warm, she was there, she was someone Hazard had never known before, and he had one hand on the small of her back while they stumbled through the pulsing crowd, but they were having fun.

Alex didn't want to go hang out with someone else. Alex wanted to be around him, and Hazard liked that. He liked how it felt to have Alex put her arms around his shoulders and her mouth on his ear. It tickled and sent shivers up and down his spine. She smelled like expensive perfume and laundry softener.

He felt the familiar warmth of pride. Hazard followed Alex down to the couch. She welcomed him in for a kiss, her hand slithering up his shirt to curiously feel his stomach. And every first kiss with someone new brought the same exhilaration, refreshing and shy, because each new mouth held the wonder of a first kiss all over again.

"I need a drink," Hazard said against Alex's mouth. She made a sound of displeasure. Hazard felt her eyes on him as he left the living room, just as Jesse had watched him leave the basement.

Somebody had made strawberry daiquiris, and Hazard poured himself a healthy cupful. Someone tapped him on the shoulder, and he was afraid it would be Alex, but when he turned around it was just someone from his art class saying hello in obligation.

He didn't go back to Alex. He sat on the kitchen counter, swinging his legs and people watching. It wasn't much later that Jesse found him, drifting between his knees and caging him in against the cabinets. Hazard blushed at Jesse's cunning smirk because he knew what was going to happen now. Jesse helped him off the counter. Hazard stumbled once. He grabbed Jesse's hand and lugged him off down the hall. He saw Alex as they passed the living room. Alex saw him too.

Hazard didn't know whose house it was, but they were in someone's room, and it was dark. Sex was sex. They made out, hard. Jesse hoisted him up to sit on the desk in the room, and by the time Hazard reached down for Jesse's pants, the feeling that he'd been thinking about something important was totally gone.

Jesse tripped over the laundry basket by the desk and got his foot stuck. Hazard couldn't stop laughing.

HAZARD should have known it was only a matter of time, really, until Emery confronted him about Jesse. It was Emery, and Emery wasn't stupid.

Emery's mom and Andrew went out for dinner. Emery and Hazard had a buffet of snacks on the coffee table and with a note of trauma in the back of his voice, Emery told Hazard about how the other night he'd heard his mom and Andrew getting it on. Hazard pretty much lost his appetite halfway through a pretzel stick, sympathizing with Emery's misery. They laughed about it as they watched TV, and Hazard still wasn't sure exactly what prompted Emery to ask, but it was something because suddenly out of nowhere the tension was there.

Emery's face pinched. His eyes clouded. He met Hazard's glance, and by the darkness in his stare, Hazard knew that whatever he was about to say had been weighing on him for some time, and that made Hazard extremely nervous. Emery licked his lips and said, "You know I've got your back, so why haven't you told me about your boyfriend yet?"

He said it tightly, notes of passive aggression in his voice that only he could make sound considerate. Hazard's stomach sank. He looked at Emery with eyes shot through with panic, feeling a crippling wave of embarrassment and shock roll through him. "I don't have a boyfriend," he said carefully, and then the panic set in, buzzing in all his nerves. Oh God, what had Emery heard now? How long had he been bothered by whatever it was?

Emery didn't answer yet. He stared. It was a look Hazard had received from him a lot lately, and it always reminded him of the way the family looked at Mary on *7th Heaven*. Emery looked more like a disappointed brother than a judgmental family, but Hazard still saw the resemblance.

"That's not what I've heard," Emery countered, on the verge of becoming patronizing.

Hazard's heart fell next, and his fingertips felt clammy in dread. He didn't want to know what Emery had heard. He didn't want to know what Emery thought of him. "What have you heard?"

Emery scowled. "Hazard, you and Jesse are inseparable. You're always together, hanging out and stuff. And I heard that—" Emery stopped short, looking remorseful for getting defensive and impatient. "Word gets around," he surmised quietly. "I mean, look at your fucking jelly bracelets."

Hazard was silent, eyes wide and heart pounding. The seconds ticked by, long and heavy. Emery's stare was critical.

"Why didn't you tell me he was your boyfriend? You think I'd judge you or something?" Emery whispered sharply, and Hazard remembered all too well how suspicious Emery had been of Jesse from the beginning. God, how long had Emery stewed in this?

Hazard almost couldn't talk. "He's not my boyfriend, Emery."

"But I heard—"

"Emery, you know as well as I do that you can't believe what people say, *right*?"

"That's not fair, Hazard—"

"He's not my boyfriend, okay? We're not gay. It's more of a benefits kind of thing. He's my best—"

Emery's eyes pierced into him, sharper. Hazard almost couldn't go on. This was torture. But he pushed forth, jaw tightening. He felt restless and powerless. "Jesse's my other best friend. We fool around, but we're not gay, and we don't have to worry about complicating things like dating."

"A 'benefits' kind of thing."

"Yeah."

"Like, kissing?"

"Yeah."

"That's it?"

"No."

"Like *sex*?"

"Yeah. Friends with benefits."

"Wow." Emery scoffed faintly. "He's really got you under his thumb, doesn't he?"

Hazard was insulted and embarrassed at the same time. He wanted to curl up and die in his misery. He didn't know what to say, so he glared at Emery, frowning darkly. Jesse had never been Emery's favorite person, especially after Hazard befriended him. That was what Hazard had been aiming for at some point, but not anymore. Not at all. And it hurt to hear Emery's cold analysis, because it couldn't be farther from the truth.

Something changed dramatically in Emery's eyes. "I get it," he said suddenly, tersely. He nodded. "What does that make me, then?"

Hazard stared, at a loss for words. What did that even mean? "What are you?" Hazard echoed, feeling very downcast and pathetic. "You're my best friend."

This seemed to placate enough of Emery's frustration. He ate a chip and then started sucking on a Lifesaver. "And you're both straight," he reiterated, looking at Hazard sideways, almost as if he didn't believe him.

"I guess you could say we're bisexual, or something."

"Hazard, it's not a joke. What if I was gay? Would you joke about that?"

Hazard blanked. He looked at Emery, throat tight in embarrassment but momentarily muted by the serious look on Emery's face. Dark-blue eyes, mouth in a firm line. Hazard wasn't quite sure what to think about it.

"No," he promised quietly. "I wouldn't. Emery, are you—"

Emery snorted. "Of course not!" he said, but looking at him, Hazard still kind of questioned it. He was a horrible friend for doubting him, but he couldn't help it. He'd grown up with Emery. He knew him too well—well enough to let something like that be.

"Emery, I'm sorry," Hazard said, horrified that he'd complicated something between them. "Tell me what you've heard."

"I used to think when people called you bisexual, they were just being mean, but I've heard too many stories about you getting close with guys at parties for it to be untrue. And, I mean, you're Jesse Wesley's friend. I heard Jesse Wesley does whatever he wants, so I guess it makes sense that you do too. I tried to ignore it all at first, but the more I heard, the more it seemed obvious that you and Jesse were going out or something. But I guess it's something totally different. Haz, I just want you to be careful. I just want you to tell me things. You know how much it sucks to find out what you do by overhearing the girls behind me in science class? I told you before: *I've got your back.* With everything. Now, stop. Just stop. Don't talk about it. Don't think about it. I won't either. It's cool. Let's just watch TV. Look, Maury is on."

Emery frowned, gesturing with the remote, and Hazard knew by the unnerving, simple candor in his eyes that what he said was the truth and nothing else. Emery wasn't upset about what Hazard had done, just that he'd had to find out the way he had. Hazard felt like he could breathe again, but he still felt kind of like Mary from *7th Heaven*. He felt guilty. He wasn't sure what was more uncomfortable, talking to Emery about doing things with a guy or just being reminded again how much people talked about him without his knowing.

Emery got way too into *Maury* for honest entertainment, and Hazard ached because he knew Emery was trying to lighten the mood. Eventually it worked, and by the time Emery's mom and Andrew got back and Hazard left, Emery's eyes weren't so dark anymore. The sense of guilt in Hazard's chest was still there, rotten and embarrassing, but it was fading considerably faster than he'd expected it to. They'd be okay. Emery didn't think differently of him. Emery had his back.

That night, Hazard texted Jesse on his way to the Elite Street and told him he needed to get his mind off some things, if Jesse wouldn't mind distracting him.

Chapter 7
October

IN SEPTEMBER, the band Panic! At the Disco came out with a CD, and if they hadn't, Hazard wasn't sure he and Jesse would have ever had sex *that way*.

Lexie's friend Jeremy was the kind of kid whose parents never really grew up, and it was only a little awkward to know that there were adults at a party where the music was loud and the air was hazy because nobody had closed the door on the toke room, and Jeremy's parents sat smoking in the kitchen, making sure nobody had more than four drinks.

Hazard was trying to get tipsy, sitting on a couch near the window. Jesse made his rounds, dancing with people he didn't know, saying hi to faces he recognized, kissing girls he knew on the cheek in greeting. Hazard blamed the vodka shots for the way his stare kept lingering on the way Jesse's hips moved to the blasting music, even if they moved behind someone else's.

Jesse came over and plucked at Hazard's glittery clear sex bracelet, a casual gesture that had become code recently. That was how Hazard knew it was time to fool around.

The song must have been stuck in Jesse's head when they retreated to a room, because he was humming it as Hazard wandered around locking the door and opening the blinds so he could see Jesse in the dark. He put his drink down and let Jesse wind his arms around his middle, and Hazard hoped Jeremy didn't mind that they'd shooed other people out of his room so they could make out on his floor.

Hazard's pants were a little too big for him. There were wide holes in them that Jesse reached into to touch his knee. It tickled. Hazard kicked him gently for it, snickering into Jesse's shoulder. Jesse tasted like booze. His hair was still grungy red then, and it tickled Hazard too.

He unbuttoned his pants for Jesse, because he really wanted it. Jesse touched him, but just as the good feeling swung from teasing to unbearable, he withdrew. Confused, Hazard kicked his jeans all the way off, lying on Jeremy's bedroom floor in just his shirt and boxers. His breath came in short bursts as he watched Jesse move away to wriggle out of his pants too, then dig around in the back pocket for his wallet. The chain rattled. He pulled out a condom and Hazard sat up, eyes wide.

"Jesse," he hissed, stomach sinking, "we're not doing it *that way*, are we?"

Jesse paused. He held the condom in one hand and his wallet in the other, looking at Hazard with something of an injured expression on his face. He looked a little offended, like he didn't know why Hazard didn't trust him. Hazard wanted to tell him that it wasn't that he didn't *trust* him, he just wasn't *gay*. He didn't really know how to do it *that way*. He just had an idea from common sense and jokes. But he didn't say anything.

"No," Jesse said quietly, looking very serious in the dark as he crawled over. "Not *that way*. We're doing it *my way*."

Hazard had to admit that when it came to being friends with benefits, Jesse knew what to do and how to make it feel really good. It was okay. Jesse was so cool, and if Jesse wanted to do it *that way*, it had to be all right. Hazard felt bad for doubting him.

The party was a muffled roar outside Jeremy's bedroom. Hazard could hear the echo of an Incubus song. He lay down again, staring up at the ceiling and thinking about how many people wanted Jesse and listening to the condom in Jesse's hands. He'd never used one before. He'd never gone all the way with anyone before. He was kind of terrified.

Jesse's breath was hot on his ear as he leaned down and whispered, just slightly scratchy and surprisingly in tune, a line of that new Panic! At the Disco song.

Hazard's eyes widened. His heart leapt to his throat and thundered there, and his fingers shook as he hooked them in Jesse's shirt and pulled him closer. Jesse was distracting him with the song as he reached into his boxers and started touching him again, and the feel of his breath and the sound of his voice and the way his hand moved, the very idea behind it all sent dangerous shivers rattling through Hazard. Jesse was sly. He knew what he was doing, but Hazard could tell somehow that he wasn't doing it just to get his way.

Jesse kept humming the song like it was stuck in his head and this wasn't a huge thing they were about to do together.

Hazard jumped when Jesse ripped open the condom. The air was cool on naked skin, and the silence in Jeremy's bedroom was deafening compared to the noise out in the house. Hazard thought that maybe he should resist when Jesse crawled on top of him, maybe he should be scared, maybe he should stop him, but then Jesse whispered, *So testosterone boys and there are no girls*, changing the last word on purpose, and it totally sold him. Hazard laughed, even though he was sick with nervousness. Jesse grinned, seemingly pleased with this reaction.

It felt really weird. It hurt, bad. Jesse held his hand over Hazard's mouth to keep him quiet, and Hazard was horrified again. It was awkward. It was potentially disastrous. Part of him was grossed out by the whole idea. He dug his fingernails into the carpet as he tried not to cry. All Hazard could think was that he was doing it with Jesse, he was supposed to be a normal guy, and *Dance to this beat....* The condom felt weird. Sex felt weird, like a vicious prodding at his belly button or spine from the inside out. But then the pain numbed, and Hazard couldn't help wondering, *Why haven't we done this before?*

Jesse found a rhythm Hazard was okay with, and they did it. Hazard's skin was so hot that he was itchy, grabbing onto the carpet and hiding from Jesse's face as his hair tickled him. After a while he realized Jesse's shoulder was shaking, muscles taut beneath his skin, so Hazard held his own mouth and let Jesse put his hand back down for better support.

Hazard felt sick with nervousness. He shivered and his heart raced and he tried to hold his hips off the floor, and it felt like he came—the jerking shudders, the fluttering heart, the tingle in all his nerves—but there was nothing wet, nothing slimy, no come anywhere. He didn't understand. His hips were starting to cramp. He grabbed onto Jesse's collar and listened to him try to stay quiet. Hazard knew when Jesse was about to come. He swore each time, right before he orgasmed. A little *Shit!* or an *Oh fuck* hissed out against Hazard's ear. Hazard pushed Jesse's punk-red hair out of his face.

Jesse swore, and then he came, and Hazard's eyes widened. He felt it all. He clenched his teeth against a groan, grabbing Jesse's hair. "*Jesse!*" he snapped breathlessly. "*Jesse—*" He wanted to say *Ew, Jesse, this is gross*, but that was all he could get out. He would have felt bad to say it, anyway. It sounded like something his mother would say.

The room was quiet except for the sound of their breath as they both fell still. Jesse waited for a long moment before he gently shifted away from Hazard's hips. He didn't even give Hazard time to roll over and bury his face in his arms. He didn't even say anything. He just caged him in on the carpet again and reached around between his thighs and finished him off too.

Hazard couldn't breathe for a minute. He lay curled up on his side on the floor of Jeremy's bedroom and kept his eyes closed. He felt perfectly exhausted like he always did when Jesse made him come, and he just listened to his heart pound and felt his muscles quivering as the momentary high faded. It left him dizzy and numb. This time—doing it *that way*—Jesse actually fucking him—and he didn't feel ashamed at all—

"Sometimes I'm scared of you," Hazard said quietly, staring up at the ceiling.

Jesse stopped, glancing at him pointedly. "Why?" he asked, sounding kind of concerned.

"Because." Hazard sat up, wondering if he'd be in pain. He felt a little awkward pulling his boxers back up from his ankle, but not as sore as he'd expected. He glanced at Jesse through a mess of dark-brown hair. Jesse watched him expectantly, his face blank in a childish, attentive way. Hazard loved him for it. He blushed and mumbled, "I'm scared of you and where you learned that and why I liked it."

Jesse smiled. He didn't say anything. He just smiled faintly, lashes lowering as he stood up and ran a hand through his hair and threw away the condom in Jeremy's little wire trash can. "Surprise, Jeremy!" he whispered, and Hazard laughed. Neither of them really had any idea who Jeremy was, except for being someone Lexie knew.

They re-dressed. They took turns in Jeremy's bathroom to pee, then went out for a smoke. Jesse handed Hazard a cigarette, sitting close to him on the cement stoop and listening to the bass and the voices from inside the house. Hazard didn't deny it. He smoked it with Jesse, shaking more with the nicotine now than the comedown from sex. Jesse ruffled his hair, and then he started to hum. Hazard smiled. Something about it was sweet, in such a teenage way.

JESSE turned eighteen the second week of October. The first thing he wanted to do was buy his first pack of legal cigarettes. Hazard gave him money for it. "So it's like I bought them for you," he explained.

Hazard helped Lexie and Felix plan a sort of "surprise" party for Jesse. The Seattle gang came down and threw it. Jesse was grinning the whole time, which made Hazard happy. There was Goldschläger and lots of rum, which were Jesse's favorites. A lot of people from school went. They practically kissed Jesse's feet.

They were at Hunter's house, in one of the sort of redneck neighborhoods of Bethany near Port Orchard, where nobody really cared about peace disruption. Shirtless from the Seattle gang knew Hunter. Everybody else knew Hunter because he threw a lot of bashes at his house. "Lose Control" pounded through the living room. Kaitlyn Roberts was kissing Kaylie Seaman, and all the guys loved it. Hazard was tipsy on rum and Vanilla Coke. He asked Jesse, "What if I smoked too, like you?"

"That's horrible for your health, you know," Jesse said.

Hazard laughed. He took Jesse's pack of Camels and dug in Jesse's hip pocket for his Scorpio lighter. Jesse smirked, moving his hips provocatively.

Hazard got out a cigarette and lit it. It stung his eyes and felt cold in his lungs until he blew the smoke out.

"You're holding that like a joint." Jesse snickered.

"No, I'm not."

"Look at you, laying down all cool like you know what you're doing."

Hazard smiled. They shared the cigarette. Jesse insisted. They made out on the couch in the corner. Jesse danced around with people after. Hazard waited to stop shaking from the nicotine. He ran around with Brianna, snapping everybody's jelly sex bracelets and playing tricks on people by moving their drinks when they weren't looking. They wrote things like *hello* and *silly* back and forth on each other with ballpoint pen, sitting at everyone's feet while they did shots of Absolut and tequila. They changed the CD to something more rock and roll and went from empty room to room, jumping on the beds.

"You're jailbait now," Jesse told Hazard when they were dancing later. He had another cigarette already, and he draped his arms over

Hazard's shoulders from behind, holding the filter to his mouth.

Hazard took a drag. It almost made him feel sick. He took a long drink to clear his throat of the itchy sensation. "So?" he said, looking up at Jesse.

"Oh, yeah? You're such a bad kid." Jesse grinned.

Hazard blushed. He had to admit that it was pretty cool to be doing stuff with someone who was legal (and really popular), even though the threat of real consequences for drinking and shoplifting and everything else he did with Jesse and his crew was always hanging there, waiting to be remembered: alcohol poisoning, social diseases, bad arguments, getting caught....

They went to find a room around eleven. They found Hunter's sister's room, where everybody who was anybody wrote on her wall in Sharpie marker between the glow-in-the-dark stars and below the little black light from Spencer's in the mall. She called it The Forum. She'd started it a few years ago, when she was in seventh grade and her brother first started throwing parties. Now she was in Hazard's grade, and her entire wall crawled with Sharpie messages in different colors. It was kind of like the wall in the bathroom by the auditorium at school where everybody wrote the worst gossip, except that The Forum was generally more frivolous. People wrote things like who was dating who, what they'd seen at the party, hellos to friends, phone numbers and random shout-outs that were sometimes too jumbled to be read or made absolutely no sense.

Jesse went over to her cluttered girly desk. He went through her drawers until he found a purple Sharpie. Hazard grabbed it from him immediately and wrote on the wall: *10-16-05 HAPPY BIRTHDAY, JESSE LOGAN WESLEY*

"How sweet," Jesse purred. He took the Sharpie from Hazard and wrote: *Jesse is king*

Hazard took the marker back, laughing. He added: *Elite Streeters suck dick.* Jesse scoffed. He got a different marker and wrote below that: *Hazard likes it.*

"You can't write that!" Hazard was aghast. "It's permanent!"

"Sorry," Jesse mumbled, smiling foolishly. He crossed out that message and replaced it with: *Make Out HERE* with an arrow pointing to the floor below the wall with all the scribbles.

They made out. Hazard undid Jesse's jeans and reached into them, but they were both too drunk to really find an end, so they just kissed hard for a while until Felix found them and coaxed them to come back out to the living room with everyone else. Hazard's fingers still smelled like sex, anyway, like his burps tasted like bottled alcohol.

"Happy birthday," Hazard whispered against Jesse's ear and all his little earrings.

"Thanks, Danger," Jesse said, and the way he ruffled Hazard's dark hair was nothing but loving.

"HEY, Hazard," Eric Garcia said.

"Hey," Hazard mumbled.

"You were *tough* out there, dude." Eric mopped at his neck with his shirt.

"Thanks. I like baseball."

The locker room was abuzz with the Lifetime Sports class before lunch, the slamming of doors and running water, riled-up voices, clothes rustling and shoes thudding. Eric sat down on the bench between the rows of lockers, elbows on his knees. He looked at Hazard with a strange expression on his face, and Hazard felt a little pang of alarm in his chest. He ignored it.

"Hazard, you're so weird," Eric said.

Hazard snorted. "I thought you were done making fun of my name."

"I am."

"Then why am I weird now?"

"Because I mean, you don't suck at sports," Eric said.

"What does that matter?" Hazard asked, perplexed.

Eric shrugged. Hazard wanted to wipe the look of furtive smugness off his face. It made him uneasy. "You can take a good beating in a game and you're not a pussy when you get hurt."

Hazard thought about the burn he'd gotten on his back from tumbling into home plate during the baseball game. It was raining out, so they'd played inside, and sliding into home on the gym floor didn't feel too hot. The red mark stung and tingled and crawled like a rug burn, but he'd felt worse, and he'd scored the point for his team, and all the guys had finally cheered his name just like they did the taller, more talented guys in the class.

"I've felt worse," Hazard said. He put his clean shirt on, feeling very uneasy. Eric sat casually, watching. Hazard glanced at him. "What?"

"I mean," Eric motioned to Hazard with one hand, "look at what you're wearing."

Hazard did, looking down at his clothes: Nirvana T-shirt, loose and faded jeans with gaping holes in the knees, Converse sitting near his backpack.

"You look like a dude, and you act like a dude. I just don't get it," Eric said.

"That's because I *am* a dude," Hazard said dryly, getting very suspicious of Eric. Whatever he was getting at, he was doing a really bad job at it, and Hazard was getting pissed—

"Well, you're gay, right?" Eric shrugged another time, pulling the towel off his shoulders. "But you don't act like it, or look like it, and you sure as hell aren't all gross in the locker room."

Hazard's stomach sank. His skin went cold. "Um. What?" he demanded.

Eric laughed like he didn't understand why Hazard was getting offended. Other guys were dawdling, quieting down, paying peripheral attention to their discussion. "Dude," Eric said, like Hazard just wasn't getting it, but there was still that underhanded gleam in his eyes. "You're all into Jesse Wesley."

"That's not what I heard," someone to the left corrected, and Hazard cut a vicious glance in his direction. He remembered the midmorning he'd been in Lifetime Sports and looked up to see Jesse at the gym doors, watching from the hall. He'd been totally embarrassed. But that couldn't be what they were talking about now. Jesse could have been doing anything there in the doorway.

"Whatever." Eric waved his hands around dismissively. "You're part of his gang and stuff. Everyone knows about his crew, Hazard. Don't tell me you don't hear all the rumors. Seriously?"

"Oh, I hear them," Hazard scoffed, fumbling with his locker's combination. His hands were shaking in bottled fury. Other guys who were suddenly interested were loitering on the other side of the bench, an audience behind Eric. They watched and hovered, like the discussion was some kind of spectacle. Hazard swallowed on a tight throat.

"Everyone knows you party with them. I've even seen you at a bash or two. What I don't get is how you don't fit the stereotypes," Eric said. He was loving this.

"Eric, *I'm not gay!*" Hazard barked.

Eric guffawed. "What the fuck ever! Look, I'm not trying to pick on you. I just wanna know how it works—how you don't *look* like it or *act* like it. I wouldn't even know you were a fag if I hadn't seen you at Zane's party last Saturday, practically drooling all over Jesse."

Someone around the bench chuckled eagerly at that, but all Hazard could think about was Jesse, Jesse, Jesse, everything was Jesse's fault and Jesse wasn't even the one taking the heat for it all. How did that happen?

Eric shrugged, smiling wickedly. He looked triumphant. He had Hazard cornered. "Is it good? Is it better than girls?"

Someone snorted. "This is sick. I'm out of here."

Eric said, "I mean, hey, if it gets you off, it gets you off. Right?"

Hazard felt trapped. A tension settled over the entire locker room. It was suddenly far too quiet to be a changing period. The air was thick with the smell of sweat and deodorants, of clothes and skin and dirty floors. Hazard felt the knots in his shoulders, skin crawling in humiliated rage. Their eyes were on him, waiting for his answer. This was all a joke to them, a scene. Something to talk about after the bell rang. Hazard shook. His face was on fire. He wanted to walk out and forget all about this or stay and say something cool like Jesse would say, like, *Oh, you hit it right on the head, man, do you want me to show you?*

But instead, Hazard just shoved Eric with all his might. Eric tumbled backward into the guys gathered behind him, and Hazard staggered back a step or two. Howling erupted in the locker room, taunts and jests and cheers and fists against lockers as Eric stumbled back up over the bench and yanked Hazard forward to fight.

By the time the coach made it through the mess of students packed around the bench, the fight had already been physical for a good minute, and after delivering both bloodied students to the office, he got an okay from the principal to keep the rest of the boys in the locker room to help clean up.

Hazard's lip was busted deep. His cheek was sore. His nose was tender and red, and he couldn't look down without his eyes watering, and there were bruises forming on his arms and back where he'd taken a few good smacks, but he was so proud of the multiple knees he'd sent to Eric's gut and the sucker punches to his eye and ear that the pain wasn't that hard to handle at all.

The suspension slip read *Fighting in the locker room. Mandatory suspension of 12 days.* When his mom came to get him, she fought tears in the middle of the office and spoke with the principal *and* the school officer while Hazard slumped in the chair outside the principal's office, praying she would just stop feigning distress and shut up already so they could go. When they got home, he suffered through a *Just wait until your father hears about this, and he hasn't been feeling good lately, so this will just be the cherry on top, won't it* lecture. He texted both Jesse and Emery behind his knee the whole way through.

"Son, it was just a normal scuffle," Hazard's dad said later, after he'd secretly patted him on the back for such a masculine thing as fighting.

"No, it wasn't," Hazard insisted. Neither of his parents would understand, but that was okay with him.

His mother gave him a list of chores to do for the next two weeks. A suspension was not a vacation, she said. It was a punishment.

"OH, COME on. Get into the spirit, Hazard!"

Emery grinned. He surveyed the pile of candy he'd dumped from his little plastic jack-o'-lantern bucket. Russell sat a foot or so away from him, sunglasses on even though it was dark inside Emery's house. Lily was having her friend Sophie fix her fairy wings in the mirror on the far living room wall. Emery's mother was out. There were microwavable meals sitting in the freezer, but Hazard knew for certain that Emery was probably going to choose candy for dinner—especially because he got a lot of Swedish Fish this year around.

Hazard sighed heavily, emptying his pockets of candy. "I am. Can't you tell what my costume is? I'm my evil twin."

Emery rolled his eyes and tore into a mini Twix bar. Russell uttered a gentle scoff, cross-legged with his own candy spread out before him.

"I don't see much of a difference," Russell said. "With the scowl you have every day, your evil twin should be a ray of sunshine or something."

"Careful," Hazard grumbled, unwrapping some of his own candy. "I might just snap and slit your throat. My evil twin lacks self-control like that."

"I see." Russell sighed, popping a pair of M&Ms in his mouth. "So you wear your costume every day, then?"

Emery pinned a disapproving glance on Russell. Hazard looked at Russell sharply in turn.

Russell just shrugged, reaching up and pushing his sunglasses to rest atop his head. "What?" he demanded, looking at Emery.

Emery shook his head, scowling bitterly. He threw his Twix wrapper at Russell and scooped up armfuls of candy, moving over to join the girls on the other side of the living room.

Silence settled over Russell and Hazard, but after a moment Russell broke it, sighing again and mumbling, "I can't believe we actually just went trick-or-treating. The things we do for Emery, am I right?"

Hazard nodded humbly. He glanced over at Russell through his lashes. Russell didn't look back.

Hazard went home later, and his house was empty again by ten. His parents were going to a Halloween party his dad's work was throwing. Hazard convinced them to let him stay at Emery's for the night and skip school the next day, except he was really going to be with Jesse. His mom had to kiss him a few times and remind him to brush his teeth and not eat too much candy or his teeth would rot and he'd get diabetes.

By ten thirty, a car screeched to a halt just off the driveway. Hazard made sure to lock the door as he wriggled into his coat, cell phone in one hand and scarf in the other, pockets of his jacket filled with suckers, bite-sized Snickers, and the house key. Jesse idled at the curb, waiting for him, and Hazard tumbled into the passenger seat with a big grin and an offering: a cherry-flavored sucker that Jesse accepted with a click of his teeth against the hard red candy on the end.

They met Felix and Lexie and Brianna at the theater. Jesse's ID, which was real this year, got them all into a late showing of *Saw II*, and then they snuck across into the midnight showing of *The Ring Two*. Hazard was completely creeped. They stayed over at Felix's house for the night. Hazard was tired, but watching *Cabin Fever* at Felix's woke him up again. By the time it was over, Hazard was scratching psychological itches all over and grimacing in disgust. He could hardly go to sleep, thinking about flesh-eating diseases and haunted TVs and torture devices. Everyone else fell asleep quickly. He tossed and turned until finally Jesse threw an arm over him to keep him still.

"I can't believe you jumped so many times at *Cabin Fever*," Jesse teased the next morning, hands shoved in his pockets as they left Felix's. Lexie and Brianna had already gone. Felix waved from the door, then went to take a shower. "It wasn't even supposed to be scary."

"It was *suspenseful*," Hazard insisted, exhausted.

"You were *scared*," Jesse argued.

"I'm *grossed out*," Hazard spat back.

"Come here." Jesse chuckled, and Hazard turned around, glaring up at him. Jesse grinned, propping a hand on the roof of his car and caging Hazard against the passenger door. Hidden from view, Jesse kissed him— casually, softly, slowly.

Hazard drew in a breath against Jesse's lips, lashes fluttering open halfway. He leaned back against the car, face puckering. He gawked up at Jesse, troubled.

"What?" Jesse asked, seeing it on his face.

"That skin disease—"

"It's fake, Hazard."

"Okay, I mean, *any disease*—if you had anything—you'd tell me, right?"

Jesse shifted, a hard look of insulted disbelief crossing his face. Curtly, he demanded, "What kind of person do you think I am?"

"I'm just wondering." Hazard shifted around a bit, uneasily. He didn't like the way Jesse stared at him. He could feel his anger growing. He nudged Jesse away so he could open the passenger door. It was locked. He fidgeted again uncomfortably, then glanced at Jesse over his shoulder. "You ready to go?"

Jesse stood there a moment, hands in his pockets and jacket hanging open, staring at Hazard in irritated scrutiny. His lip curled. With an eventual sigh of frustration, Jesse slammed his palm against the roof of his car, turning on his heel with concrete crackling beneath his tennis shoe. He got in the driver's seat and unlocked the doors—first for him, then stretching across to unlock the passenger's side.

"Come on, then," he grumbled as Hazard caught the opening door and slid in. "You want me to drop you off, or do you wanna go back to my place so you can check me for social diseases?"

"*Jesse—*"

"My place? Okay. Let's go."

Hazard hunched against the passenger door, yanking his seatbelt on. The car was silent as they pulled out of the parking lot and made their way to Redwood Court and the Elite Street, but after a few moments of nothing but the noontime radio shows, Hazard dug around in his pocket and held a leftover sucker out for Jesse. Jesse took it, tossed it into the cup holder with his lighter and cigarettes, and snatched Hazard's wrist before he could pull away. Without looking away from the road, he tugged Hazard's hand up and kissed his knuckles.

Jesse took Hazard home anyway. His mom was busy cleaning the kitchen, so Hazard hurried to the bathroom, returning her "Good morning" on the way. He hadn't brushed his teeth before going to sleep, so he brushed them twice, once before his shower and once after. He also wore a hoodie, hoping it hid the hickeys on his lower neck that Jesse had given him during *The Ring Two* to try to distract him from being scared. Then he texted Emery to see if he'd eaten all his candy yet.

Chapter 8
November

FIGHTING in public was the hardest. It was hard because it was restricted by manners and social rules, and everything that was otherwise endured in private—screaming, violence, stomping around, all the climactic moments—had to be carefully monitored. It left the fight to proceed in vicious mutters, sharp glances, and trembling self-control, so it was a very good thing that it was noisy in Fred Meyer, because Hazard had vicious enough comments biding their time in his breath and a sharp enough glare fixed on Jesse, and he was sure as hell shaking as he stomped through the store behind him.

Jesse was in one of his intolerable bad moods: scathing green eyes, caustic scowl, cruel words. Hazard wasn't sure what had set him off this time. Maybe he'd just woken up like that. He did sometimes, like the nights he'd roll over and scowl and say *Be gone in the morning*. He never followed through on those things—they were just bad moods, probably related to a lack of nicotine or something—but they still hurt. Hazard had "Blurry" stuck in his head, and it only made it easier to feel the brunt of Jesse's attitude.

"You're so *annoying*," Jesse hissed over his shoulder, winding through the aisles.

"You're an *asshole*," Hazard retorted, stopping to examine a bag of pita chips. They looked good.

"You've been calling me that since day one, Danger. I think you need to learn some manners. What if I called *you* names, hunh? You wouldn't stick around. Self-respect and all that shit, right?"

Hazard waited to respond because a lady with a full shopping cart turned down the aisle with them. They were both impatient as they watched her pass.

"Shut up, Jesse," Hazard bit back.

"Look—" Jesse motioned for Hazard to follow him. Hazard did, shoving his hands deep in his pockets. They were headed to the electronics section of Fred Meyer. Lexie's birthday was coming up, and Jesse wanted to get her a CD she'd been wanting. "Look, you're the one who wanted to fucking tag along. I told you, I'm running *errands* today."

"I don't mind," Hazard grumbled.

"Why the hell do I put up with you?" Jesse acted like he was talking to himself, but he kept his voice loud enough that Hazard could listen. "I could find someone so much better. So much *easier*. Someone who didn't bitch and whine and worry so much about me."

He said it like he couldn't believe Hazard wasted the time to do so. For a moment, Hazard was saddened by that. And then he felt a little bit of pain, frown thinning, at the deliberate derision of his worthiness. It bruised. It stung because sometimes Hazard forgot that they were supposed to be just friends with benefits, not anything exclusive. A few months ago, fighting like this would have hurt, but not this badly. Sometimes Hazard felt debilitated by it, how much these fights hurt now, and he couldn't explain why, but it was just *different*.

Jesse started going through the shelves of CDs in the electronics section, searching for the right genre.

Hazard stepped close to him and mumbled, "It's simple, Jesse. You put up with me because I'm the bad habit you can't drop. Nobody, no girl or guy, does it like I do."

He felt really cool saying it—the words just tasted right—but immediately he hated himself for it. Jesse turned sharply, red leather jacket, Seether shirt, and violent scowl. Hazard knew from the look on Jesse's face that he'd gotten the upper hand, but Jesse was certainly not going to let him keep it.

"Hey," Jesse husked, and when he spoke low and calm like that, it was cold, and Hazard knew he'd gone too far, "don't you pin all this on me. If I'm not mistaken, it doesn't matter what I do, because you keep crawling back for more."

Hazard bristled. He wasn't sure why this caught him so off guard, but it did. His face burned. His chest ached. Jesse started going through the CDs again. On the multiple TVs in the electronics section, an ad for an all-nineties collection was on, and Fiona Apple was singing about being a bad, bad girl.

"Do you remember the night you said you'd never talk to me again?" Hazard edged out between clenched teeth, needing to hurt Jesse just as much as Jesse was hurting him. "The Fourth of July. Two hours after you said that, you pulled me over and gave me a hug. You wanted to kiss. You came *crawling back.*"

Hazard thought about the Fourth of July. He thought about what happened after Jesse came crawling back, out on Felix's back patio, on the porch swing and sharing a blanket and talking for hours and hours on end about everything and anything.

"I was *drunk,*" Jesse hissed, a sudden chill in his voice. Hazard felt the sting, both from Jesse's excuse and the fact that his words hadn't seemed to stab Jesse as deeply as he'd wanted them to.

Jesse found the CD. Yellowcard, *Ocean Avenue.* He grabbed it and stalked off. Hazard hurried after him.

"God," Jesse said, "all we do is piss each other off."

"Party, fuck, and fight," Hazard grumbled, wondering if agreeing with Jesse would get on his nerves instead.

"It's pretty clear."

But Hazard swallowed and thought, *No, it's not clear, those are just words he's using to upset me, to distance himself, trying to come out on top like everyone does when they're fighting with someone.*

They bought the Yellowcard CD. There was silence between them until they were threading through the aisles again, passing frozen pizzas and pies.

"I need a cigarette," Jesse announced.

"Oh, I just stress you out so much, don't I?"

Jesse stopped, looking at Hazard darkly. A worker down the aisle unloading frozen éclairs glanced in their direction as Jesse sneered, "Fuck you, you little prick."

Hazard was so angry he couldn't even feel fazed or embarrassed. "Whatever. Fuck you too, then, Jesse. I don't care. I'm not the one making a fool of myself. You are. Anyone can see that. Don't call me. Don't text me. Don't even drive me home! I'll walk. And I don't care, because I don't need you. But I give it, oh, I don't know, three hours, tops—and then you'll be missing me—"

Jesse stopped walking and grabbed a box of popcorn off a shelf. Before Hazard could even stop talking, Jesse threw it. It hit Hazard in the stomach, but it didn't really hurt. It just shut him up. He doubled forward, holding his middle as the box of popcorn fell to his feet. Hazard looked at Jesse with wide eyes, a little shocked. Jesse raised his brows as if to say, *What?* He was already getting his cigarettes out.

Hazard scowled. He didn't mean to, but he was so frustrated he couldn't even be coherent. He uttered a little growl as he grabbed the box of popcorn and heaved it back at Jesse.

Jesse grunted as it hit him, not quite stunned. He ignored the popcorn. He grabbed a bag of potato chips and threw it instead. Hazard gave up. He was not going to throw popcorn and chips back and forth in a grocery store. They'd get in trouble. Plus, they looked like idiots. Fuming, Hazard stomped past Jesse and didn't look back.

He stayed three feet away from Jesse as they made their way back to his car. Jesse smoked his cigarette while they drove.

"Drop me off at Emery's," Hazard mumbled. He needed to see Emery. Emery could always cheer him up.

Jesse did. A few blocks from Emery's, Jesse started to laugh really hard about the fact that they'd thrown food at each other in Fred Meyer. Hazard almost didn't want to leave anymore. He wanted to stay because he loved Jesse's laugh, wild and honest. He wanted to stay because this was an opportunity to make everything better again. But he was too mad. He suddenly remembered his mom telling him the story about the Garden of Eden. *The snake tricked Eve into thinking the fruit looked good, that it tasted good, that it was good. She ate it and made her husband eat it, and they both fell into sin. And once you listen to the serpent, you fall into the snake pit with him. That's the devil's artwork.*

It was probably a little too late to worry about that. Hazard laughed with Jesse too, but neither apologized. Hazard still went to Emery's.

AS FRIENDS with benefits, they had the general guy rules of no holding hands and keeping things strictly friendly in public (unless they got drunk and couldn't remember that rule), but they took the liberty of trying new ideas out on each other when they could. Suddenly it wasn't about occasional fun. It was all the time.

Hazard worked up enough courage to touch Jesse. Jesse did all sorts of things to him that made him crazy for more, so it was the least he could do in return besides letting Jesse try it all in the first place.

Sometimes Jesse texted Hazard in class, intentionally distracting him. Sometimes he was just bored. Once, a teacher confiscated Hazard's phone because he saw him texting. Another time, Hazard agreed to meet Jesse in the bathroom by the auditorium, the one with the flickering light, the one nobody went to unless it was to make trouble, and like horny teenagers they made out in the back stall where everybody tagged the wall with gossip and complaints. They never made out in the back of Jesse's car, though. He said it was too typical.

Now and again, Jesse had everyone over at his house for drinks—Felix, Lexie, Brianna, Felix's friend Ashton. Once or twice he threw a party there, and maybe it was because Hazard was biased or maybe it was because it was on the Elite Street, but they were some of the best parties he'd ever been to. Other people agreed. Jesse was a god, after all.

Hazard never wanted Jesse over at his house. His mom already didn't like *that junior* who was now *that senior*. Jesse didn't care either way. But once—and only once—Hazard invited Jesse over when he knew for sure that his parents were going to be gone until late, and grinding together in his living room on the same couch that his parents sometimes sat on felt like such teenage rebellion that it was great. Jesse hummed. They played video games afterward. Hazard forgot to hide the little toy stuffed alligator his dad had given him years ago under his bed so Jesse couldn't see it, and Jesse wouldn't let him hear the end of it.

At someone's house one Friday, a girl and her boyfriend were having a fight over the phone, and it turned into a group effort, everyone shouting out their ideas on how she should handle the situation. Then a group of seniors left and got more drinks for everyone to just keep chilling, but then the card games came out, and the Hennessey, and the Patrón, and then around eleven o'clock the party got crashed by someone's grandma. Brianna snapped Hazard's purple bracelet, and

Hazard was kissing her when the shocked old woman walked in on the whole thing, which was totally awkward. She handed out tiny Christian pamphlets called *The Daily Bread* before she chased them all out.

Emery wanted to practice driving. Russell had his license already, and Emery wanted Hazard there for encouragement—which Emery definitely needed after he drove his mom's car into the little ditch off Fern Street, where all the lower-end houses were and the roads were usually empty. The ditch wasn't even that deep, but Emery panicked, and Russell had to switch seats with him quickly while Hazard fell down laughing in the back seat. He couldn't help it, even when Emery glowered at him and Russell drove them out of the small dip between road and trashy yard. The car was fine. Emery's pride was not.

Jesse could play the piano. He didn't like to show people, but he showed Hazard once, down the hall in his Elite Street house in his dad's study where the piano was. It was strange to see somebody like Jesse Logan Wesley sitting behind a piano creating numinous music out of silence, but ultimately touching.

Once at a party after they went to a room to make out in private, Hazard accidentally put Jesse's shirt on. It was dark. He couldn't see. Jesse laughed at him. Jesse's shirt actually fit nicely, not exactly the right size but not too big at all, and it smelled good and it was warm. Hazard didn't want to switch back. Jesse didn't make him. After that, sometimes they switched shirts on purpose just to see if anyone noticed. Felix and Lexie and Brianna did, of course. Some people looked confused. Jesse and Hazard thought it was hilarious.

Lexie worked at Cold Stone Creamery. When they stopped to see her, she gave them free ice cream, even though she wasn't supposed to. It was cold out, but the ice cream was good. Hazard liked getting coffee-flavored ice cream with crumbled pecans. Jesse liked chocolate in a waffle cone.

A guy Hazard knew from freshman English came up to him one afternoon outside school while Hazard waited for Jesse to find his car keys, and he looked at Hazard with the most injured expression on his face and said, "I thought you were my friend."

Hazard was totally confused. The old classmate left, frowning, and Jesse had to remind Hazard that a week ago, at a party, he'd blown up and berated the guy over a casual insult or two.

"It was really fucking creative—you're hella crazy when you're drunk, do you know that? And you hit him on the ear," Jesse explained, motioning with a jangle of car keys.

Hazard couldn't shake the guilt all afternoon.

The Seattle gang invited them up to party in Bellingham with other friends, and Hazard played his first game of beer pong. There was also a keg, which a group of lesbians with PETA stickers ran. The sights between Seattle and Bellingham were breathtaking, mountain highway and tulip fields. They blasted music as they drove back, smelling like smoke and yelling at Jesse to drive safely because two drinks were still two drinks, and Hazard thought it was amazing how "All That I've Got" still seemed to feel relevant.

In early November, Jesse's car broke down. His battery needed to be replaced. He texted Hazard while he waited for the tow truck, long, colorful, ranting texts. Like everything else, Jesse's dad covered all the costs. Jesse's car was running fine again by the end of the week.

Miley Baker asked Hazard out after a party, and Jesse thought it was hilarious. "Go," he insisted. "When was the last time someone asked you out? Go."

Hazard went to the Bethany Town Center mall with her. They wandered around from store to store, and it was kind of awkward, kind of stiff. Hazard didn't really know what to do. He thought about dating Olivia for a few weeks, then about how much he hated Jesse and Felix for (cruelly) convincing him to do this, and then he just tried to make Miley laugh, but that was sort of hard to do. They hugged good-bye when her dad picked her up. She didn't call him or anything. Hazard was embarrassed but kind of glad.

Emery took drama. Now and then he asked Hazard for his honest opinion about this monologue or that interpretation, and Hazard loved the fact that Emery asked *him* and not *Russell*.

There was a party at the beach by Port Orchard, the smell of cold wet sand and icy water, the November chill even through a sweater. It was mostly laid-back. There was a handful of people Hazard didn't recognize, but that was okay. They drank, sitting together on the cold beach. They had a casual wrestling match that Lexie won. Jesse let Lexie have a cigarette or two, and then everybody wanted to see Hazard have a cigarette, so he smoked one for them. He lay on Felix's blanket on gravelly sand, next to Brianna. She pointed out constellations to him while everyone else played drinking games. Hazard put his arm through one sleeve of his coat and let Brianna use the other, and they huddled together in the middle part. Eventually, they all decided it was too cold, so they just went home.

Hazard agreed to go with Emery, Russell, and Lily to the mall. It was actually fun. Russell bought lunch.

Hazard officially met Jesse's parents. They weren't uncaring at all, just a little distracted. Hazard hoped he wasn't a charity case to them with as nice as they acted. Jesse's dad liked to talk about his job. Hazard saw that Jesse looked like his mom, slim and pretty with the same straight nose and smoothly angled face. Jesse's parents thought Hazard was a very good boy, which Jesse scoffed at, and Hazard had to explain his unique name one more time before they decided it was normal enough. They weren't involved often, so even after meeting them, it still felt like he was sneaking around most of the time.

Jesse and Felix showed Hazard how they got their tattoos. Felix's aunt was a nurse and had the means to notarize parental signatures—even forged ones—and it also helped that the tattoo artist knew Jesse's Seattle friend, Max, pretty well. They also got discounts on piercings because of this connection, and that was why they took Hazard to the shop.

The shop was called *Temple Art*, playing sanctimoniously off the idea that the body was God's temple. The tattoo artist Jesse knew was really nice. The shop smelled a little bit like mold and a lot like fresh burning incense, but it looked like a professional place. Jesse paid for Hazard to get a barbell in his left brow, just like him. They all agreed it made him look less cute and much more badass.

When his mom saw it, however, she didn't talk to him for an entire week.

"YOU'RE gonna get someone pregnant one day," Jesse teased, the same way he teased about the photo Felix took when Hazard wasn't paying attention, messy dark hair and laughter on his face, the one Hazard hated and everyone else loved. Hazard knew by the way Jesse grinned that he was drunk, and Lexie agreed with his declaration with a snort and a laugh.

"No, I'm not," Hazard argued, scowling over his drink. "I only have sex with one person, you know."

"Oh, yeah!" Jesse and Lexie howled with laughter, both well aware of who that one person was: Jesse.

Hazard blushed. He didn't think it was that funny.

"You need a blue bracelet," Lexie announced.

Hazard's jaw dropped. "I am *not* getting blue."

Jesse gasped, struck by an idea. "No, you need *glittery* blue," he said.

"Yes!"

"*No*," Hazard said, blushing hotly. He snickered because he was tipsy, but he was sincerely adamant about not having any kind of blue sex bracelet. Blue meant he'd give blow jobs. Glittery blue meant he was willing to have sex *that way*. Which was all true, after all, just not something he wanted to advertise.

They were in the corner of Ashton's living room, trying to have a conversation over loud voices and music somebody wouldn't turn down a little. Jesse snapped one of Lexie's bracelets, and Lexie started babbling about hypothetically, if Hazard was drunk enough, he'd never know whom he had sex with, but Hazard didn't believe that. He never *didn't know*. He was perfectly aware of whom he went home with and who undid his pants, but it was still scary to think about party sex. He was lucky, he guessed, to have someone like Jesse who shielded him from everything else.

The cops were called on that party, right after they left. They passed the police car on their way down the street, and even though they felt bad for Ashton, they were still relieved.

Hazard remembered that conversation—about getting somebody pregnant—when he sat in the nurse's office near the end of November and waited, sick to his stomach, for her to get off the phone so he could ask her the difference between a cold sore, a canker sore, and some kind of STD.

Like the poster near the nurse's bulletin board proclaimed, the sore in his mouth turned out to just be a canker sore. The nurse said it was probably from stress, which created an imbalance in his system, and

Hazard knew it was somehow connected to his exhausting extracurricular activities. There were effects, he knew, and he felt them—hangovers and lack of appetite and a general feeling of *blah* during the day.

He was more than relieved to know it wasn't anything serious, but he still had to sit through a brief stern speech, well-rehearsed and appreciated, about how the virus that created cold sores was the same virus that created some genital warts, and it was as simple as sharing ChapStick with someone who was having a flare-up to catch the virus yourself. Hazard gawked up at her, terrified and thinking about how many things he *shared* with other people that involved spit—drinks, forks, suckers, kisses. He did not want to think about STDs, not at all.

Hazard was absolutely miserable by the time he hurried back to Chemistry, but at least he just had a canker sore. He texted Jesse, but Jesse didn't seem to really care. He was probably irritated that Hazard interrupted his nap in study hall. That was his period to sleep, and if he didn't sleep, he usually got some kind of detention for goofing off with friends. Hazard hoped for the former.

ON THANKSGIVING, Hazard's mom wanted to see her brother, so they stayed the long weekend in Seattle. Hazard's aunt and uncle lived in Ravenna, a classy neighborhood where a lot of university graduates and professors lived. The adults drank blackberry wine and sat around in his uncle's dining room eating deviled eggs, artichokes, and prosciutto. His uncle was a director at the university medical center, and his house was almost as frighteningly clean as theirs. Hazard's mom loved it. Hazard was stuck with his cousin Zoe most of the weekend, which was sort of frustrating at times. On the giant TV in his uncle's media room, they watched *Clueless, 10 Things I Hate About You*, and *Fear Factor*, then played video games.

While they all sat around an impressive Thanksgiving dinner, Hazard thought about Emery, and Jesse, and everything he had—and he knew exactly what he was thankful for.

Chapter 9
December

JESSE on Nyquil was a lot nicer than Jesse off Nyquil. He was goofy and smiled a lot more, but the deep congested cough the flu left him with for two weeks was definitely not worth a clumsy drugged Jesse who came out of class looking disheveled and high, saying, "Danger! I just had a bitchin' nap. If Mr. Lewis passed out pillows and blankets, I'd confuse US History with my bed. That's how easy it is to fall asleep in there."

On cold and flu medicine, Jesse talked forever. Hazard sat on Jesse's bedroom floor watching Fuse, knowing that being in such close proximity to Jesse meant he was going to get sick too. They laughed about what would happen if Jesse had a twin sister, if she'd be hot and if Hazard would crush on her.

"I like it when you laugh like that," Jesse mumbled, cocooned in his blanket. Hazard blushed. Jesse smirked, a drugged little smirk. "I like that too," he added, referring to Hazard's look of chagrin.

Hazard blushed again and turned up the volume on the TV. They decided that the world was not ready for two Jesses, and from that point on Jesse got really loopy. He ranted about dumb things, and Hazard sat on his floor, biting back smiles and glancing between Jesse's old beaten-up Fender (covered in stickers), his overflowing bookshelf, and the TV surrounded by hard-core posters. Jesse could have been a hoarder in another life, for all the carefully organized mess in his room.

Jesse fell asleep quickly after that. It was kind of adorable.

Thankfully, after another week, Jesse was getting better, but by then Hazard was sick too. That was what happened to friends who made out a lot. They shared flus. Hazard had a croupy cough for the same week or so, but it cleared up with a lot of cold and flu medicine. Emery teased him lovingly because it made his voice scratchy for a few days.

"It's like you're going through puberty all over again," Emery snickered when Hazard's words squeaked or rasped. Jesse and everyone else laughed too, probably thinking the same thing. Hazard felt fine otherwise, after all, and he definitely felt good enough to go to Emery's birthday party on December 2.

Everyone had MySpace now, and it was a lot of fun to stay up late leaving dumb messages back and forth on each other's pages. People from parties found Hazard sometimes. He was afraid to accept their friend requests. Felix liked to post pictures that he'd taken of them all. Lexie was good at HTML and helped them each make their profiles more badass. Once, Hazard stayed up for hours commenting whole songs line by line back and forth with Emery. They did "Pop" and other songs they remembered from when they were little. Russell called them both fags, so Emery made "Pop" his profile music for a while.

The December air was freezing, but there was no good party one night, and everybody wanted to go out. Hazard went with Jesse, Felix, Lexie, and the rest of the crew to put stickers on streetlamps and stop signs, and then they went to the park across from the Catholic school. It was decorated for Christmas, big red velvet bows on the lampposts and wreaths on the bathroom doors. The Catholic school was decorated too. Hazard sat on the edge of the playground watching Lexie and Brianna swing. Jesse sat next to him, smoking a cigarette. He let Hazard lean on him.

Everybody laughed at Hazard because he was stunned when Felix confessed he and Ashton were together.

"You didn't know?" Lexie simpered. "Seriously, Hazard, you didn't know?"

"I don't know. I just didn't think about it—"

Felix demanded to know if it was *that* obvious, and Hazard wondered what they all thought about him and Jesse.

Eventually, it got far too cold even with coats and gloves. Jesse migrated to the empty bathrooms. Hazard went with him, and they made faces at each other in the dirty mirrors there. There was a crack in one that Hazard touched curiously, and a sliver of glass fell down.

"Seven years of bad luck," Jesse admonished.

Lexie and Brianna joined them, even though it was the boys' bathroom. Felix and Ashton were sharing body heat in the slide, with tongue and wandering hands involved. Jesse started reading the tagging on the bathroom wall. Hazard could see his breath. Finally they all huddled together there in the bathrooms, sitting against the wall and listening to the sounds of nighttime, waiting for Felix and Ashton to finish up so they could go home. It was late. It was dark and it was cold, and the park was empty.

A car drove up through the park and stopped near the bathrooms. Hazard and Brianna saw it first, as they peeked out of the bathroom door. A suspicious-looking guy got out alone, scowling at the world in general. He glanced at them from his parked car. Lexie suggested that maybe he was meeting someone there for a drug deal.

"Okay," Jesse grunted, straightening up and shoving his hands in his pockets. "It's time to go."

They blasted the new Nickelback song "Animals" as they all went home.

FOR the first two weeks of December, Caelyn Westberg scared Hazard to death.

She was a senior. She seemed kind of half-cocked, wearing a little too much eyeliner and tight shirts even though she didn't really have anything to show off. She had layered brown hair and green eyes, and like a lot of other girls, she wanted Jesse.

She went to all the same parties they did. She said something funny that Hazard didn't get but Jesse sure as hell did, and he thought she was hilarious. Caelyn had a tendency to wait until Jesse was past buzzed and Hazard wasn't by him, and then she sat and tossed back beer with him like she actually belonged there at his side. She even snapped one of his bracelets. He didn't act on it.

Hazard knew she did it on purpose. He felt like all her saccharine glances and subtle smirks were directed at him, because she knew she had to get past Hazard to get to Jesse. It made Hazard sick. It made him sick when she flashed everyone one night, as if it would really help her in her cause. Jesse howled with laughter at it. He told Caelyn she had balls. He was drunk, of course. Caelyn was too, and she was flattered.

Hazard was jealous. He was furious. He was afraid. Everyone knew that *Hazard was Jesse's favorite*, and he wasn't going to tolerate anyone else trying to take his place.

He confronted Jesse the next time he spent the night, sitting cross-legged on Jesse's bedroom floor in a T-shirt and boxers while the hours crept past midnight and Jesse played video games.

"You know, crushes are supposed to last only four weeks or something like that," Hazard said.

Jesse snorted. "Dammit, and here I thought you'd leave me alone one day—"

"So don't get too involved with Caelyn."

The heat in the house kicked on, a low soughing in the vents. Jesse looked sideways at Hazard from where he lay on his bed. "Are you *jealous*?" he asked, sounding totally shocked. Hazard knew him well enough to see that he wasn't feigning surprise.

Hazard swallowed, chest tight, and voiced his first fear. "It's because she's a girl, isn't it?"

Jesse coughed, glaring at Hazard as if to say, *Wait one minute, I'm not done with you yet.* Then he grabbed his pillow and chucked it at Hazard. "*You're* a girl!"

Hazard caught the pillow and held onto it, hoping Jesse couldn't see how troubled he really was. "Why would someone like you be with me because you want to? It's just another way to get off, right?"

"No, that's not it at all. Where is this even coming from?"

"Caelyn Westberg!"

"*Oh, yeah*? Holy shit, Danger, I don't like her at all. She kind of bugs me." Jesse looked incredulous. "You're *jealous!*"

"*No.*" Hazard threw the pillow back, hitting the game controller out of Jesse's hand. Jesse was startled. "I just know that I'm lucky to have you," Hazard explained, jaw tightening. He felt the same sick vulnerable sensation he got when he thought about Emery being around Russell, and he couldn't explain why. It hurt. He felt lonely. "Everyone wants you. You could get with *anyone* but you get with *me*, and I don't want anyone taking that away from me!"

Jesse didn't say anything sarcastic like *You're a greedy, selfish prick*, which Hazard had anticipated. "Hazard," he said quietly, without hesitation, and reached down to pull Hazard closer to the side of his bed. His fingers tangled in Hazard's hair, and Hazard bristled as he pressed his mouth against his forehead, but it wasn't a kiss. It was a very mannish gesture of comfort, something like a hair ruffle.

"Nobody's taking me away," Jesse whispered. Hazard couldn't see his face with his head hung and Jesse talking against his forehead, but by the tone of his voice, Hazard knew quite suddenly that Jesse was serious. He was utterly serious.

Hazard didn't want to talk about it anymore. He didn't say anything. Jesse understood. He went back to playing video games, eventually tossing the second controller at Hazard. They found out quickly that Hazard sucked at *Halo*, which Jesse enjoyed snickering with his tongue between his teeth. They went to sleep at three in the morning, when the dog two doors down was barking at its loudest.

"OH, THOSE don't look that bad at all," Emery said, but with the bag of ice pressed to his mouth it came out a little muffled and mumbled. "I don't know why you were freaking out about them."

Hazard frowned at himself in the mirror of Emery's closet door, then looked over at Emery, who was sprawled on the floor near his charging cell phone. He was on his mom's laptop, checking his MySpace.

"Are you sure?" Hazard adjusted his reading glasses, not certain he believed Emery just yet.

Emery nodded fervently. "You look smart. Sophisticated, or something."

Hazard was content with that. Jesse and Lexie told him he looked *hot*, after all, but Emery saying *sophisticated* was definitely good enough for him. He'd dreaded reading glasses, but the headaches during homework had gotten horrible in the last few months.

Hazard scooted over next to Emery again. Emery shifted the bag of ice against his face to the other hand and pulled his mom's laptop closer. Hazard watched him, particularly the bag of ice.

"Let me see," Hazard said.

Emery lowered the bag of ice, showing Hazard his lip piercing. He'd gotten it done two weeks ago, and it didn't look that swollen anymore. Little silver stud in the tiny nook between his chin and the thin, pale curve of his lip.

"Why did you get it done if it hurts so much?" Hazard asked, honestly curious.

Emery frowned, feeling the piercing with his tongue. Then he smiled, brow knotting sheepishly. "Well, Russell said lip piercings look cool."

Hazard knew why Emery had gotten it. Emery had gotten it because he wanted to look tougher. He wanted to look meaner. He wanted Russell to think he was cool, and he wanted to prove to the high school population that, even if he was in drama and had big blue eyes, he was, indeed, just a normal guy. It soured Hazard's stomach to think about, but he had to admit it did look cool.

"You look badass," he promised Emery, fixing his reading glasses again. "Plus, kissing people with lip rings is really fun, so…."

Hazard blushed when Emery looked at him pointedly, a little startled. But Emery didn't ask. He didn't have to. He pressed the ice to his mouth again and laughed softly, looking back to the little computer against his knees. Hazard was grateful Emery didn't ask, because he remembered the party and kissing the girl with the lip ring, but he didn't remember her name.

JESSE'S house was something else. It had vaulted ceilings, broad nooks, an open kitchen, and a sunken-floor living room. With the open floor plan, the balcony of the second floor overlooked the living room where the stairs connected. The hallway downstairs led off further into the house to a study, an office, a vast bathroom, and a games room. Everything was airy and clean: gleaming linoleum, spotless carpet, cream-colored walls, smooth wood, marble, stainless steel, posh white furniture, and a big screen TV.

There were photos on the far wall of the living room, professional photos, little peeks into the family's past. They made Hazard want to see home movies or photo albums, but he was too embarrassed to ask. Picture after picture marched along the wall, from a marriage to a vacation to every other private shoot booked, and Hazard had looked at them before, but he could look at them again over and over. Jesse was in those photos, everywhere: a little kindergartener with black hair writing in the sand; a sixth grader with the same dark hair and infectious smile helping his father stoke a fire in the very fireplace just across the room; the same boy from the other photos but thirteen or fourteen now, looking smart sitting at a piano in a black turtleneck and white pants with longish black hair slicked out of his eyes. His face had always been pretty. Somehow in a simple stare, Jesse captured sarcasm and sweetness. He still did. It was just the way his features were.

Jesse was in a bad mood. He must have had something heavy on his mind. It wasn't that often anymore, but when one of his bad moods went really sour, it was enough to make all the bad days until the next time one happened absolutely bearable in comparison. His default expression for the day was one with sharp eyes, a grumpy twist of the lips, and a perpetually knotted brow. It was kind of cold.

They argued for a while, up in Jesse's bedroom while Jesse's parents got ready to go out for dinner. They argued about everything, because that was just Jesse's mood, and Hazard didn't know how to bite his tongue very well. They argued about whether they were going anywhere that night; they argued about Jesse smoking; they argued about Hazard staying over, which Jesse insisted was just because Emery didn't want him so Hazard had nobody else to annoy. Hazard told Jesse he was selfish, and Jesse told Hazard he was sick of his attitude. Finally, after his parents left, Jesse stomped downstairs like a moody kid and left Hazard sitting awkwardly in his bedroom for a moment.

Hazard wandered downstairs after him, joining him on the couch quietly. He hated it when Jesse got like this, all sulky and mean. He didn't even call him Danger.

There was nothing but the sound of the TV. He let Jesse cool off for a second, and then he glanced over at him in scrutiny, brows furrowing.

"Are you mad?" Hazard asked.

Jesse sighed, closing his eyes. His sigh was like he was gathering patience, like he needed a moment to breathe everything through. "At what?"

"That I came over?"

"*No*, Hazard," Jesse hissed. "I don't *care* if you come over."

"Do you wanna talk about anything?" It was the wrong thing to ask. It started another brief argument.

"I don't want to talk to you."

"If you don't, it won't go away."

"Why don't *you* just go away?"

"Maybe I will!"

"I don't want to talk. Let it go."

"Jesse—"

"This is great, Hazard. This is just *bitchin'*."

"What is?"

"Maybe we should just stop."

"Stop *what!*"

"Us. This isn't cool. This isn't healthy."

Hazard stopped. He recoiled for a moment. He looked at Jesse critically. "Wait," he said. "Are you saying that we should *break up*?"

Jesse turned to him, face blank. "Yeah. So what?"

Hazard laughed defensively, crossing his arms. "I think you're forgetting the fact that we're not even *going out*."

"Oh, really? Because it feels like it sometimes. Maybe we should. Wanna go out with me, Hazard? Yeah? Okay." Jesse paused for a few seconds, dramatically. He drew a breath. "Sorry, we're breaking up now."

Hazard gave him a rough shove, watching him sway into the arm of the couch. But Jesse didn't retaliate. He crossed his arms and hunched into the couch, scowling. Hazard didn't let him end the conversation that way. Instead, he snapped, "You're the one who wanted to do this 'friends with benefits' thing, so don't act like you don't want it this way."

"Of course, I forgot. That was all me. My bad. Maybe we should break that off."

Hazard was startled enough to close his mouth and take a moment to think, simply staring at Jesse. Break it off? He didn't want that. He'd never wanted that. After a year of being around Jesse, he just couldn't do that. The idea scared him. It made him sick to his stomach. But Jesse couldn't be serious—about breaking things off, about *breaking up*, or whatever. That was all a bluff. Jesse was just being nasty. It was his attitude talking. It was like the times he scorned everything Hazard did or said or liked just to spite him, even if everybody else did or said or liked the same things.

"Either way," Hazard mumbled, "I'm your friend. And as your friend I want you to talk to me."

"I just have a lot on my mind," Jesse husked. "Maybe you should go home."

Hazard was quiet. He didn't really even feel angry anymore. He was too distracted by the sudden sensation of loss the idea of breaking it off with Jesse brought on. That was fucked up. When had it gotten this way? He wasn't *gay*. He was *bisexual*. Jesse was his friend, and what they did together wasn't supposed to affect him like this. He thought about talking with Jesse about Caelyn, just a few days ago, and after Jesse saying *Nobody's taking me away*, Hazard simply could not let this breaking it off thing happen.

His eyes moved around the house, from Jesse to the TV, to his socks, to the fraying thread of his jeans pocket. He swallowed. He stood up and went to the front door, tugging his coat on. The scuffing of his Converse against the floor was the only noise besides the TV as he pulled his shoes on and laced them up loosely. He closed the door quietly behind him as he stepped out into the cold, and for a moment he just stood on the front stoop, staring at the concrete and at the toes of his shoes and at the snow on the ground, and then he sagged down to sit on the top step and pulled out his cell phone, thumbing through the digital phonebook for Emery's number. It was too cold to walk.

He texted Emery. Emery told him he had Russell over, and they were helping his mom finally put up the Christmas tree. Hazard was debating whether or not to ask him to pick him up and take him home, thumb hovering and swerving over the Send button but not pressing it just yet, when the door opened and Jesse came out behind him, silent.

Jesse reached down across Hazard's shoulder and shut his cell phone once his thumb wasn't in the way.

Hazard bristled. "Why'd you do that!"

"Because you're not leaving," Jesse grumbled. He wouldn't look at him as he stood up and held the door open. "Get back inside."

Hazard stared at his cell phone for a moment. He remembered Emery saying *He's really got you under his thumb* and considered telling Jesse that he couldn't tell him what to do, but then he just stood up and slipped back inside, limply dropping his coat and untying his shoes as Jesse closed the front door, and drifted back to the couch.

Part of Hazard was happy that Jesse had called him back inside, but the other part of him dreaded whatever conversation they might have next. The big house was quiet besides the television and the hum of the heating system. Hazard shuffled across to the couch.

Another silence settled as he sat down opposite from Jesse, pulling his feet up and propping his heels on the edge of the cushions. He felt like a baby for doing it, but he held his knees to his chest and pressed his nose against them. His shoelaces dangled off the edge of the couch, and he wondered if Jesse would yell at him for having his shoes on the furniture. But there was just the silence and the commercials on TV. And finally, Jesse held a hand out in the distance between them and said, "Come here."

Hazard fought the relief flooding through his system. He hoped it didn't show as he tipped to the side and fell into Jesse's open arm, wriggling around against his side and getting comfortable with his head on his chest. And that was it, just the simple motion.

Hazard went to kiss him on the line of his jaw, but Jesse stopped him gently.

"As the friends-with-benefits instigator," Jesse said, "I'm taking the liberty of saying please, Haz, just be my friend tonight."

The words rang with a vague, bittersweet familiarity. Hazard stared, a little embarrassed. He swallowed. "Okay," he whispered.

Jesse looked at him, lashes lowered on eyes that were dark and poignant. They pierced into Hazard with a strange sensation, something new and upsetting but somehow warm. It was a wonderful painful ache deep in his chest that was both sad and hopeful.

Hazard acknowledged it then. He acknowledged it as he shifted around on the couch so Jesse could put his feet on his lap, when he peeked at Jesse from across the couch and his chest tightened and his heart swelled and some inexplicable heat throbbed in his chest as he watched Jesse laugh and snort and chuckle at the segments on *World's Dumbest*, easily entertained like a stupid little kid.

Hazard acknowledged then that Jesse was not the demigod he'd summarized him to be so long ago. He was still the same Jesse who had waltzed up to Hazard that day during lunch and picked on him for eating cafeteria mac and cheese, but he was not at all the untouchable badass everyone thought he was. He was just Jesse Logan Wesley, and he had his regrets and his scruples just like Hazard did. For such a time now, Hazard hadn't bothered to reevaluate him. He just took him as he was every day, but Jesse was so simple. Sitting on the couch watching TV, Hazard could see that the defenses and subterfuges Jesse built around himself were down for the time being, and he loved that. There was no way they could stay this way—*just friends*. There was no way he'd *let* them stay that way. It was good, but it wasn't good enough. There was just too much about Jesse he'd miss.

It was nine o'clock when the headlights bounced off the walls and Jesse's parents pulled into the driveway. Hazard waved to them as he and Jesse hurried across the driveway to Jesse's car.

Neighborhoods, streetlamps, and street signs blurred by in the darkness as Jesse drove. Hazard watched them out the window, his brow furrowing and his stomach knotting because he didn't want to have to deal with this fear of Jesse breaking it off with him. It wasn't right, and it meant something very frightening.

"I'm sorry," Jesse said. "Sometimes I just start thinking too much, Danger."

Hazard's fingers fisted on the edge of the passenger seat. *"Hazard,"* he corrected. "And it's okay."

Jesse sighed, rolling to a stop at an intersection. Hazard frowned. His throat was raw, his chest heavy. He stared at his shoes for a little bit, watching as light passed over them when they started moving again. He watched Jesse from below his lashes, observing the way Jesse wouldn't meet his eyes. He just stared straight ahead and flicked on the right turn signal. Hazard noticed the way Jesse licked his lips and rubbed them together like they were dry, the way his fingers twitched together idly before going up to fiddle with his earrings, the way he sniffled with a stuffed nose and breathed through his mouth. He was still getting over the flu he'd had a little bit ago. They were such little details to notice, so innocent and so *stupid*—

Jesse pulled up to the curb a block away from Hazard's house. A car passed them. As it passed, the clock changed to 9:13, and Hazard unfastened his seat belt, stretched over the middle console of Jesse's car, grabbed Jesse by the shoulder, and pulled him into a kiss. Even though they were supposed to be *just friends* for the night, Jesse didn't fight it.

Hazard shifted forward to sit on the middle console. Jesse turned halfway in the driver's seat, turning the car off. The chill of the night began to seep in from outside but went unnoticed by both because the kisses were warm and frantic. Hazard touched Jesse's face. He ran his fingers through Jesse's choppy hair. He felt Jesse's earrings. Jesse's hands were hot beneath his shirt on his hips and tailbone, gentle touches just above the waistband of his pants, shiver-inducing but not too arousing. Comforting, soothing, *loving*. All of it so *loving*.

Hazard cried, but nobody would know that because they were alone in the car in the dark on a sleeping street. He choked up, trying not to let Jesse notice. He kept kissing him, snaking his arms around Jesse's neck. This wasn't good. The more he kissed him, the more he knew that his need for Jesse wasn't going away. Oh God, he liked a boy. Oh, fuck. Hazard's throat ached as his lashes grew wetter and wetter—but when Jesse's tongue nudged out against his lips, Hazard uttered a weak cry and the tears were too much to keep hidden. He sputtered, "*I want you*—"

He didn't mean it sexually. It was just the only word he could find that meant the ache in his chest. Hazard felt pathetic. He'd told his mother he'd be back by nine thirty, and it was 9:25. Jesse had just wanted a friend tonight, and here they were kissing in the car, and he was so pathetic. *I want you.* Really? He couldn't abstain for one night, just one night? What a loser, what a fag.

Jesse's fingers moved over Hazard's eyes, swiping the tears away. He didn't make fun of him for crying, even though guys weren't supposed to cry. He just craned forward and deepened the kiss—tentative tongue, grazing teeth, gentle lips. Hazard let him. He let Jesse run his hands up under his coat and into his shirt again.

"You'll be late," Jesse argued after a moment, a barely-there whisper against Hazard's mouth. Hazard had slumped forward and joined Jesse on the driver's seat, sitting hunched awkwardly against his chest while Jesse's fingers swirled through his hair, threading in and out of the thick dark locks.

"Who cares?" Hazard mumbled.

"Why did you cry?"

"I didn't cry."

"Oh, yeah? Bullshit, Haz. You're an emotional wreck, all the time. I never know what's coming next. One moment you're fine, the next you're violent, and then you're a crybaby."

"I am *not* a crybaby. I don't even remember the last time I cried."

"Well, that's because you were drunk, but—"

Hazard felt the tears prick at the backs of his eyes again, and he stared at Jesse darkly. Jesse chuckled. For a few moments it was just that: silence, a half smile on Jesse's face and a pout on Hazard's.

"Why did you cry?" Jesse asked again, persistent, peering at Hazard with utmost sincerity. His eyes pried. They commanded. There was no way to resist Jesse.

Hazard balked. He felt that strange fear tug at his stomach again, knotting it up. But he swallowed, composing himself. He gave Jesse an idle shrug and pulled away. Jesse looked a little hurt that Hazard wouldn't answer, but how was he supposed to tell Jesse that he'd cried because he realized after all this time, the really fucked up part was that he liked Jesse *that way,* and there was no way that could work out? He was a man, dammit.

Hazard hoisted himself back up onto the middle console. "I'll be late," he whispered.

"I'll walk you in." Jesse glanced at Hazard from below his lashes as he shifted around in the seat again, starting the ignition.

Hazard leaned forward, resting his forehead on Jesse's shoulder as he pulled away from the curb and rolled down the block to the wide white house with the two-story window. The car eased to a stop at the end of the driveway. Jesse put it in park, turning around and pushing Hazard from his shoulder gently. Jesse looked at him imploringly, mouth in a thin line.

Hazard's heart ached. He looked over his shoulder at the light pouring out from his house, at the front door and the windows next to it. He sighed, wilting. He avoided Jesse's eyes.

"Okay." He crawled off the middle console. "You can walk me in."

Hazard's mother watched him say good-bye to Jesse like he was talking to Satan himself. Hazard tried to avoid her cold, critical stare as he took off his jacket, waved at her, then hurried to his room to change into his pajamas.

"BISEXUAL girls are hot. Bisexual guys are just... *weird*. But maybe I just think that because I'm a guy, because Chrissy sure as hell thinks bi guys are hot. And I mean, I like it when girls kiss, so...."

"Two words. *Brokeback Mountain*."

"Maybe his name should have been *Kaitlyn*. Every Kaitlyn is a whore. Did you know Kaitlyn Hayes let Joey finger her at Noah's the other night—"

"They should make a fag island and put them all on it. Then they couldn't reproduce."

"How lonely do you have to be?"

"Maybe he can't get a girlfriend so he just takes it however he can."

"What kind of name is *Hazard*? Seriously, why not just name your kid *Loser*?"

"I know, right? It's like—'Stay away from this kid! He's a *Hazard!*'"

There was always that handful of people who found no other point in life except to make the world as miserable as them. People like Canaan Lutz, for example.

Everyone talked, but it wasn't a lot. If it was, it didn't reach the surface very often, and Hazard was relieved by that. He learned that people were hypocrites and usually didn't have the guts to gossip to someone's face. That was how Jesse created the *same rules don't apply* theory. He'd made a kind of violent monster out of his reputation that made almost everyone afraid to be mean to him. He even scared the rednecks a little when they said things like *He's a butt pirate fairy faggot* and *I heard he went to jail once. Maybe he dropped the soap or something.*

It wasn't that the *same rules don't apply* theory didn't work, but it wasn't like Jesse was totally immune to disparaging gossip either. Now and again, he heard something or somebody said something to him that really ticked him off, and when the rare cold shadow that Hazard didn't really recognize passed over his face, he knew it was one of rage and teenage vengeance and Jesse was about to get into some kind of fight. Sometimes gossip just put Jesse in a really bad mood, but others, he was two seconds away from hitting something.

When Jesse fought someone, it scared Hazard. He'd heard a lot of stories about Jesse's fights, but he'd only witnessed it three times total by that December. Watching it was nerve-wracking—but it was also kind of hot.

Hazard saw him fight Greg Pollard once, at a party. Jesse really didn't like Greg Pollard, a guy with short spiky hair and an annoying all-talk, all-bluff attitude. Hazard also saw Jesse and Felix scratch somebody's car with a key once, and another time, after school, Jesse hooked a guy across the jaw because he'd cheated on Lexie. They weren't brawls—not really—but they were still terrifying in a way that left Hazard stiff and staring, kind of nervously in awe and wondering whether or not it was bad if he was turned on while at the same time worrying about Jesse getting arrested. Was that sick? Was that weird? It didn't happen often. He tried not to think about it. Jesse only got in trouble for fighting once—but the school let him off the hook by just giving him ISS, and all night long Jesse was a little stressed out by his dad's lectures. Apparently, his dad was not in the mood for any sort of legal trouble with his newly eighteen-year-old son. He'd had enough, already.

It was different with Hazard. Hazard found that everybody either loved him or loved to hate him. Fortunately, the majority loved him. But even with Jesse's secret threats, it was still high school, after all, and although going to parties automatically made you cool and although it was cool to be gay now, everyone still spoke before they thought, and nobody cared about feelings.

Sometimes there was hope when people like Katrina Lewis or Brett Soledad asked him, "Is it true?" instead of immediately believing what they heard about parties and hook-ups and other dark, dangerous ideas. Hazard liked it when people gave him the benefit of the doubt, even though some of it was always true.

"By the way," Jesse husked when he heard about what Kameron said about naming your kid *Loser*, "the name *Hazard* is Old French for 'chance' or 'luck', so Kameron doesn't know *shit*."

Hazard sat on the hood of Jesse's car and didn't want to argue because Jesse looked especially vicious pacing around in the parking lot, gravel crunching, and flicking cigarette ash and scowling at the world as a whole. But he did. "Is that really what it means?"

"Yeah." Jesse glowered down into someone's car absently, distracted by all the McDonald's bags crumpled up in their back seat. "I looked it up when I met you."

Hazard was astonished. He blushed because he'd never known that his name was so unique. He stared stupidly at his feet, listening to Jesse finish his cigarette. Jesse had looked his name up. Something swelled in Hazard's chest. He was totally touched, and the insult didn't even hurt that much anymore.

He told Emery what the name *Hazard* meant later. Emery said, "That is so awesome! I'm jealous."

THE Seattle gang came to Max's Christmas party. Max was smart and threw it a week before Christmas, so people wouldn't have family obligations. The Seattle gang greeted Hazard like they'd known him just as long as everyone else, and Hazard kind of liked that.

Around them, Max's apartment was full of people. There was music on—Guns N' Roses, Journey, Bon Jovi. The eggnog and cider were both spiked. Max assigned Sam to the kitchen to try to concoct some hot chocolate and coffees with a recent score of Baileys. Mistletoe was hung in random places, and the whole crowd laughed when someone stopped obliviously below it. Brianna accidentally did, and Hazard beat everyone to her side to kiss her cheek. Everyone laughed, probably because they were the youngest ones there and that made them the babies.

Hazard stayed by Brianna for a while, humming rock and roll and talking about art class. He went to get some of the hot chocolate Sam made and stopped to talk to Lexie. She looked nice, all dressed up in a black turtleneck and nice jeans. She and Max were dating now.

Bentley found Hazard. He grinned at him. He said, "Still a rookie?" and Hazard didn't really get it. Thankfully, Jesse came for him then, and they went down the short hall to get a room.

It was the same room they'd been in for Hazard's birthday, but it was different. It was different because they were both more sober than last time, tipsy or buzzed at the worst, and instead of getting busy they sprawled out comfortably on the big bed, and in the dark they talked casually in low voices. Jesse wagged his foot absently. It bumped Hazard's a little.

Jesse looked serene. His eyes were soft and his mouth was relaxed. Hazard wanted to kiss his neck where it came out from the collar of his shirt.

"Hey," Hazard said.

"What?" Jesse grunted.

Hazard swallowed. For a moment, he didn't think he'd be able to ask anymore. Jesse was waiting for him to talk. Hazard shifted, looking up at the ceiling just so he didn't have to look at Jesse. He had no idea what made him want to ask, because he didn't worry about these things, but he was asking. That was that.

"Who was the first?" Hazard murmured.

Jesse's brow furrowed. He looked over skeptically, and his foot stopped wagging. "You mean, like, the first person I was with?"

Hazard relaxed just a little to know that Jesse knew what he was wondering about. He rolled over onto his side to face him, frowning solemnly. Part of him didn't want to know. Part of him was still scared of Jesse's rumored reputation even though he knew he monopolized Jesse's time now. Hesitantly, he said, "Yeah."

There was a long moment where Jesse didn't say anything. Hazard could feel him growing distant.

"It was in eighth grade," Jesse said finally. Hazard was silent. He thought of the old pictures he'd seen of Jesse in his living room and tried to imagine Jesse at thirteen or fourteen: short, choppy dark hair and younger-looking, more childish, maybe with ears newly pierced, and tinier in stature but still holding himself with as much smug, charismatic importance as he did now.

Hazard looked up. There was a poster for Warrant on the closet door. "Let me guess," Hazard mused dryly. "She was seduced by the bad boy, and you guys had a perfect summer romance."

"No." Jesse's hand twitched like he wanted a cigarette. He glanced over at Hazard. In the dark, he looked very vulnerable, and Hazard immediately felt guilty. He shut up, waiting for Jesse to go on. Jesse did.

"Her name was Jenny, and she was really smart and cute. Over Christmas break, we did it." Jesse ran a hand through his dark hair, sighing softly. "Then I found out my friend Dominic had gone behind my back and did it with her before I could. You know, after I'd told him I liked her."

Hazard was aghast. It hurt him deep in his chest to hear that and to see the look in Jesse's eyes when he said it. His fingers were cold, fisting in Max's blankets. He couldn't even say anything for a minute, but finally he stuttered out, "That was her problem! That was a really slutty thing to do!"

Jesse glared at him, scowling. "She wasn't like that," he hissed. "Either way, it's fine."

Hazard frowned in turn. He mumbled, "Well, they say first loves don't last anyway."

Jesse scoffed. He laughed dryly. He sat up for a minute, then lay back down again. "I dunno. You have a lot of different *loves* in your lifetime, but only one is *right*, you know? You can love a friend and you can love a person for the rest of your life, and it's two different things. What about, like, loving your first girlfriend and loving your last girlfriend? They're both different, but they're both love. Just because you love one person doesn't mean you can't love another person afterward, but there's only one love that's *right*."

Hazard stared at Jesse, utterly speechless. Jesse was right, of course. He was right, and it stunned Hazard to know that Jesse had such deep philosophies about things like *love*. He wondered what Jesse would think about Olivia or Tom. He thought about Caelyn Westberg, and how stupid he'd been to be upset about that, and how much it had warmed him to hear Jesse say *Nobody's taking me away*.

"Okay, Fabio," Hazard mumbled. He loved talking to Jesse deeply like this, but Jesse being so serious about *love* scared him a little.

Jesse snorted, smiling faintly. Silence filled the bedroom. After a few minutes, Jesse began to wag his foot against Hazard's again. Hazard relaxed without even realizing how tense he'd been.

"So Jenny was your first," he concluded.

"Yeah."

"Did you cry? You know, when you found out about Dominic?"

Jesse glanced at him darkly and mumbled, "Uh, maybe."

"What about after her?"

Jesse was quiet for a very long moment. He stared up at the ceiling. Hazard lay beside him, the bed bouncing as Jesse's foot wagged. There was a sense of comfort, just lying there in the silence together. Hazard liked the way it felt, as bittersweet as the moment was.

Jesse cleared his throat. "The summer after ninth grade, I had this *thing* with Gabe Donnelly. You don't know him. Or maybe you do? I don't know. Do you?"

Hazard fidgeted, stomach sinking. "A boy?"

Jesse looked at him as if he were stupid. "*Yes*," he gritted out, daring

Hazard to be more hypocritical. Hazard wasn't trying to be. He blushed miserably.

"I don't discriminate," Jesse grumbled. Hazard picked at the corner of Max's blanket. He frowned, nodding.

"I know," Hazard said. It felt like his heart was in his throat. "What was Gabe like?"

Jesse didn't look at him. He spoke low and even, narrating more than reminiscing. "We had this understanding that summer. I don't know, he just looked good in his white pants one Friday, so I told him so. I stayed over and we *experimented*. That was all it was. We slept over at each other's houses off and on all summer, and we *experimented*." Jesse fell silent. His foot stopped moving. A thoughtful frown twisted the corners of his face, and it worried Hazard because it was brooding and kind of cold.

"That was all it was," Jesse said again. "I mean, everyone experiments, right? But, yeah, there you go. My first time with a guy was Gabe, and it was just sex. I never wanted to be with him. *Ever*. He was a fun guy, he was my friend, but I never wanted anything else. I mean, we stopped talking around tenth grade." Jesse paused. "I guess maybe I just wanted to know if I could do it."

I just wanted to know if I could do it. Hazard stared up at the ceiling. He felt cold suddenly, cold and concerned. Hearing Jesse talk so apathetically about his experimenting with Gabe scared him. He thought about the night in October, when they'd done it *that way*. Now he understood how Jesse knew what to do. *Experimentation.* It hurt a little to wonder if that was what was happening between the two of them, now. He didn't want that to be all it was. He wanted to ask, but he couldn't. Instead, he said, "Did you feel gay?"

"I felt like myself." Jesse cut a glance over at Hazard. It was a little scornful in the darkness, and Hazard felt bad, because it wasn't really just about being straight or being gay. He offered an apologetic smile, and Jesse's glance softened.

"I was with Shiloh—"

Hazard's eyes widened. "You were with *Shiloh*? Shiloh Burke?"

Jesse laughed, obviously getting over remembering Gabe. He reached over and ran his fingers through Hazard's hair a few times.

Hazard let him. It soothed a little bit of his crestfallen feeling. "Jealous, or surprised?"

"Surprised," Hazard said. It was the truth. He'd heard of Shiloh before. Her name circled through the rumor mills quite often too. He heard she had really nice boobs.

Jesse's knuckles brushed along the little nook behind Hazard's ear, fingers touching warm skin and threading through layers of dark hair. Jesse smirked absently. Hazard rested his cheek on Jesse's wrist, and the feel of his hand worked shivers through him.

"Yeah," Jesse sighed in thought, "Shiloh and I dated a little bit. That was the first time I ever had sex in public too, which is exciting. We should try it."

Hazard laughed, then realized Jesse wasn't joking. He blushed, eyes widening again. "Are you serious?" he mumbled.

"I've fooled around with Lexie and Felix," Jesse said, avoiding Hazard's question and grinning like it was some great secret to be proud of. He glanced at Hazard, whispering with comical innocence, "I like sex."

Hazard chewed on his lip in uncertainty. "Who do you fool around with now?" he asked, although he really didn't have to. He just wanted to hear it.

"Just you." Jesse shrugged. The green of his eyes was honest in the dark. "I mean, there have been a few times I've been close to it with someone else before. Some dry stuff, some offers, some pretty hot make-out sessions. But then you entered the picture, and you take care of all *those* needs well enough, so why do I need anyone else to do it anymore?"

Hazard could hear that somebody had put on Nirvana's *Unplugged* CD out in the living room. Jesse's fingertips touched the small of Hazard's back. They drifted up there, under his shirt, and it was nothing but tender. But Hazard stiffened, feeling suddenly overwhelmed by guilt. He wished he could think about how much it meant that, for all of Jesse's wild reputation, he was the only one Jesse seriously fooled around with now. He wished he could think about how many people he knew at school who would give anything to be Jesse's choice partner (like Caelyn Westberg, for example). He wished he could think of Jesse and Jesse only, and all the times they were friends and all the times they had benefits. Instead, he thought about Olivia. He thought about Tom, and trying to make Emery jealous, and everything in between. He pushed Jesse's hand away from his back.

Jesse frowned. "What?"

"Nothing," Hazard said. "I just feel weird all of a sudden." He had to tell Jesse about everything. If he didn't, he might break. That's what he felt like: close to breaking. Maybe it was because the eggnog was spiked, or Sam put a lot of Baileys in the hot chocolate, or maybe he just owed Jesse for his confessions, but Hazard had to tell him. He felt like puking.

Hazard told Jesse about his first time with Olivia, when his parents had gone out of town. He told him about kissing Tom on the couch under the freeway. He told him about why he kissed Russell, and he told him that the only reason he'd agreed to hang out with him at first was to make Emery jealous. And as much as Hazard hated saying all of those things, he felt so much lighter after they left his mouth. He felt like a weight was gone. He felt like a fever had lifted. He just wanted Jesse to know everything about him too.

Jesse fell quiet, his face blank. He sat up and rubbed at his neck absently. His hand twitched again. He was really itching for a cigarette, and Hazard felt like he was the reason why. Jesse got off the bed and paced around the room for a minute. He poked and prodded around Max's room, then walked to the door and touched the handle thoughtfully.

Hazard knew what had upset Jesse. He was upset because Emery was Hazard's best friend, and Hazard had just said something that made everything between him and Jesse seem like revenge and nothing else. But it wasn't like that, and Hazard longed to say this, but he couldn't breathe. His heart was hammering in his chest, his fingers cold and numb with dread. Was Jesse mad at him? Oh God, what if he was going to end things with him? Hazard's stomach plummeted, and his heart caught in his throat, thumping there. What if Jesse was going to *end* things? Was that what this tense silence was about? Oh God, why did it hurt so much not to know the answer to that?

This wasn't right. He wasn't *gay*. He was *bisexual*. Jesse was his friend, and what they did together wasn't supposed to affect him like this. Right? That was what he'd thought before too. It wasn't supposed to hurt in such a tragic hopeful way like this, but it did.

Jesse sat down again at the foot of the bed, running a hand through his hair. His voice was low. Hazard had to sit up and lean forward to hear him when he spoke.

"You act like it's all a big deal."

"It is!" Hazard insisted, voice cracking.

"We're not going out or anything. Kiss whoever you want. Do whatever you want." Jesse's voice was thin and terse, as if he were trying to convince himself too. He paused. Hazard felt lousy. Jesse took a breath, then asked:

"Who, Hazard, do you end up with in the end, regardless?"

"*You*," Hazard said, and then he realized what Jesse was implying. He recoiled, blushing. He stared down at his knees, a little stricken. He stood up, getting his hot chocolate from the bedside table. Jesse stayed where he was, fiddling with a hemp bracelet. Hazard watched him, throat tight.

He wondered why Jesse liked him. Jesse was cool. He could have whatever he wanted. Hazard was not really anything very exciting, just a smallish dark-haired boy who wore band T-shirts, button-ups, and Quiksilver, who was tiny and didn't really look girly but wasn't really badass, either. So of all the friends Jesse had or could have had benefits with, why on earth did he choose Hazard?

What was the word for this, this weird heat in his chest, something like hope and sadness at the same time? It squeezed onto his heart and ached in his throat.

One of the reasons he'd hung out with Jesse in the first place was to get back at Emery, but that wasn't even the point anymore. That didn't matter anymore. It was Christmas. Jesse was graduating at the end of the school year. What was going to happen then? Was Jesse going to call it off with him, or was he going to wait until he found *the right girl*? Hazard didn't want to think about Jesse finding a girl he wanted to date or marry. He didn't want to think about it happening to him either. He just didn't know.

He thought about what Jesse had said, buzzed or not: *You can love more than one person in your lifetime, you know.*

Hazard skirted the edge of the bed. Jesse's unwavering stare followed him as he moved. Hazard came to a halt in front of him and reached out, resting his hands on Jesse's shoulders.

"Jesse," Hazard whispered, so grateful for the seclusion in the bedroom, the isolation and the lack of distraction. "You know that's true, right?"

Jesse tasted dry, but Hazard kissed him anyway, hooking an arm around his shoulder and kissing him quickly, pointedly. Jesse looked at him, a little confused. Hazard shrugged. He sat down in front of him and rested his head in his lap. There was a lump in his throat.

"Haz, it's true for me too," Jesse said. He ran his fingers through Hazard's hair again, then trailed them up and down the back of his neck. Hazard shifted, heart pounding.

"I think I love you," Hazard said, and then his breath wavered on his lips because he hadn't even felt the words before they came out. They stunned him just as much as they stunned Jesse. Embarrassed, Hazard felt the need to explain. His voice shook. "Not like that—well, actually, yeah, like that—I mean, even if you find someone you like and we break this off or stop being friends, even if something happens and we never see each other again, I want you to know that. You said it yourself! There are different kinds of love, and I don't know, this just feels *right* but even if it's not, I love you. So much, Jesse. *So much.*"

Jesse's hands fell still. He was quiet. He looked away, and for a long moment, all Hazard could see was the way his lips parted and dark hair fell in his eyes and his lashes were lowered, hiding a glance that might reveal what he was truly feeling. The music from the living room leaked in below the closed bedroom door, "Where Did You Sleep Last Night?" and Kurt Cobain's last scream of *shiver* wavering on the air behind the sound of everyone talking and laughing.

Hazard shook. He was embarrassed, and he wanted to cry with all the emotion swelling in his chest, but he wasn't sad. He was scared but relieved, and he wished Jesse would say something, and he was afraid of himself because if he loved Jesse like that, that meant he was gay.

Hazard didn't think it was fair when Jesse opened his mouth to say something and Lexie knocked on the door, then poked her head in. She didn't say anything at first because she was interrupting something. Hazard and Jesse stared at her. She shifted, then sighed. "Most of the party's gone, except for our crew. Max got us fucking *presents*, you guys, and he wants to give them out now that it's just us. You two coming, or should I just accept yours for you?"

"It's not the Grammys," Jesse snorted. He laughed, running his hands through Hazard's hair one last time. He poked Hazard's cheek in promise that the discussion would be continued. Hazard could see in his eyes that he had something he wanted to say, something that made him look heartrending and hopeful, something that made his smile wistful and his eyes glint. Hazard could guess what it was. He just wanted to hear Jesse say it.

Jesse stood up and followed Lexie out of the bedroom without another word. Hazard sat on the carpet, staring at his feet, for a few moments after. He sat alone in the room with the light of the hallway spilling onto him, listening to everyone in the living room. He remembered the wall at the 7-Eleven on Berkeley Street, the one whose vandalism said *we all collide*. The idea of it seemed like it could stretch forever and ever with no end. Maybe it meant something like everything happened for a reason.

Their discussion was never continued, but maybe it didn't have to be. Jesse's actions spoke louder than his words sometimes. Hazard thought about the look he'd seen in Jesse's eyes when Lexie interrupted, and he didn't push it.

Jesse and his parents went to see family in Chicago for a long weekend that included Christmas. Hazard tried not to run up his texting bill, but Jesse liked to send provocative messages. Once he even sent a picture, and Hazard surmised that Jesse had gotten a new camera phone for Christmas. Hazard sat next to Emery on his bed, watching *Adult Swim* and other late-night shows, and stared at the pixely photo for a while, smiling absently. Stupid Jesse, looking good on camera phone.

On Christmas Eve, Hazard's mom wanted to go to church. They went to midnight mass and held candles with paper around them so the wax didn't drip on their hands, and Hazard squirmed in his nice clothes, standing with the whole congregation amongst the pews, as the liturgies worked through his skin and deep down into his bones. He wondered what God thought about what he'd been doing lately. He looked around at the great crucifix above the altar and the prayer corner with the Virgin Mary painting, at everyone gathered in the sanctuary to sing hymns, and he wondered how many of them could tell he was a kid who wasn't really into going to church.

Chapter 10
Emery, Olivia, and Tom, and Where It All Began

HAZARD and Emery met in second grade.

Emery Benjamin Moore had dark-blue eyes that ate up his face and a pouty mouth that easily stretched into a bright grin or a sharp scowl. He was everyone's friend, even if they didn't know it yet. He was professional at the game of make-believe. He always shared snacks, he always thought hard about the questions asked in class, he aspired to be the line leader, not the caboose, and some of the other kids in second grade were in awe of him because he had the guts to walk right through the older kids clustered on the Four Square blocks and talk to Russell, who was one of the third graders.

Emery was in Ms. Polish's class, and Hazard was in Mrs. Kemna's. Hazard met Emery on the playground, when the rain had stopped and everyone was ecstatic that it wouldn't get in the way of their final recess for the day. The chained-in playground was filled with screaming kids and teachers huddled near the door with their whistles. Hazard was bored of kickball, so he walked along the fence, stomping through damp grass and thinking about how he hoped his dad would bring home ice cream tonight. That was when he heard:

"Hey! Hey, you, with the Spider-Man shirt!"

It took a moment, but Hazard realized that *he* was the *you with the Spider-Man shirt*. He looked up, a little shy. The boy who had called to him was at the swings, swaying to and fro. He wore a navy-and-periwinkle striped polo. He wasn't really swinging but more rocking, fingers curled on the chains and toes of his light-up Power Ranger sneakers digging into the soggy wood chips.

"Me?" Hazard asked, walking over.

"Yeah," the boy said. "Hey, I'm Emery. This is Russell." Without looking, Emery jabbed a finger at the blond boy swinging next to him, a mess of shaggy hair and deep silence. "Are you sad?" Emery asked next.

Hazard's face dimpled softly in confusion. "No," he said slowly. "I'm just bored."

The blond boy named Russell leapt off his swing in midair, landing expertly on the grass.

"What's your name?" Emery said, leaning over to Hazard. Hazard told him his name and blushed when Emery looked a little afraid of saying it.

"Hazard?" he tried. "That's cool. Hey, Hazard, I bet I could jump farther than you."

Russell had gone. Hazard took the swing Russell had been on and said, "Maybe."

They swung, and Emery demanded they jump at the same time, which was on his count of three. Hazard worried about his swing flipping over. He always worried about his swing flipping over, just like he worried about his swing coming detached in midair before he was ready to jump.

Emery screamed, *"Three!"* and with a rattle of chains, they both jumped. To Hazard's utter surprise, he jumped farther. Emery looked a little insulted by this. Hazard was somewhat shocked. His knees shook a little from jumping in the first place.

"Well," Emery huffed decidedly, crossing his arms, "that was a good jump, I guess. Why don't you be my friend?"

Hazard was quiet. Emery didn't seem to expect any other response but an agreement, looking a little upset that Hazard had jumped farther, which seemed to have been some kind of unannounced test. Hazard never thought twice about agreeing or disagreeing. He kicked at a few wood chips and grabbed the swing again, then said, "All right."

HAZARD learned quickly that Russell Leroy and Emery were sometimes inseparable. That was okay with him. He had Grant to hang out with, or Tom or Christina.

Bethany Elementary School got to go on a field trip to the museum to see real mummies, and when they were all told to pick partners, Emery chose Hazard.

That was probably the day Hazard decided Emery was his best friend.

HAZARD lived in a neighborhood called Buckingham Court. Where Easton met Walnut at the end of the street, the neighborhood bled into a collection of townhouses called Windsor Green, and that was where Emery lived. He wasn't even a five-minute walk away. Hazard was elated to discover this in the summer between second and third grade, which he spent the majority of with Emery on his cul-de-sac.

Emery had moved there three years before from Anaheim, California, after his mom left his dad. Emery's street was a lot different from Hazard's. Emery's house was two-story and a little narrower and looked like every other house on the street except for being a different color. Inside, it smelled like cinnamon sprigs and scented candles. The kitchen was stainless steel and the couch was scarlet colored, and on the walls hung decorative crosses and other pretty things from stores like Michael's and Hobby Lobby.

They played street hockey and basketball in Emery's driveway. They drew with chalk on the sidewalk. They watched Disney movies and thought they were cool kids if they said things like *damn* and *ass*. They went to the pool now and then but to the woodpile near the highway more. Sometimes Russell came over and they played hide-and-go-seek in the corners of the townhouse complex where construction on homes had stopped and they were empty inside. Emery's mom made them bananas and peanut butter, which they ate in the kitchen.

Hazard loved Emery's mom. When Hazard stepped on an industrial staple and cut his foot once, Emery's mom had Neosporin and a big fat bandage she called a *butterfly Band-Aid* that she put on his heel for him, and she was calm about it. Hazard's mom would have panicked. Emery's mom was kind of tall and a little younger than Hazard's mom, and she had blonde hair too, but her dark, dark roots were coming back. She was tan, just like Emery. She wore her hair in ponytails or half backs, and she spent a lot of that summer rearranging the living room because she wanted to be an interior decorator, but interior decorating didn't pay the bills yet, so she was a receptionist at the local veterinarian's. She smoked, but only outside. She was dating a guy Emery called Andrew, and Hazard didn't really like Andrew. From what he saw of him that summer, he had a big nose and thick hair, and his voice echoed through the house even when he wasn't yelling. Emery said Andrew wasn't that bad, but maybe that was because he had to live with him.

Emery's mom was funny and smart, and she never told Emery that his hair was too messy, that he needed to wear socks that matched his shirt, or that his name was special because he was a special boy. Hazard decided that was okay, because everyone's mom was different.

HAZARD didn't really like Russell Leroy, mostly because Russell was kind of moody, he'd known Emery longer than Hazard had, and he thought he was cool because he had a brother who was in college.

Lily was Emery's other friend, a loud girl with dark hair and dark eyes. She was in ballet and liked *Sailor Moon*, striped stockings, spaghetti straps, and Mary Jane shoes.

In Cascadia, there were regular earthquake drills at school. In third grade, Hazard sat next to Tom in Mrs. O'Connor's class. Hazard thought that it would be good to have more than one best friend, so he tried to play with Tom too. Tom introduced him to Peyton, whose family was kind of redneck. On the afternoons Emery was busy, Hazard went with Tom and Peyton to the Windsor Green park. They played Hot Lava and walked on the top of the monkey bars, trying to wrestle each other off.

Sometimes Emery went with them to the park. Sometimes Hazard tried to get everyone to play together during recess, but for some reason or another, everyone just didn't click the right way. Hazard was okay with that, and he was also okay when a girl named Olivia started playing with Tom, Peyton, and him at the park.

Russell showed Emery Jesse Camp on MTV, and Emery showed Hazard, and they thought he was a hoot. They'd roll around on the white carpet of Emery's living room, mimicking him.

Hazard's dad got a promotion, which meant he left earlier in the morning and came home later at night. His mom decided it was time for Hazard to have a key to the house, especially because she was out later now too. She ran a lot of errands, which included manicures and dinners with friends. He was told that if he went anywhere after school, it was strictly to Emery's and nowhere else. Hazard promised it would be so.

HAZARD'S mom liked to go to church sometimes. But none of the boys in Sunday school talked to Hazard, the liturgies and candles scared him sometimes, and he hated sitting alone in the pew during the Eucharist, so he tried to spend every Saturday night he could at Emery's so his mom would sigh and give in and say, *I guess we don't have to go this Sunday.*

Emery liked scary movies and movies with a lot of blood. He also liked to make living room forts, arranging chairs and couch cushions and taping sheets up over them like an inside tent. Russell, Lily, and Hazard would spend the night on weekends to marathon scary movies in the living room. Sometimes Andrew would jump out from the hall or make loud noises to try and scare them (which worked on everyone but Russell and eventually annoyed Emery). Most of the time, they fell asleep halfway through the third movie and Emery's mom had to come turn it off.

For Christmas in fourth grade, Emery got a cat. It was white and fluffy and sometimes made Hazard sneeze. Emery named it Dust Bunny.

Russell got detention once for mouthing off to a teacher. Emery thought he was so cool. Hazard thought he was dumb.

With a key of his own and the house empty most afternoons, Hazard invited Emery over a lot. Now and again he also had Tom and Peyton over, and a few times Olivia came too, which felt scandalous because she was a girl.

Emery was a klutz, and this was proven the day he fell off the monkey bars and cracked his wrist.

If Hazard's mom wasn't out, she was in her room or cleaning, so it was like Hazard was alone. Hazard didn't like his mom driving him places because she swore at all the other drivers, calling them stupid and incompetent and yelling at them to hurry up, then snapped at Hazard to stop looking so glum. So Hazard took the bus to school, and if he and Emery wanted to go somewhere they couldn't walk to themselves, they had Emery's mom drive them.

Hazard got a tooth pulled so the grown-up one could grow in. Emery made him pudding.

RED RIBBON week came to Bethany Middle School in fifth grade. Police officers passed out erasers and stickers with the D.A.R.E. logo on them during the assembly. Tom and Hazard panicked for a while that they were *drug addicts* because all through science they'd sniffed Olivia's highlighters, which were scented like movie theater popcorn and cotton candy.

There was no PE for half a semester, which everyone loved because it meant they'd have Health class instead. Everybody knew Health class was the perfect time to goof off. Emery most certainly did, making faces at the pictures in the Health books and giggling behind his hand like a lot of other students when the teacher said *penis* and *puberty*.

Hazard tried to be mature and pay attention, because he thought it was interesting. But after a while, Emery's laughter was just too contagious, and he was in fits behind his Health book too, because they'd looked up the chapter about sex.

"*Intercourse*," Emery whispered.

"*Sperm*," Hazard whispered back.

Emery went over to Hazard's house, and they made brownies one afternoon, which Hazard's mother oversaw to an almost compulsive degree. "Don't make a mess," she reminded kindly, letting them do it themselves even though the shrill note of control was obvious in her voice. "Don't eat the mix, either. You'll get sick."

Hazard and Emery didn't listen. They got stomachaches.

IN THE spring of fifth grade, Emery's mom and her boyfriend Andrew got married. Emery was the ring bearer. He invited Hazard, Russell, and Lily, and Hazard's mom was actually fun and outgoing during the reception. Hazard thought the champagne was juice and took a big sip that promptly soured his expression. His mom and dad laughed, and his mom's laugh wasn't even fake. Russell's older brother was there, holding his girlfriend's hand. She caught the bouquet. There was dancing and toasts and good cake. It was a lot of fun.

Hazard found Russell and Emery hiding in the limo halfway through the dancing, though. First, he was kind of angry that they'd ditched the reception without him. Then he realized that Emery looked torn between tears and his stubborn, dimpled frown of denial, and Russell gestured for Hazard to get into the back of the limo with them. The driver was in the reception hall, after all. They were alone in the big long car.

Hazard looked between Russell and Emery, concerned by the way Emery's eyes shimmered and the way Russell looked darker than ever.

"I kind of didn't want her to marry him," Emery confessed. "He's mean, sometimes. He jokes, but sometimes the jokes are rude, and he ruffles my hair too hard, and he thinks that I should be on the wrestling team next year."

Hazard didn't know what to say. Russell was silent too, although it seemed Emery had already told him these things before Hazard joined them. Hazard wondered if he should tell Emery that he'd always kind of hated Andrew too.

"It's okay," Hazard finally managed, putting his hand on Emery's shoulder. He thought that Emery looked very nice in his little suit with the flowers in the pocket, even if he was trying hard not to cry. "It's fine. Your mom won't put up with it if he does anything really bad, you know? Besides, you can always come to my house."

"Mine too," Russell added.

"Yeah, but my house is usually empty," Hazard murmured, ignoring the way Russell glared at him. He was just telling the truth.

Two months later, Tom's sister Emma died of an overdose. Hazard went to the funeral with him. He cried because Tom didn't—he just looked really blank—and that was when Hazard started spending a lot more time with Tom. Tom's mom got him a skateboard, like *Rocket*

Power, as if it would really ease his pain, but Tom indeed distracted himself with it. Maybe he worked through his grieving on it. By the time Hazard got a skateboard too, Tom was already really good, and he taught Hazard tricks. Peyton joined them. Olivia proved she could do a meager kick flip on Peyton's board, which earned her a spot in their ranks.

Emery didn't mind that Hazard went skating two or three times a week. He had basketball practice, after all.

As IF 2001 wasn't a big enough year yet, with a small earthquake in February and Emery's mom's wedding, at the beginning of sixth grade New York was attacked, and Hazard went through the subsequent week glued to the couch beside his mom watching the news, footage from the bombing, all the tributes afterward, and jumping every time his mom jumped, which was pretty much every time the phone rang or a car passed the house.

She was anxious about everything for a while, and Hazard couldn't go out much. Thankfully, she let up by Halloween, and he went trick-or-treating with everyone: Emery, Lily, Russell, Tom, Peyton, and Olivia.

The house was empty most of the afternoon again by Christmas break, and Emery rode the bus home with Hazard to hang out until dinner.

Puberty kicked in, hormones and changes—but it wasn't *that bad*, and Hazard tried to ignore the educational book his mom pushed at him about deepening voices and nocturnal emissions. He only woke up with the sheets wet once, anyway.

He played baseball in the fall and soccer in the spring. He wasn't the star of the team, but he liked it.

Hazard spent the night at Tom's a few times. He spent the night at Emery's more often. In the chill of winter, when the world was wet and cold and even when the sun was out everything felt pale except for the vibrant green of the trees, Emery found a new interest in sitting on the roof outside his window at night.

"Be careful not to slip," he told Hazard, hoisting up the window and popping the screen out. He set it down beneath the sill, and Hazard followed him out onto the slanted roof. Below them was grass and the generator they used to stand on when they were little, trying to reach the gutters of the same roof they sat on then.

It was cold. They could see their breath. They had their coats on, but they sat close, sharing body heat and looking down the hill at the roofs of other houses in the neighborhood. A plane passed overhead, and Emery asked, "If you could be on that plane, Haz, where would you be going right now?"

Hazard shrugged. "I don't know."

"I would go see my dad in Anaheim. I don't really remember him." Emery paused, looking a little perplexed for a moment. Then he shook his head vigorously, changing his mind with sudden zeal. "No, wait! I'd go to England or Ireland. We learned about them in geography yesterday. I wanna see the bluffs and that thing Stonehenge—"

Hazard looked at Emery, feeling a sort of ache at that. He wasn't sure why. Emery was looking up at the stars as the plane drifted by. Thick coat, shaggy hair, distant-eyed grin on his face. There was a little quiver of something in Hazard's chest then, deep and sore, and he thought with strange, chilling clarity that Emery was his best friend, and there was nowhere else he wanted to be but a few blocks away from him.

"I wouldn't go anywhere," Hazard mumbled in answer. "I like things how they are."

In January, the washing machine broke. Mechanics had to come fix it. Hazard was quite aware of the way his mother flirted with them, but he wasn't sure if that was the reason his dad worked extra late for a few days or not.

IN SEVENTH grade, there was a girl at school that had a major crush on Emery. Russell and Hazard both knew it, but Emery was totally oblivious, so when she gave him a huge Valentine's Day card, he had no idea what to do and felt guilty for a month afterward.

Emery and Hazard were old enough to hang out at the YMCA without getting yelled at by workers. They played tennis together in the big white indoor courts and goofed off on the track.

Bus routes changed that year, and all the eighth graders that had once taken bus number seventeen now took bus number three, so by default Hazard and Emery got to sit in the very back and listen to CDs that skipped every time the bus went over a big bump, while all the younger kids stared at them as if wondering why they didn't bully them like boys like Travis and Kent used to.

Hazard took art class. His teacher said he had skill. Hazard didn't know if that was true. He was just faster at sketching than everyone and liked acrylics more than watercolor. Emery was like some of his other classmates, *ooh*ing and *ahh*ing over the drawings he brought home. His mom suggested he try to paint something prettier, like the angels Michelangelo did. Hazard liked Michelangelo and other artists that he was learning about from the Renaissance, but he just didn't draw like that.

Hazard's mom had a friend named Lucy Carlson who liked to hold Mary Kay parties. Hazard's mom started going to them a lot too, which kept her out until ten o'clock sometimes. Even his dad got home before her. He made his specialty for dinner (pigs in a blanket and french fries), and Emery came over and they played video games in the living room with the volume really high. His dad usually fell asleep in his easy chair after dinner, and Hazard and Emery played *Mario Kart* and *Mario Party* and *The Legend of Zelda*. Those nights were the best.

HAZARD and Emery discovered Three Days Grace, Nirvana, and Green Day, and other bands that made them feel like they weren't the only ones going through the hell of adolescence. Hazard loved Nirvana like Emery loved Three Days Grace. His mom hated Nirvana. She said they were whiny and a bad influence and gave her a headache. When the house was empty, Emery and Hazard jumped on the couch and blasted their favorite songs—like "Just Like You" and "Heart-Shaped Box."

Emery still loved Savage Garden and *NSYNC, though, which Russell and Hazard loved to tease him about.

WHEN Emery and Hazard went to eighth grade, Russell went to high school and Emery became a troublemaker.

"I found out how to sneak in and out of my room!" he boasted. He taught Hazard how: popping out the screen of his window and getting onto the roof, leaving the window cracked enough for fingertips, sliding down the edge of the roof and onto the generator, which wasn't that far down at all, and from there it was just about stealth going past the dining room window. He demonstrated a few times for Hazard when his parents were at the store. Hazard tried it out too. It was actually a lot easier than he'd expected it to be. He found he could pop his bedroom screen out the same way too.

Russell's brother Ronnie and his girlfriend, Alice, had a baby, and Russell got stuck babysitting a lot.

Emery was afraid of spiders. Hazard loved him for it. Emery would yell and jump around and stand on a chair, urging Hazard to move faster— *"Kill it, kill it, squish it, Hazard!"*—and Hazard sometimes couldn't even stand up because he was laughing so hard.

Emery's new bad boy streak—sneaking out to go to Russell's, which led to the cops being called one night, mouthing off, detentions for sleeping in class or passing notes, a few fights and arguments with Andrew about not being on the wrestling team—meant that Emery was grounded a lot more often than he used to be. Hazard spent more time with Tom, Peyton, Olivia, and their skateboards, which wasn't bad at all.

Looking back, Hazard wished he had known that that year was the last one he'd feel free and clear. He would have spent a lot more time with Emery.

OLIVIA PIERCE was five foot two. She had auburn curls and intuitive eyes and a light dusting of freckles across her nose. It took her a while to ollie, but she could do a hospital flip and a casper flip better even than Peyton. Tom always teased her about being flat-chested, Peyton was as protective of her as an older brother, and Hazard wished he could be as oblivious as Emery was that Olivia liked him all through eighth grade.

She giggled a lot, for instance, when he talked to her. She had a certain look in her eyes when he was around. She was always fixing her hair, whereas the year before she never cared how messy it was. Hazard just knew.

"That's *karma*," Emery told him, sitting on the roof outside his bedroom and remembering the girl who liked him in seventh grade.

Hazard wasn't entirely miserable. Not a lot of girls liked him, because he wasn't cool like Grant Brown or loud like Eric Garcia, so naturally when Olivia confessed to him that she thought he was cute, Hazard didn't know what to say back, but he felt a lot better.

She told him one afternoon after Valentine's Day, so it was too late for Hazard to give her anything nice. She told him when they were at Peyton's, watching *Toonami*. Olivia was into stuff like *Toonami* and *Adult Swim*. She liked the shows from Japan. She told Hazard that he was like the pretty boys in the Japanese shows she liked, and Hazard was both dubious and flustered by this.

Emery was grounded for a week after his mom found out he'd snuck out to Russell's when they'd thought he was sleeping. Hazard watched *Toonami* and *Adult Swim* every night that week. He called Olivia, and they watched the same shows over the phone with each other.

"Are you *with* her?" Tom asked one afternoon from where he stood on top of the slide at the park.

"*No*," Hazard said, blushing. Olivia was across the park, practicing a trick on Peyton's board. Peyton was coaching her.

"Do you *want* to be?" Tom shrugged, monkeying down off the slide and pushing sandy-blond hair out of his eyes. "Because, I mean, I'd be cool with that."

Hazard wasn't exactly sure what he wanted. His dad was working long hours on an important project, and his mom was into Mary Kay and Avon with Mrs. Carlson, and Hazard was home alone a lot.

"Just *try* to be good," he urged Emery at school, wishing Emery were allowed to come over again.

"I do!" Emery grumbled. Hazard couldn't blame him. He knew how the cycle worked: Emery would be fine for a while until his stepdad set him off, which didn't take much, and then Emery's temper would snap and he'd be in trouble again.

Hazard went skating with Tom and Peyton and Olivia. They went to the mall and got kicked out when Tom threw Peyton's shoe in the fountain. They went to the movies. Sometimes Olivia put her arm around Hazard's shoulders and Hazard put his around her middle, like buddies, except maybe not. They flirted shamelessly.

They all hung around on their skateboards at the park. Once, they snuck into a few high schoolers' hangout place by the freeway and poked at used condoms and beer bottles with sticks, smelling recent pot and trying to read the graffiti. Hazard and Olivia watched TV together over the phone, and at eighth grade graduation, Olivia looked beautiful.

Her curls were softer and more carefully styled, pinned out of her face. She had makeup on, which she didn't usually wear, and in the cute black dress her mom bought her from Plato's Closet, she looked tall and thin and like she had boobs. She wore her graduation gown open like a robe, the blue shimmering in the light, and the tassel from her cap kept falling in her face, so eventually she just took the whole thing off.

Hazard couldn't help it. She looked so pretty. He kissed her before the ceremony, pulling her into the darker side of the music room, around the corner where the instruments were stored, while the rest of their grade goofed around until the principal came to escort them to the auditorium where parents waited to cheer. Her mouth was soft and warm. It was sticky and tasted sweet, like her lip gloss. The kiss was tentative and brief, but not too fast, and Olivia didn't seem to care that Hazard was a little shorter than her because she was wearing heels.

"Haz...," she said breathlessly, staring at Hazard with big brown eyes and a blush coloring the skin below her freckles.

"Sorry," Hazard said, immediately feeling bad.

"No, don't be." Olivia shook her head, curls bouncing around her shoulders. She hugged him, burying her face into his neck. Hazard hugged her back, holding her there, and for the first time he felt pretty cool. What nervous moody boy? That wasn't him. He was smooth. He pulled girls that gave him butterflies into dark corners and kissed them, which they liked. Girls liked being surprised, right? It was romantic.

For two weeks, maybe, Hazard dated Olivia. He wasn't sure if he was doing it right. When nobody was looking, he squeezed her hand, and when she thought the moment was right, she leaned over and stole a kiss. Each brush of the skin was electrifying, and sometimes Hazard felt bad because he was so shy.

Hazard didn't tell anyone but Emery when his mom and dad went out of town for the weekend. His grandma came to stay with him while they were gone. She fell asleep most of the time, watching Lifetime and the news. She was easy to persuade, anyway, and she waved at Emery from the recliner when he came over.

"She looks drugged," Emery snickered in Hazard's room.

"She's on heart medicine," Hazard explained sheepishly. He and Emery played video games until early in the morning.

The second night, Hazard invited Olivia over.

"We can watch *Adult Swim*," he said. "It'll be fun."

Olivia had her hair in French braids that were starting to come undone, little scarlet wispy locks popping out here and there. Hazard introduced her to his grandma, even though his grandma was falling asleep already.

They ate popsicles and watched *Adult Swim* in his parents' room, because they had a big TV and Hazard wanted to impress her. They watched *Family Guy*, *Cowboy Bebop*, *Big O*, and *FLCL*. Hazard didn't get as much of a kick out of everything else like Olivia did, but he liked *FLCL*. It made sense to him: loneliness, sex, and confusion. He decided he understood what Olivia meant about pretty boys.

They played solitaire on his dad's computer until *Witch Hunter Robin* came on. The show creeped Hazard out, but Olivia loved it. And maybe it was because it was very late at night, at least three o'clock in the morning, but Hazard wasn't so afraid to look at Olivia anymore, and they lay in the dark in his parents' room staring at each other. Hazard trembled with an anxious kind of curiosity, sweet and thrilling. He remembered in seventh grade, Olivia had dated Tyler Orrs for a couple weeks, but Hazard hadn't ever done anything with anyone.

He worried that Olivia could tell how nervous he was because his hands were clammy. The air kicked on in the house, and Hazard touched

Olivia's breast. It was the perfect size for his palm. She wore a green bra with little yellow bows, and Hazard was amazed at how silky soft the skin of her chest was, especially around her nipple.

She rolled over and kissed him, topless. The place between her legs was hot on his lap. Hazard didn't mean to, but when they kissed, his body rolled up. Olivia made soft noises that gave Hazard chills. She was gorgeous in the dark of the room, even without a shirt on and looking flat when she lay down.

Hazard didn't know what to do, but he wanted to impress her. He kissed her neck. He kissed her chest. He told her he liked the way her skin smelled.

Olivia took his shirt off too. She giggled. She whispered, "You're so tiny," and then apologized with a kiss when Hazard looked offended. She reached between his legs, her eyes bright, and Hazard was so surprised he couldn't even stop her. He didn't *want* to stop her. It seemed like she knew what she was doing, and he didn't, after all.

In his parents' bedroom, Olivia made him come. It was obvious on the front of his jeans, and Hazard was embarrassed. He hid his face in the bedspread. Olivia curled up next to him and breathed against his ear, kissing his cheek and whispering, "It's okay."

Hazard touched her with his face smashed against her bare shoulder. She guided his hand at first. His heart raced and his breath quickened, but not like Olivia's when she helped him finish her off with his finger. Orgasms were crazy things, Hazard thought. He couldn't get the look on Olivia's face out of his head and he smelled her on his knuckles, so he kissed her long and soft because he didn't know how to put everything into words.

Olivia slept on his bed. Hazard woke his grandma up on the recliner and helped her to his parents' room, where she was supposed to have been sleeping before she nodded off in the living room. Hazard slept on the floor with Olivia's hand dangling off the edge of his bed near his face. He watched Olivia for a little while, while she slept. Olivia Pierce was his first. He was content with that. When Hazard fell asleep, he dreamed about *Witch Hunter Robin*.

Sunday night, his grandma went home. Emery came over. Hazard told him everything. Emery was in awe.

"So is she your girlfriend?" Emery grunted, poking at a line of ants in the crack of the sidewalk.

Hazard shrugged. "I have to ask her."

On Tuesday, they went skating. They joked. They laughed. Tom teased Olivia, and she punched him so hard on the arm it left a bruise. They went to the freeway, where the high schoolers' hangout was. There were fresh beer cans littered in front of the dirty couch set up below the tagged concrete. Tom and Peyton were investigating behind the couch.

Hazard kicked at the gravel, glancing up at Olivia expectantly. With all the bittersweet maturity of a young woman, Olivia said, "I don't know if it's going to work, Hazard."

Hazard was wordless for a moment. He looked at his feet. He felt a little sore somewhere in his chest, but it wasn't exactly *pain*. Even though it meant he might be alone again, he was fine with that, because he wasn't sure if he had it in him to be her boyfriend, anyway. He didn't tell her that. He didn't ask her why it wouldn't work, either. He just nodded. He gave her a smile, and somehow, it was okay again.

Fourteen-year-olds thought they knew how the world worked.

TOM usually smelled like spearmint gum. His sister always used to give him pieces of her gum. Maybe he felt like after she died he owed it to her to carry on the habit. If that was the case, he didn't admit it. He said he chewed it so he didn't smell like pot, which he started smoking now and then in eighth grade. His cousins Gary and Craig let him do it with them when he was at their house on the weekends. Olivia didn't believe Tom, but he didn't care.

Hazard watched Tom get high only once, at the Windsor Green park. Tom dug in the pocket of his cargo shorts, and Hazard watched the hemp dance on his wrist as he pulled out a little Ziploc bag of weed. He held it out, frowning tenderly.

"Craig told me I could have this much," he said.

"That doesn't look like a lot." Hazard took the bag and looked at it curiously.

"It's not. It's enough for a good-sized joint. Do you want some, or...?"

Hazard shook his head, handing it back. "No. Go for it, Tommy."

Tom did. Sitting with one leg beneath the other, he rolled a joint on his knee with boyish fingers, and Hazard watched him smoke. Tom lit the joint and took four short puffs, held them, settled back into the grass, and squinted up at the late afternoon sky as he breathed out all the smoke. The smell was cloying. It made Hazard's eyes water, and he felt like he could taste it. He watched the way Tom licked his lips, the way he held the joint between thumb and forefinger and went through the motions so smoothly, so casually, so *maturely*. That was what Tom wanted, Hazard guessed—to be grown up and treated like an adult, because he hadn't really been a *kid* for the past few years, anyway. Hazard could understand that. They were fourteen, after all. They deserved some respect for their young adulthood.

Tom smiled stupidly. His eyes were red. He offered the joint to Hazard twice, and the second time, Hazard almost took it, but he didn't. He just wanted to be there for Tom. His eyes lingered on the way Tom's mouth moved around the stubby joint, the way the smoke drifted from his lips like silk.

It hurt him to watch, and Hazard didn't know why. Maybe it was the way Tom looked sad even though he wasn't. Maybe it was the way he stuck his gum on the tree behind them as cars passed the park now and then, or maybe it was the fact that Tom's sister Emma had died of an overdose and now Tom had a tentative habit of getting baked.

Tom liked people to think he was always happy. Hazard knew he wasn't. He was always up and down after his sister Emma died. Sometimes Hazard felt like he was closer to Tom than both Olivia and Peyton. He couldn't explain it. He thought it had something to do with being the only friend Tom invited to Emma's funeral.

Tom's favorite song was "Macy's Day Parade" by Green Day. He said it was his life. Hazard could see that. Tom's family wasn't poor, but his mom worked two jobs to keep herself busy. She had for years. Hazard remembered staying over in sixth grade and watching as she hurried through the house in her waitress uniform, grabbing Tom by the cheeks and pressing kisses to his head on the way out.

Hazard watched it again in August, just before high school started.

Peyton and Olivia weren't there. Emery was grounded for lying to his stepdad, Andrew, so Hazard had agreed to go to Tom's for dinner. Tom's dad was holed up in the den grading papers. Hazard sat on Tom's couch, watching from the corner of his eye.

Tom's mom was blonde, just like him, and she looked tired most of the time. Tom said, "Love you, drive safe," and closed the screen door after her, then slipped on his sandals and motioned for Hazard to follow him.

During summer, it stayed light out longer. It was seven o'clock but not dark yet, just dimming toward sunset. They skated to the gas station near the entrance to Windsor Green. Hazard bought Tom spearmint gum, and Tom promised him some of his Bugles.

They went to the high schoolers' hangout by the freeway. There was a cool breeze coming in off Puget Sound, and by the time dark completely fell, Tom and Hazard were sitting on the couch below the freeway among the litter and garbage and graffiti and passing gum back and forth in a kiss.

It didn't happen right away. Tom tossed down his board and started kicking beer cans and gravel on his way to the dirty couch.

"What if they find us here?" Hazard asked, talking about high schoolers as he brushed off a side of the couch the best he could before sitting on it. He didn't want to sit on dirt and grime.

"They won't. I don't think they come around here that often anymore. Besides, we're technically freshmen now too, so we count as high schoolers."

Hazard decided that made sense. Cars rushed by overhead on the highway. They sat on the couch and talked, eating Bugles and drinking Mountain Dew and chewing spearmint gum. They talked about skating tricks and Peyton's new haircut and what classes they'd been put in at orientation for Bethany High.

Tom snapped his gum. Hazard wanted to know how he could pop it so loud. Tom tried to teach him. They were talking and laughing together, as normal as ever—and it felt kind of like a movie because it was a blur, and Hazard was still never quite sure what made them start kissing, but suddenly they were. Maybe it was the way Tom's tongue moved with the gum, or the way Hazard *tried* to move his. Maybe it was because they were both kind of lonely. Maybe it was just one of those many moments in the stretch of adolescence where hormonal things happen and can't really be justified.

If Tom was gay, Hazard wouldn't hate him, but there were plenty other people to like who were better than Hazard. Hazard wanted to tell Tom this, but Tom's mouth was on his and Hazard was overwhelmed by the taste of spearmint, the slick resilient feel of gum being passed from tongue to tongue as the sound of the freeway echoed down on them and the air settled with the evening. Tom's tongue was wet and warm. His teeth were rigid on Hazard's lip.

They kissed, totally boyish kisses, tangled up on the couch with bodies pressed together and hands clutching at anything. It was a collision of curiosity and needy, biting kisses. Tom absently ran his hands through Hazard's hair. It gave him chills.

Inside, Hazard was a whirlwind of worries too. Did it mean he was *that way*? It didn't feel any different than it had with Olivia—the kissing, the grinding, the spark of delight. Suddenly he wasn't quite sure of anything, sitting with Tom on the couch in a terrifying silence after the kissing and rocking of hips was done. His heart raced, and he felt kind of embarrassed, but he hadn't hated it. Tom was a good kisser. Hazard told him so. What he didn't tell Tom was that maybe they were both just lonely, which was totally okay.

Tom finished off the Bugles. Hazard gave him some Mountain Dew. Under the freeway, eyes wide, they both agreed that they definitely weren't gay, and that was the end of it. They skated back to Windsor Green and Buckingham Court, laughing like they'd never kissed or felt the skin above the waistband of jeans or shared the same piece of gum at all.

High school started, and now it was January of Hazard's sophomore year.

Chapter 11
January and February

"OH, WOW."

One of the fluorescent lights flickered twice. Hazard softened into a frown, following Emery's finger to read the latest addition to the forum in the back stall of the bathrooms by the auditorium, where all the worst gossip was scrawled in different colors of the Sharpie rainbow. Just below the garish purple *mandy bromer gives good head*, somebody had written:

one kiss from lily and ur a fag, just ask emery moore

"'Oh, wow' is not adequate enough to describe how I feel," Emery grumbled. His eyes were frantic and skittish, the distress etched deep into his face. It looked like he wanted to be mad—he was on the verge of one of his temper snaps—but he was too embarrassed to blow up yet. Their voices echoed, bouncing off the opposite walls of the empty bathroom.

"It's okay, Em. It doesn't mean anything. 'Gay' is just the best insult stupid people can come up with."

"Maybe—"

"Plus, it's more insulting Lily, right? So obviously it was a girl who's got beef with her or something."

"Maybe it was Riley."

Hazard glanced at Emery. Emery looked positively sick with it all. "Who's that?" Hazard asked.

"Riley Parker."

"I don't know him."

"Really? I thought you might. He goes to parties, I think."

Hazard tried not to be offended. "*I don't know him.*"

"He lives in the same complex as me." Emery fidgeted. "He's *confused.*" He met Hazard's glance, face pinched up and eyes dark. "Over the summer, we broke curfew at the pool, and he… *made a move on me*. I mean, I didn't *try* to kiss him back, but I felt bad. I didn't want to push him away."

"You don't know that it was him," Hazard whispered, but then they both fell quiet. Hazard looked Emery over, red Converse and wrinkled jeans, Everclear T-shirt and lanyard swinging from his hip pocket. Blue eyes, soft face, thin shoulders. He was chewing the silver stud in his lip nervously. Hazard wanted to hug him.

Instead, he looked back at the chaos of scribbles on the bathroom wall. "I've realized something, Emery."

"What?" Emery grunted, sounding miserable. Hazard glanced at him.

"Everyone is secretly gay."

Emery scoffed loudly, but he didn't disagree. Hazard crouched down and dug through the front pocket of his backpack. He took out a Sharpie, uncapped it, and wrote on the wall:

everyone's so full of shit born and raised by hypocrites

Emery didn't say anything. Hazard guessed that was Emery's way of approving.

JESSE LOGAN WESLEY was not at all the kind of boy anybody wanted their kid to be with, but there it was. He was a hellion. He was sarcastic and mean, he was sneaky, he was controlling sometimes, he was rebellious and persistent, he knew his way around sex and drugs and alcohol, and he knew exactly how to look at someone to get his way.

Jesse was tall and thin and dangerously attractive. His favorite movie was *The Lost Boys*, and he laughed at *The Outsiders* because everyone said he reminded them of it. He said he'd rather be compared to *Gilbert Grape* Johnny Depp, or even Dane Cook or Shane West. He grew up wearing nice clothes and playing the piano, but now he was eighteen and smoked three and a half packs of Camels a week, maybe four if he indulged himself. His rough years were the years of eighth and ninth grade, when he ran with the Seattle gang, failed a few classes, and got into enough trouble to satisfy him for a while. He acted big and bad, but he

smiled and laughed like a little boy, and he had the complete seasons of
My So-Called Life, Summerland, and *Dawson's Creek* sitting with the rest
of his DVDs. His parents were from Chicago, and when he'd been
younger, he used to light leaves and blades of grass on fire with sparklers
on the Fourth of July.

On top of being a hellion, Jesse was also spoiled rotten. His father
was a building contractor and made a large amount of tax-free money each
year. Jesse got everything he asked for, including his red Celica. Jesse
knew nothing about cars, so his father financed any problem like a change
of battery or fixing the brakes. Jesse said he'd tried coke once and only
once, but his true drugs of choice were nicotine and alcohol. He'd been in
trouble with the cops before, for vandalism and shoplifting and once in
ninth grade through a bouncer at a Seattle club who realized Jesse's ID
was fake, but his father got him out of every situation. Jesse had learned
his lesson. He was careful about having fun now.

Jesse wasn't afraid to like Hole. He thought Courtney Love was a
bold, sexy woman who made good music and stood strong, and he
admired that. Jesse liked to change his hair a lot, going from dark to
scorching red to choppy black. He had seven piercings altogether, three in
both ears and one in his left brow, a red leather jacket that might have
been his trademark, and by the end of his high school career he had seven
tattoos. Nautical stars on the backs of his triceps, a flame tribal on his side,
a Bible verse on the cleft between his left palm and wrist, his favorite
numbers just below the back of his neck, his zodiac sign on his middle
finger, and musical notes around the lyrics *Fear is the heart of love* on his
inner right wrist. He refused to tell Hazard what that one was about yet.

"I will when I feel like it," Jesse insisted each time, and each time he
grinned his crooked grin, and Hazard gave up because he would never win
against Jesse's stubbornness.

Hazard hated Jesse's stubbornness. He hated how spoiled Jesse was
and how they fought together too, especially the way Jesse's eyes could
render someone speechless and then motionless and then completely
spineless. Hazard hated every little attitude, although, guiltily, he thrived
on confrontation with Jesse because Hazard loved to tick him off.
Sometimes fighting made them closer.

He hated the way Jesse's voice husked and cut and broke, the way it was gravelly when he spoke low and even worse when he woke up in the mornings. He hated the way his voice sounded when he sang in the car, tapping out the beat on the steering wheel like nobody was listening. He hated the way Jesse made him feel like an idiot sometimes, the way he didn't listen, the way he made him want *more,* and the way he just got under his skin so easily.

Hazard despised the way Jesse walked into a room and everyone noticed. He hated the way Jesse loved his reputation. He hated how girls fawned over Jesse. He hated how *easy* it was for Jesse to be cool and seductive, dancing or talking or just staring, and the way his eyes seemed to pierce right through any strong pretense, the way he made Hazard feel vulnerable. He hated the way Jesse had him sit in the front seat of his car now when they picked everyone up for a party and the way Jesse chuckled at Hazard when Hazard was drunk and traced the shape of Jesse's lips and nose. "You do that every fucking time," Jesse told him, and Hazard hated that that was true.

Hazard also really didn't like the cough that Jesse had from smoking too often, the dry taste of a smoker's mouth, and the fact that he'd only heard Jesse throw up twice—and both times, he locked the door so Hazard couldn't help him. He hated the way Jesse looked in boxer briefs, which was really good. He hated how Jesse said things like *Oh, yeah?* and *ass* with a thick Chicago accent. He hated the way Jesse loved to inspect his thin treasure trail sometimes, the way his hands felt in his pants, and the way Jesse always hummed after good sex. He hated how Jesse liked syrup on his eggs too.

He also hated the way Emery hated Jesse, but Emery was just being protective. Hazard hated the way Jesse stuck his tongue out when concentrating, especially on a video game, and the way he fiddled with his earrings when he was thinking. He hated the way Jesse's laugh tickled him and his smile stirred him. But most of all, Hazard hated the way that, unlike anything or anybody else, everything with Jesse just *felt right.*

THE Seahawks played in the 2006 Super Bowl that February. Jesse's parents went to the actual game, and Jesse threw a quiet party at his big house on the Elite Street. He called it *quiet* because it was just their crew—him, Hazard, Felix, Lexie, Brianna, Ashton, the Seattle gang—but it wasn't really quiet at all. The spacious living room was filled with their vigorous cheers, roars of approval and disapproval, the laughter at all the commercials and the jokes they made in between plays as they passed around the chips and bottles of Smirnoff Ice.

Like typical guys, they sprawled in Jesse's spacious living room, and Hazard texted Emery so much it was as if Emery were sitting right next to him in the conversation. But he wasn't; he was at home watching the Super Bowl with Russell and Lily. Hazard was okay with that. Jumping around vehemently with everyone in Jesse's living room when the Seahawks scored was so manly and overwhelmingly fun, and Hazard wasn't drunk, but he was a little tipsy, so he didn't feel that making out with Jesse in his bedroom after everything and everyone had gone home was that emasculating at all. They made football jokes all night, and Hazard loved it. He texted Emery each quip, and Emery was thoroughly amused.

"EMERY and Russell are going to marathon slasher movies tonight to commemorate Valentine's Day." Hazard zipped his coat up further, shoving his hands in his pockets. It was dark and cold out, a Northwestern winter. "Emery thinks Valentine's Day is overrated."

Jesse was smoking, leaning against the hood of his car. Hazard sat on it, cross-legged. School had let out, and they were waiting for Felix in the parking lot. Somebody down the row of cars started their engine and muffled music joined the noise outside.

"It's totally overrated," Jesse agreed.

Hazard thought about last Valentine's Day. It made his stomach hurt to remember Chase and Lexie's bedroom. Jesse laughed and pointed out a few girls laden with red and pink balloons, valentines and flowers, candy and toys.

"Pathetic," Jesse scoffed. "And what about all the kids who didn't get *any* valentines?"

"I got a few," Hazard mumbled. In truth, he only got three. Everyone knew him, but he still only got three little cards.

"So did I." Jesse sounded absolutely miserable. He hunched in his red leather, vintage Rolling Stones T-shirt beneath it. He went to the back seat of his car and got out his backpack, pulling out valentine after valentine to show Hazard. He didn't get *a few*. He got about seventeen of them. He pulled out a note folded in the shape of a heart, looked at it for a moment, then tossed it with the other valentines.

"What's that?" Hazard asked, immediately interested.

"It's so fucking old-school," Jesse said around his cigarette. He was trying to laugh it off. Hazard could tell. A teacher walked by and Jesse quickly hid his cigarette from sight, watching until the teacher had gotten into his car before puffing on his cigarette a few more times and picking up the little heart-shaped note.

His eyes looked troubled as he unfolded it. Hazard watched him, perplexed.

It was a love note from a girl in Jesse's fourth hour class. She said stuff like *You probably don't notice me* and *I think you're really cool*, and as Jesse read the whole thing to him, the wind trying to rip the paper from his hands, Hazard's chest clenched tighter and tighter. It was from the terrible honesty of the note, and the horrible way Jesse looked torn apart by it.

"That's sad," Hazard mumbled, brow knotting.

"Valentine's Day is sad," Jesse hissed, trying to fold the note up properly again. He couldn't. He just slid it into his binder so it didn't get wrinkled. He finished his cigarette and stared at his feet, arms crossed and hands tucked under his arms for warmth. Hazard watched him, not sure what to say. Jesse looked completely fraught from the note, and Hazard's heart ached because of it.

"You're going to talk to her," Hazard demanded. "You're going to talk to her and be nice to her."

"I plan on it," Jesse husked. He put all his valentines back in his bag. "God, we're all dirtbags," he grumbled afterward.

Hazard nodded. He said, "You are," but it didn't really lighten the mood. He knew why Jesse said that. Jesse didn't want to lead the girl on, but it was what he did best. Hazard felt a painful swell in his chest for Jesse because he was so distraught by the note. Jesse wasn't all bad. There was the soft side of him, so raw and unguarded, that didn't come out very often, and Hazard wanted to give him a kiss to complete the moment, but he couldn't. They were still in the school parking lot.

Felix finally came. Hazard's ears hurt from the cold. Felix thought they were fighting because they were both quiet and distant with thought, so they tried to show him they weren't. Jesse blasted Hole's *Live Through This* CD. They met Lexie and Brianna at Carl's Jr. to eat an early dinner before they went to the party they'd decided upon for the night.

Jesse seemed stuck on the heart-shaped note all night. Hazard tried to make him feel better, and by the end of the night Jesse seemed to liven up a little. He and Lexie told stories about the Valentine's Day Lexie's mom almost called the cops on them because they went back to Lexie's house so drunk they were stumbling and puking in the street. Hazard remembered not to go past tipsy, even though they played drinking games and spun the bottle and put on some really good music. It was a lot better than the party last Valentine's Day. Brianna wasn't stuck at the door the whole time, and Hazard didn't get high or harassed. He danced tight together with Jesse, and he wanted to stay the night at Jesse's house, but Hazard had promised his mom he'd be home by eleven at the latest, and he intended on keeping that promise.

Jesse dropped him off a few minutes after his curfew. His mom didn't seem to notice. "How was your Valentine's Day?" she asked, voice tight with the tension and scrutiny it always had when *that senior* was around. Hazard tried not to pay attention to her little red dress and curled hair and the fact that she still had makeup on so late at night.

"Are you and Dad going out?" Hazard countered, watching out the window beside the door until Jesse's car was gone, only then locking the door and taking off his jacket.

"No." His mother fixed her hair in the hallway mirror, straightening her dress. "While you were gone, we went out to dinner, but your dad's had a long day, so we're just going to relax the rest of the night."

Hazard had a sudden visual of what *relaxing* might mean to them on Valentine's Day: rose petals, candles, perfumes, his father sprawled on the big bed watching the TV above the dresser until his mom went in. Hazard shuddered, hanging up his coat. "Have fun," he muttered, plucking at the laces of his Converse.

"How was your Valentine's Day?" his mom asked again. The tone of her voice was bitterly maternal because he hadn't answered the first time. He glanced up at her, wiggling his shoes off. She stood at the mouth to the hall, arms folded, watching him with her face twisted in something that was supposed to be daunting but was much more condescending.

"It was fine," Hazard murmured, voice thin. He dropped his shoes at the door. He felt his mom's eyes on him as he hurried across the living room to the hall that broke off toward his bedroom. He stopped, turning to return his mom's stare from across the house.

"I told you," he said, "I was at Emery's, and we watched horror movies. No, I was not on a date. No, I did not kiss anyone. No, I did not get physical with anyone. No, I did not do anything illegal. Is that okay with you?"

His mom evaluated him for another moment. Hazard stared at her, horrified she'd be able to see he was pretty tipsy and maybe a little disheveled from kisses and dancing. He'd even chewed gum to make his breath fresh, just in case.

If she saw any of that, she didn't say anything. She scoffed softly in the back of her throat. She pivoted on her heel, waving her hand sharply in his direction as if to say *Go to bed.* She disappeared into the bedroom where Hazard's dad waited.

"Good night," she called. Hazard didn't answer her.

A week later, Jesse set the girl in his fourth hour up with his friend Eli. He told Hazard that the girl actually blushed and giggled around Eli, so Jesse was free and clear. The problem was solved. Hazard could tell Jesse felt proud of himself because he'd done something kind, and Hazard loved him for it.

JESSE dropped Hazard off at the corner of Emery's cul-de-sac. It was midnight, and it was cold and raining. Hazard could see his breath.

"Are you sure you don't want to just stay at my house?" Jesse asked, leaning across the middle console.

"I promised Emery I'd actually stay tonight." Hazard gave Jesse a wave and a smile, closing the door and holding his backpack over his head to keep him dry. He ran past Jesse's headlights. He knew Jesse waited at the corner until he saw Hazard sneak past the front of Emery's house and climb up on the generator; he heard Jesse pull away only then.

Emery welcomed him in quickly. Hazard almost slipped on the roof in the winter rain. His bag was not an umbrella. He was soaked as he fell into Emery's bedroom as quietly as he could, wet hair stuck to his cheeks and teeth chattering. Emery's light and TV were still on. He told Hazard he was going to get sick, and then he asked him if he was drunk.

"*No*," Hazard grumbled, which was true. He'd gone home with Jesse, but they hadn't partied. Felix came over, and they'd played video games for a while.

"Well, sometimes I wonder." Emery didn't ignore Hazard's insulted glance. He met his eyes stubbornly. "You look like a wet cat," he said next. Hazard looked down at himself, jeans soaked black and shirt clinging to his sides. His jacket was heavy because it was wet.

Emery went to his messy closet and started rummaging through his clothes. He handed Hazard some snap pants and a thermal, then went over to his drawers and tossed a pair of boxer briefs at him. Hazard stripped off his wet clothes and changed into the dry ones Emery gave him. He didn't care if Emery watched or not. They were close enough. They were both guys.

"I just got in your pants," Hazard joked. He laughed, fixing a few loose snaps on the borrowed pants. The clothes smelled like Emery. It was kind of comforting. It brought back memories of spending the night in grade school.

Emery snorted, putting Hazard's wet clothes in his hamper. "Tell me they're the only pants you've gotten into tonight."

Hazard looked at him quietly, wondering if Emery was teasing or if he was being grumpy. Emery met his eyes briefly, raising his brows. He seemed to be joking.

Hazard blushed, hoping he didn't look too guilty. "Maybe, maybe not," Hazard said, flopping down on Emery's bed and smiling at him over folded arms. Emery rolled his eyes and grabbed the remote so he could turn the TV channel from his bed. He flopped down beside Hazard, propping his chin on his hand. Hazard looked at him and remembered suddenly, with painful lucidity, that over a year ago he'd wanted to make Emery jealous of Jesse so Emery would know what it was like when Hazard was jealous of Russell.

It hit Hazard then, square in the face. He'd completely forgotten about that revenge, so caught up had he become in Jesse himself.

It scared him to think about it, especially so to think that maybe it was okay. No, no, it wasn't okay. He never wanted to lose Emery, but who said that Hazard couldn't have both Jesse and Emery at the same time?

That, Hazard thought, would be great.

Chapter 12
March, April, and May

"AND here, Jesse, you can have that lighter back. I don't use it anyway—"

"Don't *throw* that, Danger, you'll lose it."

"Better grab it before it falls behind your bed, then!"

"Okay, first of all, Hazard, if you're going to be this typical, *lower your fucking voice. My parents are home.*"

"You just yelled too!"

"Do as I say and not as I do and all that jazz, for Christ's sake. Hazard, if you're returning everything of mine, you'll have to return that shirt. I bought it for you."

"*Oh, that's just great!*"

"Stop yelling! Jesus, you're *crazy!* You're like a nagging, spoiled girlfriend."

"Here's *your* shirt. Oh, and those bracelets. And—don't touch me, Jesse. *Don't touch me.*"

"Hazard, please. Give it a rest. I can't deal with this."

"Because I'm so high maintenance, right? I'm *annoying*, I'm *too high maintenance*, I'm *clingy*, I'm *jealous*, I'm *crazy*, I'm *reckless*, I'm *stupid*, I'm—God, what else have you said? Oh, right. A *nagging, spoiled girlfriend*—I said *don't touch me,* Jesse!"

"Yes! Yes, you are! You are all of those things and *so much more*, and I can't deal with it anymore! You're running me ragged. You're wearing me out, Hazard. I just can't keep up, I can't figure out what it is you want me to do that I'm not already doing!"

"It's fine. It's not like…. We're just friends with benefits, that's all. Well, not anymore, I guess."

"I guess not!"

"Jesse, I can't do it either. I'm not going to sit around and be treated like I'm the mess and you're fucking perfect. Because you're *not*."

"This is it, then. Did you bring all my stuff, or is there more at your house?"

"No, I have it all in my backpack. Here's that movie, your Nine Inch Nails CD, and this shirt is yours too. I wore it home the other night."

"You looked good in it. Keep it."

"Jesse, that's not what you're supposed to say!"

"Oh, yeah? Hazard, keep it."

"I can't keep it! We're breaking it off, I can't keep it, it's yours, I don't want it—"

"Okay. Just fold it and—or, you know, crumple it up and toss it there. That's fine too."

"That's it. That's all your stuff."

"Thanks, Danger."

"*Hazard.* Do you have anything else of mine?"

"Nope, I've given it all back already—no, wait, I lied."

"Where? What is it?"

"I can't give it back."

"Fuck you, Jesse. What is it?"

"Your *virginity.*"

IT WAS spring break. Hazard had a song stuck in his head.

My inarticulate store-bought hangover hobby kit, it talks. It says, "You, oh you are so cool."

The song made him think of him and Jesse. The song circled around and around in his head like thoughts did when he was high, but Hazard wasn't high. He was very drunk, and everything was kind of foggy. He could hear the hum from the fan in the corner of the room, white noise that

Jesse liked to sleep with. His stomach was starting to sour, and he just wanted to sleep it off. He'd had too much to drink, way too much to drink. He always did when the parties were that fun, except Hazard was very emotional now, because he was very drunk.

Hazard had to puke. He rolled over Jesse. He almost fell getting out of bed. Somehow, he made it to the bathroom just down the hall a little. He tried hard not to, but he accidentally closed the door too loudly before he threw up.

Hazard started crying because he hated puking. He sat with his back against the wall and hoped to God it didn't happen again. He thought about Emery and the way Emery felt about his drinking, and suddenly Hazard was very worried that Emery hated him. He wanted to call Emery to make sure that wasn't true, but he didn't have his phone. He felt too sick to go get it, which made him cry more.

Jesse opened the bathroom door, coming after him. It hit Hazard's knee. Hazard looked up at him with his head tipped back against the wall, and he mumbled tearfully, "Ow," as he pushed the door away from his leg.

Jesse sat down in the bathroom and closed the door. It was dark except for the dim slant of light from the skylight window overhead.

"Don't wake up my parents," Jesse scolded. It was pretty slurred. "You're very loud."

"I threw up," Hazard groaned.

"In the toilet, I hope?"

"Yes. I flushed."

"Okay." Jesse reached out and pulled Hazard away from the wall. "Why are you crying? God, you always cry when you get this trashed."

"Jesse?" Hazard's voice wavered. He let Jesse hug him for a minute, and then he coughed. Jesse pulled away like he was going to puke again. Hazard started crying harder, embarrassed. Jesse always held his hair back, literally and figuratively.

"What?" Jesse finally said.

"I'm scared," Hazard mumbled, getting Jesse's shirt wet with his tears. He couldn't shake the fear of Emery hating him, and the more he cried the more he wanted to throw up again. Jesse cradled him between his knees, leaning against the wall.

"Why?"

Hazard couldn't talk for a moment. Jesse rubbed his back and rocked to and fro a little. Hazard hiccupped on a breath and paused, horrified he'd gag. He didn't. He wondered if Jesse would even understand what he was talking about, or if he'd chalk it up to Hazard being drunk. Hazard sniffled and coughed and shuddered, then croaked, "I'm scared that Emery hates me."

"Why would he hate you? You're a great friend. You guys have been best friends for, like, ever. You said so."

"I'm not Russell."

"That doesn't matter," Jesse said into Hazard's hair.

Hazard couldn't even explain. He didn't know how to, and his throat was tightening the way it always did before he vomited. He wrenched from Jesse's chest and draped himself over the toilet, breath hitching in his throat. Jesse followed him carefully. Hazard swallowed a few times, feeling horribly sick. He cleared his throat. He uttered a little breath of fear and said, "Jesse, I think I might throw up again."

Jesse rested his head on Hazard's back. "Stop crying. You're making yourself sick. I don't get what you're upset about. Okay, so you're not Russell. Of course you're not. You're Hazard. What's the deal?"

"I wanted to make him mad that you were my friend. It didn't work. He's still Russell's friend."

Jesse was quiet. Hazard just tried not to throw up for a minute, then went on. He trembled. The tears came again, and he hated himself for being this way, but he couldn't help it, he was just scared and tired and frustrated.

"Don't let him leave me. He's all I have, Jesse. He's all I've got. He's all I've ever had. If I don't have him, then I've got nothing!"

"You have *me*," Jesse said moodily.

Hazard felt guilty. He started crying harder. He didn't even know what he was saying anymore. "Don't let him leave me, Jesse! Don't let me lose him, I can't lose him, I can't—"

Jesse pulled him away from the toilet with an angry, incoherent grumble. He hugged him close against his chest and tangled his fingers into Hazard's messy dark hair. "Shut up," he hissed. "Shut up, Haz."

Hazard tried, but he couldn't. He was too tired and drunk. "—can't lose him, can't lose him, don't let me, I—"

Jesse rocked him back and forth. "You won't. I promise. Come on, Haz. Cut it out. You're totally wasted. You need to calm down and sleep it off."

Hazard shook his head. Jesse didn't get it. "I don't want to be alone," he mumbled. His nose was running. His lashes felt thick with tears. "I can't lose him, Jesse. I can't lose you, either. I don't want to lose you. Don't leave me."

Jesse fell still. Hazard was breathless. "I don't want to be alone," he said. He felt hysterical. He was shaking. He tried to calm down, body twitching with gasps and face sticky with tears and snot. "Please don't let me be alone. You guys are all I have."

Jesse comforted him a little longer. Finally he mumbled, "I won't let you be alone."

Hazard hugged him tight, heart pounding as he forced himself to breathe slowly. Jesse was warm in the dark. He smelled like his bed. Hazard felt guilty. He didn't want Jesse to think he didn't care about him. Hazard almost started crying again, but he swallowed it the best he could. His head pulsed. His throat hurt. His nose was stuffed. He let go of Jesse and twisted around over the toilet to throw up again.

They went back to Jesse's room. Jesse went downstairs to get him some water, to get the taste out of his mouth. Hazard trudged around the room aimlessly, waiting for Jesse. He looked at Jesse's posters dizzily. He looked at Jesse's desk, all the books and papers, empty cigarette cartons and a CD player. There were photographs there from that night when Felix had surprised them all with a camera. Hazard felt embarrassed to see himself in a picture, especially one that Jesse kept. He turned it over.

Hazard still had the song stuck in his head, but this time it was the line *You won't ever get too far from me*, repeating over and over. Jesse came back with water. Hazard sat on his bed and drank it, trembling.

"You need to go to sleep," Jesse whispered against his cheek. "There's nothing to worry about."

Hazard curled up tight next to Jesse in his bed. It felt good to hit the pillow again. The song circled around and around in his head. Jesse laid an arm over him protectively. It was nice. His smell was nice, and the pressure of his arm was nice.

I won't let you be alone, Jesse had promised him. Hazard believed it.

FELIX convinced them they needed to go to the last school dance of the year with him. Brianna agreed to go because she didn't care either way. Lexie agreed to go because, she claimed, Felix needed a date if Ashton was going to avoid society and hole up at home. Felix got Jesse to comply because it was the last dance of his school career too, and Jesse going meant Hazard had to go, and he was not happy about that.

School dances were awkward and stupid. As cool kids, they weren't supposed to have school spirit. They didn't go to fundraisers or clubs or football games unless it was to smoke in the back of the bleachers and give off reputed vibes of nonchalance and delinquency. That was what kids like them did, but somehow Hazard found himself in the gym dressed up and feeling very dumb.

Emery and Russell went because Lily wanted to go. Hazard talked to Emery for a while, but then Lily dragged him off to dance. Hazard spent the rest of the time sitting in the corner of the gym beside Jesse and Lexie, glaring at everyone who passed by and discussing just how unbearable it all was. After the chaperones started to lay off, the music got better, and Lexie sighed, "This is for Felix, anyway," so they tried to have a little bit of fun. They threw crumpled napkins into the crowd. They tried to see who they could recognize on the gym floor from some party or another. They laughed about the secrets they knew about some people. They loitered at the refreshment table and snickered when Lexie mimed the actions of spiking it. One or two chaperones glared at them.

Hazard danced with Brianna, like they'd come as a couple. It was nice. They whispered back and forth the whole time, talking about what they should do after.

Hazard made sure to say good-bye to Emery before they left. Pulling out of the parking lot, they intentionally drove over the pylon buffers of the exit lane, howling with laughter. They went to the park across from the Catholic school afterward and drove around there, taking turns clinging to the roof of the car and hanging out the windows. Lexie wanted to get high as a high schooler for the last time. Felix, Lexie, and Jesse were graduating, after all. Lying on the grass, smelling Puget Sound on the breeze and watching the dark sky, they got stoned. Even Jesse did, saying, "This is all for you, Felix. We're having fun tonight, and you'll always remember it."

They tried swinging while they were high. Hazard couldn't do it. He felt too much like he was going to fall off and break his neck. Brianna loved it. She and Lexie swung forever, giggling and laughing. Brianna tried to keep the end of her dress from going up. Lexie didn't care. Everybody saw her panties.

Jesse and Felix argued. Hazard laughed, feeling breathless and dizzy. His eyes itched and the world spun.

"I *am* vegetarian!" Felix insisted. He looked surprisingly blank when he was high.

"You eat chicken!" Jesse countered. "And sometimes you have burgers. And you eat tacos—"

"But *usually* I don't, and when I do it makes my stomach hurt."

"So you're only half vegetarian. You're *bigetarian.*"

Maybe it was because of the pot, but to them that made so much sense and it was hilarious. Even Felix laughed at himself.

"Wait," Felix said after a while, "guess what? I've made out with every single one of you guys except Hazard."

"*Oh, yeah!*" Jesse said, and they all laughed again. "Do it," Jesse said, leaning forward as enthusiastically as a little kid at the circus. Felix wound an arm around Hazard's shoulders, and sitting on the little wooden edge of the playground, Hazard let Felix kiss him. He was embarrassed and nervous, so he tried not to laugh on Felix's mouth. It didn't really work. Felix pinched him, and Hazard laughed more. Everything rocked to and fro. Hazard's face was hot afterward, so he pressed it to the cool grass. He looked at Jesse and wondered if his kissing Felix had made him mad, or excited, or anything at all.

"Well done, good sir," Jesse said, shaking Felix's hand. Hazard burst into laughter some more.

Chapter 13
Summer Again

JESSE bought him stuff again: some new shirts, CDs, books and magazines, a belt, a new pair of jeans that fit him really well. Hazard felt a little intimidated accepting it all, even though Jesse had looked so pleased with himself in buying them. He was quiet as they went through the mall, Jesse flashing his fat wallet and his crooked grin, and Hazard didn't mean to seem ungrateful by being quiet. He just didn't feel good.

Hazard guessed that he'd probably caught something at the party the other night. He'd shared a drink with this girl named Mackenzie after she snapped his clear bracelet. She must have been sick and now he had the same stomach bug, because as Jesse's car idled in the parking lot of the mall so Jesse could finish texting Felix, Hazard clawed open the passenger door, leaned out, and threw up on the blacktop.

Jesse jumped, eyes widening. He almost dropped his phone. "Christ, Hazard!" he said, reaching over and holding Hazard by the collar so he didn't fall out of the car. "Holy shit—"

"I wanna go home," Hazard mumbled, cringing as he cleaned off his mouth and then wiped that hand on his jeans. He really threw up way too often. He hated it. "Can we go now?"

Jesse stared at him blankly for a long moment. Then he nodded and pulled out of the parking lot. He drove with his knees part of the way, texting Felix with one hand and keeping the other protectively on the back of Hazard's neck.

"Don't you dare puke in my car," Jesse whispered. Hazard knew him well enough to recognize his pretenses. Jesse didn't really care about that. He just didn't want Hazard to puke again, period.

Jesse's graduation was the next day, and Hazard couldn't go because he was sick. Jesse came by after the ceremony was through to see him. There was a gentle knocking at Hazard's bedroom window around eight thirty that night, which scared him at first. Bundled in his blanket and achy just walking to his window, Hazard opened it for Jesse and went back to his bed.

Jesse climbed up on the cinderblocks below the window, wriggling into Hazard's room easily. "I can't believe I actually went," he said, sounding absolutely disgusted with himself, even though he looked kind of relieved and proud.

Hazard frowned. "I'm sorry I didn't go," he mumbled. His brows furrowed. He held out his hands for Jesse to come closer to the edge of the bed. He got shivers from the night air coming in through the open window. "I bet you made the cap and gown look badass."

Jesse wandered around Hazard's room for a moment, examining everything in the bouncing light of Hazard's TV. He moved over to the foot of Hazard's bed and let Hazard hug him loosely, pressing his nose into his middle. The familiar smells of cigarettes and red leather and skin, and tonight of crowds and fresh air, were comforting.

"I really wish I could have gone," Hazard said. He felt very guilty, because participating in something so formal and cliché went against everything Jesse Logan Wesley said he stood for. It meant that he actually cared about what he did with his life, and it made Hazard sad that he hadn't been there for him. It was a big deal, as much as Jesse pretended it wasn't.

"I've got my diploma in the car. I could go get it and show you. How are you feeling, Danger?"

"*Hazard.* Dizzy, cold, my head is killing me, and I've thrown up five times, and you're probably gonna catch this too."

Jesse smiled a little, threading his fingers through Hazard's hair. It relaxed Hazard. Jesse leaned down and kissed his forehead. "You're burning up," he said. "Have you taken any medicine tonight?"

"Yeah, my mom gave me some," Hazard mumbled. "Jesse, I just want to feel better."

Jesse sighed dramatically. "I know. That's why I came to see you. But anyway, my parents wanted to see me tonight too, so you should stop hogging me. I can be all yours another night. God, Danger, you're so greedy."

Hazard smiled dully and got comfortable in bed again. Jesse went to the window, watching.

"Text me," Hazard told him. "And tell your parents I said hi. And have fun. And congratulations, Jesse. You're a free man now."

Jesse cocked his head back and laughed. It gave Hazard chills. He worried his mom would hear it and come stomping down the hall.

"I've been a free man forever, Hazard," Jesse said coolly, giving Hazard one of his spellbinding glances.

"Text me," Hazard repeated.

"Sure thing."

Hazard listened to the sound of Jesse shutting his window from the outside. He listened to the familiar sound of a car starting somewhere up the block a little bit. He tried to stay up a little longer, waiting for Jesse's texts, but his mom had given him nighttime medicine, and before long, Hazard fell asleep.

WITH school out for summer, Hazard spent more time with Emery. They went to the YMCA. They went to the bookstore. Emery played with his lip ring while they sat around and read. They stayed up late posting stupid pictures and videos and comments on each other's MySpaces. They went to the mall or the Four Corners. They went to Russell's, which Hazard didn't mind because it was summer, and when Jesse was busy he didn't have much else to do. Russell's niece was pretty cute and called all of them *Uncle*, even Emery and Hazard.

They played basketball in Emery's driveway. When Emery's stepdad came out and started trying to coach them, they put the basketball back in the garage and went out again. Emery had his permit, after all. They told his mom that Hazard had his license, and thankfully, she didn't ask to see it, because Hazard really didn't have his license. He didn't even have his permit. He just hadn't gotten around to it yet.

Jesse tried to teach him to drive, though. Once or twice, on a relatively empty street. First Jesse had Hazard try to shift while he steered, cracking crude distracting jokes about gearshifts and their rather sexual connotations until Hazard was laughing so hard he couldn't remember which gear came next. Then he switched spots and let Hazard try to get the hang of the clutch while Jesse shifted. Then Jesse let him try it altogether, but Jesse ended up having to shift for him again, reminding Hazard that if he hurt his car, Jesse would hurt him. Hazard scoffed. He tried again, this time sitting halfway on Jesse's lap. He almost got it, but it was still difficult. Jesse laughed at him.

Lexie moved in with Max. They all helped her unpack one weekend, moving her into Max's apartment and wishing her the best of luck. Jesse gave her a very long hug.

Hazard's mom was bored, which meant she started to practice cooking. She got a few cookbooks and tried new recipes for dinner for a while. Hazard wasn't going to suffer alone. He had Emery over as much as he could so he wouldn't be the only one trying his mom's concoctions.

Tom invited Hazard to go with them to the freeway. The high schoolers whose hangout they used to explore had graduated and moved on, and Tom, Olivia, and Peyton had taken it on as their own. Hazard hung out with them one afternoon. It was kind of awkward. It just wasn't the same, and they all knew it.

On a day that smelled a lot like summer, Jesse wanted to wash his car. He didn't. Hazard and Brianna and Felix did, while Jesse and Lexie smoked cigarettes and watched. Felix made everyone laugh, taking off his shirt and washing the car sensually. Brianna refused to play into it. Hazard didn't mean to, but it was hot after all, and he could just feel Jesse watching him as he moved in his tank top and basketball shorts.

Felix had to go because Ashton kept calling him. Lexie took off her shirt in his stead, running around in her bra and shorts. She sprayed Hazard and Brianna with the hose. Hazard ran from it and ended up slipping. Falling on the cement hurt both his skinned knees and his pride, but they all laughed good-naturedly, so he laughed too. Jesse kissed his scraped knees later that night, up in his bedroom, before he turned out the lights and thanked Hazard for helping wash his car.

HAZARD turned sixteen the first week of July. His mom and dad took him out to eat in Seattle. Somehow, his father convinced his mom that tickets to the Warped Tour were an okay gift. Hazard was ecstatic. There was a good party at the end of the week, and now he had four tickets to the Gorge Amphitheatre on July 15.

On the Fourth of July, Hazard sat on the curb in Emery's cul-de-sac and watched Emery, Russell, and Lily throw poppers at each other. They screamed and laughed, dancing around the pops of each tiny firecracker hitting the pavement. Eventually, Hazard joined them.

The party Jesse told him about was on Friday. Jesse made sure to tell everyone that Hazard had just turned sixteen, so Hazard had to fidget through one Happy Birthday! after another until he was tipsy enough to love it. Hazard recognized the Janelle girl from over a year ago. They were at her house. She let him pick the music, going through the CD stand next to the stereo. Grinding with Jesse to "Love Addict" was really hot.

They played Circle of Death in her living room and jumped on the couches. They raided her pantry for snacks. Janelle got a lap dance from a guy named Parker, and everyone cheered. They played Clue and Monopoly, which were really hard after a few drinks. They drew happy faces and wrote notes on each other (and the walls) with gel pens. Jesse and Felix did shots together. Jesse smelled like whiskey when they kissed in Janelle's bathroom. The lights were out. Hazard sat on the counter of the sink. Jesse unbuttoned his jeans, and Hazard slipped a little bit, accidentally turning the water on. When they were done making out to the muffled sound of music and laughter, they switched shirts and snickered as they made their way back out to the living room. Hazard wore Jesse's button-up shirt. Jesse wore Hazard's Element T-shirt. By the end of the night, Hazard was very drunk, and Jesse's bed was the most comfortable place in the world until he woke up hungover.

Hazard gave one of the Warped Tour tickets to Emery, of course, and then one to Jesse. Lexie bought her own and one for Brianna. Jesse bought one for Felix. Hazard gave his last spare to Emery, who gave it to Russell, and somehow Lily got a ticket too, so they were all going. Hazard was nervous, thinking about just how poorly they might get along.

"Wear *sunglasses*," his mother insisted. "If you wear a cap, it'll attract the sun and you'll have a heat stroke. Wear sunglasses to protect your eyes. Wear sunscreen. Don't get *too* wild. Don't do anything with anyone you don't know, and don't get in anyone's car but the one you came in. Stay close to Emery."

It was warm out. They carried water bottles. There was the vague scent of weed and booze, but nothing they could find going on. People must have used before coming. Warped Tour staff members sprayed the crowds with water guns to prevent overheating. Girls ran around in bathing suits and guys stripped off their shirts.

It turned out the Seattle gang went too. Lexie split off with them at first. Jesse and Felix wandered off with them after a while. Jesse put a hand on Hazard's head and bent down to talk into his ear so he could hear him:

"Let's meet up when Fall Out Boy goes on," Jesse said. "Go have fun with your friends."

Hazard was fine with that. He wanted to remind Jesse that he, Lexie, and Felix were his friends too, but he didn't. Playfully, he hit Jesse's sunglasses off the top of his head and back onto the bridge of his nose. Jesse smirked, following Felix off to find Lexie and Max and the rest of the Seattle gang.

For the first half of the day, it was just Hazard, Emery, Brianna, Lily, and Russell. They wandered around at first, trying to look cool. Atreyu, Remembering Never, The Pink Spiders. They went from stage to stage, hopping around in the back of the crowd and holding their sunglasses or caps so they didn't fall off. Lily and Brianna held hands so they didn't get lost or trip. They saw hellogoodbye and the band Emery, where Emery sang the loudest he could because he and the band shared names. Hazard screamed along too, because he knew the songs and they were good songs and he was really happy Emery was having fun. Russell was a blur of blond hair and crooked cap beside them. When they went to From First to Last, Lily convinced them to make their way through to the front of the mob. They formed a human chain and squeezed in as far forward as they could. They jumped and sang, lost in the roar of the crowd and the song. Brianna tried to crowd surf. She drifted out of sight, and they found her again when the set was over.

Fall Out Boy wasn't on yet. They went to Panic! At the Disco's stage, which was packed. Sweaty and out of breath, they dumped their water bottles over their heads. Russell and Lily were delegated to find some food. During "Lying is the Most Fun," somebody snaked an arm around Hazard's shoulders, and he almost kicked him, then realized it was Jesse.

Emery and Brianna stayed jumping around to the band. Hazard followed Jesse to a relatively empty patch of grass a couple yards from the crowd. They sat down for a minute. Hazard understood why his mom had been worried about heat stroke. It was easy to get overheated even in a Seattle summer, getting worked up and not eating and jumping around in dark colors like they were.

Hazard watched people walk for a minute or two, listening to the bands. Jesse lit a cigarette. Hazard looked over, studying him absently. Jesse's sunglasses were gone. His hair, dark and messy and longish again, was pinned back out of his face and tucked behind his ears, but it was coming loose in a lot of places, sweaty strands around his temple and ears. Hemp and leather on his wrists, glinting silver in his ears and brow, Jesse was wearing jeans and a sleeveless button-up. He'd gotten a little bit of a tan already, maybe from days like the one in early summer when he'd lain out and watched everyone wash his car. He looked good, smooth thin arms and tattoos, red Chucks and sharp chin and straight nose, big green eyes that could be so childish one moment and then cold the next—

"Jesse," Hazard said before he even realized the question was ready to come out.

"What?" Jesse asked, taking a long sip of water while his cigarette smoldered.

"Are you starting college this year?"

Commotion blared away around them, songs and screaming fans and working staff. Hazard didn't hear any of it for a minute. Jesse looked at him sideways, a strange expression lost somewhere between pensive and petulant. He flicked ash from his cigarette, thought twice before taking a drag from it, sighed some smoke, and flicked some more ash absently. He was thinking deeply about something. Hazard could tell.

"Maybe," Jesse said, frowning genuinely. "I'd like to. I haven't got *accepted* yet, if that's what you're asking."

"What college?" Hazard plucked at some blades of grass, pulling them out nervously.

"University of Puget Sound, in Tacoma. Music History." Jesse joined him, picking out pieces of grass quietly. Then he said, "Why?"

Hazard almost couldn't talk. There was a knot in his throat, and it was aching deep down into his chest. Thinking about Jesse going away to school in Tacoma made him both happy and horrified. He liked that Jesse wanted to make something of himself, that he wasn't just some punk-ass teenager. But he didn't like that Jesse would be going so far away, and he didn't like that he wouldn't be able to just skate across town to climb through Jesse's window, and he didn't like that Jesse would be by himself on campus making new friends and going to parties while Hazard would be stuck in Bethany finishing high school alone. No, he wouldn't be *alone*. He'd have Emery and Brianna. But Jesse and everyone else wouldn't be there to keep him cool or keep him safe, and Hazard just didn't know what he'd do. It scared him. It felt cold and empty, and he realized that what he dreaded the most was Jesse starting a new life at college and leaving Hazard in the dust.

"So what happens then?" Hazard asked. It hurt him to say it, deep somewhere in his chest. He watched Jesse smoke his cigarette for a minute. "What happens when you go to Tacoma? We'll have to be just friends, right?"

Jesse looked at him like he was confused. Panic! At the Disco's set ended, and people screamed for an encore. "What are you talking about?" he muttered. "We'll always be friends, Danger."

Hazard didn't even feel like correcting him. He was too worried about Jesse going to college parties and meeting college friends and making out with them and sleeping with them and maybe finding someone he wanted to *date*, so he'd have to call off the benefits thing with poor Hazard back in Bethany.

"You'll get your license soon," Jesse reassured him.

"I need my permit first," Hazard mumbled miserably.

"Okay, whatever. My point is, Tacoma isn't *that* far from Bethany. You can come out on weekends and hang out. Or I could drive back to hang out. It's not like we'll never see each other again. I mean, this is only if I *get accepted*. I haven't yet."

"But what happens to the benefits thing?" Hazard grumbled, plucking anxiously at grass. "I find it hard to believe you of all people aren't going to have a blast at college, away from everyone and on your own—"

"Well, we'll have to figure that out, won't we?" Jesse husked. Hazard glanced at him, frowning. Jesse had a look on his face that said that was the end of that conversation. "Don't worry about it, Hazard," Jesse said, ruffling Hazard's hair. Hazard let him. He couldn't help but worry about it. He couldn't help but remember December and Christmas and anchor a small bit of hope that *we'll have to figure that out* meant something very good.

Jesse's smoke break was done. He chugged some more water. Emery found them, Russell and Lily and Brianna tagging along behind. They found Fall Out Boy's stage and sang along until their throats ached. They wandered past more stages and jumped around to sets, and Hazard stopped worrying about what would happen when Jesse went to school. Laughing with him as they thrashed to some hardcore punk bands made Hazard feel like worrying about losing Jesse was stupid and irrational.

Jesse was nice and gave Russell and Lily rides home, because Emery was staying at Hazard's for the night. Emery ranted and raved about how awesome the day was all the way to Hazard's street. He was a good friend and didn't say a word when Jesse gave Hazard a hug maybe too soft to be between regular friends.

"How was it?" Hazard's mom asked, and Hazard was comforted by how honestly excited she sounded for them. Maybe it was because it was Emery and not *that senior*, but either way she sat in the living room reorganizing her Coco Chanel and smiled brightly as Hazard and Emery told her all the bands they'd seen and how tired they were from dancing.

"I can hear it," she said, looking fondly at Hazard. "Your voice is scratchy already. You boys could have given yourselves concussions head-banging. It was really hot out today. I'm glad you're all right. Go take showers. Your dad's bringing home dinner."

After he'd showered, Hazard's mom wrapped her arms around him and whispered against his forehead, "Happy birthday. I'm glad you had fun." It felt kind of awkward, and Hazard wanted to wriggle out of her grip, but she was being incredibly warm tonight, and he didn't want to ruin it.

THE parties were hot because it was summer. There was nothing to do. Jesse, Felix, Brianna, and Hazard went to Cold Stone and ate ice cream while Lexie worked. They went to the beach and splashed through cold water and spelled their names with rocks in the sand. They went to the mall and wandered around. Hazard stayed up so late that he actually slept in until noon, which he usually could never do. Jesse was accepted to the University of Puget Sound; so was Felix. Emery went with Hazard to take the test for his driving permit.

Jesse's parents flew to New York for a week. Jesse threw a party.

It was a party on the Elite Street, which meant everyone wanted to go even if they hated Jesse Logan Wesley and his whole group of friends. Everyone wanted to say they'd gotten drunk in a house in Redwood Court. The Seattle gang came and brought lots of booze. Jesse made them act like security. If he had a problem with anyone, the boys of the Seattle gang kicked them out.

Sugarcult echoed through the house from the stereo. Some people were outside in the pool. Others were in the games room, playing video games or darts or fooling around on Mrs. Wesley's exercise equipment. There was dancing and casual fun in the living room, people getting high in the upstairs bathroom, and a lot of others just wandering around the house drinking and talking and looking at everything. Jesse locked the doors to his room and his parents' room, just in case.

Hazard made the rounds with Jesse first, bopping around the house to the beat of the music, saying hi to people they knew and people they didn't—Eli, Janelle, Mark, Emily, Liam, the twins with the red hair, and the girl with the butterfly tattoo below her ear. Sometimes people looked at Hazard sideways, and he knew they were thinking something gossipy like *He's Jesse's*, but by the end of his second drink, Hazard didn't care. He laughed with the Seattle gang. He played spin the bottle with people from his classes at school. He danced with Brianna, and he danced with Lexie, and he danced with Jesse a few times. People watched, because Jesse was throwing the party and Hazard was his sidekick.

It was fun. Somebody got pushed into the pool fully clothed. Jeff Morgan could break dance. He demonstrated in the kitchen. The Seattle gang made a wasted cheerleader leave because she was starting arguments with people. The music went from No Doubt to Kanye to Hole, which was Jesse's doing after Lexie touched the stereo. People kept snapping Hazard's bracelets, just for fun. He found a blue sex bracelet on the floor, so he put it on. He was drunk enough. He didn't care. Around ten o'clock, Jesse and Felix did shots of Goldschläger, talking about Ashton. Ashton was giving Felix a hard time lately. Jesse had Hazard try a shot of Goldschläger. It was strong. Hazard almost gagged, but he liked the cinnamon of it. They made strawberry daiquiris afterward and played blackjack for a while. It turned into a huge circle of people in the living room betting pretzels and socks and hair clips on who would win the next round.

By a quarter to midnight, Hazard sat on the island counter of Jesse's kitchen, nursing another Mike's. Jesse came into the living room and changed the CD to Nirvana. Hazard watched him. He waited to meet Jesse's eyes, but Jesse left just as quickly. He was still wandering around the house mingling with people. He was the host, after all. He also had to make sure nobody trashed his house.

"Lounge Act" was playing when Hazard saw Felix and Jesse going to the stairs. Jesse, dark hair in a sloppy ponytail, black button-up, and expensive jeans. Felix, dirty-blond hair in his eyes and The Killers shirt. They stopped a few times to talk to people on their way upstairs. It was when "Something in the Way" started that Hazard slid off the counter and left his Mike's to follow them. He just wanted to be by them. He was tired of sitting alone.

Hazard maneuvered his way past people sitting on the stairs, hand trailing on the banister. There were a few girls at the balustrade overlooking the living room, laughing as they dropped stuff down to see if their boyfriends could catch it all below them. Hazard was distracted by them for just a minute.

He looked off down the hall. He could smell pot from the bathroom. He saw Jesse and Felix down by Jesse's room. Jesse unlocked the door with a snap clip barrette, and they went into his room and closed the door.

Hazard stood at the end of the hall, by the stairs. He stared at the door. He didn't feel anything for a second, and then quite suddenly something painful clenched in his chest and he felt his heart sink far past his stomach. Slowly, he frowned. He blinked, not wanting to believe his worst fear. He started walking down the hall to Jesse's room, to open the door and show himself that there was nothing wrong, but Hazard knew. He knew with a strange quivering intuition that Jesse and Felix had gone to Jesse's room to *be alone.* Hazard knew what happened when two people left a party to *be alone.*

Hazard's fingers shook. Why was he upset? He and Jesse were friends with benefits. Jesse kissed a lot of people, and so did Hazard. Maybe Hazard was assuming things, but Jesse only ever took *Hazard* away during parties to *be alone,* and *that was the problem here.*

There was a swirl of emotion inside him—rage, disgust, the pain of betrayal. What did Jesse take Felix aside for? Why? Hazard felt sick with it all, and it was so overwhelming that he felt numb. That was the worst part. Maybe it was because he was drunk. He wanted to go open Jesse's door, but he couldn't. He wanted to cry. It hurt something deep inside him, especially because Felix had known Jesse longer than Hazard had just like Russell had known Emery longer than Hazard had, and suddenly Hazard was moving but it wasn't down the hall. He had to get out of there. He went down the stairs, stomping past the people sitting on them, and headed for the front door.

He felt very alone. He felt very cold. He felt very afraid and angry, and he didn't know why, and he didn't know what to do. The music was blasting in the living room, lyrics dancing on a riff and swaying everyone through the song after the CD started over:

Our little group has always been and always will until the end.

Once outside Jesse's house, the chaos a muffled roar behind him, Hazard didn't know where he was going. He hadn't brought a change of clothes. He hadn't brought his skateboard. His chest hurt. His fingers twitched in and out of fists. He just walked, down the sidewalk away from Jesse's house, and then he knew where he wanted to go.

He went to Emery's house, in Windsor Green. He'd told his mom he was staying there, anyway.

HAZARD texted Emery to let him know he was coming. Emery's stepdad didn't like to run the air conditioning because he claimed Washington summers were too cool for that, so Emery's window was already open by the time Hazard climbed up on the generator and monkeyed his way to the lowest part of the roof. Hazard almost fell getting through into Emery's room. He sat on Emery's bedroom floor, taking off his shoes and trying his hardest not to cry.

"Haz, what's wrong?" Emery urged, crouching down beside him. He was awake enough, tousled hair and tank top, snap pants undone at the sides and rolled up to his knees so Hazard could see flashes of his Batman boxers. It was kind of stuffy in his room. His fan was on.

"Nothing," Hazard grumbled, kicking off his Converse. He frowned darkly down at his hands, swallowing the sharp ache in his throat. Jesse and Felix, Jesse and Felix—he could feel the tears burning his eyes and the anger cold in his veins. It made him clammy. "Nothing, Em."

"You're drunk." Emery said it as if reminding him, but there was a hint of disapproval in his voice. He helped Hazard up off his floor and pushed him quietly to his bed. "Lay down."

"Don't," Hazard insisted, miserably dizzy and clinging to Emery's shoulders as the room tilted even though he'd lain down. Emery grunted, a little startled. But Emery was warm and he was there, running his fingers through Hazard's hair like a brother and trying to whisper him to sleep, and Hazard needed him because he felt alone.

"What's wrong?" Emery tried again, noticing the way Hazard stared at him in the dark.

"Jesse," Hazard said, simply enough. "I hate him."

Emery sighed as if to say *Great, not again.* He tried to get more comfortable with Hazard in bed next to him, frowning sternly. "He's not very nice to you sometimes."

"Well, you don't have to worry about that anymore," Hazard grumbled, sitting up sharply in the dark. He felt heavy because he was drunk. He felt a little queasy. He scowled, teary-eyed. "I'm done with it. I don't want to think about it. I hate him."

"Lay down," Emery coaxed gently, tugging on Hazard's arm. Hazard looked at him, face softening.

Emery was his best friend. Emery was all that he had and all he needed. Emery looked back at him, worried frown and messy hair and gray tank top, smooth sun-kissed skin, thin mouth with the silver ring at the corner.

Maybe it was the fact that Emery had fought with Russell earlier in the afternoon, or maybe it was because Hazard was drunk and Emery looked good, or maybe it was because Hazard felt lonely and cold and needed to get back at Jesse, and maybe it was all of those things in one. Whatever it was, Hazard leaned down and kissed Emery on the mouth.

Emery stiffened. Hazard's fingers tightened in the bed sheets. After a moment, Emery touched a comforting hand to the back of Hazard's neck, then tilted his head and kissed him back. Hazard didn't know what justified it. He didn't want Emery like this—he didn't even know if Emery was *that way*—but kissing him felt so good right then.

Jesse texted a few times, then called twice, but Hazard didn't pick up because he was kissing Emery. Tangled in Emery's bed, they made out, kicking back blankets and taking breaths between kisses, wet lips and tentative brushes of tongue after their teeth knocked together. It sent off sparks of delight in Hazard's nerves, warm and dangerous. Emery reached up Hazard's shirt and curiously felt around his chest and stomach. Hazard kissed him over and over, feeling Emery's lip ring on his mouth.

After a moment, Hazard reached over and texted Jesse to let him know he'd gone to Emery's.

Emery rolled over on top of him, and they kissed a while longer, hips shifting. Breathlessly, skin flushed. Emery smelled kind of like sunscreen. Hazard's heart thundered in his chest.. He felt very drunk, but Emery's kisses woke him up. They were dangerously tempting. They were kind of boyish and rough, just like the way his body twitched with each one.

And then it was one o'clock in the morning, and Emery stopped. He looked at Hazard like he wanted to talk about it, like he wanted to know why it happened and what it meant, but he didn't say anything. There was something dark in his eyes, not like regret but more like guilt. Hazard smiled at him, hoping to alleviate it. Emery smiled back. He sat up on his elbow and played with Hazard's hair until Hazard fell asleep.

Half an hour later, Emery played with Hazard's hair again as he sat by him in the bathroom. Hazard threw up three times before he felt steady enough to follow Emery back to his bedroom.

"I'm sorry," Hazard croaked miserably.

"It's okay," Emery whispered, helping him back into bed. He didn't sound mad at all.

HAZARD woke up with a horrible headache. He also woke up to the sweet smell of sunscreen and skin around him, face shoved in Emery's pillow. Emery's bed was empty.

Hazard waited for him, sitting against his wall with his eyes closed and feeling the headache pulse in his temples. He couldn't get up and go downstairs. Emery's stepdad would be there, and they didn't know Hazard was in Emery's bedroom. Emery's mom probably wouldn't mind, but Andrew would.

It took twenty minutes, but Emery did come back upstairs. He brought some water and painkillers with him.

"Do you want toast?" he asked, brow knotted.

Hazard shook his head, taking the Excedrin and pressing his face to the cool plaster of Emery's bedroom wall.

"Do you wanna borrow some clothes?" Emery asked next, opening his closet. "Just pick whatever. I don't care."

Hazard wondered if Emery thought he didn't remember that they'd made out the night before. Hazard watched him as he chewed his lip ring and went through his closet, holding out shirts he thought Hazard might like. Hazard almost told him he remembered it all, but he bit his tongue and decided against it. If Emery didn't want to talk about it, they wouldn't.

"Drive me to Jesse's?" Hazard asked, feeling very tiny and pathetic with the way Emery looked at him so darkly, reproving because he'd mentioned Jesse. But Emery didn't ask. He just shrugged, then nodded in agreement.

It was just after noon when Emery pulled up outside the big house in Redwood Court. "Don't wait for me," Hazard said.

"Are you sure?" Emery asked, frowning.

"It's all right," Hazard promised.

Emery left as Hazard tried the front door. It was unlocked. He went in immediately, closing it behind him. The house smelled vaguely of cigarette smoke and alcohol. A large amount of empty bottles were stacked in a little cardboard box at the end of the island counter. A trash bag full to bursting sat next to it. Everything was still slightly askew, not yet cleaned up all the way. Jesse's parents wouldn't be back until mid-Monday. It was unsettlingly quiet.

Hazard went upstairs to Jesse's bedroom, steeling himself all the way. He heard the TV on in Jesse's room. He was watching *Foster's Home for Imaginary Friends*. Hazard's resolve faltered just a little when he stopped in the hallway outside Jesse's open bedroom to watch him slip into some loose Levi's. Jesse had just gotten out of the shower. His hair was still wet. Hazard watched all his tattoos dance on smooth skin, and he wanted to just give up on all this injured anger and make up with Jesse right away so they could sit down and laugh and watch TV together.

But he couldn't. It hurt too much. Jesse looked at him, buttoning his jeans. He looked pretty hungover still. He didn't even act surprised. He'd probably heard Hazard walking all the way through the house.

"Don't you knock, Danger?"

"The door was unlocked. Call me by my name, Jesse. *Hazard*."

"I left it unlocked, *Hazard*. I figured you'd be coming over. We need to talk. Where'd you go last night? I was worried."

"I left."

"Why?"

"Jesse, you went to *your room* with Felix."

"Yeah. We need to talk."

Hazard flinched. Any part of him that had wanted to calmly talk it all out withered away in a new spark of fury. Jesse didn't seem remorseful in the least. He didn't even deny going to his room with Felix. He knew he had and the implications it held, and he was hardly sorry.

We need to talk. Wasn't that the notorious line of *breaking up*?

Hazard felt sick. "Yeah, we really do need to talk."

"We're friends with benefits, Hazard. Don't act like I cheated."

Hazard bristled. His heart sank sickeningly. Jesse had a point, as horrible as it was, and it shut him up. It *hurt*. Hazard thought about Christmas, talking in Max's bedroom about love and other simple truths like that. He gawked at Jesse, feeling the fear on his face. Jesse stared back. He looked like he wasn't quite sure of himself either, which made the hurt worse because Hazard could read him like a book. Jesse was being stubborn. He was pushing Hazard away on purpose, and Hazard didn't know why.

Hazard stood up straight, feeling the cold vindictive frown as it crossed his face. "I fucked Emery," he said.

Jesse stared. He looked completely shocked for a second, arms sagging away from his chest. Then he leaned forward like his hearing was poor. "*What?*" he said curtly.

Hazard swallowed. He was lying. He wanted to talk it out. He wanted it to be okay. He wanted to forgive Jesse, but he couldn't let himself. He was too mad. He just wanted to hurt Jesse like he'd hurt him. "Last night, I saw you and Felix go to your room. I got pissed. I left. I'm not yours, Jesse. I went to Emery's and—"

Jesse pointed out into the hallway. "Get out of my house," he edged out.

Hazard's heart fell. "If you wanna get technical, though, Emery fucked *me*."

"I told you to get out of my house." Jesse's growing fury was evident on his face and in the way his shoulders jerked. He gritted his teeth, jabbing his finger at the hall.

Hazard felt sick with adrenaline. He scowled. He couldn't stop the lies from bleeding out, even if he was just speaking them to hit any sore spot he could. "It was kind of awkward. He's not experienced like you. He doesn't know how to move—"

"*Hazard, shut up!*" Jesse was across the room in a flash. Hazard stumbled backward, away from that pointing finger. Jesse was breathing hard, face twisted in anger. Hazard was scared. He was scared and upset, and he wanted to remind Jesse that it wasn't *cheating* because they were just friends in the end, anyway. Then he wanted to apologize and come clean for his lies, but he was wrong and he knew it and he didn't want to face it.

"You said we need to talk," Hazard said. Blue clashed with green as he met Jesse's eyes, shaking. "So I'm talking."

"I'm gonna be with Felix."

Jesse said it so quickly and casually that Hazard thought he was just trying to get back at him, another lie for a lie. Hazard hoped that was what it was. He opened his mouth, but no words came out. Jesse stared at him, as if challenging him to doubt. Hazard was dumbfounded, and then it hit him with painful clarity.

Jesse wanted to *be with* Felix. He wanted to start a relationship with him. He wanted to drop his bad habit for a permanent routine, and *that hurt*. It *wasn't fair*.

Hazard backed up into the hall. He stood against the wall beside a walnut stand with a rococo-like figurine on it and stared at Jesse. He was in utter disbelief. He didn't want to believe it. Something in him longed for Jesse to be lying, to be playing the same dirty game of arguments: hit below the belt. Hazard felt discarded. He felt like puking. His heart hammered. His chest ached. Who was really wrong here?

Jesse stared at him with a deep injured look on his face. He knew exactly what Hazard had done. "You went to Emery's to get back at me," Jesse guessed wearily. Hazard remembered Jesse in Max's room over Christmas and realized he'd already incriminated himself. Jesse knew how much Emery meant to him.

Hazard's eyes widened as he realized the depth of that. He felt the ugliness of it as if it was the first time he'd heard the idea. "I *lied!*" Hazard sputtered, feeling the tears welling in his eyes. His voice shook. He hated that it cracked and wavered. Crying was stupid and pathetic and meant that he cared. "I lied, okay? I didn't *do* anything with him. We just made out—"

"*Jesus Christ, Hazard!*" Jesse roared. He hit his door, so angry. Hazard uttered a tiny sound of surprise, breaking down. His vision doubled, then trebled with tears. What was the sudden crime? They were friends with benefits, so why did it hurt so bad? Because maybe, possibly, it was something curious like betrayal? Was it because Felix was not a stranger, Felix was one of Jesse's best friends, just like Emery was to

Hazard? Was it because just because nobody had the guts to put certain feelings into words, it didn't mean that those certain feelings weren't there and weren't true?

"I'm gonna be with him," Jesse insisted below his breath, sounding so apologetic that it was unsettling. He sounded as if he still had to convince himself. "So we're going to have to end it, Hazard. We can still be friends, though. Just not *beneficial* friends."

Hazard thought about when they all went to the Warped Tour. He thought about what Jesse had said, about going to school in Tacoma, about nothing changing what they had. Hazard laughed cruelly. He did on purpose. He wiped the tears from his eyes, but more came, and he grinned at Jesse angrily. "You, with Felix. Do you know what people will say about you now?"

"Do you know what people say about *you*?" Jesse hissed.

Hazard's breath caught in his throat. Jesse hit below the belt again, intentionally. Hazard glared at him from across the hall. "I can't believe you. Fuck you."

Jesse scoffed, so coldly that Hazard remembered the day in the cafeteria that they'd met. "Look, if you like me more than a friend or whatever, I can't do anything about it. I can't be in something so serious when you never know what you want anyway—"

Hazard didn't listen. He turned and stormed down the hall, heading for the stairs. Jesse followed him. His footsteps were heavy.

"Hazard, *wait*."

Hazard's breath quickened, bringing his voice with it in desperate little sounds. He felt like he was going to get sick. He wanted to scream. His hands shook. He was overcome by the weight of betrayal and pain and confusion, and it was suffocating him, crushing him. Hadn't Jesse been happy? Had Hazard missed all the signs of him getting bored or moving on? Was he that stupid? Felix had been accepted at the university in Tacoma too, and they'd be together all the time. How great! They'd probably planned it that way. The two of them and nobody else and the whole college scene to explore—

Jesse grabbed him by the wrist before he reached the stairs. He twisted Hazard around and pushed him to the wall. Hazard scowled up at him. Maybe there was something like panic in Jesse's eyes, but Hazard didn't care. Jesse was ending everything, so he didn't deserve pity or patience or anything like that. He was ending it all to be with *Felix*. He was throwing it all away without even considering the way Hazard felt, and it just *hurt*.

"*What?*" Hazard yelled. "What's wrong? You have more to say? Do you wanna tell me how annoying I am, how I was a waste of time, how horrible I am in bed, how I'm a little fag, how I'm nothing but a burden, how you've been fucking around with Felix or someone else the entire time and didn't tell me? Which, by the way, I wouldn't care about, seeing as we were never *together*, we just had a benefits thing going on, but a *real friend* wouldn't have kept it all a secret!"

"Shut up, for Christ's sake, Hazard!" Jesse's hand tightened, hot on Hazard's arm. Even though it was vicious, Hazard liked the fact that it was there. Jesse's eyes narrowed. His jaw tightened as he seethed, "If you *shut the fuck up* for just a second or two, just breathe for a minute, just calm down, we can go out—and I'll buy you a coffee or something—and we can talk about this, I don't know, calmly and shit. You're right. You're right, okay? About being a real friend. Because that's what you are, you're my friend, even though you're being really awful right now—"

Hazard jerked out of Jesse's grip. The tears came again. Maybe some of them fell. His throat hurt from yelling and trying to stifle the emotion. "Don't try to cover your ass, Jesse. I know you don't mean any of that. If you did, you wouldn't have told me to get out of your house—which I'm trying to do if you'd just leave me alone!"

"Fine." Jesse threw his hands up, scowling. Back in his bedroom, his cell phone started to ring. He ignored it. "Fine, Hazard. Go. I'm not keeping you. When you calm down, maybe I'll still feel like talking this out with you, but I don't know. You'll just have to see."

Hazard wondered who was calling him. He shrugged roughly, glaring at his feet. He didn't want to leave. He wanted to go with Jesse to talk it out, because if Jesse was willing to, maybe it wasn't over yet.

"Good luck with your new fuck buddy." Hazard glowered up at Jesse, shaking. He hated himself for saying it. He wanted to bite his tongue, but he just couldn't stop himself. He felt on the verge of hysteria now. "But I wouldn't expect too much if I were you. Look around, Jesse. Your house is empty. Your parents don't love you. Your friends don't love you. I'm the closest thing you had to a relationship lately, and I don't care about you at all. Nobody *wants* to love you, so why are you even going to try?"

Jesse stared at him in absolute shock. His eyes were big and green and empty. He looked childish for a minute, then slowly grew cold with a frightening shadow of pain and guilt. He looked calm, dangerously calm, and Hazard immediately regretted his words. He gawked up at Jesse, horrified at himself, because he'd just exploited Jesse's secret.

Jesse Logan Wesley had everything, but he also had nothing.

It was just a short instant of silence, and Hazard didn't expect it in the least when Jesse hit him. There was an explosion of heat on the side of his face, something between a slap and a punch. Hazard lost his balance. He stumbled down against the wall, then out of instinct shot back up and shoved Jesse backward.

There was a brief scuffle between them. Hazard's ear rang. The place where Jesse hit him stung and itched. His chest was tight. Jesse was stronger. He wrestled Hazard back against the wall and seethed, "You're one to talk, you fucking crybaby! Isn't that why you cling to me? Nobody else cares about you either. Nobody's ever home, Emery likes Russell more—"

Hazard jerked out of Jesse's grip and pounded down the stairs. He stopped at the foot of them, staring up at Jesse in shock and betrayal. There was another silence that lasted only a few moments but felt like eternities. It was volatile and heavy.

Jesse looked down at him apathetically. He'd hit him, and he didn't seem to care in the least. He still didn't have a shirt on. He looked well aware of his lack of remorse and compassion, and it wasn't Jesse, it wasn't Jesse at all. Hazard believed that, but he was still horrified—at Jesse, and at himself.

Jesse seemed to calculate him for a moment. Chest heaving with his breath, he husked, "You're a little slut, Hazard. As a *friend*, I'm telling you that. Get out of my house, okay?"

The words pierced Hazard directly in the heart. His head spun. He trembled. He stared up at Jesse, eyes wide and empty, and he thought— how could someone hate someone else so much that they'd even say something like that to them?

He waited for Jesse's face to change, for the coldness to fade—but it didn't. Hazard looked away. Jesse watched him silently, arms crossed and waiting patiently for him to go. Hazard left the stairs and moved across the living room. The hush was deafening. He left, closing the front door quietly behind him.

It was over.

What was over?

Hazard walked. He walked, feeling dazed and sick. His throat ached. He'd bitten his cheek on the inside when Jesse hit him, and it was sore. He wanted to cry. He blinked the tears away easily enough, but they kept coming back. He opened and closed his phone a few times, not knowing who to call or why.

He walked to the 7-Eleven on Berkeley. He stood at the side of it, looking at the vandalized wall that said *we all collide*.

Hazard sat down on the sidewalk and looked at all the writing. The summer sun beat down on his back. The warmth felt good because he was shivering. He wondered who had written that *we all collide*. He wondered why. He wondered if they had ever imagined that their simple vandalism would influence someone's life so profoundly.

Olivia, Tom, Russell, Jesse, Emery, all those other frivolous moments at parties that Hazard could barely count. What had he become? He felt like he didn't know himself anymore. Was he really a slut? What made someone a slut? He knew people called him that sometimes. Even though the word was usually reserved for girls, he'd heard it. And now Jesse had said it, but maybe just to hurt him.

We all collide, the graffiti said.

They'd all collided, most definitely. Hazard knew it. He'd collided with Olivia and Tom. He'd collided with other people, random, insignificant people at parties who had collided with him too, with drinks in hand and worries on the back burner. People like Russell Leroy, or Liam, or Amy, or Alex, people who just wanted to forget about the world for a while.

He'd collided with Jesse, and in turn Jesse had collided with him. Hazard loved Jesse as a person. He also hated Jesse as a person sometimes. Something flourished between them, but they repelled each other. Their collision didn't link them together. It shot them apart, like the first law of motion: *An object at rest tends to stay at rest and an object in motion tends to stay in motion with the same speed and in the same direction unless acted upon by an unbalanced force.*

Felix was an unbalanced force, and he changed the directions of both Jesse and Hazard. Was Hazard supposed to hate Felix? He wasn't sure. He just hated everything then, hunched on the sidewalk and feeling very lost.

He'd collided with Emery too. Emery was his best friend, but curiosity killed the cat. Hadn't he learned that by now?

Hazard's head hurt. His cheek hurt where Jesse had hit him. His heart hurt too. He felt the same cold scary ache that he'd felt a few times before, when he'd been afraid he and Jesse were going to call things off. He'd felt it that December night, sitting on Jesse's porch. It was just a little more painful than the hot swell in his chest he'd felt in Max's room, talking about stupid things like love and what it meant. It felt like his chest had been ripped open.

There was really nothing very special about him, so how had he managed so many screw-ups?

He had to pull it together. He didn't want it to be over. Jesse had just said all those things to hurt him, the same as Hazard did. They could talk this out. This was just all their denial blowing up in their faces, after all. Maybe this was just a turning point in their friendship or something, an obstacle they had to get through together. But Hazard was afraid to know what that meant, and he was *furious* with Jesse for everything, especially for calling him a slut. Guys weren't sluts. Girls were sluts.

Hazard couldn't think about it anymore. It hurt too much, even thinking about it positively. He had a sudden desire to be by Emery. Just to have Emery there to distract him would be so much comfort. Hazard wanted to cry again, feeling suffocated by all the pressure in his chest, but he also felt strangely empty, like a substantial weight had been lifted from his shoulders. It made him feel disconnected from the world, insignificant and ready to float away at any moment. After all, he wasn't that special anyway.

"WE USED to be so close," Emery said, watching ants march by in the crack of the sidewalk.

Hazard looked at him, brow knotted. "I like to think we still are," he mumbled. He passed the bag of ice back and forth from hand to hand. Emery had insisted he ice his face when he saw the mark Jesse's hand had left, a tiny little bloom of black and blue. It was hardly noticeable, Hazard thought, but it shocked Emery. They told Emery's mom he'd run into a door, which was typical and stupid, but she believed it.

"I hope we are," Emery said decidedly. He sat up straight again, looking at Hazard. The sun was setting. In the shadow of the summer evening, the darkness in Emery's eyes was obvious. He played with his lip ring, in deep thought. Behind them in the house, the sound of his mom loading up the dishwasher echoed through the open windows. Two little girls were riding scooters with their dolls around Emery's cul-de-sac while their mom watched from their porch.

"A lot has happened since high school started," Emery murmured.

"Yeah." Hazard leaned down over his knees to toy with the laces of his shoes. He held the ice to his face again with the other hand. Emery's words made him feel guilty all over again, a sick, rotten, horrible guilt.

"It happens." Emery shrugged, brow dimpled in a sincere frown. "Best friends drift apart. There's just a point where we all grow up and we're not the same anymore."

"That's not happening to us," Hazard said honestly.

Emery smiled faintly, like he was embarrassed to look relieved. "I know. I just…. You started dating Jesse, and I thought you weren't going to be my friend anymore."

Hazard's stomach soured, but he was feeling pretty numb about it all by then. He took a deep breath, bracing himself. "I wasn't *dating* him, Em. I told you that."

Emery looked at him quietly for a minute. He seemed to think everything over again, watching him. Hazard fidgeted under his stare.

"Let's talk more later," Hazard mumbled, glancing up at the little girls screaming and riding around the cul-de-sac. They were riding ever closer to where Emery and Hazard sat on the curb by his mailbox.

Emery laughed. "I was just thinking that too." He waved at the girls. They waved back, then rode their scooters over to show Emery and Hazard their baby dolls and all the teeth the tooth fairy had taken from them.

IT WAS nine o'clock at night. In the living room, Emery's mom and stepdad were watching a movie. Upstairs, Emery sat cross-legged near his pillow and Hazard sat across from him at the foot of the bed. The room was dark except for the slithering shadows Emery's lava lamp cast.

"I've had a really, really bad day," Hazard husked.

Emery watched him. The dim light lit up his face, and his eyes shone clear in the dark. Hazard felt him looking at the bruise on his cheek. "What happened?"

Hazard shrugged. How did he explain the argument he'd had with Jesse, or the fact that he told Jesse *I think I love you* a few months ago, or that he'd fucked all of that up and Jesse didn't want him anymore? How did he tell Emery that, and then everything else?

You're a slut.

Hazard picked at the hem of his shirt. It was Emery's. He'd borrowed it earlier. "Emery, it's hard to talk about."

"You'll feel better when you tell me."

Hazard knew this was true. Emery knew that he knew. He swallowed around the lump in his throat. "You wanna hear from the beginning?" Hazard murmured, voice paper-thin.

Emery nodded. The way he looked at Hazard relaxed him. He just had a feel of openness about him, and it made Hazard want to talk. Hazard hung his head. He cleared his throat. He was talking before he realized he'd known where to start.

He reminded Emery about all the afternoons he'd spent with Olivia two years ago, where his curiosity always got the better of him and he snuck peeks of her not-so-girly slants and angles, the afternoons that had eventually led up to that weekend his parents were out of town. He reminded Emery of that, and then he told him what he'd never told him before. He talked about that summer night with Tom, out under the freeway at the old high schoolers' hangout. He told Emery about the way it felt like a movie because he still didn't know why they'd kissed. They just had, and it had been fun.

Hazard glanced up at Emery, wondering what he thought of this. Emery didn't say anything. He gestured kindly for Hazard to go on.

It felt so good to just talk about it, even if he was scared to admit it all. Hazard told Emery about how everything was fine then, until high school started. Hazard explained how he was jealous because of Russell and how much Emery looked up to him. And everything was still fine then, until he met Jesse and went to his first party, and made out with Russell later to try and piss Emery off. Hazard insisted that he didn't know what had come over him, but it had been wrong and he knew that and he was still so, so sorry. Emery *had* to have something to say to that. Hazard looked up.

Emery regarded him through his lashes, still silent.

Hazard took a deep, deep breath. He told Emery about hanging out with Jesse because he wanted Emery to be jealous. He conveniently left out the fact that he liked being with Jesse. He swallowed hard and told Emery about how he danced and flirted with other people as well as Jesse, and that sometimes he kissed them but mostly he kissed Jesse.

"You're probably sick of hearing about all that, though," Hazard mumbled miserably down at his feet, thinking about gossip and how much Emery already distrusted Jesse. The bruise on Hazard's face probably made that worse.

"Not really," Emery whispered. "Besides, this is the truth."

Hazard admitted that he'd started staying over at Jesse's and they decided they'd be friends with benefits. He almost couldn't talk for a minute. He told Emery that the parties continued and the benefits thing continued, and then somehow that summer after ninth grade everything changed. He didn't specify that things changed most drastically in the way he didn't need Emery anymore, but instead Hazard explained that the parties got harder and things between him and Jesse got more serious, and just last night Jesse had thrown a party and it had been great, but then Felix—and then he'd come to Emery's house—and—

Hazard couldn't talk anymore. He was crying. He tried his hardest not to, but he couldn't hold it in any longer. He felt alone and discarded, unworthy even for Emery to understand. He still felt that rotten guilt pooling in his gut, that horrible *ache* in his chest when he thought about Jesse and the forty-eight hours that had just passed.

Hazard crumpled forward and choked on a breath. Tears overflowed, running down his cheeks as he gripped at Emery's blankets with shaking fingers.

Emery jumped, eyes widening. He put his arms around Hazard's shoulders and didn't care if it was a manly thing to do or not. Hazard loved him for it, because pride sure as hell wasn't in his way, either. He sobbed as quietly as he could. Emery let him lean on him.

"I'm sorry you were jealous," Emery mumbled. He sounded anguished. "I know I ignored you a lot in the beginning of ninth grade. I'm sorry. I told you before, though, no matter what, I've got your back—"

Hazard took a long breath, trying to stop crying like an idiot. He loved Emery for his heartfelt words, but he couldn't say anything. Emery didn't get it. He didn't understand how lonely Hazard felt. Emery just didn't get that he was all Hazard had and ever would have, now that Jesse hated him too. Emery was what Hazard thought of when he imagined a life without problems. Emery, coming over after school, sitting on the roof outside the window, playing video games or anything else that wasn't important because what mattered was that Emery was there and Hazard was not alone. But sitting in Emery's room in the dancing shadows of his lava lamp, Hazard felt like he was losing Emery too. Something was shifting. Something was going to happen.

Things had changed.

Hazard didn't want to accept that, but it was true. Things had definitely changed. Hazard was dumbfounded. He stared at Emery, afraid. He really wasn't sure anymore what Emery was to him. The whole reason Hazard had even talked to Jesse had been to make Emery mad, but that plan had failed from the start because, there at the end of it, Hazard was okay with Emery and Russell, and Hazard ached for Jesse more than he ached for Emery right then.

Hazard swallowed. He was scared. This wasn't how it was supposed to be. This wasn't how it had been. When had it changed? When had he no longer felt the need to have Emery around him? Why didn't it matter to him anymore?

"It'll be okay." Emery shifted. "Hazard, it'll be all right."

"Maybe," Hazard whispered. He felt numb again. He didn't care. He didn't fight it.

They watched TV until early in the morning. Hazard pretended to be okay again so Emery would feel better. He didn't know if Emery truly believed he was okay or not. He didn't worry about it.

When Emery was asleep, Hazard went through his bag and made sure he'd packed everything he needed. Clothes, toothbrush, his favorite books, his cell phone charger. Emery's mom's laptop sat on the bedroom floor. Emery had borrowed it earlier. Hazard got on it as quietly as he could to check the ferry schedules.

He changed back into his own clothes and put on his shoes and backpack. He stood by Emery and watched him sleep. Dawn was creeping in through the blinds, pale and gray.

It was all okay. Emery had Russell. He had Russell and Lily, and he was doing okay. Jesse was okay too. He had Felix and school in Tacoma, and he still had Lexie and Brianna, after all. Hazard's mom had his dad and all her friends. Everyone had somebody, but Hazard felt very, very alone and forgotten.

Hazard snuck out through the window and down onto the generator. He took the bus from the entrance of Windsor Green to the ferry dock. He called his uncle when he got there and told him he was coming to Seattle.

In Seattle, his aunt and uncle didn't know he'd run away until Hazard told them. They were horrified. They scolded him, then called his parents and came to middle ground a lot faster than Hazard was comforted by. Hazard would be staying with them in Seattle for a while to *shape up*, which were his mother's hopes.

Hazard and his uncle drove back for the rest of his stuff later.

Chapter 14
Seattle

WHEN Hazard first moved in with his aunt and uncle, his cousin Zoe was really quiet. He remembered her being louder and more annoying, but now she wore lots of black and spoke so politely and softly that it was almost unsettling. Sometimes she would stare, as if looking right into his soul. She stared at him a lot at first, like she was observing him, like he was a spectacle: her cousin, the bad kid who ran away from home, the son her aunt said had given her so much trouble maybe some time away from home would straighten him out. Hazard didn't like being stared at like he was a delinquent or some kind of show.

His cousin Zoe had huge ice-blue eyes like his and white-blonde hair. Her face was kind of narrow and sharp, but in an intelligent way. She was two years younger than him. She was going to be a freshman, and Hazard was a junior.

Hazard moved in with them just a few weeks before school started. Mostly he stayed inside the house, slumped on the couch, watching TV or watching out the window as everyone moved in the University District hurry. He was horrified he'd run into someone from the Seattle gang at the grocery store. It never happened. He surfed the Internet on his uncle's desktop computer. He found out a lot of the shows Olivia and he used to watch at night were also comic books, so he read some of them online. Sometimes he played Zoe's Sims game.

He arranged his new room in his uncle's big expensive brick house and lay curled up on his bed listening to sad music. He found October Fall's song called "If We're All Alone Aren't We In This Together?" and immediately decided that if any song was the song for him and Jesse, it wasn't Fall Out Boy or Taking Back Sunday or Three Days Grace, or any of the others that made him think of them. It was that plaintive October Fall song. He played it over and over and stared at the ceiling and kept his phone across the room so he wouldn't cave in and call anybody from Bethany, no matter how much it hurt. He had to forget. He had to start over. In the real weight of things, the last two years were small and insignificant. There were bigger and better things that would happen to him, right?

His uncle took him back to Bethany to get some of his things. He stayed in the car while Hazard ran inside. His mom said "Hello, again" coldly and went outside to talk to her brother. She gave Hazard a kiss before he left, but she wouldn't look him in the eyes.

Hazard grabbed all the most important things from his room and put them in a cardboard box: books he wanted to read, clothes, his reading glasses, skateboard, CDs, his pillow, his stuffed alligator. He couldn't touch the pictures he kept in his desk drawer. Pictures of him and Emery, pictures of him and Jesse, and Felix and Lexie and Brianna and Tom and Olivia and Peyton. He left the pictures there and promised himself he'd delete any pictures on his phone, but he couldn't bring himself to do that either. He couldn't even bring himself to take off his jelly *sex bracelets*.

Hazard did manage to ignore his MySpace a lot. Emery messaged him once, making sure he was safe somewhere. Hazard promised he was, and after that nobody tried to contact him. Hazard was thankful. Eventually, after he met Drew and Oliver and Zack and everyone else, he made a second MySpace that was pretty much a copy of his first, but it didn't have the same friends on it, so it was like starting with a clean slate.

At his aunt and uncle's, Hazard helped with chores. He helped with dinner. His aunt and uncle didn't ask him to talk about things; they just let him adjust. His aunt was sweet and kind of klutzy, which meant there was always a lot of laughter. His uncle was just as friendly, which meant it was always comfortable. Zoe stared.

Sometimes Hazard sat and scribbled stuff out onto a steno pad, just thoughts and random ideas that marqueed through his head. Sometimes he drew, sketching stuff that his aunt and uncle smiled at, but Hazard had a feeling they thought he needed counseling. He couldn't help it, though. When he picked up the pencil, he just drew stuff like people colliding together in an explosion of pencil marks, or leaning off rooftops about to fall, or more gothic images like dead trees with clocks hanging from them and people hung on crosses with stakes through their hearts, not their hands. He remembered his mom asking him to draw angels like Michelangelo. He wasn't trying to be creepy. He wasn't trying to get attention. Those were just the things he liked to draw, like the dark poems he jotted down.

Maybe that was why Zoe stared at him those first few weeks. Maybe, unintentionally, Hazard *made* a spectacle of himself. He didn't try to. He just felt *numb*. Creative and sad and angry, but numb. Numb like he'd slapped something over the wound and was ignoring it but hadn't actually mended it and appeased it and worked all the pain out just yet.

"You're *not* going to do this once school starts," Hazard informed Zoe one night. She stared at him with those soulful eyes for a long, long moment. Then she shrugged and went back to the book she was reading.

But Zoe obeyed. She kept her distance at school, and although Hazard was wary of her presence, he found that she wasn't as quiet and creepy with her friends as she was with him. At school, she was totally different. She was scholarly and ambitious and outgoing.

When he introduced himself to people, he intentionally left out the fact that he was Zoe's cousin, but they all knew because Zoe openly told everyone. That was okay. Hazard was fine with that after a while, as long as she didn't start telling people he was weird, or troubled, or a runaway or something.

High school in Seattle was a lot different from high school in Bethany. Roosevelt High was much bigger. Hazard got lost a few times and hid out in the bathroom once or twice, skipping math class at first because he didn't know where the room was and he didn't want to ask.

He didn't understand why people talked to him when he didn't talk back, but they just kept it up, so Hazard shrugged and nodded and picked at the eraser of his pencil. He drifted along, scribbling and sketching his thoughts and rolling his eyes when his aunt and uncle tried to pamper him for fear of him being emotionally unstable. Some nights he cried, face shoved in his pillow. Some nights he *almost* called Emery, and then *almost* called Jesse, and then shoved his face back in his pillow and cried some more, because some nights it felt like someone reached down his throat and ripped his heart out from there, and some nights he felt so blank and bored and okay that he worried himself too.

Hazard met Drew one afternoon when he was skipping math class in the bathroom. He'd just settled into the back stall with a book and his feet pulled up off the floor so nobody would see him when someone knocked on the stall door and asked him what his name was. Hazard was horrified it was a teacher, but the voice was far too young, and Hazard couldn't talk for a moment but finally mumbled:

"Hazard. Who's asking?"

"*Hazard*, like *choking hazard*?" the boy outside the bathroom stall asked. Hazard could see his shins and his shoes. He was wearing black jeans and gray Converse. Hazard fidgeted, dropping his feet down to touch the floor again from where he sat on the tank of the toilet.

"No, like the Old French for 'chance' or 'luck'," Hazard explained, unlocking the bathroom stall. He opened it up to Drew, whom he recognized from his history class. They stared at each other for a minute, Drew looking just short of St. Jimmy and Hazard awkwardly holding the bathroom stall in one hand and a book in the other. Hazard's heart fluttered excitedly, because he felt like he might be making a friend or something, but he also felt sick and guilty with it. He tried to ignore that part.

"What are you cutting?" Drew asked.

"Math," Hazard whispered.

"Let me guess," Drew said, opening the bathroom stall door a little more so Hazard could get his things and walk out, "it's Mr. Cassidy's class. His room is a pain in the ass to find, and he's a pain in the ass to deal with sometimes."

Hazard nodded dumbly, wondering how Drew knew that. Drew helped him find Mr. Cassidy's class, and that was it. He and Hazard didn't really talk to each other yet. When one of them came into history class, the other waved, and now and again they exchanged glances when the brainiac Isis Marshall answered every question for everyone, but they didn't start really talking until they were learning about yellow fever, in October. Drew was kind of quiet too, but he had the same humor as Hazard, so they got along right away.

Hazard felt kind of guilty for it, like he wasn't supposed to like anyone else. But he had to forget Bethany and everyone there, so he tried. He was fed up with being alone. He was scared of it. He tried to talk to other people in other classes too, which made school a little easier.

When Halloween came around, Hazard asked Zoe if she was going to go to her friend's house and contact spirits with a Ouija board or perform a séance or something. They were in the media room, and Zoe turned from her homework, nailing him with a glare. She said, "No, but you're free to join us on our midnight picnic in the graveyard. We'll be dining atop the grave of Cheryl Devereaux, an infamous mistress who was into Satanic rituals and killed her husband for his insurance benefits, who people say has been spotted now and again around the cemetery."

Hazard stared at her over his shoulder. He tried to decide whether or not she was serious, brow furrowing.

"I'm just teasing," he mumbled, going through the video games again: *Castlevania, Metal Gear Solid, Silent Hill 4, Dirge of Cerberus, Grand Theft Auto*. His aunt and uncle had everything.

"That's okay. So am I," Zoe said and smiled at him.

"It's Halloween." Hazard pulled out *Fable* and turned the Xbox on. "Aren't you going to go do something?"

"Mom and Dad said they'd take care of trick-or-treaters for a while," Zoe said. Hazard stared at her. She put down her pen, face pinched in confusion. "What, you mean *go* trick-or-treating? Why?"

Hazard frowned over his shoulder at her. "I went trick-or-treating when I was your age."

"All the kids my age want to go trick-or-treating just to egg people's houses," she said.

Hazard turned around more, scowling. "Why do you think I'm such a corrupted youth?" he demanded.

Zoe studied him with such surprise in her eyes that it even confused Hazard for a moment. "I don't," Zoe said, a concerned frown slowly crossing her face. "Do I seem like I think that?"

"All you do is stare at me," Hazard grumbled, fumbling with the cord of the controller. "Like you're scared of me or something."

"Mom said that Aunt Laura said—"

"That I gave her trouble, right." Hazard frowned tersely. He gestured in Zoe's direction with the game controller. The opening screen of the game flashed on the wide TV. "But what *you* don't know, Zoe, is that *she* gave me more trouble than I ever gave her."

"Trust me, Mom and Dad don't really believe her. Uncle Brian even said that she's probably overreacting, but he also said that he doesn't know what you've been doing lately so he can't say for sure. Just that you and your mom were fighting a lot and she says you've been disrespectful and ungrateful."

Hazard frowned down at his bitten nails and the game controller. His dad defended him, but it still made him mad that his mom's words hurt so much, because he *hadn't* been disrespectful or ungrateful. "I'm sixteen," he mumbled. "What do they want from me?"

Zoe looked at him silently, another one of her deep and probing stares. Hazard let her stare for a while before glancing up to meet her eyes darkly. It was like she was waiting for him to fess up to something, asking without asking. Maybe that was why she always stared at him, because she was waiting for him to open up. Hazard sighed. He ran a hand through his hair. He guessed now was better than ever to start talking. He was tired of keeping it to himself, anyway.

"I partied a lot," he confessed, shrugging. "And drank a lot. But my mom didn't really *know* about all that. I did it secretly. She just nagged at me nonstop."

Zoe didn't say anything, but there was something totally open in her face that just prompted Hazard to talk. It was like the words were alive and needed to be spoken or they'd rot inside him. A lump formed in his throat, and he dropped his gaze, watching his thumbs wiggle the game controller's joysticks to and fro.

"She didn't like one of my older friends." Hazard glanced at Zoe. "Not Emery. She loved Emery. No, he was…. Okay, is there a kid at school who's like, really popular, but on a completely opposite side of the spectrum from say, Brad Reynolds? Like, you would *never* see him at a football game unless he was there to pull a prank, but he's still one of the coolest kids. Is there anyone here at school like that? I don't really know everyone yet…."

Zoe nodded. "Connor Schmidt."

Hazard shrugged limply. "Well, yeah. He was—one of my best friends. We met when I was in ninth grade, and I started going to parties with him. He ruled that scene, Zoe. He was the king. He was on top of his world, I swear. And I guess we were kind of like a boxed set. We were untouchable. My mom didn't like him, so we fought a lot. She'd say, '*That junior!*'" Hazard screwed up his face, trying to show Zoe his mom's disapproving expression. "It was fun, though. Everyone knew me, and even if they hated me, I was cool because I was with Jesse." He paused, chest feeling tight. He looked over at Zoe. "That's his name, by the way. *Jesse Logan Wesley.*"

"Cool," Zoe peeped respectfully.

Hazard stared at his fingers for a while, thinking back over the things he'd admitted and the things he hadn't. It felt good to talk about it, but there was so much more he could say. Maybe one day he'd tell Zoe about the way he and Jesse had had a *benefits* thing, or maybe more. Maybe one day he'd tell her about how much Emery Benjamin Moore meant to him and about the real reason he ran away.

"I wasn't a delinquent or anything. I wasn't a bad kid," Hazard whispered.

Zoe was quiet. It was obvious in her silence that she wanted to say, *I never said you were.* But then her silence ended and she murmured, "You talk about everything in the past tense."

"That's because it's over, Zoe." Hazard was embarrassed by how thin his voice sounded. He swallowed, the resolve he felt still a horrible pinch in his chest. He turned back to the TV and finally started his game.

"Don't be mad if I come into your room tonight." Zoe barely spoke above a whisper. "I don't like hearing you cry and feeling like I can't go comfort you."

Hazard stiffened, eyes widening. He dropped the game controller. He went cold with shock and chagrin and a lonely ache. He wanted to turn around and tell her not to say something like that, then deny any kind of crying because he was a *guy*, for Christ's sake. But Hazard was frozen, his throat tight. Even though he was embarrassed, it kind of touched him that Zoe didn't look down on him for crying and that it upset her.

"Okay," he finally managed, sounding very tiny and weak. He didn't know what else to say. Zoe did her homework, and he played his video game, listening to the last of the trick-or-treaters ringing the doorbell for candy.

At school, Drew eventually introduced Hazard to Zack and Autumn, and then Oliver, Jamie, and Elizabeth. Hazard still couldn't figure out how they all became friends or how he somehow fit in with them, or how they all stayed friends for the next two years, but it happened—and he needed it. They distracted him in good ways.

SOMEHOW, when you got older, New Year's wasn't as fun anymore.

Seniors especially were used to staying up late anyway—at least well past midnight, and on a regular basis—and all the noise of the party crackers and horns that Jamie insisted they use were wearing away at Hazard's nerves.

The ball dropped in Times Square. They all watched it on the television in Zack's living room. His parents were out at their own party, and Hazard had given in and joined everyone to bring in the New Year even though he didn't really like dark living rooms and the sound of drunken teenagers anymore.

That was sort of a problem, then, because New Year's Eve, Hazard was a very drunk seventeen-year-old, and he thought it was great. The music was low and the TV was on. There were good snacks and good drinks. It was casual, just the normal crew, even though Zack had invited a few people Hazard didn't know and so had Oliver. Whoever they were, though, they were funny, and Hazard didn't kiss them, even though he was working on his third Green Jesus, and by then he was pretty fiercely tipsy. That was good. It meant he was comfortable with his friends. It meant that New Year's was great (except for Jamie's annoying persistence with those little plastic horns) and he was okay lying around on the floor with Drew and Oliver, laughing like hyenas at Zack's friend's impression of the principal in all his bloated glory. Zack's friend's name was Roscoe.

It was great to feel this way again—fun and liberated, dizzy and a little too full of laughter. And nobody asked him about his old friends, because they knew that was not something he'd talk about; and nobody asked him why he chose that of all nights to get drunk with them when he tried so hard not to otherwise; and Jamie dropped one of her stupid noise makers in the toilet when she went to pee, and everybody thanked God; and it was great to laugh this hard and to feel like he was a part of everything.

Around the end of his fourth drink, Hazard started to get emotional.

He was the smallest of all the guys, so when he stumbled around the edge of the couch (it happened about three times), both Oliver and Drew held out a hand to steady him just because it was natural. They were like older brothers like that, and Hazard was five foot five and their resident runt.

"For your size, you can really hold your own!" they'd all joked before, the first time Hazard had cracked a drink open with them. They'd chalked him up as a lightweight, and he surprised them. He might never stop surprising them, but that was why he didn't talk about Bethany, Washington.

Around the end of his fourth drink, Hazard put on his coat and sat on Zack's steps alone, feeling the brisk air of a winter nighttime biting at his nose and cheeks. *What's wrong?* they asked. *Are you all right? Do you feel sick? You're not ditching us already, are you?* That was right, because usually before he got this drunk, he ditched them for safer places. Hazard fumbled in his pockets for his gloves, but it was too hard to punch in a number on his cell phone with gloves on, so he abandoned them next to his knee.

Who did he want to call, really? Did he want to call his mother? If he did, he'd probably argue with her and have to deal with it with a headache in the morning. It wasn't good to call your mother out of nowhere after weeks of grudges, no matter how much Hazard longed to talk things out with her like a normal family might.

Did he want to call his aunt and uncle, or maybe Zoe? Zoe would come pick him up. She was an angel that way, his cousin. But Hazard didn't want to be picked up. He just wanted to hear a familiar voice that would quell the bad feelings bubbling up in his chest, bad feelings that were ruining his good night. He could call Emery, but Emery would worry way too much. He could call Elizabeth, but no, Elizabeth was inside Zack's house delicately nursing a drink. He could call Jesse, and Jesse would humor him for a little bit. Jesse always humored him for a little bit.

With cold fingers, Hazard started dialing Jesse's number. He didn't remember all of it, maybe because he was drunk, or maybe because it had been that long since he called him. He went through the little digital phonebook in his cell phone, slowly, heart jumping with each name he scrolled down: Brianna, Isabella, Jack, Jamie, *Jesse.*

His breath shuddered in the air in front of him as he listened to the connection ring. He could still remember the day he'd put Jesse's real name into his phonebook, changing it from that rude nickname and trying to ignore that there was meaning in doing such. Fuzzy, ring after ring, and with each one, Hazard's heart throbbed in his throat. He didn't know why. He couldn't name the feeling thick in his chest. He was too drunk.

The other line picked up. Hazard held his breath. A familiar voice, bridging the gap between cell phones, crossing the distance of the connection just slightly higher than it would have been in real life, face to face:

"Hazard?"

Hazard broke into a stupid smile, brow knotting above relieved eyes. Alone on Zack's stoop, he squirmed down tighter into his coat, but he didn't feel as cold anymore.

"Hi, Jesse," he mumbled, maybe too eagerly. "Hey, how are you? What's up? Having a good New Year's? Are you wasted yet?"

"Good, nothing, yeah, and maybe."

Oh, that timbre—that light and gravelly voice, thick with sarcasm and booze. It wasn't that deep at all, but it was just right. Sometimes it sounded soft and young; other times it was coarse and sharp. Tonight, it was somewhere in between and a little slurred. Jesse sounded confused, doubtful, and grumpy. Hazard could hear the sound of a party in the fuzzy background of the phone connection. He heard voices, a buzz of incoherence that he could make out as faint music. Jesse was probably angry that Hazard had interrupted his fun.

"What about you?" Jesse asked.

Hazard wanted to cry. He wasn't sure why. He was just so happy that Jesse was talking to him. "I'm good," he said. "I'm sitting outside. It's pretty cold. I'm at Zack's. We watched the ball drop. I'm a little drunk, though. I just wanted to call someone—"

"This is the second time you've done this."

Jesse's voice was curt and caustic over the phone. Hazard shut his mouth with a click of his teeth, frowning at nothing in particular but remembering the scornful expression that invariably accompanied that tone of Jesse's voice.

"Done what?" Hazard mumbled.

"Called me because you're drunk and lonely." Jesse's scowl was almost audible.

Hazard's throat tightened. "Oh," he whispered. "I'm sorry."

"It's fine." Jesse sighed. Hazard cringed. There was a brief click as Jesse shifted the phone to another hand. Hazard waited with bated breath, and Jesse's farewell came mercifully enough:

"Look, Haz, I appreciate you calling, but neither of us will remember this in the morning. That's probably for the better, because it would really piss me off and it would probably fuck you up and you'd want to call again. Don't do it, though. Don't call me. You don't miss me. You're a masochist, that's all...."

Jesse was starting to ramble. The alcohol was talking. Hazard waited through it, nodding with each *Don't call me* and *I'm sorry, Haz*, and *Happy New Year's, man, I'll say it once, I miss you too*. Hazard didn't really hear anything else, casual insults or frustrated grumbles, or subtle glimpses at what Jesse really thought of the phone call, because all he could think about was *This is the second time you've done this* and *Neither of us will remember this in the morning.*

No, he wanted to say. No, I'll remember this in the morning. I *always* remember it in the morning.

When he hung up, Hazard felt tired and sick. He sat in the cold and he thought about Bethany, Washington, and New Year's parties happening there, and really, he didn't want to be alone after that phone call and the way it left him feeling shaky and nauseous.

Drew saw it first, the way Hazard came in with a pinched face and troubled eyes. He took away the last of his Green Jesus and made him drink water instead.

Hazard fell asleep on Zack's easy chair with the same pinched expression on his face. Zack was letting them all stay the night, anyway. Nobody drove when they were drunk. They were all good kids, after all.

And when Hazard woke up feeling icky, he remembered it all. Because he always remembered it in the morning.

A FEW days before graduation in June, Hazard had a dream. In the dream, he was at school, but it was Bethany High, not Roosevelt. All his friends were there, old and new. Everything was foggy like dreams always were, and he sat on a desk in a relatively empty classroom. He looked over, and Jesse Logan Wesley was in a desk a few rows over. He waved. Hazard smiled and waved back.

When Hazard woke up, his chest hurt. It wasn't the first time he'd dreamed about seeing old friends, but maybe that was when he subconsciously realized it was time to go home.

Chapter 15
Bethany

THERE was nothing really special about Hazard James.

After the graduation ceremony at Roosevelt High was over, Hazard conceded to a shower of hugs and kisses from his aunt and uncle and cousin Zoe, promising to be home by midnight, and then he ducked out of the crowd and hurried after his friends to the parking lot. They weren't going to the school graduation party. They were meeting up with Oliver, Jamie, and Roscoe at Red Robin. They all stripped off cap and gown in the parking lot, shoving everything hastily into the trunk for later.

Zack nearly got into two accidents trying to get out amongst the rest of the graduated students and the families that had come to watch them. Everyone clung to the seatbelts for dear life until they finally made it out on the road. They were about twenty minutes from the restaurant where the others waited for them. The lights of the city flashed by, bright and blinking and multicolored.

Drew wiggled across the middle console from the back seat, pushing Green Day into the stereo. The car filled with the trite melancholic melody of "Good Riddance." They were laughing—Zack, Drew, Elizabeth, Autumn—laughing about something Elizabeth had said, something sweet and innocent but completely hilarious, but Hazard wasn't really paying attention. His thoughts were elsewhere.

There was nothing really special about Hazard. Not like his friends. They'd known each other for years, and Hazard had been the transfer kid junior year—and there were a lot of students at Roosevelt High, after all. Nobody was required to care about the new kid, but they had.

They all had it together. Zack was tall and cool. He already had offers from the Air Force. Drew was the shortest just before Hazard, but despite a misleading appearance of flannel and denim and childish eyes, Drew was very grown-up, contemplative, and talented in everything he did. Oliver was confident, and he had hair that always fell perfectly. Then there were the girls, who were so down-to-earth and unique. Elizabeth didn't have a mean bone in her body. Jamie was always full of energy. Autumn was as quick-witted as Zack.

They were all strong and mature and held their heads high. They had their goals set and their wits together, plans and achievements and *certainty*.

Hazard didn't have that. He'd received an award at the assembly a few weeks ago, something about Outstanding Passion from his art teacher, but that didn't count. He was just a scrawny seventeen-year-old with a weird name and dark-brown hair that was always in his eyes and very often a thick, tousled mess. He was tiny in stature, so nobody ever expected him to be able to do anything in the weight room. He still wasn't truly shaving yet. He had to wear reading glasses when he did homework, he didn't really get pimples (which his mom had said was a gift he got from her), and his face was set in a perpetual frown that everyone noticed, everyone commented on, but nobody fully questioned. His eighteenth birthday was coming up, and he didn't have plans, he didn't have memorable accomplishments, and he sure as hell didn't have *certainty*.

In Zack's backseat between Drew and the armrest, Hazard watched the world stream by outside the window. Drew stretched over and skipped forward on the CD. *Today's the Macy's Day Parade, night of the living dead is on its way.*

Hazard's parents hadn't even come to his graduation. Everyone else's parents came.

His aunt and uncle came, of course. His cousin Zoe had yelled his name the loudest when he'd walked to get his diploma—but Hazard was feeling that way again, old sensations of being a nuisance and being unneeded.

"You're spacing out," Drew told him as they lurched to a stop at a traffic light. Bright lamps lit up shopping plazas on either side of the intersection. "You haven't spaced like that in a long time."

Hazard watched the way his mouth moved around the words. He felt Zack's eyes hover over him in the rearview mirror. Drew wanted to say, *You haven't spaced like that since you moved here.* Hazard had seen the brief twitch of his lip during that pause. He could just see in his eyes that that was what he'd wanted to say. *Since you moved here.*

They weren't dumb. They all knew there was something wrong. They had all day. They were good friends like that, and Hazard didn't deserve them.

"What's the matter?" Zack demanded, paying more attention than he should have to the conversation, since he was driving. "You'd better tell us now, because the restaurant's right up here somewhere—"

"I don't know," Hazard lied. The light turned green. Everyone in the back seat clutched onto something to keep from rocking forward at Zack's sudden acceleration.

"Maybe you're in shock," Autumn guessed. "You know, from graduation. Maybe he just can't believe it happened, guys."

Hazard nodded. His friends murmured in agreement, as if they didn't buy it—but they did. They believed him. They teased him and comforted him. Hazard let them. He let them believe him even though he knew for sure he wasn't feeling this way because of graduation. They'd never understand what he meant if he tried to explain it.

They joined Oliver and the others at a big booth table amidst a restaurant bursting with activity. They ordered drinks. Their table was loud. They were graduated seniors, after all. High school was over. This was a celebration.

But something was different.

He'd known them for almost two years, but they were all still foreign to Hazard. Drew, Zack, Autumn—they all had their own lives, their own baggage. He was their friend, but Hazard still felt detached from them. He felt like he didn't have a right to be included. He felt like a sore thumb— not only to his friends, but to his aunt and uncle and his cousin Zoe. He'd just shown up one day, after all, announcing that he'd run away, and they'd made sure he was comfortable, and he thought that after two years, the awkwardness and discomfiture would be gone. But here it was again, and it was just as heavy.

Maybe he *was* feeling this way because he'd graduated. There were decisions to be made—weighty decisions about school and work and life choices—and suddenly Hazard felt very tiny and insignificant. He felt *out of place*. He wasn't excited at all. He dreaded his newfound freedom. No school meant no distractions, which meant more time to think, more time to accept that he was imposing on his mom's generous brother and these open peers he called friends, more time to see that these friendly peers had it all together and he *didn't*. More time to remember summers skating in the Windsor Green park, of playing basketball in Emery's driveway, of waking up in a room that smelled vaguely of cigarettes and familiar skin, of teenage rebellion and empty evenings to fill—more time to acknowledge that he was missing his old friends, that he was jealous of his new ones, and that he didn't belong here in Seattle.

Around the table, everyone else was having a grand time. Hazard frowned at the appetizers, wondering now if he really knew any of them here at all. They were friends, but he didn't *know* them. He didn't know about the memories they shared when he hadn't been around. He didn't know about their family beyond what he saw when he was over at someone else's house, or what somebody complained about Monday morning. He didn't know about their innermost desires, fears, regrets.

And on that note, *they* surely didn't know *him*. They'd all probably reconsider their friendship with him if they did.

The people that really knew him were back at home. Not here in Seattle, but back across the sound in Bethany.

It hit Hazard then, slouched in the dining booth of a noisy restaurant. Maybe he wasn't *supposed* to fit in here with his new friends. Maybe he needed to go back home. Maybe that was why all the memories were welling up in the back of his head, straining to get out of the neglected corners of his mind reserved only for the things he didn't want to deal with.

The revelation left Hazard more winded than he'd expected. He actually had to keep himself from grinning at this thrilling new idea. Go back to Bethany and see everyone? If his friends here asked, he'd never be able to explain. They wouldn't get it. He told them he'd moved because he didn't belong, and now he was going to go back because he didn't belong *again*.

He was lonely and scared and his heart ached, and Hazard decided he was going back to Bethany in the morning.

"Party with us tonight," Oliver urged at ten fifteen, in the parking lot outside his car.

"I think I'll pass." Hazard laughed. "I don't want to party with you losers."

"Oh, come on!" Zack cried, fumbling in his dashboard for his lighter. "You don't mean that. You know you want to, man."

"Whatever." Hazard allowed Drew to give him a rough hair-ruffle. He relaxed under Drew's arm. "My aunt and uncle want to see me too, you know."

They didn't force him. Zack dropped him off, and Hazard got his things out of the trunk. He felt bad for not hanging with them just one last time before he left, but it was okay. He went inside and tossed his cap and gown on the couch. He took his diploma to his room and stared at it in privacy for a long moment, remembering the night a few years ago when Jesse graduated. He almost changed his mind about going back to Bethany.

His aunt and uncle kept congratulating him. Hazard blushed. When they went to bed, Hazard joined Zoe in the living room with some ice cream, sitting cross-legged on the carpet in front of the TV and searching for something good to watch.

"I'm leaving tomorrow," Hazard announced plainly.

Zoe choked on a spoonful of ice cream and looked at him. Hazard kept going through the channels. He glanced at her, then back at the television.

"Back home?" Zoe supposed quietly. She stared at Hazard, waiting for him to cave and look at her in return. Eventually he did, with a defeated sigh and a tight frown.

"Yeah," he eased out. "I'm sure my mom and dad want to see me—"

"You're mad they didn't come," Zoe surmised. Hazard shrugged, not wanting to confess that. "That's understandable," she said. "When are you leaving?"

"I dunno. I'm gonna surprise them." Hazard shifted a little, staring at his spoon just to avoid her piercing eyes. "Maybe after lunch, or something."

"I guess that's okay." Zoe's teeth clicked on the spoon as she ate more ice cream. They watched TV together for a few hours, curled up on the sofa and laughing together. Hazard remembered coming up for Thanksgiving two years ago, when lounging with Zoe had been awkward. But not anymore, not even with knowing that Zoe knew about everything, even the fact that Hazard had cried so much when he first moved to Seattle. He actually relaxed a little.

Hazard was up until two o'clock packing. He started around a quarter to one, then stopped to text Emery with clammy fingers and tell him he'd be in Bethany tomorrow afternoon. Emery told him to text when he left. Seeing the message, Hazard regretted everything, unpacked, and tried to sleep, because he got scared and decided not to go anywhere. What was he expecting, anyway? If his parents wanted to see him, they'd call. And they hadn't. So he shouldn't go.

He tossed and turned for ten minutes, then got up, turned the light on, and packed again. He stared at his suitcase for a moment before closing it and putting it by the door. Tomorrow. He was leaving tomorrow.

He did. Over breakfast, Hazard announced, "I'm gonna go see my parents for a while," and it wasn't as awkward or upsetting as he'd expected it to be. His uncle said, "That's a great idea, bud," and ruffled his hair hard. His aunt hugged him more sincerely than his mom ever had, and Zoe promised not to touch anything in his room.

Hazard texted his Seattle friends and told them he was going to visit his parents for a while. He lied and said his mom had asked him to. Emery sent him a message to meet him at the Carl's Jr. at the Four Corners back in Bethany.

Hazard didn't know what he was getting himself into, but the fear he was feeling as he drove off the ferry and remembered his way to the Four Corners was a good kind of fear. It was totally debilitating but so, so sweet. He was excited to see them all again—Emery, Jesse, Brianna, Felix, everyone else—but he didn't know if they would feel the same, and that was the horrifying part. He didn't want to look like an idiot coming back to people who hated him.

It was more numb nostalgia than anything that prompted Hazard to stop for a coffee at the gas station down the street from the Four Corners, the secluded 7-Eleven on Berkeley Street tucked in against the corners of neighborhoods. The breeze coming in off the water felt delicious, and Hazard wandered over to look at all the vandalism on the side of the gas station. Nobody had cared to paint over it over the years, Sharpie messages scrawled between bathroom doors near the ice and stacks of starter logs. It gave Hazard a weird sense of déjà vu to taste the coffee and look at the names and dates and solicitations like *Call me for a good time.* And amongst them all was the phrase, neatly tagged:

we all collide

It gave Hazard a shiver. He hurried back to his car. He needed to be at the Four Corners, anyway.

It was shuddering déjà vu again when he saw Emery, rubbing at his forehead with the ball of his palm and smiling shyly as he trudged over from his car to Hazard's. Hazard opened his door, unable to suppress a big smile. His heart thunked nervously, a clammy little chill zipped down his spine, and his stomach started to knot sickeningly, but he couldn't stop the smile. He sat there like an idiot. It felt like having to get up in front of the class and answer a question, with all eyes on you, judging and evaluating and piercing. What was he supposed to say? What was he supposed to do?

"*Haz,*" Emery said, as if chastising, but the impending grin was obvious in the corners of his face. "Holy shit, it's *Hazard Oscar James.*"

"Shut up." Hazard beamed. He couldn't help but sound excited. Part of him didn't want to believe Emery had come to meet him, but there he was, and Hazard was frozen in place for a moment, overwhelmed by the familiarity and the awkward, anxious sense of distance between them.

Emery looked so familiar but so different. He was eighteen now, and he didn't look like he was *trying* to be cool anymore. He was an inch or so taller, the little silver ring from his left ear and the stud from his lower lip both absent. Their disappearance made the mature angles of his face come across more plainly, but with his sun-kissed skin and soft features, he still looked more like a kid on the beach than a young man. He stood there in his sleeveless Adidas hoodie and faded jeans, blue Converse peeking out beneath. Details stood out to Hazard—faded scribbles on Emery's knuckles like he still had the habit of doodling on his hands when he was bored, the way his wallet was an obvious oblong in his pocket with his phone.

Emery looked at Hazard like he was feeling just as overwhelmed by nostalgia and relief and apprehension all at once, his hair a little shorter but still sticking out in all the wrong places. Emery had never been friends with cowlicks, and there was a strange shadow in his eyes that was almost too serious for Hazard's liking. But it was still Emery, the same Emery from summers of basketball in the driveway and nights on the roof talking about serious things, and Hazard's heart felt sore.

There was a short hush. Another car or two pulled into the Carl's Jr. parking lot with them. Someone honked out at an intersection, voices and motion and all the background fuzz of a city. Was someone supposed to say something? Weren't there certain questions to be asked first? Was it wrong to feel the sense of falling into place again so naturally and fearlessly after two years? Trite, but maybe that was just what it was like to have a best friend.

Emery grinned a familiar dimpled grin and pulled Hazard into a sloppy, boyish hug. "You're the same as always," he said decidedly, as if he'd known Hazard was evaluating him too.

Hazard didn't really know what to say after that, still kind of in disbelief. That was okay. Emery motioned to Hazard's car. "You have to follow me."

Hazard's brow knotted. "Where are we going? Don't you want to talk?"

Emery shrugged. "Not yet." He smiled again, not at all too kindly. "I know you better than you think, Hazard. I'm not stupid."

Looking at him, Hazard felt a sudden bleak pang of guilt or bittersweet nostalgia. It was so weird to be face to face with Emery again after two years. He felt a little impatient, but maybe he was expecting tension when he shouldn't have.

In his car, Hazard followed Emery to the Bethany Town Center mall, which brought another whopping blow of melancholy with its towering Macy's and JCPenney and the broad glass façade of the food court. Hazard felt a very strange sort of nervousness, biting his nails a little as he parked a few spaces down from Emery. He felt clammy and he felt anxious, alone but not alone, like it was a first date or something. That was all he could think to compare it to, but that was far from the truth.

"Lunch first," Emery decided, waiting for Hazard to lock his car. The breeze coming in off Puget Sound was refreshing. "Massage chairs second, and bookstore third. And then whatever else you wanna do, like

Spencer's or Best Buy or whatever."

Hazard met Emery's eyes, smiling faintly. God, he wished he could just relax. But there was an obvious shadow in Emery's smile too, like this nostalgic triteness was going to buckle into some horrible awkwardness soon. You weren't supposed to just *hang out* again after two years, right? There was bound to be tension or something at some point.

They talked about graduation while they ate Chinese in the mall, snickering at the girls in the photo booth near the sub shop who couldn't figure out how to pay for their pictures. Hazard drank his coffee from 7-Eleven, and Emery drank Dr. Pepper.

"So your uncle is on Professors' Row, right?" Emery asked after a while, and Hazard understood nervously that their conversation was taking a turn for the serious. It had been inevitable from the start, and although he was dreading it, he was relieved because it meant the pressure would ease soon.

"Yeah." Hazard shrugged. "Ravenna. It's really busy all the time."

"What's Roosevelt like?" Emery asked, grinning around his straw. "We beat their ass in soccer the last five years, you know."

"It's *big*," Hazard said, and his expression must have been funny, because Emery laughed. The sound made Hazard relax, smiling meekly.

"You grew a couple of inches," Emery noted.

"So did you."

"Do you have a girlfriend?"

"No."

"Neither do I."

"What about Lily?"

"We haven't tried dating again since that one summer. Face it. You and me? We're losers."

Hazard laughed. "Yeah, we are."

Emery sighed dramatically. "But you probably think you're so much cooler, living in Professors' Row."

"Nah."

"Did you miss us?"

The question struck Hazard sharp in the chest, and he slouched at the table, brow knotting guiltily. "Why else would I be back, Emery?" he mumbled under the buzz of mall noise, poking at his chow mein.

Emery smiled crookedly, a boyish little half grin. Hazard could see relief in it. Emery sighed, fiddling with his straw. "I missed you, man. You don't know how boring it was without you."

"It was not. You had Russell," Hazard argued without really thinking about it, and Emery looked at him pointedly, almost injured. But Emery didn't say anything, and for a moment they ate in silence, a precarious kind of hush about their little food court table that neither really knew how to mend just yet. They could talk and laugh as comfortably as ever, but Hazard had a hunch that these moments of awkwardness would still settle now and again, just reminders that it had been a few years and a lot had happened.

"Yeah, but…," Emery said slowly, more to his food than to Hazard, "whether or not Russell was around, I still missed you. Being friends with someone since second grade, you can't just *not miss them*, you know?"

"Yeah," Hazard mumbled, "I know." And he did know. He felt guilty for ever supposing differently.

They went to the little outlet on the mall's second floor where the massage chairs were set up for passersby to try out. The automated massages were amazing, and Emery and Hazard laughed together as the movement of the chairs made their voices vibrate. It was like they were twelve again, pointing out people across the mall atrium and snickering like idiots at them. They watched a little girl throw a tantrum. They watched someone drop all their bags and have to pick them up, a group of middle schoolers trying to act cool, and a flamboyant man pass by quickly, which set them into peals of laughter that attracted one of the store workers. She shooed them out of the massage chairs and back into the mall with a very stern scowl on her face.

They went to the Barnes and Noble entrance on the first floor, navigating directly to the funny books.

"Just like old times," Emery said with a grand sigh. They flipped through those for a while, then wandered off together to the art section, where they perused anthologies of Caravaggio and van Gogh, then books of Annie Leibovitz and other interesting photography. Of course, they also had to walk through the self-help and sexuality sections just to pause and snicker together at all the funny titles and book covers (this was something of tradition for them, ever since Health class in fifth grade), and of course it was when Hazard had pulled out a book with two men and a woman tangled together on the cover to show to Emery that familiar faces passed by the shelf aisle, and Hazard's laughter immediately stopped as he realized that he'd just seen Tom, Peyton, and Olivia. And they'd seen him too.

Hazard started panicking. He put the book back quickly, leaning over around the shelves and trying to see where they'd gone.

Emery cocked a brow. "What's wrong?"

"Nothing," Hazard mumbled. He really didn't even have to explain because Olivia came around the other corner of the shelves, arms full of books and leading Tom and Peyton behind her.

"*Hazard?*" she cried incredulously, her whole face lighting up.

Hazard's heart fluttered, and he felt very bad for being so stiff when Olivia hugged him. Emery waited patiently a few feet away, watching from an arbitrary distance. Hazard met Tom's eyes over Olivia's shoulder, feeling kind of inept and not knowing what to do or say to them.

"What are you doing here? Are you moving back? Or just visiting?" Olivia was full of questions, passing off her books to Peyton and holding both of Hazard's hands in her own. Her eyes danced. Hazard found it hard to swallow for a moment, let alone answer.

"I'm just visiting," he said quietly.

"You were in Seattle, right?" Tom asked, crossing his arms.

"Yeah." Hazard nodded.

"How long are you staying?" That was Tom again.

"Is it more fun in Seattle?" Olivia interrupted.

"Obviously not as fun as here or he wouldn't be back, Olivia," Peyton grunted, joining the conversation. He smirked dully, holding all the books Olivia had shoved at him: parts of the Harry Potter series, Japanese comic books, *Wuthering Heights*, and *Twilight*.

Hazard glanced over his shoulder at Emery, helpless. Emery motioned a little and raised his brows as if to say, *Go on, talk to them.*

Hazard glanced over at them again. Tom didn't look high, just a little tired. He was chewing gum. Hazard smelled the spearmint now. His hair was curling a little over his ears. Peyton had gotten even taller, something of a goatee on his chin. Olivia's hair was shorter. The reddish locks ended in wispy curls near her chin. It was cute. And that ring on her left hand—what did it mean? Promise ring, maybe. Peyton wore one too. Maybe they were together.

Did any of them think about old times when they looked at him? Hazard did. He thought about the high schoolers' hangout under the freeway and Windsor Green park, the way the light of his dad's TV had flickered in the room when he'd taken Olivia's shirt off, and the pinched look on Tom's face when he'd asked, *Are you really friends with Jesse Wesley?* Just little things like that. They made his heart ache.

Hazard shrugged, trying to stay cool and collected when his heart pounded nervously. He definitely hadn't expected to see them today. Coincidence was cruel. He said, "I don't know how long I'm staying. Just a little while, I guess. Graduation was yesterday, so I'm here to see family."

"We should grab our skateboards sometime while you're here and kick it like we used to," Tom suggested.

Hazard stared at him a moment, seriously considering asking if Tom remembered how poorly the four of them had kicked it in the past. But he swallowed the words and smiled a little, mumbling, "Yeah, sure. Why not? I mean, if you guys have an extra board."

"Aw, man, you didn't bring yours?"

"Nope."

Tom scoffed and shoved his hands in his pockets. He pursed his lips in a scowl, looking more like the Tom Hazard remembered. "Well, whatever," he teased. "Just make sure to call me when you figure out when you're leaving so we can plan some stuff before then."

"Me too," Olivia added.

"I will," Hazard promised.

They left with a hug, a wave, and a fistbump between them, disappearing amongst the other aisles. Hazard stood there, watching them move over to the cash register. There was a lump in his throat that made it hard to swallow and a weird embarrassed shiver twisting down his spine.

"You okay?"

Hazard glanced over at Emery. Concern dimpled his brows, something not a smile and not a frown on his face. Hazard swallowed hard, nodding. He didn't ever want it to be as awkward between him and Emery as it was between him and Tom, Peyton, and Olivia, and that determination was just as strong as it had been before. He was going to have a good day with Emery, and that was that.

"Yeah," he said quietly. "That was just... *weird*, you know? Seeing them."

"I know, right?" Emery laughed. He paused for a moment, peering at Hazard with a curiosity that made Hazard clam up. "Do you plan on seeing anyone else while you're here?"

Hazard thought about it. It was a daunting idea. He didn't know if he could handle it at the moment. "Maybe," he mumbled.

They went to Best Buy on their way out. They wandered around listening to music for a bit, then decided they should get a movie to watch sometime. Emery bought *Saved!* "It's really good," he promised. "It's hysterical. Where are you staying? We should watch it tonight."

"My uncle booked me a room at the Hampton." Hazard shrugged, getting out his keys as they made their way to their cars.

"You're staying at a hotel?" Emery raised his brows, a little skeptical. "Stay at my place. We have a comfortable couch."

Hazard shook his head, smiling apologetically. "My uncle already booked it."

"Cancel it," Emery insisted, and Hazard remembered how persuasive Emery could be. He sighed. In the parking lot of the mall, he called the Bethany Hampton and cancelled the reservation his uncle had made for him, then looked at Emery pointedly.

"Happy?" he asked.

"Very." Emery opened his car door and tapped his hand absently on the roof. "Follow me. I don't live in Windsor Green anymore."

Emery had gone from a Windsor Green townhouse to a modest-looking duplex near the middle school. Hazard didn't see Emery's mom's car in the driveway. He figured she was at work. Emery helped him with his things even though he only had a backpack and a duffel bag. Inside, the duplex actually felt pretty spacious—a nice open kitchen and living room, a flight of stairs that led to two bedrooms and the second bathroom.

It was nearing seven o'clock already. Hazard felt like he should call his mom and let her know he was there, but he couldn't yet. He had to ease into Bethany again, not jump in full force.

They watched *Saved!* sprawled on the cozy red couches in the little living room. There were pictures from places like Hobby Lobby and Marshall's up around the house, a few posters on the wall near the stairs like Emery had needed to add his finishing touch to his mom's décor. Hazard was reminded of the afternoons they used to spend in Emery's living room before, avoiding Andrew and laughing with his mom. And this was going to be okay, Hazard thought. If it felt this comfortable with Emery again after so long, it was all going to be okay. He just had to take it slow.

Just after nine o'clock, while Hazard was telling Emery about Drew and Zack and everyone else in Seattle, the sound of the front door being unlocked came, and Hazard bristled out of habit. He couldn't wait to see Emery's mom again. She'd probably want to talk. Except it wasn't Emery's mom that came through the front door; it was Russell Leroy.

"Hey," he said casually, and then he stopped halfway and leveled sharp scrutiny on Hazard.

"Hey," Emery replied. "How was work?"

Hazard didn't really know what to do. He took his feet off the coffee table and sat stiffly against the arm of the couch, feeling like a guilty child. Russell didn't seem to have any better grasp on the situation. He closed the front door behind him slowly, locked it, and held Hazard's stare a moment longer over his shoulder before dropping his bag by the door and crouching down to take off his shoes.

"Work was annoying," Russell finally answered. He still had his same moody sense of indifference. His hair was a little longer, maybe too long, and he kept sweeping it out of his sharp blue eyes with what looked like frustration on his face. "How was your day off?" he added after he'd stood up, propping his hands on his hips and peering at Emery with brows raised.

"Good." Emery pointed at Hazard. "Look who's visiting!"

Russell nodded, meeting Hazard's stare again. It was a gesture of greeting, Hazard knew. He returned it coyly. He didn't really know why he felt so callow below Russell's eyes. It actually kind of alarmed him more than it angered him.

"I'm gonna take a shower," Russell announced, heading upstairs in a tense silence.

The moment he was gone, Hazard finally forced himself to speak. He didn't want to ask, because he kind of knew the answer already, but he looked at Emery pointedly and said, "You live with Russell?"

Emery stared at him shamelessly. He gave a vague nod. "Yeah."

"Are you going to the same college?" Hazard ventured, uncertain of how he felt about this information but not sure why.

"He's doing OSU online," Emery explained quietly, inspecting the fading pen marks on his knuckles like he didn't want to meet Hazard's eyes. He took a short breath, hesitated, then went on, "I wait tables at Claim Jumper. I actually pick up *a lot* of tips. It's really awesome." He tapped his feet against the edge of the coffee table and glanced at Hazard as if waiting for him to find something to be upset about. "I'm applying all over for college—Tacoma, Bellevue, Bremerton, even the UW. I'm not sure what I want to do yet. Probably theatre and European history."

It was odd to hear Emery sound so decisive and organized. Hazard told him that, and they laughed about it. In the duplex next door, somebody slammed a door, and it echoed. Hazard didn't know what to say next. Sitting there listening to Emery explain his plans made him feel a slight sinking sensation of dismissal, because Emery was just like his Seattle friends.

Emery had it all together. He had plans, and accomplishments, and certainty, and to top it off, he was perfect. Hazard realized that now. Emery was smart and handsome and had good morals, a contagious smile, and the right amount of pride. Emery had always been perfect. He would always be perfect, no matter what he did, and Hazard had no idea what to do about anything.

There was a brief hush, in which he knew that one of them was going to say something important, but he didn't know which of them it would be. He thought about Russell, upstairs in the shower he could hear. He thought about Emery and Russell and the way they used to be, the way they used to look at each other, and the way they'd looked at each other when Russell came through the front door.

"Felix is gone, you know," Emery whispered, completely out of the blue.

Hazard glanced at him skeptically. Emery had a look on his face that Hazard recognized, an expression torn between tears and pride where his eyes shimmered and his mouth was in a tight line, his big heart and his masculinity at war. Something intuitive in Hazard knew exactly what Emery meant, but he said, "What?"

"He, um—" Emery's brow knotted. "It was four months ago—"

"No way," Hazard argued. His voice wavered on his breath, and he held his head for a moment, incredulous. Emery's head was hung. Hazard felt a cold quiver of frustration. He didn't have to ask again; he knew what Emery meant. Felix was gone. Felix had died.

Why had nobody contacted him, if only to tell him? Why hadn't he been invited to the funeral? Most importantly, why hadn't *Jesse* told him? Because Jesse hated him, of course. Hazard's jaw tightened in disbelief. He couldn't blame any of them. He'd left, and nobody had talked to anybody after that. But he felt kind of betrayed, and it made the pain in his chest wither into weak rage.

"It was a car accident." Emery paused, foot wagging tensely. "Drunk drivers."

The ominous phrase soured Hazard's gut, and he looked somewhere else, emotion thick in his throat. All of them were guilty of drinking, he was very positive of that, and the phrase *drunk drivers* was pinning the blame on them as much as it did on the real criminals. Hazard fidgeted. He'd been wanting to apologize to Felix but just hadn't pulled up enough courage to do so—not like he'd been able to pull up enough courage to talk to *any* of them in the last two years—and now there it was. Felix was gone. Hazard's heart fell below his stomach and his fingers shook. His eyes stung, and he stared at his hands, lost.

Emery looked vaguely pissed, probably because he'd been stuck as the bearer of bad news. Hazard felt just as bitter. He didn't want to be. He tried to change the subject.

"How's Russell doing?"

Emery softened immediately, like he was shocked Hazard even cared to ask. He visibly relaxed, clearing his throat. "Good. He works at the YMCA. He got one of those certificate things for personal training. He bugs me about eating my vegetables, but I'm like—I'm eighteen. You're not my mother."

Hazard laughed with Emery, because he knew how much Emery hated healthy food. But Emery didn't talk about why they were living together—they were probably just roommates—or maybe it was Russell's house and his parents just weren't home—but whatever it was, Hazard dropped it. He needed to talk about something that would make his heart stop pounding as anxiously as it was and his throat stop aching so much. He'd rather laugh than think about Felix at the moment.

Russell came down to get something to eat, hair wet.

"Are you staying here?" he asked, leaning over the island counter and raising his brows at Hazard.

Hazard exchanged a glance with Emery. The way Russell looked at them, he really did feel like they were two kids in trouble. It was kind of amusing and unsettling at the same time.

Emery looked at Russell expectantly. "He was staying at a hotel, but I'm making him stay here instead."

Hazard searched out Russell's eyes, curious as to his opinion on this. Russell was busy making a sandwich, a curtain of blond hair around his face. There was something that was almost tension thick in the air, and then Russell put away the peanut butter and said, "That's cool. At least you're not blowing money on a room."

That was approval. Emery relaxed again. Hazard remembered him saying years ago, about Jesse, *He's really got you under his thumb, doesn't he?* He was tempted to say the same to Emery now, but that would be mean.

Russell ate his sandwich in the kitchen, then went back upstairs to do his week's classwork on the computer. Emery put on some funny TV. "I'm glad you're back," he said, breaking the silence.

"Really?" Hazard murmured.

"Really."

Hazard smiled faintly. Emery glanced over at him, his eyes clouding like he had something deep he wanted to say. He shrugged, brow knotting. "I hope you had fun today. I'm sorry it was kind of awkward."

Hazard shook his head, feeling something nostalgic and warm and very bittersweet. "No," he said, "it's okay. It wasn't that awkward. It was great."

"I'm glad." Emery practically beamed, seeming to wilt like a weight had been lifted from him.

Around midnight, Emery brought down pillows and blankets for Hazard. The couch was actually very comfortable. Hazard got settled in quickly.

Emery frowned worriedly. "You sure you're okay down here alone? You can turn on whatever light you want, there's movies, and here are the remotes, watch whatever, the bathroom's there, the kitchen is right there, so feel free to get something to eat or drink—"

Russell passed through the living room to get a glass of water. "Good night," he said curtly as he headed back upstairs.

"I'm fine," Hazard told Emery. "Seriously."

Finally convinced, Emery retreated upstairs too. Hazard's bags were behind the couch. He brushed his teeth in the bathroom next to the kitchen, then switched his jeans for some pajama pants and wriggled into the blankets Emery had given him. Curled up on his side with his cell phone and wallet on the coffee table, he flipped through the channels for a bit, lingering on late-night *NCIS* before watching *Adult Swim* and thinking of Olivia.

He watched until his eyes began to itch, lashes drifting shut. He turned the light off and buried his face in the pillow. He closed his eyes. He frowned. The pillowcase smelled familiar, like sunscreen and Emery's hair.

Hazard remembered staying over at Emery's house before, the lava lamp and the generator below the window. He remembered staying at Felix's house once or twice, which ripped open that new, accosting pain in his chest that he was going to have to get used to because Felix was gone. He teared up a little and tried to think of something else—living room forts, summers with Russell and Lily, staying over at Jesse's, and the way Jesse looked in the darkness, smoking at the window while his video game was paused.

The little living room was comfortable, but Hazard felt out of place in it. He didn't want to impose. It was Russell and Emery's house, after all. The light upstairs had gone out. He was alone on the couch and he was alone in the room and he felt small and vulnerable and couldn't help it. It was overwhelming. He'd felt the same thing when he'd first left Bethany, except a little worse.

He needed to sleep. It was late, and he was probably overtired now. He left the TV on because it was too quiet otherwise and he couldn't understand why, but he just felt scared to be back.

The digital clock above the TV read 2:42 when Hazard finally fell asleep.

Chapter 16
Emery and Mom,
and Freudian Theory

A TINNY rendition of "Scotty Doesn't Know" echoed for three lines, then paused and repeated again. Hazard's eyes fluttered open, then closed. He thought for the umpteenth time that he needed to change his ringtone before going back to Bethany. It would save him from making the wrong impression. Then he thought that if it was Drew calling him again for a ride to his girlfriend's place, Hazard was going to punch him.

Hazard woke up fully, and he remembered where he was. He was in Russell and Emery's living room, where the light of early morning was spilling through the shades, and there was Russell in the kitchen eating an egg sandwich, staring at Hazard because Hazard's phone was ringing and "Scotty Doesn't Know" was a terrible ringtone.

Hazard blushed, chagrined. He threw an arm out of his cocoon of warm blankets and grabbed his cell phone, silencing the ringer. Wary of Russell's presence just across the room in the kitchen, Hazard stayed curled up on the couch. It had been Drew calling. He texted shortly after, wanting to know how Hazard was.

Russell must have turned the TV off for him at some point. Buried in the blankets again, Hazard almost fell back asleep. He listened to Russell's keys jangle. He heard Emery come down the stairs quietly. There was a bit of whispering, the rustle of clothing. The door opened, then closed again. The sound of a car starting told Hazard Russell must be headed to work.

Emery hovered over the couch. "You awake?" he asked tentatively.

Hazard opened his eyes and looked at his cell phone. The clock on it read seven o'clock in the morning. He mumbled, "Yes, Emery, I'm awake."

"Good," Emery said. He drifted into the kitchen and started making cereal. "I'm off today. You wanna do something again?"

Hazard sat up slowly, groggily looking at his bedhead in the mirror across the room. Emery sounded far too chipper for such an early hour, especially in the summer. A few years ago, Emery wouldn't get up until noon unless he was dragged out of bed, but this morning Emery had already been through the shower and was fully dressed. The smell of his soap followed him with each step.

Hazard lay down again and stared up at the ceiling. "Emery, it's *seven o'clock.*"

"Yeah, I know. Russell gets up early for work, and he always ends up waking *me* up, and I can never get back to sleep. Let's do something."

"I guess." Hazard rubbed the sleep from his eyes, listening to Emery eat. "What do you have in mind?"

"Does your mom know you're in town?"

"No."

Emery gasped. He might have dropped his spoon, overdramatically. "You're a horrible son!"

Hazard chuckled softly, closing his eyes for another moment. He couldn't help it. Emery made him laugh. But, he supposed, there was his day's first plan: visiting his mother. Thinking about it made him sick with nervousness, his chest tight.

"Take a shower first," Emery said. "Upstairs. You can use my soap and stuff. And we can take my car, okay?"

Hazard smiled meekly, kicking the blankets back and forcing himself to sit up. "Okay," he conceded with a sigh.

HAZARD was not very happy standing on the sidewalk outside his old house at nine o'clock in the morning. He hadn't been very happy driving there, either. He *was* a horrible son for not telling his mother first thing that he was back in town, and he was scared to see her.

When Hazard's mom opened the door, she raised her brows at first, not quite sure what was going on. It dawned on her slowly. It was apparent on her face when she understood. She almost dropped her coffee cup, icy complacency melting into disbelief, and then she fell absolutely still.

"Hey, baby," she said quietly, eyes wide.

"Hey," Hazard whispered, fidgeting slightly.

She glanced over and smiled primly in Emery's direction. "Emery."

"Hi," Emery said, returning the thin smile.

Hazard couldn't look away from his mom. She looked much older than before. Maybe she hadn't changed in two years. Maybe he just hadn't *looked* at her for so long. Something emotional caught in his throat, and Hazard glanced away, remembering the way she'd acted when he'd come back with his uncle to get his stuff.

"Your uncle told me you were coming." His mom clutched at her coffee mug and turned, opening the door further. "Come in, guys."

Hazard's old bedroom was still the same, completely untouched. It choked him up to see that, standing in the doorway while his mom made them cups of coffee. There, all his posters—and his bed, neatly made—and all his old things, scattered around the room. TV, games, box of old photos on his desk. Hazard had to walk away from looking at it all. It hurt in a strange way to know that his mother had left his room set up the way it was the year he left, like she was afraid of changing it should he ever come back home.

His parents had gotten divorced without telling him. Apparently, they hadn't even told his aunt and uncle, or his grandparents, for that matter. They'd done it quickly and come to quiet agreements, one of which being that Hazard's mom didn't have to work because of Avon and the Pampered Chef, his grandparents, and the healthy child support payment she got each month. Nobody knew about it. His dad had moved to Seattle to be closer to work, and he'd never even told Hazard. He'd given him money for his car a few months ago, a little black hardly used 2004 Mustang, but it was Hazard's uncle who had taken him to the dealership to find it. And that hurt, because Hazard had thought he was closer to his dad than that.

They sat with his mom in the living room. They talked a little bit. Hazard told her about what he'd been doing for the past two years—the classes he'd taken, how his aunt and uncle were, how mature Zoe looked now.

His mother touched his shoulder as she stood up, hugging her robe closed. "Let me finish my makeup really fast, hon," she said, leaving Emery and Hazard alone in the living room for a short while. Hazard understood vaguely that being interrupted midroutine drove her crazy.

Hazard stared at his feet. "So I guess I really missed a lot," he said after a moment. The hush that had fallen in the clean living room was tense.

Emery nodded. He tapped his toes on the carpet. "I guess so."

"Maybe it wouldn't be so bad if people cared to, you know, call me. And fill me in on stuff. Like, I dunno, divorces or *death*—"

Emery scoffed loudly. Hazard looked at him, affronted.

Emery shrugged. "Don't be mean, Hazard. Phones work both ways."

"Exactly! I can't believe nobody called me about anything! I mean, Felix *died*—"

Emery put down his cup of coffee and turned, fixing Hazard with a stormy blue glare. "*You* left *us*, Hazard. We figured that meant you didn't want anything to do with us."

"I don't understand. When I left, none of you hung out together."

"Well, when you left, we all lost the same thing, and I guess that's worth something. Things change, you know. Sometimes for the better."

Hazard recoiled, confused. "What—"

"No, Haz." Emery frowned. He closed his eyes as if gathering patience to deal with it all. Hazard was briefly speechless. The last time he'd witnessed Emery so defensive and obstinate had been when he'd found out about Russell and Hazard's drunken kiss, or when he'd asked about Jesse that one afternoon.

Emery tried again, gentler. "I'm saying that we all hang out now, and that's better than being separated."

"*All* of you are tight," Hazard surmised skeptically.

Emery shook his head. "No. Me, Russell, Jesse, Lily, and Brianna. You leaving just... I don't know, we all just started talking." He paused, brow knotting. He looked over at Hazard, mouth in a thin line. "I'm still really pissed off at you too, Hazard. Don't think I'm not."

"Just let me know what I've missed," Hazard mumbled. He looked at his feet. He didn't really feel all that wronged that nobody had told him anything, and he wasn't upset that Emery was mad. In fact, he just felt inept. He felt like everything was still his fault. He didn't mean to argue with Emery, not after the day before, but being around his mom made him feel really tense.

"Well, I sat in a cop car for the first time in my life." Emery ran his finger over the arm of the couch. "Andrew's been horrible lately. We got in a lot of fights, and one night he called me some bad names, so I punched him. He called the cops. I almost got in big trouble. I cried in the back of the cop car, like a baby. After that, it just wasn't okay with Andrew at all, so I moved in with Russell."

Emery looked at Hazard through his lashes, as if demanding he challenge any part of that—the part about Andrew, the part about punching his stepdad, or the part about moving in with Russell. Hazard swallowed. He'd always hated Andrew, and so had Emery, and he'd always kind of known Emery was never letting go of Russell. He just wished he could have been around when Emery was going through a really tough time. He felt like a bad friend.

"You know I've got your back," Hazard insisted quietly.

"I know. Ditto." Emery sighed and leaned forward on his knees. "Anyway, that's that." He paused uncomfortably. "You already know about Felix. He was living with Jesse in Tacoma when it all happened."

Hazard fought a cringe, but he smiled. He smiled because Jesse had made it to Tacoma for school. He smiled because Felix had been there with him. *When it all happened*, Emery said, meaning the crash that killed Felix. Hazard felt his throat tighten at the thought, but thankfully, his mom came out into the living room again. She was still in her pale-pink robe, but she'd brushed her hair and clipped it into a half back. The strands that hung down along her temples and ears were curled, and her makeup was nearly done.

"How about we go out for lunch?" she asked, fiddling with a bottle of concealer.

"Sounds good," Hazard mumbled, still not quite sure how to interact with her, especially now that she wanted to do things with him.

His mom smiled at Emery. Her smile was thin, one of nearly condescending approval. "And you come along too, Emery. You've always been such a good friend to Hazard, even when he went through those horrible teenage stages and was obsessed with those *junior* friends of his."

Hazard sighed. It wasn't like he'd expected her to have changed over the course of two years, even with a divorce and Hazard leaving. That wasn't that upsetting, really. It was actually kind of comforting, her awkward and snide charm. It reminded Hazard that he was indeed back home and it was all really happening.

Emery said he had to make a phone call, so he stepped outside. Hazard waited for his mom to disappear again, hoping for silence that would help him regain a bit of his composure in this situation, but it never came. His mother didn't leave. She lingered between the hall and the kitchen. Finally, after a few long seconds, she smoothed her robe out along the backs of her thighs and eased down to sit in the easy chair to his left.

Hazard glanced at her through his lashes. She was smiling nostalgically. Hazard didn't quite know what to say. Was she going to apologize, or maybe berate him for his decisions?

"Thank you for coming back," his mother said, refusing to meet his eyes. She stared at the coffee table, a plaintive little smile still pinching up her face. She twisted the bottle of concealer around and around in her grip, and for the first time, Hazard noticed how thin and bony her neat hands were. Her wedding band was gone.

Hazard looked back down at his feet, a weird pressure spreading in his chest. "You're welcome," he mumbled.

"Are you still mad at me, or has that phase finally passed?"

Hazard's shoulders sagged. He couldn't help but smile in weary recognition of that tone. "I'm not mad at you."

She crossed her arms and leaned down against her knees. "Baby, you know I love you," she insisted, tapping her nails against the concealer bottle. Her brow knotted. Hazard nodded mutely. "But you were just such a hard kid to deal with. I thought that maybe letting you do what you wanted, something that drastic, would be best for you."

"Oh, you mean, me running away?" Hazard asked. His mom frowned tightly. He frowned in turn, shaking his head quickly. "I didn't mean it like *that*, I was asking honestly."

His mom looked at him a moment, thinking. She nodded, toes curling idly. "I had an angry stage too, you know. It's not like I didn't understand it."

"You just didn't know how to deal with it, right."

"Right."

Hazard smiled thinly, lacing his fingers between his knees. Of course his mother hadn't caught on to his bitter tone. It was too close to her own.

"But you graduated high school," his mom murmured next. The pride was subdued in her voice, but Hazard saw it in her eyes. It made him blush. If he hadn't still been holding a grudge that she hadn't gone to the ceremony, he might have liked the warmth there between them.

"I did," he said quietly. "Did you think I wouldn't? Why didn't you come?"

She skirted that intentionally, countering with, "I have a question, baby."

"Shoot," Hazard mumbled. He didn't really think he wanted to know what his mom had thought about his academic career, anyway.

"How much of the problem was *that junior's* influence?"

His stomach fell, and then his smile, just at the sound of the word coming from her mouth and the way it made him feel like he was a freshman again. Hazard glanced over at the front door, frowning. "Should I tell Emery to hurry up? He's probably talking to Russell—"

"Hazard James."

"You know, Mom, he wasn't always a *junior*. He was a *senior* too."

"All right. Are you going to avoid my question forever, or what?"

Hazard closed his eyes. He pressed his knuckles to his temple and searched for composure. This was supposed to be some kind of closure between him and his mom, right? He'd come back to Bethany prepared for closure, so he couldn't push it away just because his mother was unbearable sometimes. She was trying. It was obvious she'd missed him.

He needed to just suck it up. She wasn't going to change, after all, and she didn't know how uncomfortable it was for him to talk about *that junior*.

"I don't know," Hazard whispered. He looked at her defenselessly. "I don't know, maybe a lot of it was him. But he was my friend, Mom. You get that now, right? He was one of my best friends, whether you liked him or not."

"All right, calm down." She raised her brows. Hazard sighed, because he *was* being calm. "It was just a question, Hazard. Believe me, at this point, I'm quite aware there are things you'll do whether I like it or not."

"Mom, I'm not a bad kid, I *wasn't* a bad kid—"

"You weren't a bad kid, you just made bad decisions."

"Mom, *seriously*—"

"I know that you would sneak out. And drink, and smoke. And maybe do other things."

Hazard froze, staring at her. His heart sank and a strange shock set in. He swallowed hard.

His mom had *known*. He totally believed that. He was horrified by the idea—and then he saw the way his mom's eyes had taken on a little sheen. She was tearing up. Hazard didn't know what to do or say. He was not prepared for the way it hurt him so much to see his mother that close to tears, and because of him. He husked, "What are you talking about?"

"After a while, I caught on. Parents always do. We're not a different species, you know. We're the same as you, and it's not like we're stupid. We were there, and we know our kids, and we know that it's only natural for a person to do what they want to do whether they're allowed to or not."

His mom looked away and blinked rapidly until she felt confident her eyes were no longer as clouded by tears. She cleared her throat, turning back to him. "I wouldn't be able to sleep until I heard you come back home. And the nights you'd 'sleep over' at Emery's house, I'd barely be able to sleep at all because I'd keep wondering what you were really doing, if I'd wake up to a police officer at my door or something."

Hazard stared, completely dumbfounded and rendered speechless. Guilt settled in his stomach as sharp and cold as fear. It crawled anxiously beneath his skin. He swallowed again, searching for the will to talk. "Well, I *did* stay at Emery's. Sometimes."

"I saw you once." His mom stared at the concealer bottle with her face pinched into as nonchalant an expression as she could manage.

Hazard's brow furrowed further. "Saw me what?"

"Kissing that junior. Excuse me, that *best friend* of yours."

As if he couldn't feel anything worse, Hazard's stomach lurched and everything else he was feeling plummeted into a sick amalgamation of embarrassment, horror, and shock. Hazard stared down at his shoes and wondered where Emery was. His breath quickened. His skin crawled with a rotten little heat, something next to clamminess. He wanted to get out of there, now. Fuck lunch. He wanted to leave, hug and kiss good-bye, and go wallow in humiliation elsewhere.

But instead, Hazard licked his lips. He whispered stupidly, "Oh."

His mother hummed a bit, brusquely, looking at her concealer bottle just so she didn't have to look at him. "It was one night when he dropped you off. I guess you didn't think I could see you out there on the curb next door."

Hazard flinched at the subtlety of her bitterness. He swallowed on a raw throat and held his head in his hands, fingers curling into his hair. Suddenly he felt very small again, very young and scared. Maybe he still was, after two years. It wasn't like the jump from sixteen to eighteen was *that* long.

"Maybe you just thought you saw it, Mom. Maybe it didn't really happen."

His mom went on without even considering this possibility. "I didn't know if that *best friend* of yours was over eighteen or not then, but I might have considered pressing charges for carnal knowledge of a minor if your dad hadn't convinced me to just pretend it never happened. Which was easy, I guess, because I'm definitely not equipped to handle *something like that*. I mean, I sensed *something* going on between you two, but I just couldn't bring myself to believe it, I guess. God, something like *that*, I could never—I just—"

She broke off into a weary sigh. Hazard thought he might die of embarrassment. He wasn't sure what appalled him more—that his dad knew too, or that his mom had thought about pressing charges. *Carnal knowledge*, really? What if she knew about everything else? What if he told her she still had to deal with *something like that*, because he still felt stirred up when he thought of Jesse Logan Wesley, and that didn't seem to be changing?

"And then you ran away," his mother finished with a curt nod and a little perk of her shoulders. She stared at her hands. A silence fell, and although he wanted to deny it all, Hazard couldn't think of anything strong enough to stand up against the opinion she held. Her opinion would remain unyielding in the end, anyway.

Hazard figured Emery knew they were talking. He was probably staying outside on the phone intentionally.

His mom sighed again. Hazard cleared his throat. The hush went on for another moment, and then his mother offered decidedly, "Well, I've heard of the Wesleys. At least you were smart and... *associated* with someone who was rich. I guess."

Hazard sputtered for a moment, so stunned by the statement that he actually laughed at it. "*Mom,*" he mumbled. "Honestly."

"Honestly," she agreed cutely. Hazard shook his head, smiling sadly. She was trying to lighten the mood.

The front door opened. Hazard silently thanked a higher power as Emery stumbled inside, already apologizing. "I'm sorry, I'm sorry, I was trying to hurry, but Russell kept talking."

Hazard glanced at his mom, and they laughed. Emery looked between the two of them, lost.

"I'll be out in a few minutes," his mom said, going back to her bedroom. The door closed. Emery smiled awkwardly and searched out Hazard's eyes, confused. Hazard shook his head, waving his hand in dismissal.

"Closure, or something," Hazard mumbled.

Chapter 17
The Way Things Are

THEY parted ways with Hazard's mom after lunch at Red Robin. They stopped at Subway to get food for Russell, which Emery was going to drop off at the YMCA. Hazard didn't have much else to do, so he tagged along with Emery. He felt guilty for it, but he preferred wasting time with Emery to sitting through an awkward day with his mom.

"Well, she's as uncomfortable as ever," Hazard mumbled, watching the city pass outside the passenger window. He still remembered everything like the back of his hand. He remembered the streets, driving them and walking them, in daylight and at dark.

"Yeah," Emery said. He laughed below his breath, steering with one hand and leaning on the other. "But she's your mom. You have to love her."

Hazard couldn't argue with that. They laughed a little, listening to the radio. When they got to the YMCA, Hazard waited in the corner of the lobby as Emery went to the front desk and asked for Russell.

"Get some coffee," Emery said to Hazard, leaning against the front desk to wait. Hazard did. He trudged over to the free coffee bar and made a cup. The smell was comforting. The taste of it brought back memories of goofing off in the indoor tennis courts or on the track upstairs.

Hazard lingered by the bulletin board in the lobby, between the front desk and the coffee bar. Russell wandered in from a hall near the entrance to the pool and met Emery at the desk. He played with a pen absently, smiling at Emery like he was the only one in the room. Hazard couldn't hear what they were saying below the buzz of the busy gym. Whatever it was, Emery laughed, leaning on the counter. Russell pulled his shaggy hair back into a little ponytail and took his lunch from Emery.

They looked happy.

Hazard frowned, looking down. He looked at all the dust bunnies gathered below the coffee bar. The layers of sound in the YMCA faded into white noise, a hum in the back of his head as Hazard stared at the scuffed rubber toes of his Converse.

He wasn't supposed to feel this. He'd felt like an outsider here before. He'd felt like an outsider in Seattle. He'd felt like a loose end or a last-minute addition, and Hazard had been so sure it would be different coming back after two years, but in fact it felt a little worse. Emery waited tables. Russell was in school and worked at the YMCA. Peyton and Olivia were probably together, his parents had gotten divorced, and God knew what everyone else was up to. Hazard had left that August, and they'd all moved on without him. What had he expected them to do, wait for him?

Hazard understood.

He was just a speed bump in all their lives, or a little detour. They all got along just fine whether he was there or not. He was just collision, like that graffiti on the 7-Eleven: *we all collide.*

Hazard felt eyes on him. Russell was looking at him. Hazard straightened up. He swallowed, throat raw, then forced a friendly smile and waved idly.

Russell muttered something to Emery. Emery turned around. He gestured for Hazard to come closer, but Hazard shook his head. Emery stared at him hard until Hazard gave in and walked over.

"Hey." Russell tipped his chin in greeting.

"Hey." Hazard shifted to his other foot. "What's up?"

Russell began to unwrap his lunch, shrugging. "Work. What are you guys doing after this?"

Emery glanced at Hazard, then back at Russell. He frowned thoughtfully. "Just hanging out. What time do you get off, Russ?"

"Three." Russell looked over at Hazard. "If you're up for it, you can have dinner at our house again, Hazard. We can watch a movie or something."

Hazard tried to swallow the feeling of being an outsider. It wasn't fair of him. Russell was trying to bridge the gap, uncomfortable as he seemed, which had to mean something.

Hazard smiled meekly. He mumbled, "Sure. That sounds great."

They wasted time until Russell's shift was over, wandering from room to room before finally sitting at the pool with their feet in the water, watching kids run around and splash while their parents swam laps.

Hazard called his mom to let her know he was at Emery's for dinner. He felt bad because he didn't want her to think the old routine was starting again. Russell made Totino's pizzas for them all. Just like old times, Emery picked out a horror movie. There were no living room tents, but that was okay. Emery and Russell shared a couch. Hazard curled up with the throw blanket on the easy chair. He'd prepared himself for an incredibly awkward afternoon and evening. He'd expected there to be tension of some sort still, it being just the three of them, but in reality it felt okay. Hazard told them that. Emery looked guilty, but Russell smiled kindly enough.

Hazard let himself relax. He didn't feel like such an intruder anymore. In fact, he felt nostalgic. He felt comfortable. He felt like he had years ago, when he'd spend time with Emery and know deep down that Emery would never really be his best friend because he was already Russell's best friend.

It was fun. They watched *The Ring*. Hazard jumped more than any of them, although it seemed roles had switched over time: Russell was a little freaked, but Emery scoffed a few times, maybe only to hide how scared he was. Russell cleaned up afterward, while Emery asked Hazard more about living on Professors' Row, about high school in Seattle, about what he was doing now and what he'd done lately. They laughed. They remembered together. Russell joined them again and actually laughed about afternoons of long ago too, like the time Emery had puked on his shoes or Hazard had gotten stuck on top of the monkey bars.

Sitting at the coffee table talking about being little, Hazard didn't hate Russell. He might have been good at everything and really attractive and moody and Emery's best friend, but he wasn't that bad. Hazard felt okay with the two of them. He felt warm and at ease. He was having fun. He felt like everything was going to be all right again—except that there was something missing, and Hazard wasn't sure what.

Hazard didn't think about it, this missing something, until after Emery drove him back to his house in Buckingham Court. Hazard got out, dragging his backpack and duffel bag. Emery got out too, leaning on the open driver's side door with a smile. He rapped his knuckles on the roof of the car absently.

Emery said thoughtfully, "Haz?"

Hazard closed the passenger door, meeting Emery's eyes over the hood of the car. The road was dark, but the streetlamps left pools of light here and there. "Yeah?"

Emery licked his lips. "Promise you won't leave again without telling."

Hazard's chest tightened. "I promise," he murmured. Emery smiled again.

His mom acted surprised to see him, but he caught a glimpse of the smile on her face as she held the door open for him to bring his things in.

"Your uncle told me you had a hotel," she said curiously.

"I cancelled it." Hazard glanced at her through his lashes, shrugging. "Plus, I watched *The Ring* with Emery. There's no way I'm sleeping alone."

Hazard watched TV with his mom, curled up on one side of the bed in his parents' old room. They talked for a while, feeble colloquial conversation. His mom said, "I'm feeling rebellious tonight," when she got some snacks to eat in bed. Hazard was saddened by it, but he snacked with her. He didn't want to imagine that this was how she spent her time after everyone left her: alone, curled up in bed.

Thinking about that, Hazard couldn't leave her to sleep in his old room. He changed into his pajamas and lay in a ball beside her. They laughed together. Hazard realized their laughter was very similar, and so were their smiles, flanked by very faint shared dimples. It made him feel kind of sad that it had taken him so long to notice those things.

He let his mom run her fingers through his hair like he was young again. In truth, he felt young again. He felt little and innocent, and he liked the way it felt as his mom's hands tangled in his hair. It was soothing. Hazard fell asleep to it and the sound of his mother giggling to herself at *The Nanny*. He hoped she didn't feel so alone that night. Nobody wanted to go home and be alone. He knew that from experience.

HAZARD woke up wanting to call Jesse.

Sunlight filtered in through the blinds. His mom was already up. He could smell her curling iron, beyond the closed bathroom door. There was the sound of her little radio, low and muffled, playing soft hits that she hummed and swayed to as she did her hair. Hazard lay curled in her blankets a while longer, staring up at the ceiling fan with hooded eyes. He felt very awake, but he was too comfortable to move yet. He was afraid of the decision he had to make.

Eventually, Hazard leaned out of his mom's bed and got his phone from the bedside table. He opened it up and went to the digital phonebook. He'd switched phone models in 2006, just before he'd moved in with his aunt and uncle, but the SIM card was the same, so all the old numbers were still in there. He scrolled through them. He was stalling. He knew he was. He was balking horribly.

Hazard found the number he wanted. He stared at it, suddenly feeling very clammy. His heart fluttered and his stomach tightened nervously. Hazard got up. He moved quietly, so his mom didn't hear him. He went out into the living room and sat on the couch. He realized he was holding his breath. He let it out, brow knotting. Finally, he hit the call button. The answer was coarse and unwelcoming when the line connected:

"What?"

Hazard bristled. He frowned, glancing at his mom's bedroom, wary of her coming out. She didn't. For a moment, Hazard couldn't talk. His throat was clenched. His mouth was dry.

"Hey, Jesse," he managed, not sure what to expect next in response.

He heard Jesse sigh and shift with the phone. "Do you know what time it is?"

Hazard gritted his teeth anxiously. He looked over at the clock across the living room. "Nine o'clock," he mumbled. "I was wondering if I could come see you today."

Hazard was met with silence. His stomach dropped. He hoped he wasn't making the wrong impression. Maybe Jesse expected that Hazard intended much more than a friendly visit. The line was still silent. Hazard blinked, wondering if he'd lost the connection. He checked his phone. He hadn't. He still had full bars.

"Hey…," Hazard whispered hopefully.

"Still here," Jesse husked, then fell silent again.

"It's not what you think," Hazard hurried to explain. He felt very stupid. "This isn't like that. I'm in Bethany seeing my mom and stuff, and I just thought maybe we could do lunch or something and catch up—"

There was a clatter on the other end of the phone connection. Hazard jumped, eyes widening. Very vaguely, he heard muffled voices. They might have been arguing. One of them was a female voice. Hazard tried not to assume anything. He couldn't make out what they were saying. There was a thud, somewhere far in the background of the voices. There was more fuzzy clatter over the phone, and then suddenly Brianna was there.

"Come over," she said, sounding tired. "I'll give you the address."

Something pinched in Hazard's chest to know that Brianna was with Jesse. He swallowed, glancing over at his mom's room again. His resolve faltered. Did he really want to go see Jesse? What did he expect? He didn't even know. He frowned down at his toes and said, "Okay. Hold on. Let me get a pen."

Brianna gave Hazard the address. Jesse was in Tacoma. Hazard wrote it down, then looked up directions on his dad's old computer.

HAZARD got dressed.

"Where are you going?" his mom asked.

"Jesse's," Hazard replied cautiously.

His mom didn't say anything. She stared at him from the doorway of his bedroom as he buttoned his jeans and looked for a clean shirt. He glanced over at her. He hoped she hadn't had anything planned to do with him that he was ruining.

Hazard got out his toothbrush. "I'll be back sooner than later, Mom.

I promise. I just wanna catch up a little."

"I feel like you haven't even been gone for two years," his mother said, arms crossed. She wasn't picking at him; she frowned genuinely, as if feeling very sentimental.

Hazard understood what she meant. Standing in front of the sink in the hall bathroom with his toothbrush and toothpaste in hand, he looked at his reflection in the mirror. He still looked like a teenager, not a young man who had just graduated high school. He hadn't gotten much taller. He was still kind of smallish, although his jaw was a little more defined, which made him look older. Sullen blue eyes, dark-brown hair still crowding in on his face. And his mom, lingering outside the bathroom door, wanting to know what he was doing, why he was doing it, and why she couldn't change it. He understood exactly what she meant when she said it felt like he hadn't even been gone. He felt the same way for a moment or two.

Hazard brushed his teeth and put on his shoes. He felt very nervous, so it didn't help that his mother kept wandering between the kitchen and the bathroom while he got ready, sipping her coffee and smiling at him like she wanted him to stay. Hazard fidgeted in front of the mirror, hoping he looked okay. Part of him wanted to impress Jesse. Part of him hoped he'd make Jesse miss him, or prove to Jesse that he was doing all right without him.

He got the directions and his phone. He hugged his mom tight, keys jangling in hand. He promised, "I'll be back later. Love you."

After he said it, Hazard felt kind of shy and awkward, so he hurried out to his car. His mom smiled and waved from the stoop. He smiled and waved back, pulling out of the driveway.

Hazard drove to Tacoma. He fiddled with the radio for a while, settling on the alternative station. Afentra was hosting for the morning. She talked for a while, and Hazard was too nervous to laugh at all her funny quips and outrageous laughter. "Nine in the Afternoon" played, which made Hazard think of "Lying is the Most Fun" and having sex on the floor of a stranger's bedroom.

He almost got lost because he was distracted by the University of Puget Sound campus. It was gorgeous and majestic.

Jesse lived in an apartment a mile from the school, nice white buildings surrounded by rich green. It was well taken care of. Jesse was on the third floor. With each stair he climbed, Hazard felt more and more sick with nervousness. He stopped twice and almost turned around to go back to his car. He didn't.

Hazard stopped at the right door and knocked. He looked out over his shoulder at the view from the third floor, deep green trees and scattered buildings, the college in the distance and the sun reflecting off the water. There was a dirty ashtray on the edge of the banister.

The door opened, and Hazard felt his heart sink. Slowly, he looked back around. Jesse regarded him coolly. He looked like he'd just rolled out of bed, his dark hair in a sloppy wannabe ponytail because it was too short to be anything else, and was that a tiny bit of stubble there by the line of his jaw?

Hazard couldn't breathe for a moment. It was Jesse. Oh God, he was standing in front of Jesse Wesley again after two years, and he felt like puking. Hazard knew those eyes, and that nose, and that stubbornly set jaw, the piercings and the hands and all the little hidden tattoos, and the way there was a distance in Jesse's stare. He looked rather harsh and unrelenting. He was twenty now, Hazard knew. He'd be twenty-one in October.

Below Jesse's dismal stare, Hazard felt very small and pathetic. His heart pounded. He was terrified and excited at the same time, and he fidgeted. Jesse looked him up and down and Hazard swallowed, mouth dry. He didn't have a clue what to expect next. He could smell the familiar scent of lingering cigarette smoke from inside the apartment.

Jesse shifted. He said plainly, "'Flat Out Fucked.'"

Hazard's face pinched. The voice sent chills racing up and down his back, but it was not so much the memory of the voice as it was the ghost of the memory that spoke. It was just different, that was all. Everything was different now. He mumbled, "What?"

"'Touch Me, I'm Sick,'" Jesse said next, frowning.

Hazard frowned back. Were those supposed to be insults? Feeling even more nervous, he mumbled, "What are you talking about?"

Jesse smiled thinly. It wasn't relieving in the least. He pointed at Hazard. "That's what I thought. You don't know any of the songs. That's *my* Mudhoney shirt, stupid. Thanks for returning it."

Hazard blanked. He blushed, looking down at his shirt, and realized quite too late that he was wearing one of Jesse's shirts that he'd worn home drunk before. He stared at his feet, totally embarrassed to have worn it today of all days. He just hadn't thought about it. It was a comfortable old shirt.

Brianna was there suddenly. She pushed Jesse out of the doorway, giving him a frustrated glance and Hazard an apologetic smile. "Hi, Hazard," she said, sounding very pleased to see him. Her hair was shorter, little blonde curls near her chin and purple barrettes at her temple.

Hazard smiled dumbly, relieved she was interrupting. "Hey."

She led him into the apartment. It was weird to be there with them. Hazard had a feeling Jesse's dad financed it completely, right down to the furniture. It was too nice for a simple college student, even if Jesse had a really good job. In the corner by the little fireplace, between the TV and the hearth, was a stack of textbooks. There were a few dishes in the sink, framed pictures scattered about on end tables and shelves. It smelled like Jesse everywhere.

Brianna closed the door. The TV was on. Jesse wandered off to the couch to watch it. Hazard studied him uncomfortably, wondering if he'd meet his stare. Jesse didn't. He looked frighteningly serene, like he was unaffected by most everything.

"I made coffee," Brianna announced, moving into the kitchen. Hazard noticed for the first time the way she sounded older, very much like a young woman. It was pretty. Hazard followed her, not sure what else to do. She got out cream and sugar for him.

It was horrifying to be in Jesse's apartment. He didn't know what to do. He felt scared to be around them and worried about Jesse. He suddenly felt very sad and very *guilty*. He thought of Felix again, which ripped open that pain just below his throat another time, and he looked down at his cup of coffee, trying to regain composure as tears stung his eyes. He could think about that later. It wouldn't do him very much good to break down around Brianna and Jesse, would it? It just wasn't fair that they hadn't told him—

There was tension in the air. Brianna seemed to notice it. She tucked hair behind her ears and drifted off down the hall. "I need to finish folding laundry," she explained, and Hazard wished desperately that she would not leave him alone with Jesse—especially now that he felt for sure this Jesse was *not* the Jesse he was used to.

Hazard shrugged limply. There was a photograph of Jesse and Felix on one of the shelves near the kitchen. He fidgeted, jaw tightening. "I heard about Felix," he husked feebly.

Jesse was quiet for a long time. Then he said, faintly, "Yeah."

"You didn't call me?"

"Nope."

"So I guess you were still with him." Hazard shrugged again, mouth in a firm line. "That's why you didn't want me there when he died."

Jesse didn't seem fazed. If he was, he hid it well. "Know this, Hazard," he edged out, ignoring Hazard's enthusiastic glare. "I'll kick your ass if you piss me off any more." Jesse paused, as if imagining the scene, then added with childish spite, "Oh, and I'll laugh too."

"Give me a cigarette burn while you're at it?"

"Just shut up. Your attempt at sarcasm makes me want to barf."

"Good, I'm glad."

"Look, just because we were friends before doesn't mean we're friends again now that you're back all of a sudden."

"*Perfect*, because I don't wanna be your friend."

"Oh, yeah? Good."

"So you're still at school here, Jesse?"

"Yeah."

A silence fell, heavy. In it, Hazard's glare softened into a culpable frown. He fidgeted, picking at the rough skin near his cuticle with absent distaste. He looked up at Jesse, studying him again. His hair was choppy and dark, naturally dark. He had a new tattoo there on the instep of his foot. His earrings glinted in the living room light. He still had the barbell in his brow. Hazard had taken his out. Jesse looked long and thin and barely there in his T-shirt and jeans. Where was his usual flair? It was just a plain gray T-shirt and dark blue jeans today. Nothing eccentric, nothing special. Just a gray shirt, jeans, and bare feet. Hazard didn't know why it hurt to acknowledge those things.

Hazard's heart fluttered as he braved his next question. He almost couldn't voice it. "Did you love him? Felix, I mean?"

It sounded stupid spoken man to man, but who cared? He knew it would sting and he knew it was bold, but he needed to know.

"Yeah." Jesse didn't hesitate to answer. "And get this. Ashton was *fine* after Felix told him to fuck off. You know why? I don't know, something like, he consulted all these books on stars and psychology and finally came to the conclusion that the two of them had never been compatible in the first place. Maybe it had something to do with him meeting this girl Katie." Jesse scoffed. He grumbled, "God, I had so many friends like that. *Gay*, I mean. What was wrong with me?"

Hazard smiled in bitter amusement, but it faded quickly and his heart sank. There was a lump in his throat. He kept seeing Felix's grin in the back of his head, and the guilt in him for hating Felix when he left Bethany for Seattle was too much. He'd never get to see Felix again, or joke with him, or talk to him seriously like they sometimes did. It was probably worse for Jesse. Jesse had known Felix for years and years.

Hazard fidgeted. He took a few sips of coffee. The TV echoed, *Full House*. Hazard opened his mouth and really considered asking, *Did you love me too? Like you did Felix?* But before he could gather enough courage to so much as begin forming the words, Jesse picked up the frayed end of the silence.

"I don't drink as much anymore. I still smoke though, if you didn't notice."

Hazard thought of the ashtray on the railing outside and the pack of Camels on the table to his right. "I noticed. Your humor is astounding."

"I believe it was more sarcasm than humor, Hazard." Jesse actually laughed, briefly.

Hazard hung his head. He had to smile, simply because Jesse had laughed, and as bleak as it sounded, it was a familiar laugh. It meant his stopping by wasn't meaningless or inappropriate. His chest still ached for Felix. Finally, Hazard choked out:

"I'm sorry, Jesse."

Jesse shrugged. He turned halfway, looking blankly at Hazard from the couch. Then he smiled thinly—but it was a smile, after all—and lovingly gave Hazard the bird.

Hazard was somewhat aghast but quickly returned the obscene gesture. Over his coffee, he laughed too. "I saw Emery," he announced. "Russell looked pissed when he saw me."

"Yeah, they're living together now," Jesse mumbled.

"I know." Hazard met Jesse's eyes as he took a sip of coffee. "I stayed over there the other night."

Jesse shook his head, uttering a dry chuckle. He understood what Hazard was implying: he'd made Russell mad by staying over and he'd liked it. "You know," Jesse said, "I hated you the moment you opened your mouth that time in the lunchroom. About the spoiled milk and all. And you're *still* quite the little prick, Hazard."

The faint smile on Hazard's face faded. For a moment there, he'd felt as though he'd gone back in time for a few seconds, gone back two or three years to a time when that tone of Jesse's voice meant something along the lines of *I really like you.* Hearing it again made Hazard feel even sicker—a little nostalgic, a little hopeful. He wanted to say something, return the feeling, but he didn't know what to say that would mean the same thing without outright stuttering *I like you too.*

"So where's Lexie? Did she die too?" Hazard asked, glancing over at Jesse and immediately regretting his disrespectful sarcasm for such a sore subject. Whatever progress he'd been making in talking to Jesse withered a little.

"She and Max moved to fucking Florida." Jesse shrugged rudely.

Hazard stared down at his coffee, disconsolate and startled by all these changes and feeling sort of left out. The heavy sense of it settled on his shoulders. How could things be so different here after just two years?

"I just realized something," Hazard said, trying to mend his blunder. Jesse stayed silent, but Hazard knew he was listening. "You never, ever told me why you got that tattoo." He pointed to Jesse's right arm, where the lyrics *Fear is the heart of love* were visible on his inner wrist, surrounded by little music notes and bars.

Jesse looked a little surprised by the sudden recollection. "You're right. I didn't."

"Care to tell me now?"

"Not really."

Hazard's brows furrowed. He wilted into a defeated frown and cast his eyes elsewhere, absently running his thumb over the rim of his coffee cup. "Okay," he mumbled.

Brianna came back into the living room with a laundry basket full of folded clothes. "You need to put these away," she said to Jesse.

Hazard didn't mean to seem grumpy or challenging, but it was just the way the words came out when he asked, "Do you guys live together?"

"What if we do?" Jesse sent a scathing glance at Hazard. Hazard frowned darkly back at him. Jesse's attitude was incredibly touchy, like it had been a few times before, but this was ultimately more vicious.

Brianna cleared her throat. She tucked her hair behind her ear. "Not officially. I helped him get set up when he moved in. Every Friday I come in here and clean because I know that he won't. I make sure he's eating—"

"It's not like I'm an *invalid*," Jesse grumbled, scowling on the couch like a child. Hazard couldn't believe he was going to be twenty-one in a few months. Then again, he could.

"So you're like a free maid service," Hazard surmised, glancing over at Brianna.

Brianna couldn't get the words out. Jesse interrupted, "She's a good friend."

Hazard was in disbelief. "You're using her," he murmured, and immediately regretted saying it. He stared down at his coffee with wide eyes, feeling the tension in the air snap. Brianna was silent. Jesse got up and stormed over to the kitchen.

"Oh, yeah? Is that really what you're here for, Hazard? You wanna pick on me? You wanna make judgments and assumptions?"

"No." Hazard frowned at him firmly, even though he really just wanted to sit down and hide his head in his arms. "I'm sorry, Jesse. I'm not trying to start anything."

"Sure, you're not." Jesse scowled. "God, you haven't changed at all."

"I have too!" Hazard yelled. He had to stop himself from stomping his foot, he was so mad and insulted and a little bit scared of Jesse. He glowered up at him, and Jesse stared back just as angrily. "Everything's different now!"

"Of course it is! It's called growing up and getting smart and accepting changes instead of running away from them."

"*Please stop*," Brianna hissed. "This is stupid!"

Hazard scoffed. He had a feeling Jesse was referring to his own acceptance of Felix's death, or maybe he was referring to the night Hazard left Bethany.

"That's what I did, right?" Hazard edged out. "I *ran away* from change."

"If you want to get technical," Jesse snorted, "then yeah, you did."

A cold, familiar ache was rising in Hazard's chest again, and it scared him. They'd just been talking relatively civilly moments before. Now he just felt so overwhelmed. Of course it couldn't stay civil. This was the first time they'd seen each other in two years; *of course* they were going to argue. Hazard pointed at Brianna, scowling fiercely. "Then explain this, Jesse. I left and you had Felix. Felix died, and now you have Brianna—"

"*You don't know anything!*" Jesse howled. Both Hazard and Brianna flinched away. Jesse glared at Hazard. It made Hazard's skin crawl. It made tears sting the backs of his eyes and his throat tighten to see the hurt in Jesse's eyes and know that he'd inflicted some of it. He looked down at his feet. This was not what he wanted to do. He wanted to fix things, not make them worse. He needed to think before he opened his mouth.

Jesse left the kitchen. He grabbed his cigarettes and went onto his patio, pushing the curtains aside and closing the glass doors on the rest of the house. In the tense, volatile silence, Hazard and Brianna heard him light a cigarette.

Brianna stared at Hazard pointedly. Hazard felt like he was about to get a lecture. His stomach hurt and the adrenaline soured. He knew what he had to do. He was just horrified to do it. He didn't want to screw things up any further.

Hazard moved the curtains at the doors to the patio and went outside. He sat down on the chair opposite Jesse, smelling the sharp, sweet scent of cigarette smoke. It scared Hazard now, that bad habit of Jesse's, a lonesome little worry. He wanted Jesse to cut down. He looked out over the guardrail of the patio. He could see Commencement Bay. It was pretty in the early summer light.

Hazard looked at Jesse. Jesse took a long drag on his cigarette, pretending Hazard wasn't there. He looked tired in too many ways. Hazard ached because of it.

"I'm sorry," Hazard whispered. "I didn't mean it, Jesse."

Jesse smoked silently for a minute. It was a nice day, but Hazard kind of felt cold. He watched the waves of the bay and listened to Jesse smoke. He swallowed. His throat felt raw and his chest felt tight.

"Look at us, sitting down and talking it out together like two mature adults." Jesse smiled bitterly and sighed a silky stream of smoke. Jokes aside, his brow furrowed above dark eyes and his smile faded. "Don't apologize. You don't know anything."

Hazard couldn't help it; he rolled his eyes. "Jesse, I get it. I don't know anything. You can stop now."

Jesse shook his head. He spoke kindly enough. "No, I mean.... You really have no idea what happened."

Hazard watched the smoke swirling in the air, from Jesse's lips and from the glowing end of his cigarette. Jesse ran a hand through his hair and was quiet for a minute. Hazard wasn't quite sure what to say. He just stewed in it a bit, touched that Jesse was calming down and troubled by what he was saying. He itched to understand everything that had happened, but he was a little afraid to know.

"You did a few times, because you'd been drinking, but why didn't you ever really call me, Hazard?"

Hazard stiffened. He looked at Jesse, startled. Jesse sounded very upset, and the look on his face was the same. His green eyes were distant, and his face was set in a sharp frown.

Hazard shrugged limply. He remembered the few times he'd called Jesse, drunk. He felt guilty for it. He started biting his nails, anxious. "I didn't think you wanted to talk to me, Jesse. I thought you'd call *me* if that was the case."

Jesse shook his head. "You just *left*, Hazard. I get not telling your parents, but you didn't even tell *Emery*."

"I know—"

"I thought you needed time, to calm down or cool down or whatever. But you *never called*."

Hazard stared at Jesse in disbelief. Something hurt deep in his chest to hear that. "You *hit me*, Jesse. You said some really mean stuff to me. I didn't think you'd care either way if I called or not!"

"I was wrong," Jesse mumbled tersely, avoiding Hazard's frantic eyes. He glared at his cigarette. "I was wrong to do all that, and I get it if you don't ever forgive me, but you have to understand that you don't know the whole story. You only know your own half."

"You wanted to *be with him*," Hazard insisted in a whisper. It felt rotten to say. All the old feelings were coming back, especially because he was in front of Jesse again after so long. "That's what you told me."

"I did...."

"And you didn't want that with me."

Jesse flicked ash off the end of his cigarette, scowling. He looked like the old Jesse with that expression. "Goddammit, Hazard, I never said that. You *assumed* that. You said some really damn hurtful things to me too, you know."

"I was scared, Jesse!"

"Oh, yeah? So was I, Hazard." Jesse's eyes glinted fiercely as they met Hazard's. "I was scared of making the wrong decision."

Hazard was confused, and he hated it. He looked at Jesse coldly, brow knotted. "The *wrong decision*? You said you loved him."

Jesse closed his eyes and rubbed at his head like he was gathering patience to deal with Hazard. "Felix was my best friend for years, Haz. That's what I meant. Not like *a relationship*. You should understand that, with Emery and all. He was having such a hard time with Ashton that summer, you know? I wanted to talk to him seriously about it, without anyone else around, but we were fucking drunk, Hazard. We were *drunk*, and I thought that the best thing I could do for him was to be with him. At that point, I thought he needed it from me."

At that point.

Hazard's eyes widened. He stared at Jesse, cold with shock. Jesse kept talking, something about how it only lasted for two months or so and he didn't have to worry because they didn't *do* anything, but Hazard wasn't really listening. His heart fluttered uneasily and he felt sick with it. His chest hurt. He could feel the emotion knotting in his throat, and he was scared he might cry like an idiot, like a fag, but it was just too much. Jesse was saying that he only wanted to be with Felix that summer because he felt obligated to. Because Felix was his best friend and Felix was confused and Felix needed someone to remind him that Ashton was a loser. All the old feelings of stubborn jealousy and betrayal made Hazard want to demand, *Wasn't there a way you could have helped him without dating him?* But he couldn't talk. He could hardly breathe with all these realizations blooming in his mind, painful and guilty, and on top of it all there came the ache, knowing that Felix probably died thinking Hazard hated him.

Jesse watched him, somewhere between harsh and sad. He could see that Hazard was making realizations. He flicked ash off his cigarette and took a long drag from it. Thankfully, it had calmed him down. He whispered, "I told you, Hazard. You have no idea."

There was a long silence. It wasn't empty. It was bitter and significant, full of deep thinking and the strange comfort of being around an old friend. Jesse finished his cigarette. Hazard focused on breathing, even though it hurt to. He held out his hand, and Jesse knew exactly what he wanted. He handed him his lighter and his pack of Camels.

Hazard lit a cigarette too. He let it rest on the edge of Jesse's ashtray after a moment or two, pulling his legs up Indian style on the chair. "You're different," he mumbled, glancing over at Jesse. "You're, uh...."

"Skinnier?"

"Yeah." Hazard swallowed, looking Jesse up and down. He was definitely skinnier. He was paler too, and his eyes just looked very tired. "You look sick," Hazard whispered.

Jesse smoked a little of the cigarette Hazard had lit. Hazard let him even though Jesse's smoking worried him, then took a drag too. Jesse sighed slowly. He met Hazard's eyes, and Hazard held his stare even though it made him sad.

Jesse shrugged. "When Felix died, I really lost it. You were gone, and then he was gone, and I didn't really know what to do anymore. I changed apartments, and Brianna's been, um, taking care of me since February."

More guilt settled at the bottom of Hazard's gut for what he'd assumed earlier. It collected there and soured his stomach. "Oh," he whispered, breath wavering on his lips. Finding all these things out, he felt like such a brat.

Jesse shifted uncomfortably in the patio chair. He picked up his lighter and fumbled with it. He watched as Hazard took a small drag from the wasting cigarette again. Hazard's chest was tight with a familiar sensation, the cold ache that he used to feel when he was afraid Jesse would not need him anymore. There was a song stuck in his head, one that he'd listened to many times after leaving Bethany—*I thought that I could change you, but you changed me.*

It hit him then, like a ton of bricks. Hazard sat back in the chair heavily and stared at his feet.

Jesse was a lonely person too. All he'd really wanted was security, or maybe assurance, and that security came from a serious relationship— which Hazard had denied but Felix had needed. Jesse had hoped it would fill the spot he wanted it to, but it hadn't. It hadn't, and the only memory Jesse had had of the security he'd *almost* had was Hazard telling him that nobody loved him, that nobody wanted to love him, that he had never loved him in the first place, and—

"You left," Jesse husked out. His face was blank, but his voice was very fragile. He tapped his lighter on the little glass patio table. "You fucking left."

Hazard couldn't take it anymore. Whatever dammed up his emotional reserves cracked under the pressure of it all. He was overcome. He choked up. He threw his hands in the air and croaked, *"You didn't need me, Jesse!* You didn't want me! You had Felix, and you didn't want me anymore! Emery had Russell. He's always had Russell. God, even my *mom* had my *dad*, you know? *You didn't need me!*"

"I never said I didn't need you." Jesse spoke slowly and evenly, like Hazard was a child on the verge of a meltdown and needed pacifying. He reached over and put out the cigarette Hazard had lit because he wasn't smoking it anymore. "I never said that. Emery never said that, either. Nobody said that."

"I've changed." Hazard's voice trembled awkwardly. His vision was blurry and his chest was tight. He gritted his teeth. "I'm not the same."

"I know."

"It's been two years. It's been so long, it's been *hard*, Jesse—"

"It has been."

"I still need you."

Jesse shook his head. "No, that's not it."

Hazard scowled, glaring at him. "What are you talking about?"

Jesse didn't say anything. He stared back at Hazard, and his eyes were unreadable. Hazard felt like he was panicking, shaking all over. He knew this sensation. He'd felt it before, that one night in December of his sophomore year when he'd cried on the way home, and the night of Max's Christmas party. He didn't wait for Jesse to talk. He was too afraid.

"I'm telling you the truth now. Aren't you happy? I'm not *running away* from anything. I need you, Jesse. I always have. Don't you get it? *I* didn't even get it. But I do now. It's not Emery I need anymore, it's you, and I *want* to feel that way."

Hazard emphasized each word and stopped for a breath. Jesse gave him nothing but silence and a blank stare. Hazard choked up. He started to cry. He felt pathetic and stupid to be crying, but he couldn't help it. He cried for Felix, and for Jesse, and for all the misunderstandings, and he cried because he was embarrassed to be crying. He felt guilty for being loud when they were outside and everyone could hear them, but he couldn't stop. He was finally letting it out now, and confessing had a power of its own.

"Jesse, I miss you, I need you, I told you before, I love you—"

Jesse waved a hand sharply. "You can't just say that. Stop.

Seriously."

"*Why?*" Hazard yelled. His voice was abrasive, but it broke emotionally. His pride hurt a little.

Jesse shrugged. "Because I'm tearing up," he mumbled timidly, and Hazard was shocked into silence. He stared at Jesse, troubled. He saw the way his eyes were bright with emotion, maybe ready to form into tears too. He wiped at his own eyes, feeling kind of sheepish and childish.

"I made you cry?" he asked quietly.

Jesse looked away stubbornly.

"I never even thought you were capable of crying." Hazard smiled meekly, brow knotting. It was like that simple idea made it easier to breathe for a moment. Jesse glared off in another direction, chin in hand. But there was a spark of something in his eyes, something different, something alive. Hazard sniffled dumbly and husked, "Do you want a tissue?"

Jesse pointed inside the apartment. "There's some in the living room."

Hazard went inside and got them, avoiding Brianna's curious eyes. He probably looked like an idiot, eyes red and mouth in a tart line. He closed the door behind him and put the tissues next to the ashtray. He sat down again. Jesse reached for a tissue but just crumpled it up in a fist. Hazard watched him.

Jesse met his eyes sharply. "That's a lot to take in, Danger. Don't look at me like that."

Hazard looked at his feet instead, but he relaxed a lot. Jesse's voice was livening up, just like his eyes. There was that old ring of dry sarcasm in it again. He'd called him Danger.

A long silence fell then. They both patched up their pride, waiting for the awkwardness to fade away. Jesse stared out at Commencement Bay. He reached for his cigarettes, then just left them on the table. Eventually, Jesse looked over at Hazard. Hazard fought the urge to look up, fingers twisting in his lap. Jesse waited long enough, then reached over the little glass table between the chairs and forced Hazard to make eye contact, lifting his face by the chin. His stare was stern.

"Don't leave like that again," Jesse edged out.

Another wave of emotion hit Hazard, and he held his breath against it. His eyes stung, but he smiled. He tipped his head out of Jesse's grip. "I guess I won't," he said. It was mostly to appease Jesse, but after the words came out, Hazard had no doubt they were true. They took a weight away with them.

Jesse pointed to the musical notes and *Fear is the heart of love* on the inside of his right wrist. "Do you wanna know why I got this?"

Hazard looked between Jesse and his tattoo, eyes wide. "You're going to tell me?"

Jesse held his arm out so Hazard could see the tattoo in full. "Remember when that Death Cab for Cutie album came out? When I started senior year?"

Hazard nodded mutely.

"Well." Jesse cleared his throat gently. His voice was gravelly. "One night, I was just laying in bed listening to it, right? I don't know. 'I Will Follow You into the Dark' came on. It moved me, I guess, as stupid as that sounds. I just remember thinking, *How can music do this to someone?* And then I got to thinking about how imperative and strong music can be, and I realized that I wanted to study it. I guess that was like, the moment I decided I wanted to *do* something with my life, you know? I went to Temple Art and got the lyrics on my wrist so I'd never forget the way I felt that night, or that it's okay to feel that way."

Hazard stared at him. Jesse looked wistful. His eyes were bright with emotion again. Sometimes there were moments that Jesse spoke so deeply it left Hazard reeling. He wanted to say something that might pinch up Jesse's chest the way Jesse's confession had his, but he didn't know what. He mumbled stupidly, "I missed you, Jesse. I missed you so much."

Jesse really started to cry then, finally. Hazard watched it build in his stare and then shatter, honest tears that weren't pathetic or emasculating in the least. They welled up and slid down his face, across his nose, and he rested his face in his palm and stared at nothing in general.

"I made them play the song at Felix's funeral." Jesse's voice was shaky. It scared Hazard. He stared, a little cowed to see Jesse so fraught. His glossy eyes flickered over to meet Hazard's, and Hazard choked up again too.

"I wish I could have gone to the funeral," he whispered.

"No, you don't." Jesse shook his head, laughing caustically. "No. We couldn't even have the casket open. He was too fucked up from the crash—"

That really broke Jesse. He pressed both palms to his eyes and bit his lip, crying so mannishly that it made Hazard ache for him. The legs of the patio chair scraped on the concrete as Hazard stood up. He ran into the table. He didn't care. He put his hand on Jesse's shoulder to comfort him as he cried, and that was it. Hazard teared up too, especially when Jesse mumbled, "The song, the fucking song, the whole reason I'm here—"

Hazard sat down in front of Jesse and rested his head on his knees. Tears and snot fell a few times. Hazard watched them, little dark dots on Jesse's pants. They cried silently together, not like idiots or fags, but like friends, and after Jesse calmed down for the most part, he tangled his fingers in Hazard's dark hair and cleared his throat. Hazard heard him get some tissues. He handed them down and Hazard took them, blowing his nose at the same time as Jesse. Jesse laughed about it, a very childish little laugh.

Hazard looked at the tattoo on Jesse's foot, the peace sign with the date *2-22-08* beneath it, and he knew immediately it was in commemoration of Felix. Hazard swallowed, looking away. He met Jesse's glance, sitting cross-legged at his feet. Jesse's eyes were red and still watery. Hazard wondered if he looked the same way, all exhausted and weak.

"So Brianna's been staying with you?" Hazard played with his shoelaces.

Jesse sniffed roughly. "Yeah."

"I'm glad," Hazard whispered.

"Why don't you stay tonight?" Jesse lit a cigarette. Hazard heard it, then smelled it.

Hazard blushed. He looked at Jesse skeptically, but Jesse was not joking. He didn't seem to be expecting anything like kisses either, which Hazard decided he could be okay with for a while, even though he really wanted to bury his face in Jesse's neck and just stay like that all day. Jesse looked down at him patiently, and Hazard wondered if the question was Jesse's way of inviting him to take over Brianna's role as caretaker.

Hazard murmured apologetically, "I can't. I promised my mom I'd be back sooner than later."

"Oh, yeah? I'll stay with you, then." Jesse shrugged.

Hazard thought it all over carefully. It wasn't like things were all back to normal yet. In fact, maybe there was no *normal* to get back to. The way things had been was over, and this feeling in his chest—the feeling he'd had since he'd come back—was the feeling of starting again.

Hazard took a deep breath, hesitating, then nodded slowly. "Sure," he murmured. "That's cool with me."

BACK inside with Brianna, they ate corn dogs and macaroni for lunch. Jesse got dressed. Brianna gave them both tight hugs before she left.

"I have Smirnoff Ice in the fridge," Jesse said. "Do you want me to bring it?"

Hazard looked at him, appalled. "*No.* You're staying at my house, Jesse. *My mother* will be there."

Jesse smiled, like he'd been joking anyway. "Can I drive?" he asked quietly.

"My car?" Hazard raised his brows. Jesse nodded, and it didn't take much more than the pinched expression on his face for Hazard to realize that it had something to do with Felix and the car accident, like a paranoid compulsive fear of being out of control because he wasn't driving or something. Hazard almost started imagining what Felix might have looked like under the casket at the wake, but he stopped himself. He gave his keys to Jesse.

Jesse drove his car, and Hazard was a little embarrassed of the Ed Hardy seat covers and pop tab chain around his rearview mirror, gathered from a number of Red Bulls and Vanilla Cokes. All the way back to Bethany, they blasted music. Hazard went through his book of CDs. They talked about how they both loved Ronnie Radke, listening to Escape the

Fate for a while, and then Nirvana. Jesse rolled down his window, made Hazard roll down his window too, and turned the volume up. On the Tacoma Narrows, he smoked another cigarette. They took the highway past Gig Harbor, toward Port Orchard and Bethany. It amused Hazard how comfortable Jesse seemed while Hazard was full of nerves still. Maybe Jesse was pretending. Faking or not, it was comforting.

Hazard thought he might puke when he walked into his house with Jesse and his mom stared as if the devil himself had just waltzed right in too.

"Mom," Hazard said, closing the door behind them and feeling queasy as Jesse offered a handshake, "this is Jesse Wesley. Remember him?"

She remembered. It was awkward at first, especially after what they'd talked about the day before—*something like that* and *carnal knowledge*. Hazard texted Emery a little, telling him where he'd been all morning. Hazard's mother kept looking at Jesse like she hated him, like she wanted to discipline him, like she wanted to tell him to take a shower. Hazard was mortified every time one of them moved. He remembered what his mom had said about seeing him and Jesse kiss once. He hoped Jesse impressed her. It might make her feel better.

They all talked for a while. His mom did seem impressed. She seemed surprised that Jesse could actually smile or say things like *Mrs. James*, or that he was going to be *that junior* in college now instead of in high school. Jesse didn't pull anything. He was polite. Hazard was kind of proud of him for that. He watched them, Jesse and his mom, both wary of one another but talking comfortably. His mom was trying, and Hazard realized that she was trying for him.

They were there all day. Jesse and Hazard ran out and grabbed something quick for dinner. They separated to eat, his mom going to her room while they ate at the coffee table. By eleven o'clock at night, it was just Hazard and Jesse on the couch. Hazard's mother was in bed, door closed and light off. She smiled at them both and gave Hazard a huge kiss in front of Jesse before she retreated to her room, just in case he wasn't embarrassed enough already.

Hazard took Jesse into his bedroom and went through his suitcase. He pulled out his October Fall CD, which he'd brought on a whim. He put it into his old CD player. He played the song he'd listened to on repeat, in Seattle at his aunt and uncle's. He sat with his head hung while the track played, feeling something pivotal and tacit swell in the room, maybe something like the beginning of something better.

Jesse didn't say anything. He ruffled Hazard's hair and let the simple quiet between them last another moment or two.

There was something almost dreamlike about sitting on the couch in a dark living room, watching late-night TV and lying with his feet tangled up in Jesse's legs. Hazard wagged his toes against Jesse's knees. Jesse flipped through the channels. He took two smoke breaks out on the stoop. In the shadows filtered between the blinds, the talk ranged from times long ago to how things were now, Jesse playing piano and other strings at school and working as a photographer's assistant part-time, and how he hung out with Emery a lot after Hazard left, to *Do you remember this?* or *Do you remember that?* and all the way back to fragile silences and tense stares and the eventual warm smile at the end.

"You should come to school in Tacoma too," Jesse said.

Hazard wanted to tell Jesse that he had no idea what he even wanted to go to school for, or what he wanted to do with his life at all, when suddenly he realized that he *did* know what he wanted to do. He looked over at Jesse, a little stunned by this moment of clarity. "Yeah," he whispered in the dark, shadows from the TV dancing. "I think I will. I'll take over for Brianna too."

Hazard sat by Jesse on the stoop for another smoke break at around midnight. He told Jesse about the vandalism on the wall of the 7-Eleven. He told him that it said *we all collide*. He told Jesse all about his theories, and Newton's laws of motion, and how he'd collided with everyone so viciously.

"Maybe *you* weren't the collision, Haz." Jesse shrugged, blowing a stream of velvety gray. "Maybe you were the unbalanced force to act on everyone, and not in a bad way." Jesse thought deeply about it all for a second, then looked at Hazard gravely.

"What do you think we are, Hazard?" Jesse asked then, quietly. "Are we moving forward, or are we standing still?"

"I don't know," Hazard whispered, stomach in knots, and he really didn't. But Jesse was content with that.

They watched more TV and talked. Hazard fell asleep on the couch in the knit throw blanket from the easy chair. He woke up early the next morning to his mom getting coffee. Sleepily, he watched her until she went back to her room, to make sure she wasn't staring at them. She glanced over curiously a few times as she made her coffee, but her eyes were never *totally* suspicious.

The pale light of dawn filled the living room. Hazard's muscles were stiff and his back ached, but he also woke up with Jesse sprawled on the other side of the couch from him, the sound of his quiet snores surfacing now and then.

Hazard carefully maneuvered off the couch. He didn't wake Jesse up. He went in and said good morning to his mom. She looked at him like she was checking for hickeys, then smiled and offered him coffee. Hazard took a shower in her bathroom. He settled down on the couch again afterward with cereal in a mug. He watched the morning news on low volume until Jesse stirred, shifting around and blinking sleepily and sighing in that early-morning way.

Hazard waved at him. Jesse mumbled, "Oh, hi," after he woke up enough to stop staring.

we all collide

NOBODY had painted over the 7-Eleven's tagged wall, between the bathrooms. All the old stickers and flyers were still there, worn off or smeared, and the writing had all faded a little over two years. Hazard took a sip of the coffee he'd gotten from inside and tilted his head, studying it all. The breeze was nice today. It tickled his skin.

Newton's third law of motion said that for every action there was an equal and opposite reaction. When two people collided, they would not be in the same position as they were. Everyone equally affected everyone else.

Hazard had collided with Tom and Olivia. They'd always be

connected because of those moments and all the afternoons they'd spent together.

He'd collided with Emery, in so many ways. Emery was his best friend and always would be. There was no reason to fear losing him. Hazard understood that now.

He'd collided with other people. Random, insignificant people at parties who had collided with him too, with drinks in hand and worries on the back burner. People like Russell Leroy, or Liam, or Brandi, or Alex, people who just wanted to forget about the world for a while.

But none of those things mattered, because he'd collided with Jesse, and in turn Jesse had collided with him. Hazard had thought they'd repelled each other. He'd thought their collision hadn't linked them together but instead shot them apart, like the first law of motion. *An object at rest tends to stay at rest and an object in motion tends to stay in motion with the same speed and in the same direction unless acted upon by an unbalanced force.* He'd thought that Felix had been that unbalanced force, that Felix had changed their directions.

But Jesse might have been on to something. Maybe it *had* been Hazard who was the unbalanced force working on everyone. Maybe he hadn't been pushed away but had been the one to affect people in the first place. Maybe that was how it worked with everyone. Maybe everything happened for a reason.

What do you think we are, Hazard? Jesse had asked the night before out on his stoop. *Are we moving forward, or are we standing still?*

Hazard went around the corner to the front of the 7-Eleven. He waited for a few cars to roll by before he jogged over to the pump where Jesse was waiting by his car, gas paid for and everything. Hazard was letting Jesse drive again.

"You done?" Jesse asked, raising his brows. Hazard nodded, climbing into the passenger seat of his car.

In June of 2008, Hazard Oscar James was almost eighteen. He had a weird name that started nicknames like Danger. He had thick dark-brown hair that was usually in his eyes, which were big and ice blue and framed by long lashes. He was pretty small for a seventeen-year-old guy, and he was afraid that that and his face made him look kind of girly, even though he wasn't girly at all. He got nervous very easily and had a bad habit of biting his nails. He still wasn't shaving his face. He sometimes needed to use his reading glasses. His parents were divorced. He was learning that he could live with his mom if he really tried.

Hazard liked Vanilla Coke, Nirvana, and dancing to a good beat. He wanted to go to school in Tacoma when the fall semester started, for a degree in humanities. He wanted to be a writer. He had a little black 2004 Mustang. His best friends were Emery Benjamin Moore and Jesse Logan Wesley, and Hazard used to think he was lonely, but he was coming to find that if he wasn't stubborn, he wasn't lonely at all. He was still technically jailbait, he'd gotten high a few times, he liked to draw and paint, he'd been suspended once, when he drank he could certainly hold his own, and he hadn't been a virgin since he was fifteen. Maybe he was *gay*, or maybe he was *bisexual*, but whatever he was, he wouldn't ever consider himself to be single, either.

And midmorning on a pleasant late June day, Hazard was going with Jesse to the bookstore to hang out with Emery before his shift at Claim Jumper started at two.

If E.L. Doctorow was on point when he said, "Writing is a socially acceptable form of schizophrenia," J. R. LENK is a self-confessed pretty boy severely in need of a psychological once-over.

Cursed by a height barely scraping five foot five, he is a culture connoisseur. He's a sucker for overcast skies and the smell of books, particularly good old-fashioned horror and gothic thrillers, à la Rice or Michael Cox. He enjoys a lot of things from movies about castrati to smoking cigarettes on the roof of his house, to classy sweaters and wayward glances, to successful sex hair and hobo chic. He's an old soul with a little bit of a potty-mouth and a friends with benefits relationship with Red Bull and Microsoft Word that goes hand-in-hand with his love for Vivaldi and alternative rock in equal parts.

J. R. has been penning stories of the M/M or bisexual persuasion for years. He's known to sometimes spontaneously burst into song, go off on twenty-minute tangents, and quote Sherlock Holmes (usually assuming the Robert Downey Jr. interpretation).

He currently lives near Pike's Peak with his family and his one and only better half, but Seattle is his hometown and he finds himself inexplicably thinking about the West Coast every day.

Visit J. R. on Twitter at http://twitter.com/prettyboysays/ or on Tumblr at http://mainliningsunsets.tumblr.com/.

Young Adult Gay Fiction at

http://www.harmonyinkpress.com